The
Wrong Girl

The Wrong Girl

Rik Wuyts

authorHOUSE®

AuthorHouse™
1663 Liberty Drive
Bloomington, IN 47403
www.authorhouse.com
Phone: 1-800-839-8640

Published by AuthorHouse 12/08/2014

ISBN: 978-1-4969-4853-3 (sc)
ISBN: 978-1-4969-4852-6 (e)

Library of Congress Control Number: 2014918799

Chapter 1

A Jamesville Police car cruised by the Witherspoon High School. The driver, Stan Bott, a seasoned officer with the Jamesville police department, and his rookie partner, Jeff Cooper, who very recently had joined the force, noticed a red sports car parked halfway on the curb. Jeff was immediately filled with excitement and adrenalin seeing the opportunity to score his first ticket.

"Stop the car. We have to issue a citation. That car is clearly in violation. We've got to fine that asshole, parking halfway on the curb like he owns it," he said with fervor.

Stan just chuckled but kept on driving, ignoring his rookie partner's outburst.

Jeff exclaimed, "What's the matter with you? Why aren't you stopping? We can't just let him get away with that."

Stan simply responded, "Writing a ticket would be a waste of time and probably result in a serious ass chewing from the chief. Since I'm the senior officer, it would be my ass getting the brunt. If you are going to be riding with me I obviously need to fill you in on some of the dirty secrets of the Jamesville police force. Some citizens of this fair city are above the law and untouchable when it comes to minor infractions. The red Corvette you saw belongs to John Witherspoon Jr. He's one of the members of the club that is immune to traffic violations. Writing him a ticket would be severely frowned on by the brass, ignored and never see the light of day. We'd be deemed idiots for such a ridiculous act of futility. This may shock you but that's just the way it is in Jamesville. This town belongs to the Weatherspoon's and if you can't live with it you should seriously consider a transfer to another town, because this town won't ever change."

"Thanks for the heads up, but I have to admit I'm shocked. This just goes against everything I was taught in the academy. I'm gonna have to think about this for a while. I don't want to make a rash decision." Stan looked at his partner, shook his head but refrained from making a comment.

What kind of bubble did this guy live in? Did he really think that the real world abides by what we are taught in the academy, especially in a town like Jamesville.

"Where is it you said you grew up?" he asked his partner.

"I've pretty much lived in the Dallas-Fort Worth area all my life, why."

"Just wondering."

Well that explained things. Jamesville, Texas is a far cry from the high class metropolis of Dallas-Fort Worth.

Jamesville was a small town located Southwest of Houston with a population of about 40,000, most of whom had lived there for generations. Predominantly white, but over time it had become a little more diverse. There were now some Hispanic and a couple of black families. Actually, compared to the early 1900's, that was true progress.

The major employers were the Jamesville Rice Growing Company, which had been in Jamesville for many generations, and computer manufacturer Alltech Computers. Other employment was sometimes available from the retail stores, building contractors, various offices, city administration and legal firms. Rumor had it that both major companies were owned and managed by the powerful Witherspoon family, which was no surprise to the people familiar with the Jamesville politics and history. Every paycheck issued in this town seemed to be somehow linked to the Witherspoon Empire. The majority of the residents' paychecks were above the average Texan worker, so in all Jamesville was a good place to live, and most of the locals would agree with that.

The Witherspoon's owned at least half of Jamesville's real estate and businesses including the local bank. The John Witherspoon Bank, named after the founder of the Jamesville Rice Growing Company.

The John Witherspoon Bank was the most important bank in Jamesville, which made sense since most of the money earned and spent in Jamesville eventually ended up in the pockets of the Witherspoon family anyway. There were a few smaller local banks but none close to the size of the John Witherspoon Bank.

Jamesville, of course, had all the amenities you find in most American small towns, two Grocery stores, a couple of decent restaurants, most of the fast food joints, a few bars, a decent size mall, an athletic club, a golf course, a bowling alley, movie theatre, a fairly well equipped medical center, and whatever else the citizens of Jamesville would had a need for.

Jamesville was situated far enough from any major city to risk annexation by them. But nobody worried about that possibility because if that ever became an issue the Witherspoon's friendly relationship with the Governor would take care of it. The Witherspoon fortune was established in the late 1890's during the Texas oil discovery in the Beaumont area. The Witherspoon clan was fortunate in that they had substantial interests in the Spindletop fields and when in 1901 the Lucas Gusher blew and produced 60,000 to 80,000 barrels of oil a day their future was secured.

The Weatherspoon's invested this windfall profit not only in the oil industry but in many other, nonrelated businesses such as rice cultivation, banking, automotive, and various other enterprises all of which were very successful. The Weatherspoon's seemed to have the Midas touch and it was no secret that the Witherspoon family was filthy rich, by any standard.

The summer vacation had not started yet but the teachers and students from Jamesville's Alfred Witherspoon High School were already making plans and dreams of the things that they were going to do during the coming summer vacation. As with most dreams and plans very few would actually materialize. The majority of students and faculty members would come back and start the new school year in the fall, unsatisfied with how they had spent their vacation and realizing that another boring year lay ahead of them.

This day was one of those hot, humid, lazy days that only the Texas gulf coast area seems to produce. Although it was only early May, the temperature was in the high eighties with the usual high percent humidity and not a stitch of wind. The few puffs of clouds high up in the sky looked like they were anchored in place and unable to move.

John Witherspoon Jr. and his buddy and cousin, Glenn Evans, were hanging out in front of the high school unaware that a police car had passed by and the cops were talking about them. Not that this would have scared them one bit as they were well aware of what they could get away with in Jamestown due to their family's status. Both boys were juniors, both good looking, fairly intelligent and players on the high school varsity basketball team. They were by no means superstars, with no chance of NBA recruitment or even any of the major universities. But being on the varsity team in a town the size of Jamestown and the fact that they were the offspring of two of the most affluent families in the community multiplied their popularity tenfold. There wasn't a student or faculty member who did not know who they were and how important it was to remain in their good graces. Of course, the female students all aspired to much more than that. To be the girlfriend of either was a sure ticket to instant popularity and the envy of their friends.

They never seemed to be low on cash, so dating them assured they would be treated to the best Jamesville had to offer. It wasn't uncommon for their dates to end up in bed after a night out, but the girls knew in advance that was part of the deal. After all, there is no such thing as a free lunch. The few girls that refused to go all the way with them were never invited again and were soon labeled as possibly being lesbians and became social pariahs.

The conversation that afternoon between John and Glenn was focused on how boring and non-eventful this Podunk town was and always would be. Getting drunk, drugged and laid with the same girls no longer excited them. They were sure there must be something new and different to be found. There must be something exhilarating that they had not experienced yet. John was the one doing most of the complaining while Glenn just nodded his head in agreement.

"Look," John said pointing at the kids streaming out of the school. "Look at all these damn foreigners. What are they doing here? Why don't they all go back to their shit-hole countries where they came from? We don't need them here".

Glenn just listened to John's tirade. John frequently felt the need to vent his dislike of various people, especially those who looked different than he did. He always claimed that he was not a racist but Glenn knew better. Glenn knew all too well that John's views mimicked those of his father and grandfather. However, Glen knew better than to challenge John or point out that they weren't living in the 19th century anymore. John had always been the leader of the twosome and Glen usually just went along for the ride. So it wasn't surprising that once John finished his tirade he informed Glen that they must come up with something that would rejuvenate and excite them, sexually or otherwise. It was not a suggestion, but a statement.

Glen responded, "Well, what do you think we should do?"

John stared at Glenn with exasperation. "If I had a plan, I would have told you already. I swear you can be such an idiot sometimes. I just know there has to be something we can do to make this summer exciting and one we will never forget. That's why I'm mentioning it now. We have to start thinking and thinking hard. Summer will be here in no time and I want to have a plan in place."

"Okay. I just thought you already had something in mind." Glenn said in an apologetic tone.

"Well, you thought wrong. So put your shit for brains to work and come up with some helpful ideas. Surely between the two of us we can come up with something that will juice up our miserable lives here. I've got to do something different this summer before I go nuts."

This was the way most of the conversations between the two of them ended; John walking away asking himself why he was friends with an idiot like Glenn and Glenn wondering why he tolerated being friends with an egomaniac like John. John knew that he was going to be the one who came up with the brilliant idea and Glenn knew that even if he came up with a great idea it would be shut down by John simply because he hadn't come up with it.

Glenn also left feeling hurt by the insults his friend always seemed to throw at him, although he didn't know why he took it personally. John treated all his friends that way. Glenn could never find an appropriate response but then again even if he could he probably wouldn't say it. Pissing John off and risking being his enemy was not a situation he wanted to be in. This is a lesson Glenn learned by witnessing the wrath of John towards friends that had crossed him in the past. There were always consequences and none of them were good and you can forget ever earning your way back into John's good graces. That was something he would never allow. Once an enemy, always an enemy was his motto.

The weekend passed without the two of them seeing each other. John was out on the water sailing with his father and a couple of his father's friends, the usual assortment of lawyers and other business acquaintances. John did not really enjoy these outings but his father felt that it was necessary for his future development; John was slated to join the Witherspoon Empire after graduating from college with a degree in business.

Glenn's father who by the way was the son-in-law of John's grandfather and CEO of the Witherspoon Banks, was less demanding and let Glenn decide what he wanted to do on weekends.

So this weekend Glenn spent most of his time with his girlfriend Melissa and also racked his brain to come up with something that John would approve of. This was not an easy task because there was little left that John had not already tried. Glenn came up with a list he hoped John could be interested in:

Skydiving

Deep sea diving and fishing

Speedway racing

Week-end at the beach house with some hookers

Party at the beach house with high school kids

Week-end in Houston or Galveston

Go to Vegas for the week-end

After that Glenn gave up, knowing that none of the above would be daring or exciting enough for John. Those were the activities that John claimed were boring and they had done before. So, Glenn said "To hell with it. Let the fucking smart ass know-it-all come up with something himself."

Monday during their lunch break at school John and Glenn got together and John immediately asked. "Well genius, are you going to tell me what wonderful ideas your imagination has come up with?"

Glenn showed him the list he composed and immediately knew by the look on John's face that all hell was going to break loose, he was not disappointed.

John, with a look of disbelief and anger on his face said with a malicious grin, "This is exactly what I expected from you. Absolutely nothing. What you suggest is something we have been doing for years and what we agreed upon was boring and we needed something new."

Glen mumbled, "You said it was boring, I never did." John did not think that this deserved a response from him but instead said. "Well I came up with something that will blow your mind. I'm not going to tell you any of the details because I will present you with a perfect plan for something exciting, sexy, maybe against the law, something we have never done before. All I will tell you is that it is all about a sexual experience you or I never had and probably will never again have in our lives."

Glenn said," I hope it's not like the last time you had this great idea that would spice up the Baptist church members."

John's idea was that he would replace the video that was projecting the pastor's sermon on a giant flat screen with a porno flick.

He managed to sneak into the church early in the morning and switched the disks in the projector system. This caused quite an uproar in the Baptist community and nobody suspected John or Glenn but John was so proud of it that he started bragging in school that he was the man and that was when all hell broke loose.

Glenn's father was one of the Baptist church laymen and when he heard that his son could have been involved he went ballistic and took all Glenn's privileges away. No car, no allowance and a curfew. But since there was no proof that they were the guilty parties, this storm blew over after a couple of weeks.

John chuckled and said, "Okay, it was a close call but you have to admit that it was funny."

Glenn said, "Funny, not for me it wasn't. My dad still doesn't trust me."

"Well, this is nothing like that. Let's go to our beach house this weekend and I'll tell you all about it. Count on spending the weekend so we can plan our strategy and timing in detail, John sensed that Glenn was not excited, looked doubtful and maybe a little scared. John said. "Well, are you in or do I have to look for somebody with guts to do this?"

Glenn responded, "How can I tell whether I'm in or out if you won't tell me what it is we are planning to do."

"It's not important what it is. "John said" It's a matter of trust. We have a non-written understanding that whatever we do we will do it together. No ifs or buts, no excuses. A total commitment to each other. Have you forgotten what we did a couple of months ago, when that little bitch Marissa dumped you for that football jock. I still remember, you had that brilliant idea of setting her parents house on fire. I also remember that I told you that this was a stupid idea but I went along with it and helped you torching the place. It backfired and we almost got our asses thrown in jail. Thanks to my dad's interference we got away with it. But if loyalty to your best friend means nothing to you, just forget it, I will handle it by myself. I don't need you. You are easily replaceable."

Glenn, afraid of the consequences said, "No that's not what I mean. Of course I'm with you all the way.

Whatever it is, we do it together". Glenn's thoughts went back to when they had set fire to Marissa's house. He had just wanted to start a little fire, cause some damage to the garage as revenge for the misery he felt at that time. He really liked Marissa and was hurt when she broke up with him. The real reason, she had said, was John. She did not like him and she felt that he was a bad influence for Glenn.

That night at Marissa's house, John was the one who felt that a little fire would not get the message across and that there should be some fireworks involved; he was the one who went inside and opened the main gas line that caused the explosion and destroyed the whole house.

The arson investigator quickly found out that this was no accident but the work of an arsonist, and a thorough investigation took place. Every kid in school was questioned and had to show proof that they were nowhere near the house the night of the fire.

One kid, who lived close to Marissa's house, remembered seeing a red sports car parked near the house at that time. John happened to drive a red Corvette, so they started to question John and Glenn more seriously and things looked real bad for them. They were interrogated by the arson inspector and the local police, questioned one at the time or together, probed and asked the same questions over and over again, with the hope that they would make mistakes and give them conflicting answers. And then suddenly, the police left them alone, stopped asking questions and the whole thing died away. John called it the Witherspoon Magic. Glenn said." We were damn lucky that I made sure there was nobody in the house when we set it on fire or we would have been in deep shit if someone would have been killed in the fire, Witherspoon magic or not."

Chapter 2

John's father, J.A. Witherspoon Sr., was in his office contemplating whether he should call his lawyer and ask her if she could spent the afternoon with him discussing some of the litigation issues. Jane has been his corporate lawyer for the last six years and besides handling the company's legal issues, she also took care of John's sexual needs. Jane was a very smart, attractive and sexy girl, an early thirties divorcee who knew how to take care of herself.

He decided to call her and said he was coming over to her office and for her to be sure that she cleared her calendar and that they would not be disturbed. The not to be disturbed request was the signal that no legal issues would be addressed that afternoon.

Jane's offices were not in the corporate building but in a townhouse in a quiet part of town, on the ground floor with her very luxurious living quarters upstairs. This was very convenient to accommodate both the legal and sexual activities, all under one roof and more or less discreet.

When John Sr. arrived Jane already had changed from her business outfit into a more sexually attractive and tight outfit. She informed her secretary that she could leave early for the day. After making sure that she had left, they went upstairs where a bottle of chilled champagne and two glasses were waiting for them.

They went through the usual, not very exciting short love making part. John always felt insecure that Jane's participation was not as spontaneous or steaming hot as he was hoping it should be. He, of course, was convinced that he was the perfect lover and the reason he was not all that satisfied must be her fault. He never had the courage to come right out and say so, but it lingered in his mind every time they had sex. Jane once jokingly said that she felt like a prostitute because she billed him the usual hourly fee for her services. John became very upset and angry and she quickly had to retract and said that it was a joke and tried to explain what she meant.

"John," she said, "when you walk through the front door, Alice logs you in and out and at the end of every month your company gets invoiced for the hours I spent with you regardless of what we are doing. Alice, I'm sure is already asking herself why we have so many not to be disturbed meetings. She would become very suspicious if I told her that some of the hours that you spent here should not be billed."

As a matter of fact, Alice knew exactly what was going on, but John was unaware of this little secret between his lawyer and her secretary.

"And don't worry," she said laughingly."That way our romantic sessions are legal expenses and therefore tax deductible for your company." She was never sure whether John thought this was funny or not. His sense of humor was almost non-existent and most of her jokes went right over his balding head.

Jane knew that this affair would never go anywhere; she understood that John would never leave his wife, and she definitely did not want him to divorce his wife and marry her. She was content, for the time being, with the arrangement they had.

Jane realized that what she did was maybe not called prostitution, but she was well aware that she took advantage of her relationship with John. Nowhere else would she be able to make the kind of money she got paid and receive perks like a car, her office rent paid, and serious bonuses for work that was pure and simple just doing her job. No, life was good the way it was right now. She had her freedom and could do whatever she wanted. She was well on her way to becoming financially independent, and when that goal was achieved, everything was possible. John Sr. was most likely not part of whatever she decided to do in the future.

John Sr. never even thought about divorcing his wife, not that his marriage was such a great success or a great failure. It was neither. It always was a marriage of convenience rather than a torrid love affair and this suited John Sr. just fine. The reason he never considered a divorce had little or nothing to do with the feelings he had for his wife or children. John Sr. had political ambitions for which a divorce would certainly not have a positive impact. His goal was to be the next Governor of Texas, and a divorce would upset a lot of people in the Bible belt. There was also the fact that his wife came from a wealthy and well-known family, which could be very helpful in his quest for office.

Shooting for Governor was quite a lofty ambition for someone with very little or no experience in the political arena. John Sr., of course, was counting on the numerous business connections he had to support him on this journey. The only governmental position he ever had and currently held was on the City of Jamesville Community Council. Not much of a reference for the position of State Governor.

The relationship John Sr. had with his two children was at best described as amicable but by no means lovable.

He was not very proud of the achievements of either one. John Jr. was a constant pain in the ass due to his perpetual run-ins with the law for speeding, drinking, drug possession and several other misdemeanors. He had also managed to get a 16 year old girl pregnant. This problem was resolved with an abortion and a costly settlement with the parents in order to keep the incident from becoming another embarrassment for the Witherspoon family.

He was also disappointed that John Jr. never made the high school football team, and this being a Texas small town environment, Friday night football was the only sporting event that really counted with the citizens of Jamesville. This gave the football players a certain swagger and celebrity status that a basketball player could only dream of. John never told his father that he had no interest in being on the football team and had not tried out for it. Being crushed by a 280 pound line backer was not something he wanted to experience just to please his dad.

His daughter, Monica, was another disappointment to him. She was not very bright, not very pretty and had zero personality. She was a year younger than John Jr. Monica behaved and looked exactly like her mother, shy and ill at ease at parties or other gatherings that they could not avoid attending. Monica's friends were all like her, not sexy, not flashy and not close to the type of girls John Jr. would look at, let alone date. The two siblings had very little in common and their relationship was very cold and remote. In fact, they seldom spoke to one another.

Elisabeth Witherspoon, who had married John Sr. when she was 19 years old, was the daughter of another oil baron from Port Arthur, Texas. A wealthy family in its own right, they approved of this marriage whole heartedly, content that she would be part of the powerful Witherspoon family. A close relationship with the Weatherspoon's could do nothing but improve their status in the area.

Elisabeth's life as the wife of John Sr. did not change much from the life she had led at her family home. Elisabeth never showed any interest in going to college, partly because she liked the life she was living and also because she thought she was not smart enough to get decent grades. She felt that she did not need a degree for the lifestyle she had planned for herself.

Her married days were filled with frivolous events such as parties, ladies committees, bridge, tennis, horseback riding and once in a while fulfilling her duties as married women to John Sr.

These duties became less and less frequent as the years went by and her husband had found women who were more exciting than his wife, so sex became no longer an obligation.

Elisabeth loved her children dearly but did not spend much time with them because she was just too busy. A nanny was assigned to take care of the kids when they were young and when they got older and went to school they needed and preferred less attention from their parents. All their material needs and wants were always taken care of without much questioning from their parents. Strange as this may sound considering their wealth, the Witherspoon children were actually mentally neglected by their parents and never experienced a real family environment. They lived in the same house but that was it. Their lives were disconnected.

Chapter 3

The weekend at the beach house, planned by John, needed to be postponed because a hurricane was threatening to hit the Gulf coast. Neither John nor Glenn was inclined to drive 60 miles in pelting rain and high winds to spend the weekend inside the beach house. So John decided to have a talk with Glenn and unveil part of the plan, just enough to see his reaction and gain a feel for whether he could trust him or not.

On Saturday night they met at Glenn's house because his parents were out of town and they could talk without fear of being overheard by his parents.

John started by saying, "Listen and let me explain the whole plan before you start making comments, or objections or some other shit that you don't like. Since we already have done everything that you came up with on your list of things to do, I felt I had to take the bull by the horns and propose something that you could never imagine doing. So here we go, I want us to get a girl and make her our sex slave."

Before John could continue Glenn asked, "What the fuck are you talking about? What do you mean by getting a girl and making her our sex slave?"

John calmly said, "What did I ask you to do? I asked you to let me finish without interruptions, so do me a favor and shut the fuck up till I finish. Is that too much to ask?"

Glenn nodded and mumbled, "Please, continue I will keep my mouth shut and listen to what you have to say."

"Thank you very much; I really appreciate it." John said sarcastically.

"So back to the sex slave bit. What we have to do is discreetly look around and select the girls we believe would qualify to participate and be part of this debauchery. I know for a fact that there are a number of these little sluts who would love to do this. The problem we are facing is that we can't approach them and then get rejected. It would be emailed to the whole school and we could well end with a suspension, which neither of us need or can afford in our senior year.

"Once this is broadcasted to the whole school we won't be able to recruit another girl. None of these bitches would come near us even if they would love to be part of this game. Their precious reputations would be at stake and none of them would take the risk".

John did not mention that he knew that this would be the case anyway and if they wanted a local girl they would have to kidnap her to be their sex slave. He felt if Glenn was aware of this now he would back out. John wanted Glenn to participate, just in case something went wrong and he needed a scapegoat to take the blame, Glenn would be the ideal person to fit the bill.

Glenn spoke up and asked, "Well, how can we approach these girls then?"

"John said let's first select the sluts who we think could go for this, and then eliminate the dogs we don't want. We are aiming for a good looking sexy bitch, nice body, boobs, the whole works and willing. It has to be fun for all three of us. We don't want to face rape charges."

"Let's both make a list, a list of four girls, girls who fit the requirements we just laid out. We meet again in a couple of days and consolidate the two lists. I'm sure we will have some of the same girls on both lists. Once we have decided on the girls we have to rank them in order of our preference."

John got more and more excited while they were talking about this venture, while Glenn became more and more nervous and unsure about this whole slave girl bit. He, of course, said nothing about his doubts and the insanity of this plan, knowing that would create another violent outburst from John, belittling and insulting Glenn further.

They parted with their assignment and agreed to get together two days later, make their selection and finalize the procedure on how to find out which one of these girls would go along with it. This probing had to be done in a careful manner so that when the girl showed no interest at all she would give it no further thought thinking that is was just another joke from these two maniacs. This girl would be crossed off the list and never be approached again on this subject.

Glenn found it difficult to compose a list like this because his reluctance to participate became stronger and his thoughts were more focused on finding a way to convince John not to pursue this sure to fail adventure. Telling John that it was too dangerous too complicated and impossible to pull off would only fuel John's desire to do it. When John has his mind made up to do something, nobody could change it, on the contrary, it would increase his desire and stubbornness and he would definitely go ahead with it. Glenn's only hope that this would go away was that none of the girls would agree to be part of this "off the chart" lunatic idea. Glenn decided to select girls who he was certain would show zero interest or girls that

John would outright reject because they did not fulfill his sex fantasies.

When they got together, John felt that they should add to the girl's names their qualifications and why they should be on the list in the first place. Glenn reluctantly agreed to do so before they would look at the infamous list. John had already done this so he showed Glenn his list with the added qualifications. The girls he selected were:

Brenda: Extremely good looking, very active sex life, party girl, a little mysterious.

Bridget: Sexy looking, willing to please the guys, not very smart but good between the sheets.

Charlene: Great body, will do anything to be popular with the guys

Sandy: The high school slut, not bad looking, loves to get laid by anyone available.

"This is what I want you to do with your list." John said, "We can finalize the four candidates and select the one we want to contact first and she should be the one that we think would be the most fun." "Glenn said. "Well I need a couple of days to do that. I never thought about qualifications".

"Then how did you come up with girls on your list?" John asked.

Glenn did not really have an answer because his criterion for selecting the girls was not what John would approve of or what they had agreed upon during their last get-together.

He said, "I just need some time to do this; it will not take more than a couple of days."

John annoyed with this response angrily said, "Well don't take forever or I'll do it for you. You seem to find any excuse to sabotage this project. If you're too lame to be part of this just say so and I'll find somebody else. I don't need you. There are plenty of other guys more than willing to join me."

Glenn knew that he should have said at that time. "Okay find somebody else. I'm sick and tired of being your lackey." But he didn't and instead said, "No I'm with you. I was just too busy the last week. I'll take care of it by tomorrow."

John left and on his way home started to think about his relationship with Glenn and how far he could really trust him. The more he thought about it the more he became uncomfortable having Glenn involved in this risky adventure. He knew from experience that when Glenn was under pressure he was at the least, unreliable and could collapse at any time. This would be catastrophic in a situation like this and could easily result in a messy court case, where even the Witherspoon's powerful influence would not be enough to keep them out of jail or worse.

John kept thinking. How can I pull this off without Glenn's help? Even if I could, how can I be sure that Glenn will keep this a secret? Truth is I can't' but what other options, besides Glenn do I have to make this caper work? To be honest, I don't have any options, Glenn is the only one. I at least have some power over him and once he is involved I wont let him back out. If common sense had prevailed John would have had to admit that this was a harebrained idea that should be abandoned and classified as "Mission Impossible." But nobody had ever accused John of having much common sense, so the gig was still on despite the obstacles and risks involved.

John then decided that Glenn, by default, was the designated partner for his sex slave project. But he thought by the first sign of serious trouble, John would save himself and make Glenn the major player, and he would claim that he was just an innocent bystander. He was convinced that with the help of his father's lawyers and fortune he could escape with minor damage if need be. Although John remembered his father saying after the fire fiasco that if John Jr. ever got involved in something like that again, he would be on his own, and his father would simply ignore him. John, of course, knew that this was grandstanding and that his father could not afford a scandal like this, not if he ever wanted a political career. John just ignored that statement and filed it under "Dad's bullshit." This would never happen.

John was very good at taking care of numero uno, and making somebody else pay for his foolish mistakes would not bother him at all.

Chapter 4

The day after Glenn reluctantly went to John's house with his list that without any doubt would be ignored and ridiculed, the project would go ahead with John's list of preferred ladies. Glenn's prediction was right on and none of the girls picked by Glenn were on John's list. They now had to discus in detail how to approach these girls. Since Glenn didn't have a clue it was John again who took the lead and explained how to do it.

"You or I will have to start chit-chatting with Brenda."

"Brenda being the first choice, we have to tell her that we had a very strange dream, a dream so ridiculous that we just wanted to forget about it, but strangely enough the next night we had the same dream but this time one of the characters was Brenda. The guys in the dream were unidentifiable.

"If Brenda is the type we believe she is, she will want to hear more about it. We, of course, then refuse to tell her. We are counting on the female curiosity that this is now something she has to know, no matter what. We will stall and pretend that we are not going to tell her ever. She will persist and we then reluctantly will explain what this dream was all about.

"Depending on how she reacts will determine what our next step will be. If she shows any excitement or interest we continue pursuing this with her. If on the contrary, she shows disgust or fear we back off permanently from her.

"Our next step then will be to use the same strategy with the next one on the list. But first one of us must start with Brenda and see what happens."

Glenn said. "Since Brenda is on your list and you developed this strategy, I feel you should go first. You can evaluate our strategy and possibly modify it if necessary." John, convinced that he would do a better job then Glenn, did not argue and agreed to approach Brenda at the first good opportunity.

This opportunity came sooner than expected, Brenda ran into John at the library the next day. She plopped herself into a chair next to him and started to talk about the next party she was planning at her house. She invited John and he, of course, saw this as a golden opportunity. This couldn't be better. After a couple of drinks at the party he would approach Brenda and tell her about the dream. If she reacted negatively and called him a pervert, he could always pretend he was drunk. End of story. But if her reaction was positive, talk could continue more seriously and maybe lead to an agreement. Who knew?

John got all excited and immediately told Glenn about it. Glenn's first reaction was negative and he thought what if she is drunk and starts telling everybody at the party about it. Before he said something to John he changed his mind and figured that if she tells everybody this stupid idea would not survive and John would have to give it up. Glenn also knew that Brenda would never go along with this. Brenda had a little secret of herself, a secret Glenn knew about but John had no idea. Glenn knew because when he and Marissa were still an item, she told him about it. Glenn was not going to tell John because he assumed that was one less candidate on the list, reducing the viability of the project by 25 percent.

The party took place at Brenda's house on a Friday, a night her parents were out of town; it was a typical Jamesville high school kid's party. Alcohol, drugs, sex and extreme uncivilized behavior from both sexes. John was wandering around at the party making sure he did not get too much involved in any of the bacchanalian activities. He observed Brenda to be ready for when he felt she had consumed enough alcohol or used drugs so that he could make his move.

Finally after hours of boredom, because he could not fully participate and party with the crowd, he thought the time was right. Brenda was starting to slur her words and became a little unstable on her feet.

He approached her when she was sort of lying on a coach away from the main activity. He pretended that he was somewhat intoxicated and ready to make a move on her. She jumped up and said with a sexy smile on her face, "John, don't even think about it. You're not my type and I'm too drunk to enjoy it. Come back some other time."

He said, "If I'm not your type why do you ask me to come back some other time?"

She said laughing. "Maybe some other time I'll let you fuck me, sort of a mercy fuck, you know."

John seething on the inside said, "I'm not here to jump on you. I wanted to tell you about a dream, I had two nights ago and you were the main character. Do you want to know what it was about?"

"She asked" Was it fun? did I like it?"

"I was not a character in the dream so I don't know whether you had fun or not. The two guys who were banging you looked like they had fun and you did also by the look on your face and the moans and screams when you had an orgasm, which by the way happened many times, so yes, I believe you had a lot of fun."

Brenda said, "Well too bad I don't remember any of it. Are you sure you didn't watch too many porno flicks before you went to bed?"

"Listen," John said, "last night I had the same dream and while I did not recognize the guys in the dream the night before, this time I did."

"So who were they and was it the same type of dream?"

John smiled and said, "You had more fun because you kept asking for more. It was unbelievable. It was a smorgasbord of sex and it never ended it kept going and going until I finally woke up. I did everything to fall back asleep so the dream would continue." John looked at here and said. "That's where you're wrong.

Last night Glenn and I were the guys in the dream and Glenn and I want to repeat this fantasy in real life with you."

Brenda said quietly, "Keep on dreaming, John, but this will never happen, not with me as the main character in your play. I'm pretty much convinced that these dreams are made up and this is just you, not Glenn, who fabricated this scheme hoping that I would fall for it."

John stood up. "Never say never. Just give it some thoughts. You will never again have an experience like that in your life. You may want to consider this. We can make it happen."

Later that night when the party was over and Brenda and her friend Tammy were the only ones left, Brenda told Tammy about the scheme John came up with and that he expected her to reconsider and become their playmate.

"Why did this pervert choose me? What kind of person does he think I am the campus slut?"

Tammy moved closer to Brenda and said, "Don't let this perverted motherfucker upset you like this." She took Brenda in her arms and lovingly kissed her softly on the lips. This went on for a while and when Brenda responded the kissing became more passionate and urgent. Tammy slowly undressed Brenda and tenderly kissed and stroked her whole body. Brenda started to shake when Tammy began using her tongue and fingers on Brenda's more intimate parts. This continued until Brenda reached orgasm after orgasm.

"See, my love, we don't need anybody else."

"Brenda held on to Tammy. Don't ever leave me. I would not survive without you."

Tammy assured Brenda that she loved her too much and that they would be together for life. They had already decided that they would go to the same college, room together and come out of the closet with regards to their sexuality.

Tammy was an orphan who had gone through the system and was declared an adult at the age of sixteen. She was abused by the older boys in the orphanage and became a loner turned off by any male who came close to her.

She landed in Jamesville not by design. She was on her way to California, where she had some distant relatives, and stopped in Jamesville to find a motel to spend the night. She walked around town to kill some time and thought that this looked like a nice little place. Maybe I should try my luck here. She decided to stay for at least a couple of days to check it out. On the second day she found a part time job with the Summersville local paper and got enrolled in school without any trouble.

She now had to find a furnished room because she could not afford to stay in a motel for very long. Again she lucked out. The news paper owner and editor had a small apartment on top of his garage that used to be his son's digs. It was furnished and she could move in right away.

Tammy was a very attractive, distinguished young girl, looking older than her 18 years; she was also a very intelligent person who was determined to go to college on a full scholarship. Tammy kept to herself most of the time and had no close friends. This however, changed the day when she met Brenda. They were paired and had to work together on a school project. In no time they discovered that there was a common bond between them that they could not explain.

Their backgrounds were so different yet still they felt they had so much in common and in a few days they became inseparable. Brenda's party friends could simply not understand what was happening to her. Some of them were convinced that Brenda was on some sort of a drug and that Tammy was responsible for it. Others became jealous and said that this was a lesbian relationship, not aware that it would eventually turn into that. None of it was true at the time, and the two of them just wanted to be together, not realizing that they already were in love with each other. Brenda avoided the wild parties and slowly separated herself from the rowdy crowd that she used to hang out with.

It was Tammy who told Brenda to have that last party, saying that this would silence the rumors on why they were so close. They could pretend that they were having a good time but not really participating, not drinking too much, no drugs and definitely no sex.

Everything was working out well until John appeared and made Brenda aware that in his mind she was still considered a first class slut, although she never was.

Brenda and Tammy spent that night together making passionate love and swearing that John and Glenn would pay for this, no matter how powerful he thought he was.

On his way home John felt convinced that things could not have gone better. She was going to come back to him for more particulars. She was hooked and turned on by what John had said to her. It was just a matter of time before his so called dream became reality.

He couldn't wait to tell Glenn all about it and as soon as he got home he called him. After hearing John's version of his talk with Brenda, Glenn was flabbergasted and could simply not comprehend what had really happened. Marissa had told him that Brenda would not have a guy touch her with a ten foot pole anymore, and that she was close to coming out in the open and letting everybody know that she and Tammy were lovers.

This did not make sense at all, but it made Glenn even more nervous and scared about this sex project and more determined than ever to bail out before the shit hit the proverbial fan. He just had to figure out how to do that. He started to realize that John was obsessed and that nothing would stop him, no matter what. Glenn wanted no part of this, no way, no how; this was no fun anymore and way too dangerous.

A week went by and John still had not heard a word from Brenda. He felt that she was avoiding him in school. John was still confident that she would come along and that this silence was just a hard-to-get ploy from her.

After a couple days, John contacted Glenn and wanted to get together to discuss the situation and how to continue. Glenn, of course, knew exactly what was going on but could not find the words to let John in on the little secret that Brenda was not and would never be a player in this game. Glenn was afraid how John would react to the fact that not only was Brenda a lesbian but more so that Glenn knew it all along and never told him.

Another week went by without any sign from Brenda, positive or negative. John's patience ran out and he called Glenn to say that he should talk to Brenda and let her know that John was getting pissed off and threaten her that they could make her life very miserable if they had to. John was so excited about this sex slave thing that he simply disregarded the fact that Brenda never said that she was gone call him, Glenn panicked with the idea that he had to do the dirty work, knowing that it was not going to change anything. It was time to let John in on the secret life of Brenda and Tammy, hoping that John finally would come to his senses and that this plan of his was a pie in the sky and could never be executed.

Glenn gathered his courage and drove to John's house.

John opened the front door. He looked at Glenn and said, "What's going on? I can tell from that confused and scared look on your face that something is wrong. Come on, let's have it."

Glenn took a deep breath and with a shaky voice said, "I think I know why Brenda is not responding to you. There is a rumor going around that Brenda is a lesbian."

John looked in disbelief at his friend, shook his head and burst out laughing. "Who the fuck put that nonsense in your tiny head? Brenda the party girl is playing for a

different team. That's rich. I could accept that she is AC/
DC but lesbian no way. Half of the seniors had sex with
her. As far as I know that's not what lesbians do he said
mockingly. You know what they do, don't you? They play
with each other's pussy, that's what they do. They don't
let guys fuck them. Do you have any other pearls of
wisdom you want to share with me or is that it for the day.
And by the way, when and how did you find this out?"

Glenn did not respond to the last part of the question
but asked John, "How can you be so sure that all these
guys really had sex with her? I know for a fact that you or
I didn't, so why do you think that anybody else succeeded.
You tried hard enough and couldn't get to first base and
neither could I."

John's first reaction was that he hadn't tried to get
her, but Glenn saw doubt creeping into his face and knew
that he would check it out before making any more moves
on Brenda. This suited Glenn just fine. More time for him
to get out of this crazy scheme.

Chapter 5

Carla had left her home when she was 16 years old. She was told by her father to respect the rules of the house or ship out. She had no intention of following rules that dictated she be home at a certain curfew, stop smoking, stop doing drugs, drinking, or dating guys her dad did not approve of. The no drinking part was a joke coming from somebody who had not been sober for as long as she could remember.

One morning after another shouting match among her mother, father and herself, she left the house at the crack of dawn while her parents were still asleep. She took all the money she could find from her mother's purse and her father's money that he had left on his night stand, a total of $54. Together with the $25 she had saved it came to a total of $79. She felt guilty and left a note to her mother saying that she would send money to her as soon as she got a job and that she loved them both but could no longer live with them. She said she was afraid that one day she would be hurt by them.

Carla took a public bus to the French Quarter and started looking for a job. She got really lucky and soon found a restaurant that had a sign in the window that said "help wanted." She walked in and asked about the sign, the manager looked at her and asked how old she was and what waiting tables experience she had. She told him she was 18 years old and used to work in a restaurant called "The Round Table," knowing that this restaurant was closed and the owner had left town deep in debt. It would be difficult to check this reference.

The manager spent more time evaluating her looks and body than checking her credentials as a waitress. He told her that she could start immediately at an hourly wage of $2.15 plus tips. Carla did not hesitate and immediately accepted this offer. The first night she worked she made $70 and was ecstatic about it. She had never had that kind of money. At the end of her shift she asked one of the other waitresses where she could find a cheap room for the night because she had just come into town and did not know where to go. The other waitress, a more mature woman, said, "Well it's almost midnight it will be hard to find a place now. Look, why don't you stay with me for your first night and we will find something more permanent tomorrow."

An apartment or even a room that Carla could afford was not easy to find. Her new friend told Carla that she could stay with her for $400 a month including the cost of the utilities. Carla thankfully accepted this generous offer and moved in with her. This worked out very well and both were happy with the arrangement.

Carla quickly became a good waitress. Her looks helped her to get tips far exceeding the normal 15 percent. She made an average of $500 a week and was able to send her mother some money.

One evening a handsome young man was having dinner at the restaurant and started to talk to Carla. He asked her if on her night off she would like to go out with him, maybe to a movie or whatever she wanted to do. Carla thought why not? I haven't been out of the apartment for months except to go to work. So she accepted the invitation and they would meet on her next day off, which happened to be the following day. They would meet outside the restaurant at 7:00PM. Carla was a bit nervous. The boys she had dated before were all her age while this guy was at least 10 years older than she was.

That first night they went to see a movie and had a late dinner after. He behaved like a real gentlemen and told her that he was 27 years old and was a salesman for a large insurance company. He lived in a small apartment in the French Quarter, was single, never married before and that he was attracted to her the moment he walked into the restaurant the night before. He walked her to her place and asked if she had a good time and if so, could he see her again. Think about it, "he said," and we can talk next time I come to the restaurant." Carla gave him a peck on the cheek and thanked him for the lovely evening and she looked forward to seeing him again.

When she came home that night her roommate was still awake and Carla couldn't wait to tell her everything and how much she liked him and was going to see him again.

Her roommate said, "I don't want to rain on your parade, but be careful don't rush it. Go slow and give it some time. This is New Orleans and we have a lot of smooth operators here taking advantage of young good looking girls like you. I'm not saying he is one of them but if he really likes you he will be patient and understanding. He must realize that the age difference is scaring you a little.

Carla was a little disappointed that her roommate, Susan, didn't share her enthusiasm and wasn't happy for her but was pleased at the same time that she cared about her and wanted to protect her.

This once a week dating with Philippe continued for about a month at the same pace. Carla became more and more enamored and loved the way he treated her. But on the last date, while they were having dinner, Philippe asked if she was satisfied with being a waitress and said that he felt she could be so much more. There were so many opportunities in a place like New Orleans for a smart, sexy and above all beautiful girl like she was. Carla was flattered but at the same time a little worried and confused about this question and wondered what Philippe had in mind. She answered that she would, of course, like to have a better paying job but she had never finished high school, and had no other working experience than being a waitress, she said "why do you ask, everybody wants to have a better paying job?"

Philippe answered, "I know some girls half as pretty as you who make a lot more money than you do. I was just curious to know if you would be interested in work like that. But if you're happy with what you're doing that's fine with me."

That night in her room Carla pondered the question, did Philippe asked her that because he wanted to know if she had ambitions, or because he wanted their relationship to progress further. She simply could not figure it out. The following week Philippe couldn't make it on her day off. He had a meeting and dinner with a potential important customer; Clara was concerned. Was it something that she said on the last date when he asked her whether she was interested in making more money. So far their dates were amicable but had not progressed romantically. Carla was willing to take their relationship to a more intimate level but Philippe seemed to hesitate doing so. Maybe he did not have a lot of experience with girls or was naturally shy.

She decided on their next date to take the initiative and ask him to go to his apartment, saying that she was interested to see where he lived. She would tell him that she would ask him to come to her apartment but that was more complicated because she had a roommate and they would not have much privacy. That should give him a hint that it was okay to be more romantic, even go all the way if he wanted to. Carla had limited sexual experiences, mostly with 16 or 17 year olds, experiments which made her wonder what the big deal was about sex. For her the sexual act had been something that was finished before it began. She hoped that it would be different with the right partner, but she had her doubts about this sexual thing. She started to like Philippe a lot and wanted this relationship to continue and hopefully lead to being loving and permanent.

The next date with Philippe would be different because he asked if she would mind having dinner with one of his friends and his girlfriend. Carla was somewhat disappointed because she had other plans for that night. But she agreed and they decided to have dinner at their favorite Cajun restaurant in the French Quarter. Carla was excited to finally meet one of Philippe's friends. She had often wondered if he had close friends that he spent some time with when he wasn't working.

His friend wasn't there yet when they arrived in the restaurant but Philippe told her not to worry. His friend was always late; he had a busy schedule and worked strange hours.

They arrived almost an hour late and Carla could not believe that this guy who walked in was actually a friend of Philippe's. He was the exact opposite of what she pictured him to look like. She had expected somebody conventional like Philippe. This friend was dressed like a rock star, or rapper or one of the other entertainment celebrities you see in the movies, a lot of bling, and the girl on his arm could very well have been one of the ladies you see plying her trade on every street corner in New Orleans. Carla was shocked and could not believe that Philippe had invited this guy to have dinner with them.

His name was Mike and the girl friend was Mary. Mike immediately ordered a bottle of champagne and instructed the waiter that it had to be ice cold and he wanted it now and when I say now I mean now. Carla, herself being a waitress, found his behavior very rude and she immediately disliked Mike. Mary must have been used to this boorish behavior because she nodded in agreement with the way he ordered. Mike saw the look on Carla's face and told her that you have to let these lazy bastards know from the start who's the customer and they are only the waiters. The remark hurt Carla even more and she whispered to Philippe asking if he was always like that or was he trying to impress them.

Philippe lowered his voice and responded, "That's Mike. You have to take him the way he is."

They placed their order and Mike said to Carla. "I understand that you are interested in changing jobs and making some real money. If you do you are talking to the right guy. I run an escort business and my girls all make plenty of cash." He turned to Mary. "Isn't that right honey?" She enthusiastically nodded her head.

Mike said that his escort business was called "Full Satisfaction". He did not say exactly what services his outfit provided.

Carla liked the idea of making more money but was annoyed that Philippe had put her in this position without telling her about this before. She would definitely not have wanted to work for a jerk like Mike.

Carla replied, "Yes I'm interested in making more money but I want to know more about what this escort business is before I can decide."

"Well that's why I brought Mary along. She has been in this business for a long time. She can tell you all you need to know, and she may even tell you how much cash she makes every week."

Mary smiled, "it's really easy money but before you even consider this kind of work, you will have to change your appearance, clothing, hair style and make up. I'm sure with your body you won't have any trouble at all fitting in. Maybe we should get together some time without these guys around and I can explain the tricks of the trade to you."

Carla nodded. "That would probably be better than talking business during dinner." She wanted to get out of there as soon as possible.

The guys started to talk sports and she and Mary discussed movies and Carla's job, which did not seem to interest Mary much. Mike picked up the tab and Carla was surprised that Philippe did not offer to split it. It was a pretty steep bill because Mike and Mary guzzled down the wine like it was water, and the main courses Mike and Mary ordered were the most expensive on the menu.

On the way home Carla voiced her surprise about Philippe being friendly with Mike. "You two are so different I can't believe you guys are friends. You have nothing in common." The look on Philippe's face told her that she had touched on a subject Philippe was not willing to discuss with her. She asked Philippe whether he thought it was a good idea to meet with Mary to find out more about the escort service job.

He immediately said, "Of course you should. This may be an opportunity of a lifetime for you. I know for a fact that Mike is making a lot of money with it."

"How did you and Mike become friends?" Carla asked.

Philippe seemed hesitant to answer but after a while he said, "Mike and I know each other from high school, and Mike helped me out when I was in a bind, and needed help."

Carla did not asked anything further because Mike had said during dinner that he was relatively new in the area. Besides he seemed to be a lot younger than Philippe to be in high school at the same time. She thought it was strange for Philippe to lie about something like that but did not pursue it any further.

Carla met with Mary a couple of days later for lunch and a briefing on what an escort girl's job description was. Mary started out by stating that when you meet a client for the first time you need to be at your best, that includes looks, attitude, behavior with the emphasis on looks and being sexy.

Carla asked, "Why is sexy looking a major requirement?"

Mary rolled her eyes. "These guys who can afford that kind of money they want to show you off. They have wives at home who in most cases feel securely married with a bunch of kids. Sexy looking is no longer high on their priority list. So for the middle aged successful business man, being seen with a good looking sexy, half his age girl is an ego booster which they all seem to have a need for. That's why you have to look sexy."

Carla nodded, "Yes, I can see why that is important, but what if they want more than just companionship for the evening?"

"Well," Mary said, "that's entirely up to you. If you want to make a lot more money you can go that route. If you don't, you just tell him this is an escort service not a whore house. In this business you will encounter three different types.

The wary business man who just doesn't want to have dinner by himself and wants some good looking company to spend the evening with. This guy will want to meet you in the hotel lobby or at a restaurant, for these clients you dress chic but not too sexy.

Second category is the same as category one but in the back of his mind is sex, and if he feels that you could accommodate him, he will pursue this and again you can accept or refuse. He also will want you to meet him at the hotel lobby or a restaurant.

Category three is the one that is not looking for companionship but wants sex, pure and simple. You will know that before you have even laid eyes on him. You dress the same way unless you want to accommodate him and have sex with him, in that case you need to dress sexy.

He will want you to come to his room in the hotel, a bottle of champagne will be in plain view, and his greeting will be with a French kiss or a grab at your ass. You will know immediately what he has in mind. So you can stay or run. If you're planning to stay you can't dress sexy enough and show your attributes."

Mary saw the concerned look on Carla's face. "Category three guys are the exception. Most of our customers are in category one or two."

She did not mention that 90 percent of their clients were in the category two and three sections. She felt that

Carla was not ready to process that information, and her instructions from Mike were to tell her anything you want as long as she comes on board. She would be a moneymaker from day one, with her innocent young gorgeous face and terrific body she will be high in demand. Mary knew that Mike was counting on her and there would be unpleasant consequences if she failed.

Mary also stated that the agency had a list of regular customers and they selected the girls in accordance with the preferences of the clients. If for instance she was only interested in category one clients, they would only assign that type of customer. After all, it is in the agency's best interest to match the customer with the type of girl he prefers. That was only good business. But she had to keep in mind that category two and three customers are a lot more lucrative than the companionship only clients. Some of the girls were making $2,000 a week for their services.

Carla still felt somewhat uncomfortable working for an outfit that delivered part time hookers to their clients. She assumed that this operation must be illegal and she could get in trouble with the law working for them.

She mentioned this to Mary who said, "No, this is not how it works; the girl who agrees to satisfy a client's sexual needs does that entirely on their own. The agency is not involved and will bill the client only for the companionship part of this arrangement. We don't even want to know about it. This is nothing to worry about, and this agency is running in full compliance with the law. If one of our girls has sex with a client she collects from him and the agency will not know about it."

Mary continued by saying that Carla would have to buy a set of outfits needed for an escort girl. She assured her that she would go with Carla when she went on this buying spree."

"I don't have that kind of money to buy expensive clothes and other accessories that go with it," said Carla.

Mary assured her that Mike would lend her the money if he could count on her to stay on until at least the loan was paid off.

"What about training?" Carla asked. "I've never done anything like this before. What do I say? How do I handle myself?"

"I will coach you." Mary replied. "There's nothing to it. The client usually does all the talking. You just listen and nod your head. They like it when you agree with them. Never get into an argument with them. They usually have enough of that at home. Another topic to avoid, never talk politics. The weather, restaurants, movies, health issues and whatever sports he is interested in are usually safe topics of conversation."

Carla was still a bit nervous but decided to go ahead anyway. She could always bail out if she wanted to|.

She told Mary that she was in and asked her how to proceed from there?

Mary assured her that she would take care of the paperwork and only needed to know when she wanted to start, her birthday and Social Security number

Carla said, "That she was 18 years old but would have a problem with giving her SS number. She at left it at home and did not know her social security number. She was afraid to go home to ask her parents because her father had told her never to come near him again. Maybe I can call my mother and ask her."

Mary waived it off. "Yes, that's OK. Just give it to me whenever you have it."

This sounded to Carla like it wasn't all that important. The restaurant never had asked her for it because she was never officially on their payroll and was paid in cash every night.

It was Mary's intent to let Carla handle the companionship only customers first. She did not want to scare her off by exposing her to the core business the agency specialized in.

Mary told her that she should quit her waitress job immediately because she had to take care of buying the outfits needed for her new job, and she might have clients for her as early as next week.

Carla was hoping that she could keep her job while trying out the escort business but that seemed to be impossible. She was actually afraid to give up her present employment for something she really was not sure she could handle.

She decided to talk to Philippe first and ask his advice before making that decision. Philippe; knowing Mike as a friend, was in a better position to gauge the risk she was taking with this new job. She called him that same evening and when she explained the situation he said, "Do you realize the opportunity you've been offered? This could bring you from borderline poverty to a very well to do young lady. I recommend you don't jeopardize this chance in a lifetime deal, because you want to keep your minimum wage job. I can't believe you even hesitate. Sometimes you have to make decisions and take risks. You by leaving your home at the age of 16, know about risks. You took one and you never regretted it. Take this opportunity baby otherwise you may regret it forever."

In spite of Philippe's endorsement Carla still had doubts but she had already made the decision to take the job. She might as well quit her waitress job.

When she told her roommate about the escort job, the woman looked at her and said, "I know you're young and inexperienced but I thought you were very smart for your age. Obviously I was wrong."

"What do you mean?" Said Carla I can get a job paying at least three times what I'm making now and you try to make me feel stupid."

The woman said, "Don't you understand that an escort service is just a more sophisticated and elegant name for a prostitution ring run by crooks and pimps?"

Carla cringed and felt small and dumb. Deep inside this was exactly what she thought at first, and now hearing that gave her the horrible feeling that she had made a terrible mistake by accepting this job.

Maybe she could talk to Mary and say that she had second thoughts and hopefully they would let her out the agreement she had signed.

She called Mary and told her that she had inquired further into jobs like that and repeated what people said about the reputation of these escort agencies.

Mary immediately went on the defensive but agreed that some agencies operated that way. "Total Satisfaction was definitely not one of those. Carla could be assured about that and Mary vouched for her agency and said she wouldn't be working for Mike if it was not a reputable enterprise."

"Why don't you ask for a couple of weeks off at the restaurant, tell them that your mother or father is seriously ill and that you need to go home to help out? If they agree and you don't like working for the agency you can always go back and you keep your job."

Mary also reminded her that she had signed a contract and if she negated this agreement Mike could give her a lot of trouble. "And believe me she said you don't want to be on Mike's shit list."

Carla gave this some thought and decided that she really had nothing to lose. The people at the restaurant were very understanding and agreed to let her take a couple of weeks off, and when she came back her job would still be there.

Carla was thrilled with this arrangement and told Mary she was ready to start and to get the clothes and other accessories needed.

They decided to go shopping the next day and she could be in action one or two days later. She called Philippe to tell him the news. He seemed to be very happy and said she had made the right choice. Philippe also told her that he would be out of town for a couple of weeks on business and that he would call her during the coming days from wherever he was at that time. He said that his itinerary was not yet cast in stone so he couldn't tell her where he would be.

Carla was a bit disappointed because she wanted to be able to talk about her first day at work and how it went, but she could tell him that on the phone. That will have to do till he came back from his business trip.

The call came to Carla around noon time. She picked up the phone and somehow knew this was Mary calling. It was Mary.

"This is the day," she announced. "You're on tonight. Ready or not here you go. I'm just kidding, of course, you're ready. I will come over around 6 o'clock to refresh with you the things we talked about the last few days."

She hung up leaving Carla in a panic mode. She herself was surprised that she had reacted like this. She was always a kid that was self assured, always ready to be adventurous, never afraid to experience the unknown. So why was she so nervous about getting into this escort job? She didn't know the answer but was determined to do it and do it right, after all it was just having dinner with a middle aged lonely man.

By the time Mary arrived she had her nerves under control and felt almost calm and collected. Mary gave her some information on the client. He was a 62 years old businessman from Detroit, CEO of an automotive parts distributor, married with two children not living with them anymore. He had no specific requirements from the escort girl, except that she was good looking, not too flashily dressed. Mary felt that he was looking for a girl that if need be he could present as his daughter. Excellent customer for a rookie escort girl.

They would meet at the New Orleans Marriott hotel lobby. Mary escorted Carla and introduced her to Mr. Tom Crosby. She then left Carla with her gentlemen for the evening. Mr. Crosby was the fatherly type, gray thinning hair, a bit of a pouch, but overall a pleasant enough looking mature man.

He said to Carla," I understand that you are fairly new in this business and I want you to understand that all I want from you is your company and conversation."

This reassured Carla that this was something she could handle and made her feel comfortable.

She answered," Thank you Mr. Crosby I will try to make this a pleasant evening for you and hopefully we'll find something in common to talk about."

"Please, call me Tom. That will make me more at ease he said. I don't very often have dinner with such a lovely lady like you. Calling me Mr. Crosby reminds me too much that we have a business relationship. Using my first name make me feel that we know each other and are friends."

"Now we have to decide where we want to eat or more important what do we want to eat"

Carla said, "It really doesn't matter. I'm starved. I was so nervous all day I couldn't eat. You put me so at ease and relaxed that my appetite came back. I'm usually a good eater and eat almost anything. The only thing I'm not too fond of is Sushi."

Thank God," Tom said, "I never understood people eating raw fish; see we already have something in common. The restaurant in the hotel is apparently quite good. This way we can have a drink in the bar here and move from there to the restaurant and we don't have to bother taking a taxi or using my rental car."

Carla agreed with this whole heartedly. She felt comfortable and safe in the confinements of the hotel and with Tom's company, she thought this is actual enjoyable. He was good company and seemed to like her. He was obviously curious to know why a young attractive girl would spend an evening with a middle aged men, she must have better things to do than that. Carla thought I better be honest and tell him why I'm in this position. She said, "You probably wonder why I chose to become an escort girl."

He looked at her and said, "Was I that obvious? I'm sorry but, yes it crossed my mind. It is really none of my business."

"No it's okay. I want you to know, I come from a very dysfunctional family. My father is a Vietnam veteran and when he came home he needed psychiatric care but never really recovered. He became an alcoholic, an abusive and violent man to the extent that my mother and I were afraid of him. He took most of his frustrations out on my mother, verbal and physical. Unfortunately, my mother in turn then started to take it out on me. I took this for a long time but when I turned sixteen I decided to leave home and got myself a job as a waitress. I was a waitress till about a month ago when I met somebody in the restaurant where I worked. He came in for dinner and we started talking and before he left asked whether I would like to go to movie or have dinner with him. I accepted and we were dating once a week on my day off. He was the one who introduced me to one of his friends who owns the escort agency. He offered me a job as an escort girl. At first I said no, mainly because I didn't even know what an escort girl was. To be honest, I thought they were high priced hookers. His friend had a girl with him who said to me don't say no. Find out first what it's all about and then decide. These girls make quite a bit of money, I bet at least twice or three times what a waitress make, I know she said, because I did both. So I decided to find out more about it and she said let's have some lunch together and I can explain the job to you. So we did and she convinced me that Mike's outfit was above board, and well the rest is history and I'm here with you being an escort girl."

Tom said, "That was quite a story. I hope this will turn out well for you. You deserve some happy times after what you've been through in your young life. Let me tell you a little about myself so that we are more or less even when it comes to our backgrounds.

I'm the owner of a small company in Detroit. I'm married and have two daughters. They are both married, happy I presume. They both moved out of Detroit and I don't see them that often. I suppose that's what happens when your children have their own families, but I still wish we were closer, and I could be part of their lives. After the children left the house my wife became a different person, and I was either in my office at the plant or away on business.

"She was lonely and started to become religious to the point that she was in her church more than she was at home. I didn't object to that at first till it got out of hand and she became a religious fanatic. I'm not much of a church person but she insisted that I should go to church more often and I also must become an active member of the church doing things I had absolutely no interest in. That's when our marriage fell apart and we started living separately although still in the same house. I spent more and more time at my plant and traveled more often and things are getting worse.

"Well" he said, "I think we could use some food after revealing our dark secrets." Carla thought that he sounded embarrassed opening up as he did to a total stranger."

"Yes," she said, "let's change the subject and focus on the menu."

"Excellent idea. Let's order a drink first or do you prefer just have a good bottle of wine with dinner?"

Carla hesitantly said, "I'm afraid I can't join you in a drink. Contrary to what some people say, in Louisiana the legal drinking age in public is 21 not 18. There was a time that it was 18 but the US Court in New York overruled The Louisiana Court somewhere around 1998. I believe,

49

and brought the legal drinking age back to 21 in public. I know a woman should never tell a man her age but now you know I'm not 21 yet, but please, if you enjoy a glass of wine with dinner I will have a ginger ale that looks like a Chardonnay. This really is a silly law because it is not illegal for an 18 year old to drink in private."

The rest of the evening was pleasant and Tom told her that she was a very intelligent and sharp young lady with a good sense of humor. He asked her if he was in town again if she would she be his escort. The smile on Carla's face said it all. She couldn't say yes fast enough.

This delighted Tom and he said, "So we have a deal."

It was time to end the evening and Tom asked how she was going home. He offered to drive her, because New Orleans was not exactly the safest city to walk around at midnight.

"That would be very nice but the agency insists that we call their limo to pick us up, just for safety reasons," said Carla, "and to make sure we did all right."

Tom said, "I don't know if this is in accordance with escort protocol, but I want you to have my business card and if you need some advice or anything I can help you with, please call me."

"I don't know either since you are my first escort, so I'm giving you my cell phone number if you want to call me."

Tom again told her how much he loved her company and was looking forward to seeing her again.

He left her and Carla waited in the lobby for her ride home. She couldn't believe how much she enjoyed the evening and how ridiculous she had been to be so afraid of this first escort experience.

Chapter 6

Mary called her, first thing in the morning, to find out how everything went on her first day on the job. Carla was still in heaven and described the evening in detail, Mary was very pleased and told Carla her net income for that one evening was $100.

Carla was happy $100 for 4 hours of talking with a pleasant individual was not bad at all. It was about half of what she made as a waitress for a week of hard work.

Mary said, "You have another client for the day after tomorrow. He is younger than Mr. Crosby and usually wants to go out and show off his girl of the night. But don't worry he never caused any trouble with any of the other girls we supplied him. He is a lot of bark but no bite if you know what I mean. So dress accordingly. He likes his girls to look sexy and hot. That should not be a problem for you; you look hot and sexy no matter what you wear."

Carla was concerned. She had not heard from Philippe for a couple of days and he didn't answer his phone when she called him on his cell. She hoped he was OK and would call her soon. She was also dying to let him know how her first escort assignment went. She still couldn't believe it went so well and she couldn't stop thinking about Tom. He being her first escort would always be special to her.

The next time, following Mary's advice on what to wear she had chosen a pair of tight designers jeans, a low neckline orange shirt and short black boots, the result was spectacular and very sexy. She hoped it would not give the wrong signal.

Again Mary took her to the lobby of the hotel where he was staying and introduced her to Charlie. He was dressed up in obviously expensive clothes but lacked class. It was an Armani suit but it would have been more appropriate for a young rock star than for an aging businessman in his late forties. The first words out of his mouth after the introduction were, "They were not kidding. You're built like a brick shithouse."

Carla had never heard that expression and had no idea whether this was a compliment or disapproval of her looks. But he immediately followed up by saying that he had never seen a chick looking as sexy and beautiful as she was, so she assumed that it was a compliment. However she could not see the connection between looking sexy and beautiful with a shithouse. Strange duck she thought.

He obviously was not the type that wanted a quite dinner in the hotel restaurant. He announced that he had picked an expensive Creole restaurant in the French Quarter for dinner. His car, he said, was parked in front of the hotel and he was ready to go. His car, of course, was one of these foreign sports jobs. A bright red convertible that matched his personality. On the way out he put his arm around her shoulder to show everybody that this hot number was his. He got into the car, never thinking that a gentleman would open the door for his date. Carla was not used to people opening car doors for her, but she thought it would have been a nice touch if he had.

The restaurant he had chosen was first class and expensive. The moment they were seated, Charlie immediately grabbed the wine list and started looking for a wine of his liking, never asking her whether she had a preference. This escort was going to be different than her first one, no doubt about that. But the fact that Charlie was different did not mean it couldn't work out.

He ordered the wine and she was going to tell him that she legally could not drink wine but figured that in a classy establishment like this nobody would be interested and ask for proof of her age. It turned out that she was right and the waiter poured the wine in their glasses without any questions. She had to admit that either Charlie knew his wines or maybe just ordered the most expensive one on the wine list. Either way it was very good.

Dinner was excellent. Charlie did the ordering and they started with Bisque d'homard followed by Sole Normand, ending with a Crepe Suzette for desert.

During dinner the conversation was one sided, Charlie doing all the talking and Carla listening, nodding and saying a few words when she felt she needed to.

After dinner when Carla thought her job was done Charlie insisted that they visited a couple of bars and a club where he had a membership. They followed more or less the same pattern as during dinner. Charlie talked, Carla listened. She asked him what business he was in and he gave her a vague answer about being in the Import and Export business. She wasn't really interested in his business but thought that she needed to show some interest in what he did.

When they got to his club, he wanted to dance with her. He talked to the crooner of the small band that was playing and the next song was a slow song and Charlie asked her to dance, he held her very tight and started to softly kiss her on the cheek and neck, Carla figured that this was the time to let him know that she was an escort, nothing more and that she didn't kiss or have sex with somebody she'd met for the first time. He took this surprisingly well and said that he understood, but that the people at the agency told him that if he wanted to have a more romantic ending of the evening it was certainly possible.

Carla responded and told him that some of the girls would do that but that she was not one of them. She apologized and added that the agency made the wrong match up; if he used the agency again he should make it clear to them what he expected.

He said, "No I won't do that because next time I'm in town I will demand to have you again as my escort. This was a fabulous night for me, spending the evening with a girl like you was just unbelievable."

They drove back to his hotel after Carla told him the agency's rule was to pick her up there. When they kissed goodnight at the hotel he gave her a small envelope and said, "This is a little surprise for you." He then walked into the hotel and she waited for her pick up.

Carla was curious to know what the envelope was all about and quickly opened it. There was a little note that read "Thank you for this lovely evening you gave me. Take this as my gift to you." A $100 bill was attached to the note. First Carla was offended but on second thought realized that was just Charlie. He didn't give her the money to make her feel bad or to belittle her, he was showing that he had a good time.

That evening Carla made $240 it almost made up her mind to never go back to the restaurant to wait on tables. This was too easy.

The morning after she tried again and again to contact Philippe to no avail. She feared that something had happened to him.

When Carla went to the office to get her money, she saw Mary and told of her concern about Philippe not answering her calls.

Mary gave her a strange look and said, "Well I believe Mike and Philippe had dinner together last night."

Carla answered, "No, that's impossible Philippe would have called me if he was back in town."

Mary look puzzled and said, "Why would Philippe call you. His job is done."

She glanced at Carla Oh no, you didn't, did you?" she asked. "You were romantically involved with Philippe. Oh, sweetheart, she said, "It could not have been serious. I'm sure he never really kissed you did he?"

Carla admitted that it never happened but that she thought perhaps he was shy and needed more time.

Mary said, "This is going to hurt, but here it is. Philippe is as square as a $3 bill. He is gay. He is a faggot. He has had a live-in boyfriend for years. Philippe never kissed a woman. He hates women. How could you not have seen this?"

Carla couldn't say a word. She thought she was going to pass out.

Mary ran to the water cooler to get some water. Carla was white as a sheet and needed to sit down. She wasn't sure what she was feeling. Was it embarrassment, humiliation, anger? Was she really in love with this person was it the hurt that made her feel this way? She slowly recuperated and was able to ask Mary why he had done this to her. What did it accomplish? She had no money and obviously he didn't want her for her looks or body. So why?

Mary said quietly, "Philippe works for Mike. He is Mike's recruiter. His job is to find extremely good looking, sexy, vulnerable young girls like you. When he finds one he brings Mike into the picture. I had no idea that you were unaware of this process when we first met. I now feel bad that I encouraged you to join the agency."

Carla walked home, her mind working full speed with no specific goal to focus on, just jumping from one thing to another. She finally slowed down and pure raw anger mixed with hate took over. This anger and hate was focused on all men. She would never trust any of them again. From now on they were all enemies, and every single one that crossed her path would pay for this.

Her initial reaction was to quit this job, but then she thought that would be foolish. She could make good money and all these guys that needed escorts would be handed to her on a silver platter. She would just have to manipulate them, and she knew by now that with her looks that would be easy. They would eat out of her hand and then the hand would disappear, leaving them wanting more. Revenge was the name of the game and the rules were hers.

She called Mary and said, "In order for me to get over this creep I need to work as much as I can. Work will take my mind off this disastrous situation and get me out of this depressed mode I'm in."

Mary said, "I will do everything I can to help you, but all of the clients I have on the books for the coming days are category 2 clients."

"That's OK." Answered Carla "I understand the rules. Just for my information how much do I make if I sleep with one of them?"

"$500 at a minimum." Mary responded. "It depends. If you spend the whole night with them it's $750 a pop."

Carla thought, "How does she know that? She told me that this was strictly between the girl and the client and the agency had no part in these transactions at all. Then the light went on. Of course Mary knows. She used to be one of them and obviously was not restricted to category 1 customers."

The next escort for Carla was again a middle aged man, on the pudgy side, also a business man away from home, ready for a sexual adventure in the big city, using the agency to supply him with the merchandise to achieve this. In this case it was Carla.

He told here from the start that she was beautiful. In fact, she was the girl of his dreams. Keeping him company in a restaurant or bar was not his priority. He wanted her in bed right then, but didn't know how to tell her that. She didn't look like a hooker. She behaved like a classy girl; she actually intimidated him a little. Although he was the paying customer she seemed to be in charge and she made him feel that he should be grateful that she accepted him as an escort. Shouldn't this be the other way around? He thought.

Carla sensed that he was a guy, with a lot of money who was not very sure of himself and was willing to let her make the decisions. She suggested a restaurant and he immediately agreed without asking what type of restaurant it was. It did not matter to him. Eating was just a prelude to the real action.

Carla asked him how long he was going to be in town. He replied that he would be there the whole week. Carla made up her mind that sex was not on the menu that night for this gentleman, who's name was Mark, no last name. They would have dinner, go to a couple of bars, dance a little, get him inpatient, horny and than tell him that the party was over.

The evening progressed more or less as planned by Carla. Mark drank more than he could handle, which worked for Carla. He started to be more amorous as the evening went on and she encouraged him. This made him believe that the night would end with her in his bed making passionate love. It never got that far because that was not what Carla had planned.

When they got back to his hotel she said, "Well it's time for me to go."

Mark sobered up instantly when it registered that this gorgeous, sexy woman was not going to sleep with him. He loudly protested but she explained that the contract with the agency was for five hours of companionship and the time was up. She could not change the rules and was bound to the arrangement he made with the agency.

He became belligerent and shouted, "What the fuck agreements are you talking about."

She calmly replied, "If you can't behave like a civilized human being, this conversation is over. I will inform the agency of your behavior and I doubt that you will ever be able to use our services again. Good Night."

She walked away, leaving the poor bastard in disbelief. Lesbian bitch he shouted to her as she disappeared into the dark night.

The following morning Carla informed Mary about the incident.

Mary said, "This happens sometimes. I just hope we haven't lost a client.

"I don't think so. I would be very surprised if he doesn't call later today and wants another date with me for tonight. He had a taste of me. He felt my ass, my tits, and I'm sure he wants more of it. Just tell him that you will have to talk me into seeing him again after last night. You guys shouldn't complain. You have two bookings instead of one this way."

Carla was right, Mark did call and Mary told him she had to ask Carla. She said that Carla was in tears when she told her about what had happened.

Mary said, "You have to understand, Carla is not one of the girls waiting for a $50 trick on a street corner in The District. That's not what she is. She asked me not to, but I will give you her cell phone number and it would be better if you called her and apologized yourself for your behavior last night. I understand these things happen but Carla is just not used to it. People in general realize that she is a charming, sophisticated girl and they treat her as such. If you're going to act like she is another sexy looking piece of ass, you better forget her and I wouldn't bother calling her. Think about it before you pursue her any further and remember she is very special."

Mark did give it some thought and his first reaction was. Fuck that slut. Who needs this? I can get laid anytime I want. She is not the only good looking whore in this city. There are a lot of professionals better looking than that Carla bitch. But while he was saying that to himself, she got into his mind and he felt an instant erection developing. Just like that, he knew that he would never get her out of his mind. He had to get her. He tried to picture in his head how she would look naked with him on top of him making love. He at least had to see her again and hopefully restore the damage he had caused.

Mark was a good businessman, but the problem he was having had nothing to do with closing a business deal. This was a mind game and he was no match for Carla in that department. Unfortunately for him he was not aware of this. That uncomfortable feeling he had was only the beginning of what was in store for him.

He picked up the phone and called Carla. She had caller I.D and it read New Orleans Hilton. She knew this was Mark and did not answer, knowing he would call every 15 minutes until she finally answered the phone. That wouldn't happen for at least another hour or so.

Carla was new at this game, but she was learning fast and focused on creating as much damage to every male who had the misfortune to come into her life.

The phone rang again and Carla decided to talk to him. "Hello," she said in a voice as cold as ice, "who's calling?

"This is Mark. Please don't hang up. I need to talk to you."

Carla replied, "Give me one reason why I should ever talk to you again. You insulted me, called me names and treated me like a two bit prostitute."

With that she hung up and decided she would not answer his succeeding calls for at least two hours. As she expected, he kept calling and calling for the next two hours.

When she finally answered the phone she said," I don't know why you keep calling me. We have nothing to say to each other, so what do you want. Please leave me alone and go back to your wife. I assume she is used to being treated that way."

"Please," Mark said. "Can we see each other? I need to talk to you one more time. I apologize, but that's not enough. You must forgive me or this will hound me for the rest of my life."

Carla said "Don't be so dramatic. Last night you called me a slut and now all of a sudden you sound like you can't live without me. Give me a break."

She then realized that she had probably reached the point where she should show some compassion before he realized she was impossible to reach.

"OK, I will meet you but it has to be during the day, not at night. I can meet with you tomorrow at your hotel for lunch and we can talk there, I don't trust you enough to meet somewhere private. It has to be in a public place where we are surrounded by other people."

Mark immediately agreed and said, "I will cancel the meeting I had scheduled for that time and meet you at 12:30 for lunch."

She said okay and hung up the phone.

Carla felt that she had him wrapped around her finger and now she had to decide what to do with him next. She knew for sure that she would never have sex with him, but she wanted to find a way to keep him thinking that someday it would happen.

Carla was aware that she was playing a dangerous game, but she was consumed with anger and felt she would only find peace with revenge. Monetary gain was secondary to her and she would only separate them from their cash if that would really hurt them. Her goal was to make them feel the same she had felt when she found out how Philippe has used her.

Mark was waiting for her in the hotel lobby. As usual she had made herself look irresistible and unapproachable. What little self confidence Mark had mustered disappeared when she walked in. He smiled at her but only received a cold stare in return. She looked at him as if he was one of the bell boys from the hotel, which is how Mark felt anyway.

This was not going to be easy, he thought. He had no idea how correct he was. Carla had no intention of making this easy; on the contrary she was going to make this as difficult as it could be and take away what little self esteem he had left.

They sat down in the dining room and she asked him straight on.

"What do you want to talk about? I don't have all day and as far as I'm concerned there is not much to talk about anyway, so what is it you could not tell me over the phone?"

Mark felt like a school boy in the principal's office. He stammered, "Well I was hoping that you would forgive me for my stupid behavior and that maybe we could go out again and start all over. I promise that was not the way I normally behave. I had too much to drink and you looked so beautiful and desirable. I was infatuated and thought you would spend the night with me and when you turned your back on me I just lost all self control and went berserk. I never wanted anything in my life as bad as I wanted you last night."

Carla said, "And you are so spoiled that when you want something you have to have it, no matter what, even after I made it clear that you could not have me that night. Is that it?"

"You know what Mark? What happened last night is all too recent for me to get over it. I accept your apology but I don't want to see you for a while. If you really want to see me again, you will have to give me at least two or three weeks to forget what happened. If you want me that bad, call me and maybe we can give it another try. That's all I'm willing to do right now."

She stood up and walked out of the restaurant without even looking back.

Mark shook his head in disbelief. What was wrong with this creature? He was her customer and she treated him like shit. She must be crazy or on drugs. He knew he should get her out of his system and forget that he ever saw her. He also knew that he couldn't or wouldn't be able to do that. She was like poison for him, she must be Satan's daughter, he concluded with a chuckle.

He decided to call her back in two weeks. He must and would have her, not for one night but as his mistress, no matter what it cost him. He wondered what he could buy her, maybe jewelry or a flashy car. She must have a price. Every bitch has one and was for sale.

He was in for a very nasty surprise. Carla was not for sale.

Chapter 7

Things in Jamesville were more or less at an impasse. John was still recovering from the news that Glenn had revealed about Brenda. He still had a hard time believing that he had misjudged Brenda that badly, and blamed Glenn for not telling him about it earlier in the game.

But he secretly admitted that after talking to all these guys who claimed they had sex with Brenda, none of them had convinced him that it had actually happened. It could very well be that she was a dyke. That bitch really had everybody fooled.

The end of the summer was approaching fast and John had envisioned that the event would take place during the school vacation. That way nobody would know what was going on. People went on vacation or visited families out of town. He and Glenn would tell their parents that they would use the beach house for a couple of weeks. This had happened during previous holidays, so there would be no suspicions there. John was afraid they were running out of time to make it happen this year. He had not found a girl he wanted for this caper, and worse, he did not know how to make contact with any of the candidates left on his list. They were all friends with Brenda and if Brenda found out that John had told them about his dream the shit would hit the fan and he could forget the whole thing.

So he felt he had to find a girl from the outside, not a Jamesville high school girl. That was too risky. The problem was how did he approach a stranger with a proposition like that? She could go to the police or tell her parents or friends. Either way, it would create serious problems for him.

Deep inside John knew that for this to happen it would have to be with a stranger, a girl that could not identify John or Glenn after the happening. John also knew that the only way was to kidnap a girl and bring her to the beach house. How they were going to do this was a different story altogether.

Glenn, of course, had no idea that kidnapping a girl was something John was even contemplating. He would have flipped and probably refused to be part of it, so John kept this a secret for now. No need to upset Glenn even more than he already was. There was also the possibility of hiring a hooker for a couple of weeks but John felt this should definitely be the last resort. It would be less of a thrill and more of a make believe situation. A professional prostitute would not react and be scared like a girl who was there against her will. No it could not be a hooker. That would ruin the entire thrill that he expected from this adventure.

John's intention was not to hurt this girl, just have fun with her for a couple of weeks and then let her go. He was convinced that at some time the girl would have fun too. His twisted mind never considered the fact that the traumatic experience of being kidnapped and repeatedly raped would leave this girl with serious psychological damage for the rest of her life. He was so used to doing whatever he wanted to, he did it without worrying about the possible effect it could have on his victims. He disregarded the consequences because there never were any. Consequences were taken care of by the family lawyers or his father's checkbook.

He was aware, though, that this was something that could have serious repercussions. But the danger made him want to do this even more. As far as he was concerned, this was going to happen. It may have to be rescheduled for a later date but he would go ahead with it. No matter what! And Glenn would be part of this venture whether he wanted to or not.

Time went by and they went back to school for their senior year. Same routine as the year before, classes, basketball, parties and boring home work.

John and Glenn were still friends and hung out together. Their relationship had changed somewhat. Glenn was seeing Marissa again, so some of his spare time was devoted to her. John didn't like this too much, although there was a positive side to it. Marissa knew all the girl's gossip and told most of it to Glenn, so without knowing it she was a source of information for John. John's devious mind stored this gossip for eventual use in the future. He believed strongly that the more you knew about someone's private life the more power you had on that individual. This was probably a philosophy that ran in the Witherspoon family.

John's latest run in with the law was a DUI charge and refusal to take a breath analyzer test. This would normally be a six month suspension of your driver's license. This case never went to court and John got off with a stern talk from his father. This was proof that all men are equal with justice for all, but does not mean that justice is equal for all men. That's a common misunderstanding shared by many people. But the point is that even John had to face the consequences. He had to listen to his father for at least 10 minutes. How boring!

Since John couldn't come up with a solid plan, he didn't talk much about it with Glenn. Consequently Glenn had the wrong impression that John had given up on the "sex slave" project and that was good news, because he had always had really bad feelings about this crazy shit from the beginning, and he was relieved that John had given up on it. He should have known better. When John has an obsession he never gave up. Bad judgment on Glenn's part.

The project was in a holding pattern, not abandoned but simmering on the back burner, waiting for the right time to be rejuvenated.

The year 2005 came to an end, and John and Glenn both spent the holidays with their parents at their ski chalets in the Rockies, each doing their own thing, John drinking and whoring and Glenn doing pretty much the same. This was more or less a contest between the two. They would embellish and exaggerate the erotic encounters they had with these sexy woman at wild parties when they were back home, each trying to outdo the other, and both knowing they were lying.

Entering the year 2006, John told Glenn that would be the year we have to make it happen. Glenn pretended not to understand what John was talking about and said, "Happen what?" John sensed that Glenn knew exactly what he meant.

John using a menacing tone of voice said." Listen you little weasel. Don't start this crap again. You know what we are going to do this summer vacation and when I say we I mean we, as in you and I."

John then decided to let Glenn know that there was a change in the plan. Concerning how to get a girl. He tried to explain but when Glenn heard the word kidnapping he went ballistic, unable to talk coherently and choking on his own words. John patiently waited until the storm calmed down a little and Glenn started breathing again before he said," I know this comes as a shock to you, but I considered all other possibilities and there are no other options."

Glenn shook his head and said," Yes there is another option. You go see a shrink and after he officially diagnoses you as insane we can forget this off the wall plan of yours. This way we can live our lives free instead of being locked up in an 8 by 8 foot cell for the rest of our days."

Seething inside, John decided to stay calm, although he was ready to beat the living daylight out of Glenn for doubting his sanity.

After cooling down for a few minutes, he asked Glenn to tell him where they could find a girl that would be willing to be their sex slave, never touching on the option to forget the whole thing, acting like Glenn never mentioned it. Glenn understood that nothing had changed and John would continue planning and scheming. Glenn also knew that he had to be very careful because if he stood his ground by refusing to be part of this, John would retaliate and find a way to get Glenn in more trouble than he could handle. He already had hinted that Glenn could easily be found solely responsible for the fire that destroyed Marissa's house last spring. He must convince John that he was still game and would do whatever was necessary to pull this venture off.

Glenn some time ago had suggested that they should go to the trailer park just outside of town and pick up one of the trailer trash bitches and use her as a sex slave, give her a few hundred in cash and that would be it.

John asked him not too politely if he had gone completely crazy. Do you have any idea, "he said, what diseases this little whore could carry around? Besides where is the adventure in that? It would be just like paying a professional hooker. Forget that shit. That's not what I have in mind."

John, of course, had his doubts about Glenn's commitment to the cause and would make sure that Glenn was involved to the point that even if he bailed out, he was still be found guilty if there would be an investigation, or worse, a conviction of kidnapping.

John would continue investigating and planning for when the right victim came along. They could strike at short notice and start living his sick dream.

Chapter 8

Carla's life as an escort and part time hooker became routine and in most cases uneventful. She made really good money for very little work, and enjoyed and cherished the pain and discomfort she bestowed on the wife cheaters and perverts who had the misfortune to fall into her hands.

She was by far the most in demand girl from Mike's agency and she took full advantage of the situation. She could pick and choose her clients, work the days of her choice.

One week every month she only accepted the "Companionship only" customers. She told Mary that she needed that week to purge her soul from the nastiness she had to endure the other weeks, weeks when she had to have sex in order to hurt the ones who deserved her hate and anger. She was not aware that she did probably more mental damage to herself than to the people she targeted. She had days of depression when she asked herself if this revenge was worth the agony she went through. Did she receive the satisfaction she so desperately sought or was she just kidding herself and going through the motions because some faggot had hurt her, and was too dumb to see it?

The days she suffered from depression seemed to happen more frequently, and when she talked to Mary about it she said, "You can go see a psychiatrist or another doctor and they will prescribe anti-depressants that will make you feel like a zombie most of the time, and make you want to sleep twenty hours a day. Or you can just smoke a joint once in a while and feel better immediately."

The thought of doing illegal drugs made her hesitant to take Mary's advice, but when she looked on the Internet about the possible side effects of the anti depressant drugs. She decided to try the marijuana way and see if that would change anything. Marijuana was in some states prescribed by doctors, so the illegal aspect of smoking a joint didn't seem that serious.

The next time she had a spell of depression she smoked a small five dollar joint and actually felt better. Little did she know that this was the beginning of something that would make her life a living hell.

Things began to change when some of the agency's clients started to complain to Mike about Carla's attitude and the way she treated them. These complaints came mostly from the so called category 3 clients. Those were the men that were being ridiculed and verbally abused by Carla because they were the ones, according to Carla, not worth living on this planet. This did not sit well with Mike because they were his most profitable customers, and losing them was simply not acceptable. He warned Carla that she had to change drastically or she was out of there. He demanded that she apologize to some of the guys who she apparently had insulted the worst.

She had no intention of apologizing to these scum bags, and told Mike that he couldn't fire her because she quit, but don't be surprised if you lose them as customers anyway, she said."

Mike got angry and said, "If you dare to steal his customers she will regret it as long as she lives, which may not be much longer. I have more connections and power in this city than she can even think of, and to be careful not fuck with him."

Carla was well aware that Mike was a dangerous man and one would be better off not to cross him. She, however, was in a mental state that would and could not alter the course she had set for herself, so Mike's warnings were not heeded or taken into consideration. Carla was staying on course even if that was a path of self destruction.

Mary, of course, was no longer scheduling Carla for any of the clients who were her regulars. When Carla started to contact these clients she either got the cold shoulder or a response that they were not interested in a crazy bitch like she was, and definitely not with someone who had a disease.

She put two and two together and concluded that this was Mike's work to keep her from infringing on his clients. Nothing was beneath him, that miserable son of a bitch would sell his mother for a buck.

Carla soon realized that once a rumor like that spread, people got scared and nothing could reverse this. No matter what Carla said it didn't matter. The damage was done. If she wanted to continue in this business she would have to build her own client base. She soon found out that this was easier said than done. For a while she did fairly well by hanging out in the upscale hotel lobbies. There, of course, the concierge had to be bribed for her to operate. Most of these clients were well to do people who discreetly told the concierge that they wanted an escort for the evening and asked if the concierge could provide one for them. Not only did the concierge pocket a nice tip from these gentlemen, he also collected from Carla, so this was a lucrative business for him.

She also had started to use cocaine and was on the road to becoming a full blown drug addict.

The hotel lobby scene worked for a while until one night, the client was a fairly young, good looking guy and Carla wondered why he needed a paid escort. He could have picked up almost any girl in one of the French Quarters bars. Maybe she figured he got his kicks using a professional escort or call girl. He turned out to be an undercover detective who took her out for a good dinner, a couple of drinks and then asked her if she was interested in sleeping with him. Carla agreed and when they went to his room he asked her if by any chance she had any drugs she could provide him? Carla had a few small bags with cocaine with her, which she occasionally used.

He then asked what the going rate for sex was with her. The moment she said $500, he grabbed her arms and clipped the handcuffs on her wrists, saying she was under arrest for possession with intent to sell illegal drugs, prostitution, and for consuming alcohol under age. Carla started cursing the detective and tried to hit him while handcuffed. She managed to kick him in the crotch. He pinned her down on the floor with his foot on her neck. He was angry and yelled." Listen you little slut. You give me any more trouble I'll shoot you." He then added assault of a police officer to the charges and called for a squad car to pick her up.

Carla had difficulty coming up with the $500 bail, but managed not being locked up. A preliminary hearing was set for a week later, but she never showed up and a warrant for her arrest was issued.

Life began spiraling downward for Carla. She could not show her face in hotel lobbies any longer, because the police were now looking for her and she would end up in jail if they found her, something she was deathly afraid of. She had heard stories about what happened to good looking girls in jail.

The only way she knew how to make fast money was by selling her body. She decided to try the street corners in the quarter. That turned out to be very dangerous because the police were there in force and she would be picked up in no time if she was working there.

She needed protection from the police, so one of the other street walkers told her one way to get protection was to have a pimp who paid off the cops. Carla didn't like the idea of working the streets and then giving most of the money she made to some low life who drove around in a fancy car with expensive jewelry draped all over him.

She finally admitted that there were no other options so she reluctantly became a working girl for a pimp. She swore that this was definitely temporary and she would run away from this life as soon as she accumulated a bit of money.

She also realized that drugs were part of the reason for the bind she was in and she decided to go cold turkey right then. Simply "say no" as the slogan went.

This would be a lot harder than she could imagine but she was determined to stop using drugs. They were ruining her life and doing a hell of job of it. She knew that she could do it and she would, that was all there was to it. She went to meetings at Narcotic Anonymous, but decided it was a waste of time for her. If she wanted to quit she would have to do it by herself.

The NA people had given her some good advice, some of which was that if the urge to do drugs got to her the best thing to do was to call a friend who also used to be a user, and visit or talk with him until the urge subsided. Carla remembered that the woman she had lived with for a while told her that she was a drug addict in her youth. She asked her if she would be her mentor.

She said, "Of course, I still consider myself a drug addict, although I have been sober for a number of years. I will be more than happy if I can help somebody to kick this disease."

Her mentor reminded her that once an addict always an addict. "You must be aware that you will have to fight this battle for the rest of your life. Yes, it will get easier, but it will always be there and will attack you when you are the most vulnerable. Going to NA meetings is one way to remind you that you are an addict and that all the people who are there are in the same boat, all fighting the same war. I would never have been able to stay sober if it wasn't for the support I got during those meetings."

Chapter 9

The TV weather forecast now indicated that hurricane Katrina would make landfall within the next 4 to 5 hours and was heading straight to New Orleans as a category 4 storm it had been downgraded from a 5 to a 4, still plenty dangerous and capable of creating serious damage. Some low lying areas would be completely flooded. There was also a risk that the flood gates could not withstand the water pressure and if they broke a large part of New Orleans would cease to exist.

Evacuation of the city was now mandatory and the police were trying to enforce it, but were not successful this far. Older and sick people simply refused to leave or didn't know how.

The weatherman on the screen had said with a smug look on his face, "I have been been reporting this over and over again that people should evacuate and now, of course, it's too late. The highways are jammed and traffic is going nowhere." Carla thought to herself "Yes, try to evacuate if you don't have a car or money, you moron. It's easy for the rich people to get out of town. For the poor and the sick it's a whole different ballgame."

The Mayor announced that the Louisiana Super Dome would be opened and accepted people who were unable to leave town. Food, water, sleeping cots and sanitary facilities would be available and free to the people seeking shelter in there.

Carla thought that a shelter like the Super Dome would probably be a better place than the fleabag motel room she was in. Being with other people would be more desirable than facing this Katrina bitch by herself.

She gathered whatever valuable belongings she had and headed for the safety of the dome. Thousands and thousands of people were already in there when she arrived, but this was a big place and she found an area that was not too crowded and a sleeping cot free for her to use. It was not exactly the Hilton but it would have to do. She had no other options, so she would adjust. The places where she had stayed in the last months were not exactly luxurious either.

The dome was slowly filling up and people became jittery and upset because nothing seemed to be organized, it was chaos and the volunteers were running around in circles trying to help people. You could see that the idea of using the Super Dome as a shelter was a last minute decision and the volunteers were not trained or properly informed and didn't know what to do with this mass of people, all needing something. Carla was proud of herself that in a situation like this she was able to face it without the make believe support that drugs would provide.

When the storm finally hit, heavy winds tore a piece of the Dome's roof and water started to come down on the people below. This, of course, created a stampede in order to get away from that area. What was chaotic before became now panic. Fights broke out, people argued for space they said was theirs. People fought for sleeping cots. It was a nightmare. Carla managed to keep away from most of it and stayed in her area, which was somewhat remote from the mass of panicked people.

The following day more problems surfaced. The sanitary system was unable to accommodate so many people for this long a time. Carla realized that it was designed for usage not longer than 4 to 5 hours of occupation, not for that many people and children spending the night there.

Water became scarce, toilets were overflowing, air condition units overloaded, nothing worked. Rumor had it that over 100 people had died in the dome due to heat exhaustion and that the bodies were outside just lying on the sidewalk.

One of the problems Carla faced was that the young studs discovered her and became permanent visitors in her space. She was probably the best looking girl in the dome and as usual she attracted the male species present.

Carla was getting somewhat scared and promised herself that she would get out of there as soon as the situation outside improved. It was impossible now because the streets around the dome were still flooded.

Carla was still a looker in spite of the life she had lived and looked younger than a 19 year old. She still had a terrific sexy body that made heads turn when she walked the streets. Men were always trying to get her attention.

While she was standing in line for dinner a familiar face, a neighbor, from her parent's trailer came to her, hugged her and said, "I am so sorry about your ma and dad."

Carla stared at her and asked, "What about my parents?"

The woman looked confused till it dawned on her that Carla was not aware that her parents perished in the storm.

Carla now scared, and impatient repeated, "What about my parents?"

She then saw the woman crying and immediately understood that the worst had happened and that her parents had not survived the hurricane. The woman saw that Carla was aware and nodded her head. She explained that none of the people in that area of the trailer park had survived. She and her husband did because they came to the dome before the storm hit.

Carla numb and not able to talk just nodded and walked back to her cot where she felt down. Tears rolling of her face, her eyes closed realizing that she was alone in this world and that her parents were gone.

All she could think off was, if she would have stayed with her parents this would not have happened. She was convinced that she had killed her parents.

An announcement was made in the dome that buses would be arriving to bring people to Houston where housing, clothing and cash would be provided to all whose living quarters were destroyed during the storm. Since her parent's trailer was destroyed and nobody could proof that she was not living there she qualified for this evacuation to Houston, she immediately put her name on the list. She assumed that with her trade she could make a better living in a thriving city like Houston, much better than in a mostly destroyed New Orleans, she also would be free of the pimp she left behind, what money she made would be hers alone. There was also another good reason for Carla to leave New Orleans, there were several warrants out for her arrest, and since she was well known by the local cops, being arrested was just a matter of time if she stayed in New Orleans. The warrants were for:

Soliciting for paid sex

Possession of drugs with intent to sell

Alcohol use as a minor

Assault

Missing court hearings

Before she left New Orleans she went to the site of her parent's trailer in the hope that there were some valuable things left that she could claim as the only survivor, not expecting to find much because her parents did not have many valuables to begin with. She was still disappointed when she saw the total destruction of the trailer and its contents, she did find a small brief case that was stuffed with what looked like official papers, she decided to take it and give it a look over when she was in Houston.

The transfer to Houston finally took place and after a 7 hour journey they rolled into the Astrodome parking lot. The facilities at first looked better than the ones in the New Orleans dome and it seemed like the staff was much better organized. But in all fairness they had a few more days to be prepared for this influx of people, while the New Orleans dome got flooded with people all at the same time.

Nevertheless, Carla decided that this would only be for a couple of days, as soon as she could get an apartment and the money they were promised she would be out of there. She was never the type that was comfortable with people telling her what to do, what to eat, when to sleep, and above all obeying a curfew. There was talk that in a couple of days the families with children would be moved to furnished apartments in the city. That would still leave the single people in the Astrodome for God knew how long. Carla found this extremely unfair and decided she was not going to wait that long to move out.

She examined the contents of the briefcase she had taken from the rubble of the trailer and found nothing of monetary value. But there was an address of one of her father's army buddies who lived close to Houston in a small town by the name of Jamesville. There were also several letters from this army friend Robert Pott, revealing the fact that her father had saved his life on two occasions during the Vietnam War, the letters also repeatedly told her father that whenever there was something he could do not to hesitate to call him.

Robert apparently has done well for himself and was the owner of half a dozen Mc Donald's franchises. Her father, Carla was sure, had never responded to these letters, although he could have used all the help he could get, he was a raging alcoholic with many issues resulting from his experiences in Vietnam. He was never able to hold on to a decent paying job. Her father was either too proud to ask for help or he had never even read the letters. Carla who had a lot of street smarts, felt a phone call to let him know that his hero died in the Katrina hurricane could not hurt.

This could lead to something, Carla didn't know exactly what but she sensed that there were opportunities worthy of being explored.

She wasted no time and examined the brief case in more detail until she found Robert's phone number.

She called the number and a woman answered. Carla asked if she could speak with Robert Pott and the woman answered "Robert is not home but if she would tell her what this was about and give her the phone number she would make sure that he calls her later today.

Carla said, "I'm the daughter of Harry Jones. Your husband Robert and my father were together during the

Vietnam War." Before she could continue the woman said, "Oh yes, you must be Carla. I talked to your mother not too long ago. Are they alright?" Carla said with a quivering voice, no they are not. Both of them died when the hurricane hit New Orleans."

The woman said, "My dear, I'm so sorry to hear this. Are you alright?" No Carla said, "Not really. Our house was totally destroyed. Nothing was left and I am now in Houston in the Astrodome, which is a shelter for the hurricane victims who lost their homes."

Carla heard a man's voice asking his wife who she was talking to. The woman told Carla that Robert just came home, I want to tell him. The woman asked if she could call her back in a few minutes? There is no way we are going to let you live in a shelter."

Carla gave her cell phone number and said." Talking to somebody who knew my parents made her feel better already. I can't wait to talk to her husband. Not more than five minutes later the phone rang and a man's voice said, "This is Robert Pott do I speak with Carla Jones?"

"Yes, you are and I am so happy to talk to someone my father was so close with during a very difficult time in his life."

"Your father was a very special man and I for one can never repay him for what he did for me. I understand that you are in Houston in the Astrodome, in a shelter for the Katrina hurricane victims. Mary, my wife, and I would like you to come here as soon as possible and live with us for as long has it takes to get over the trauma you are under right now. I feel good that I can finally do something for the man who saved my life, please accept this invitation it would make Mary and I very happy. We have no children and will welcome you as our daughter. I can be at the

Astrodome in less than an hour. Can you be ready by then?

"I don't know what to say," Carla said. "I'm all choked up and crying. Five minutes ago I was desperate not knowing what was going to happen with me and now it's like I'm getting a new change. It sounds like a dream. I can't believe this is happening to me! I could be ready in five minutes but I'm sort of baby sitting for a young mother with four children who had some problem getting the medicine for her baby. I just can't walk away and leave her little kids here by themselves. If you can come and get me in the morning I'll be ready and waiting for you."

Robert assured her that he would be there around ten in the morning

Carla had to pinch herself in the arm to make sure that this was not a dream but reality. Her immediate challenge was that she had 12 hours to transform herself from a 19 year old prostitute into a 16 year old sweet and innocent schoolgirl.

The main problem was her outfit, fishnet stockings, and a miniskirt up to her crotch, black leather boots and a blouse that barely covered her nipples would not be something that the Potts family would expect her to wear.

Another issue was her hair. she was naturally blondish but not a peroxide blonde as she was now. Clothes were maybe not so difficult to find. She had noticed before that there was an area in the dome that had lots of clothes donated by the local Houstonians. She was sure that she could find something that would fit for now. She could always tell the Potts that all her outfits were blown away in the hurricane and that what she was wearing was all that was left.

Carla had about $30 cash, probably not enough to go to a beauty salon to get her hair back to its natural color she would try anyway.

Clara first took care of the clothing and found exactly what she needed, a worn but clean modest outfit. She then inquired and found a salon within walking distance of the Astrodome. She walked in and told the lady at the desk that she was a hurricane victim and needed her hair done to look presentable, because she had a job interview in the morning and wanted to look good. The problem she said, "Was that she only had $30. The lady called the owner of the salon and explained the dilemma. The owner immediately said don't worry, we will take care of it. This will be my donation. I needed to make a donation and this way I know for sure it is going to somebody who needs it.

Carla was thrilled with the job they did on her hair. It looked just like she wanted it to be. She profusely thanked the hair stylist and went back to the shelter.

She couldn't fall asleep, curious to meet the Potts and determined to make them like her. This was one opportunity she could not afford to mess up. Not only would she have a home to live in, she would also be safe from her pimp and the New Orleans police. Nobody was going to look for her in a small Texas town, living with a respectable family. This would be something that she never had or at least could not remember ever having.

Carla was not afraid that she could play the role of a 16 year old innocent girl. She just had to be very careful, watch her language and play it by ear. From what she could sense from the short telephone conversations, they seemed to be more than happy to have her live with them. It was up to her to make them like her even more. Carla needed to make sure that she became a member of the family, at least for the time being.

Robert showed up promptly at 10 in the morning at the Astrodome's parking lot, in the section they had decided to meet. Robert was wearing jeans and a Hawaiian shirt. They found each other without any problem. The first impression for Carla was that Robert looked so much younger than her father. It was hard to believe that they were basically the same age. Robert's first impression was that Carla looked very mature for a 16 year old girl, but he thought she had gone through very hard times and that had speed up the maturity process.

It was a bit awkward at first but very soon they got over it and their conversation became easier. Both felt more comfortable with each other as they came closer to Jamesville.

Robert said, "We will be home in another ten minutes or so and I want to warn you that Mary was convinced that you have not eaten in a while and is determined to fatten you up. You looked more than okay to me but be warned she thinks you're a skeleton. I don't know where she got that idea."

"She must have detected that over the phone." he said laughingly.

"I was not starving, but cafeteria warmed up food becomes very unappetizing after a couple weeks, so I'm looking forward to a good home cooked meal."

"Excellent! She'll be very pleased with that."

The area they were driving through had some beautiful, and no doubt, very expensive houses.

Robert said, "This is our neighborhood. We live on the next block."

Carla thought this can't be true but when he drove up to the house, she managed to say, "Oh what a beautiful home!" Still not believing what was happening to her. This was a dream house. Carla had never set foot in one like this and thought she never would.

The front door opened and Mary came rushing out with arms wide open to welcome Carla with a hug,

"I'm so happy you decided to come to us!"

Mary looked like she was at least ten years younger than Carla's mother.

They went inside and the interior of the house was even more impressive than the outside, with wooden floors, high cathedral ceilings with molding all around.

"Now you just relax and Robert will show you your room while I prepare lunch for us."

Robert winked at Carla. "Just follow me and I'll show you the room and bathroom we think you will like, and if not tell us. We have plenty of empty rooms up here, rooms that were never used. With you around this big house will feel better for us. We always said that this house needed more people and more activity and I think you will provide that for us."

Again Carla was in awe. This room with the bathroom felt like she had her own apartment, much bigger than the places she had ever lived in. The room had a wide flat screen TV, telephone, CD player, built-in cabinets. The bathroom had a shower and giant bathtub that looked like a spa equipped with jets.

She felt that something was happening in her life, something good and that was foreign to her. She never had good things just fall into her lap. She almost felt that she should pray that this was real and not some cruel joke someone was playing with her. And maybe for the first time in her life she felt sorry for her mom and dad that they had to live like they did in a rundown trailer, never enough money to enjoy a normal live. This made her feel sad and guilty for the way she had behaved while she was living with them. This was all a new sensation for her. It dawned on her that she had lost them forever and would never see them again. In the past when they had argued or fought there was always tomorrow. This time there was no tomorrow to patch things up.

Robert brought her back to earth by saying, "I hope you have everything you need for the time being. We know that you lost everything you had. We realize that the pain you must be feeling will be with you for a long time. Losing your parents like this is awful, and we can't fill that void. But everything else can be replaced and Mary is dying to take you shopping as soon as you feel fit to go out."

She became teary eyed and Robert put his arms around her.

"I'm so sorry I made you cry," he said. "I always talk too much."

Carla recovered and said, "No Robert it's not you. It's me. Maybe I can explain this to you and Mary, just not yet."

Feeling a man's arms around her in the past was normally followed by a grab for her tits or ass. She never even thought about that when Robert hugged her. This also was new for her.

With that they went downstairs to have lunch. It was just as Robert said it would be delicious food and more than enough to feed an army. Obviously Mary was a good cook because everything was prepared by her from scratch. None of the precooked deli stuff. Carla felt that she should eat like a pig in order to do justice to Mary's cooking, but the food was so good that this was really easy. No pretending was required. Eating too much came naturally.

After the meal Mary said, "We have an awful lot to talk about, but for now I think we should put this on the back burner and let you get comfortable in this new environment. What this means is that for the next couple of days, you just relax, do whatever you want. Watch TV, play music, read books, take a walk in the neighborhood, play with the dog or chat with me or Robert."

"That reminds me. You have not yet met our other part of the family. We also have a dog. She is at the vet right now, but Robert is just about ready to pick her up. It's a big Golden Retriever but as sweet as can be. She doesn't have a bad bone in her body. When she comes home be prepared. She will want to lick your face. I hope you're not afraid of dogs, but even if you are she will win you over in no time. She's that kind of a dog. She is also a very good listener so if you want to talk to somebody and don't want an answer she is ideal."

"While Robert is getting Ginger, that's her name, I will give you a quick tour of the house. I don't want you to get lost, and please consider this your home. There are no restrictions. As the Latinos say, 'Mi casa es su casa' and we mean it."

The estate was enormous and awesome, a beautifully landscaped backyard with a pool, a stone patio, an outdoor kitchen with a barbeque and refrigerator, big mature oak trees that provided shade for the outdoor furniture all surrounded by a luscious green lawn.

The interior of the house itself looked like it was done by an expert home decorator, but Mary said that she and Robert did it by themselves and the only help they needed was with the drapes and blinds.

Carla was overwhelmed and speechless.

When Mary noticed that Carla was quiet she immediately said, "Oh dear, I get so carried away with my home that I forgot that this is too much to digest for you after the horrible things you went through during the last months."

"I'm so sorry, why don't I leave you by yourself until dinner. You can go to your room, take a walk or explore the house by yourself. I need to go to the store to get some things. So the house and the yard are all yours."

Carla said, "You don't have to leave the house because of me. This is your house I'm the one who has to adjust not you or Robert."

"This is not adjusting, sweetheart. This is for me to make sure that you realize that for the near future this is your house as well."

Carla once more thought. What have I done to deserve this? I was a whore, a drug addict, a mean bitch and all of a sudden I'm showered with goodness by people who don't know the real me.

Mary went out, leaving her by herself for a while. She then realized that this was exactly what she needed, time by herself, time to absorb all this and ask herself how she could possibly fit in. She was scared that she won't be able to meet their expectations and didn't want to hurt people like Mary or Robert. Carla had only known them for less than a day but felled that they cared for her and were willing to take on the burden of making her whole again. She either had to leave here soon or totally change her life style, and she didn't know if she could do that.

Her inner feelings were telling her to take this opportunity and change her life; it could very well be her last chance to do so. But what if some how they found out about her past? That would hurt them so much.

She wondered if she should tell them the truth now. Did she have the courage to confess and tell them about her past or should she try to keep that a secret forever?

Carla decided that she needed time and should not make a decision on such an important issue when her mind was in turmoil and things were happening so fast that her head was spinning.

She went to her room and lay on the bed trying to adjust to the present and at the same time planning the future. Carla fell asleep and woke up when someone was wiping her face with a warm rag. This turned out to be Ginger's tongue licking her face, trying to get her attention, Mary was right. It took less than a minute and Carla was sold on Ginger. It was virtually impossible not to love this dog. She was irresistible and she knew it.

Maybe it was Ginger who was the deciding factor that Carla was going to try to fit in and live a normal life. She convinced herself that it was already too late to tell them her true story without hurting them. She was going to gamble and keep her past a secret. She also knew that she needed to adjust to a normal life style in order to survive. She also knew that she would not survive living on the streets of New Orleans or Houston. Her options were limited.

A few days passed and Carla was getting adjusting to the Potts's household routine. She helped in the kitchen and in the yard and went grocery shopping with Mary. This was an eye opening experience as well. Mary just loaded up the cart without ever looking at what things cost or whether they were on sale or not, asking Carla every minute, what kind of snacks she preferred, what drinks she liked, what her favorite meal was. Carla said," Mary the amount you feed me every meal, there is no room for snacks, and the drinks that are in your refrigerator are just fine. I'm not much of a soda pop drinker, but if you want to buy me something I like to look at these fashion magazines they have, Mary told her to go ahead pick a few of them that she liked.

Carla started a routine with Ginger. Every morning they went for a walk around the lake that bordered on the back yard. It was about a half hour walk and Ginger could run free because there were no streets. The lake was surrounded by trees and stocked with geese Ginger could chase. Carla looked forward to these walks every morning and she and Ginger started bonding.

Carla never was much of a dog or cat lover but that was because they never had a pet in the house. But with Ginger it was different and Mary was right, she was a good listener and never talked back. Carla suspected though that she sometimes must have thought, what the hell is she talking about?

But Carla could understand that because sometimes she thought the same thing. She still struggled with the fact that she was living a lie, and there were days that she said to herself I'm going to tell them, and then, of course, chickened out. Truth was, she loved the life she was living, and couldn't imagine going back to the life she had lived before.

After a couple of weeks the subject of school came up when Robert asked what grade she was in, when Katrina happened. Carla was prepared for this and without hesitation answered that she was a sophomore which was only half a lie. She actually had been a sophomore when she left home, but it wasn't when Katrina struck; it was a couple of years earlier when she really was a sweet sixteen year-old girl.

Mary said, "You should really go back to school and at least get your High School diploma, don't you think."

Carla was now skating on thin ice and had to be careful how to respond to that. She said, "I want to go back to school, but I missed so many classes that I'm afraid I will look like a stupid fool if I do."

Robert said, "You would not be going back. We want you to go to school here in Jamesville, not in New Orleans. Let me rephrase this," he said. "We would like you to go to school here but this is, of course, your decision."

Yes," replied Carla. "But I will still look unprepared because of the classes I missed. It was not only during the hurricane period. I missed a lot of school for various reasons, problems at home, visible injuries, stuff I have a difficult time talking about."

Robert said," Listen, you couldn't go back to school now anyway. It's the middle of the school year but what if you took some private lessons to bring you back on even par with the other kids. How would you like that?"

The only reason she could think of to kill this offer was to say that she didn't have the financial means to use a private tutor and that you guys have done enough for me. She wouldn't think about them again helping her with this schooling. It was time for her to find a job and stop taking advantage of them.

There was an uncomfortable silence after she said that, and she almost regretted doing it. Robert and Mary looked at each other and Mary nodded at Robert who then said. "What I'm going to tell you is something that Mary and I have discussed and we were going to talk to you about it after you felt at home here. But we might as well tell you now. Mary and I both have come to like you very much to the extent that if you would leave, we would have a tough time readjusting. To come to the point, we would love to have you live with us permanently, not just until you're over this sad period of your life. We think that you like it here but are afraid that this life may soon be boring for you and that eventually you may want to go back to New Orleans."

At first Carla was speechless and then she quietly started to cry, which turned into sobbing and when she tried to say something it was incoherent. Mary and Robert looked at each other wondering what they had done to this poor girl. Had they overwhelmed her and she was not ready to make this decision? Finally, Carla was able to say that she was overcome with happiness but at the same time feeling sad and guilty, happiness she said because she had been thinking that she could not stay much longer because she felt that she was exploiting this situation. They had done more for me than she had the right to expect, but she didn't know where to go if she left here.

But, she said, "I have to tell you some of the things that I have done and that you should know. That's why I said those were tears of happiness and sadness at the same time."

Mary and Robert were of course anxious to know why Carla was so sad.

Carla continued, "When the hurricane came I was no longer living with my parents. I left about six months earlier and became a waitress in a restaurant to support myself. The reason I left home was that the situation there became unbearable for me. My mother had joined my father in his drinking bouts and I just could no longer live there. Now I feel that I abandon them and acted very selfish. I feel I should have stayed and helped them with their drinking problem, and now they are dead I feel guilty and sad. Guilty that you offered me a life that they never had and sad that they're gone and that I wasn't there when they died."

"I'm a mental wreck and you do not deserve to be saddled with me. I don't know how to handle my past. I have these periods of depression that make me moody and you don't need somebody like that in your life."

She started to cry again and rushed upstairs to her room, her future looking dark again.

Downstairs, a similar feeling of sadness developed and Mary started to cry. She stammered to Robert, "She definitely has to stay with us. We can't let her go like this."

Robert fully agreed with her but said, "We can't force her to stay. We have to convince her that none of this was her fault, and that sadness is sometimes needed to get over the death of your love ones. But she should not feel guilty. These were circumstances that a sixteen year old can't handle. Many mature adults can't cope with a situation like that. Let her calm down for a while and then we should have a long talk with her. She is a smart girl, very mature for her age. Her emotions are guiding her right now, but she will understand things happen and in a lot of cases there is nothing we can do to stop it, it's just life."

Carla thought, why did I not tell them the whole story? She answered her own question. You are too ashamed to tell them about your life as an escort, part time hooker, or worse, working on the street corner for your pimp. You know that they couldn't handle it. She tried to justify for herself that she had done the right thing because she felt this would make them unhappy and sad, and they shouldn't be confronted with this dark side of her life.

She knew that this was all bullshit and the honest truth was that she couldn't tell them or anybody else about her past. She promised herself that someday she would confess and tell them the whole story, the truth and nothing but the truth.

When she went downstairs, she apologized for her meltdown to both of them.

Robert said, "No need to apologize. Maybe Mary and I should apologize to you. We should not have put you in a position like we did. We know that when you are ready you will tell us everything you want us to know."

"Now back to school. The reason we got side tracked from it was your refusal to let us pay your private tuition, right? Well we have to tell you something you should know about our financial situation. We have never talked about it with you because we were afraid that you would feel that we wanted to flaunt our money or even worse that we could buy your affection. This may sound pretty stupid, but it wouldn't be the first time that I did something stupid. But again I'm sort of avoiding the issue. To put it bluntly Mary and I are very rich. I was very lucky when I bought about a dozen McDonald franchises while they were still cheap. I then sold half of them when they were very expensive, and later when I didn't want the hustle and bustle to manage them I sold four more of them at a very high price. Now we have two franchises left that are managed by a manager and all I do is collect the profits every month. The money that I made by selling the franchises I invested in the stock market and there again I was very lucky with buying Microsoft and Apple stocks when they were very cheap and again sold them when they were very high. Now you know our dark secret. I'm not a money making guru. I was just extremely lucky."

"What I'm trying to say is that we have more money than we can ever spend. Yes, we could live in a house twice the size of this one, have a cook, a maid, even a chauffeur to drive us around in an expensive foreign car or buy a yacht that would sit unused in some Marina, but that's not us. We wouldn't feel comfortable living like that."

"I'm not trying to impress you. I just want you to know that money is not important to either one of us I know that sounds very blasé but it happens to be true."

"So we now finally found somebody we can spend a little of that money with, somebody who in a very short time has become dear to us, and if you decided to leave us, we would miss you very much. Don't get us wrong. We have no intention of trying to run your life or interfere if you want to do something. We just want to make it a little easier for you, and we feel you deserve this break. You would give us more than you think you can."

"Mary and I feel that you like it here and could be happy. Both of us like you being here, so wouldn't it make sense for the three of us to try to make it work? Give it six months or so. By then we will know."

Carla said. "This would make me very happy if you are sure, after what I told you, that you still want me in your life."

Mary simply said, "Carla, we don't want you out of our lives, so let's start today. We never explained to you our family status for the simple reason neither of us have much family. Robert has none. Robert grew up in an orphanage and then later in various fosters homes. When we got married I was the only family he ever had. As for myself my parents died when I was very young and my older and only sister became my mother. Her name is Katherine and she lives in Florida. She is not very healthy and prefers to live in a warm climate. So having you here with us is like a godsend. We needed somebody to take care of, and when you came into our life we couldn't have been happier."

Mary said, "Now that the financial problems you had are resolved, let's go and do some serious shopping, Jamesville is no big city but there are some really nice stores that I'm sure have clothes and other things you will like."

On the way to their shopping spree, Mary asked if Carla had a valid driver's license. This threw Carla for a loop. She had one but was afraid to show it. If for one reason or the other she got stopped by the police and they checked her out on their computer, the warrants for her arrest would show and that would be the end of it. So she told Mary that she had one but had no idea where it could be. She didn't have a car when she was home so the license was in the house during the flooding.

She said, "I have a bunch of paperwork that I found in a briefcase in the trailer after Katrina. It may be in there, I'll look for it."

"It would be a lot easier for you if you did. There is a spare car in our garage that nobody is using. It's in good shape and has insurance on it. Robert used it when he was managing the two stores we still have. Check it out. Having wheels in Texas is almost mandatory. Jamesville has practically no public transportation."

The next thing on her agenda was looking for a tutor. Robert said that was something she had to do, because she was the one that would spend considerable time with him or her. He asked her if she was computer literate and if not that was another thing she had to put on her to do list.

"It's a lot easier than it looks," he said. "After a day you know the basics and can start using it, and from there you learn as you go, so to speak. The PC has become a necessity and is a very useful tool for a student; your tutor will probably insist that you have one. I have two fairly new laptops in my office at home. I bought one for Mary but she is the exception to the rule and claims she will never touch that instrument, so whenever you want to try it let me know. I can teach you the basics."

Carla looked for her driver's license in the briefcase but only found her mother's license. The picture of her mother on it was probably 15 years old if not older. She looked remarkably like Carla and if it was not for the birth date on the license, Carla could have easily used it.

Maybe there was a way; she thought to get a license in Texas. She remembered a guy she met in the Astrodome saying that getting papers or licenses renewed was easy. He said when they asked you for proof of identity all you have to say is that you're a Katrina victim and lost all your papers.

The Department of Transportation in Houston had given up on trying getting proof because they knew from experience that chaos was still rampant in Louisiana and getting any type of information from them was an exercise in futility, so they didn't bother going through the motions.

Of course there were risks involved, but Carla decided to give it a try. She looked at her mother's driver's license and if she somehow could damage the license in a way that the date of birth could not be read, the picture should not be a problem. This could work out after all. She had to find a manner to doctor up her Ma's license in such a way that nobody could see that the damage was done on purpose. She thought that hitting the driver's license all over with a rock with emphasis on the date, this damage could have been caused by the hurricane. She worked on it and after a couple of hits with a rock she found the result satisfactory. She told Mary that she had found her drivers license but that it was slightly damaged. She showed it to her and Mary thought she should have no problem renewing it.

Carla went to the local Texas Department of Transportation office, and they said all license renewals for the Katrina victims had to be handled in Houston or New Orleans. Mary and Carla decided to go to Houston the next day and get this done.

They showed up early in the morning and after filling out a two page application form and waiting three hours in line they finally stood in front of the clerk who glanced at the driver's license and told Carla to stand in back of the yellow line so she could take a picture, after that she told her the driver's license would be mailed to her within 5 working days to the address on her application form.

Mary said, "This is cause for a celebration. Let's go for a real Mexican lunch at Pappasito's. You like Mexican food don't you?"

"I never had Mexican food before, but I'm willing to try. If you say it's good, I believe you."

They had a nice meal and a very good time. Mary could not resist and asked Carla if she still have doubts about living with them.

Carla said, "I never had doubts. I was just afraid I wouldn't measure up."

"Silly girl," Mary said and hugged her. "We wanted you to stay with us from the first day we saw you."

One day Robert came in and said, "I have a little present for you."

He gave her a little box and said, "I have one also, but I haven't figured out how to use it, so you figure it out and then you can teach me."

She opened the box and it was one of those new cell phones that was not just a phone but had a lot of other things you could do with it. She had heard about it but had never seen one. She was thrilled and gave him a thank you hug and said, "I promise to get right on it. I know it's a phone that can do lots of other things. We just have to learn what they are and how to use them."

Carla had found a lady tutor who would prepare her to attend Jamesville High School for the next school year. After a couple of sessions she told Carla not to worry, she would be ready, probably more so than the present students. This encouraged Carla to study even harder because she wanted to make Robert and Mary proud of her.

As time went by they all became closer to each other and it began to feel that Carla was one of the family. Carla at times still felt that she was an imposter and had no right to be there. She also was afraid that her past

100

would catch up with her and that this fake scenario would crumble like a house of cards.

Not being able to tell the truth to Robert and Mary was also something she had to struggle with and made her feel unworthy of their affection. Some day she would tell them her real life story.

Chapter 10

One day after a couple of months of tutoring, her teacher said, "Well, I believe my job is done and I can declare you more than ready to start as a junior at Jamesville High School. You were a brilliant student and I'm sure you will be doing better than most students in your class. By the way, I have a 17 year old daughter who is in high school and since you don't have friends here it might be a good idea if you two got together, maybe do something, I'm sure she could give you some idea how things are done and prepare you before you start school, Just let me know if you want to, her name is Stella Baker."

This was not the sort of thing that Carla wanted to experiment with, but then again it wouldn't hurt to get the lay of the land before venturing into it. Nobody knew her so there wouldn't be any surprises like. Oh I know you. You're the hooker off the corner of Bourbon Street and the Market. None of that will happen.

She called her tutor and said, "I'm taking you up on the offer of hanging out with Stella if she agrees to it."

Her tutor said, "No problem. Hang on I get her on the phone so you can both make the arrangements on where to meet and when."

Stella got on the phone and said. "Hi, Carla I heard a lot about you and I'm dying to meet you. Listen, the weather is gorgeous and I was thinking of going to the Municipal pool by myself, would you be interested in joining me?"

Carla said, "Yes that would be great. How do I get there?"

Stella answered. "No problem I will pick you up, is one o' clock OK?"

"Yes, that's fine but if this is out of your way I can find it."

"It's not out of the way and to be honest I would like to see the house. My mother said it is beautiful. So I'll see you in a little bit."

Stella arrived right on time. Mary showed her in and Carla could see that Stella was impressed with the house. She said, "Ma wasn't kidding that this was one of the most beautiful houses she had ever set foot in."

"Well, thank you." said Mary. "We are very proud of our house."

Mary asked," Did you have lunch yet? If not please sit down with us I won't let Carla leave the house before she eats something and I can see you rushed out of your house before lunch, so please sit down."

Carla said," Stella, you might as well. There is usually enough food for the entire neighborhood."

Poor Stella didn't have much of a choice, so she accepted the invitation and they had lunch together. This was really an excellent way to break the ice and soon they were all talking like people who had known each other for years.

Stella and Carla had hit it off almost immediately. This was very unusual for Carla as she always had a difficult time getting along with other girls

She asked Stella if she had a lot of girlfriends.

Stella started laughing and said, "This is so strange. It was on the tip of my tongue to ask you the same question. No, I do not have a lot of girlfriends. How about you?"

Carla replied. "I have no girlfriends, none right now and very few when I lived in New Orleans."

She almost started to tell her life story but restrained herself at the last moment, thinking it's a little too early to go that far.

Stella said," The reason I don't have many girl friends is that, according to the girls in school, I'm stuck up and I think I'm too good for them. Now, to be honest with you, they are half right. I'm not stuck up but I do think I'm too good to hang out with them. I'm a junior and most of the juniors and seniors girls are jock admirers and they have some sort of high school sorority. They go to all the parties that the jocks organize. Most of them get drunk, do drugs and get laid at these parties."

"That doesn't bother me but listen to this. They call themselves the Party Bimbo's and yes. I think I'm too good to be called a party bimbo."

Carla burst out laughing and said, "You're pulling my leg!"

"No," she said" "this is the sad truth. And what is really incomprehensible is they themselves came up with that name."

"Well," Carla said shaking her head, "I don't think I'm going to have too many friends here either."

They both were lying in the sun in their bikinis and Stella looked at her and said, "You may not have had too many girlfriends but I'm sure you were never lacking any boyfriends."

Carla asked, "What make you say that?"

"It was Stella's turn to laugh. "Now you are pulling my leg. Don't tell me that you're unaware that you are beautiful with a body to match."

Carla felt a little uncomfortable with this remark and mumbled, "Yes, I've heard that before but always from guys and always with an ulterior motive, the motive being getting in bed with me."

Stella laughed and said. "Rest assured that is not why I said it. I'm straight. I don't bat for the other team."

Carla looked like she was embarrassed. Stella grew serious again and said, "Don't worry. I like you a lot already and I believe we can become good friends but we need to know each other and sometimes I'm a little clumsy. So forgive me if I embarrassed you."

With that she reached for Carla and hugged her. Carla responded by putting her arms around Stella. When they returned home Stella asked Carla if she would to do this again next Saturday.

Carla said, "I would love to. We can also sit by the pool at our place if you prefer that, but it's probably good for me to go somewhere where there are people other than Robert or Mary and that way they get some time alone with each other."

Carla mentioned that by next week she should have her driver's license back and she could pick up Stella.

"I need some driving practice real bad and prefer somebody with me when I start driving again."

When Carla was back in the house, Mary asked her how it went.

"It went real good," Carla said. "We're going to make this a weekly thing, seeing each other on Saturday. Stella mentioned that once in a while after the pool we can go out, eat something and maybe see a movie together, if that's all right with you."

"Of course that's all right with me. I love it that you met somebody your age and seem to like each other's company. That's just great and something I believe will be good for you."

Mary had another surprise for her. She opened her wallet and gave Carla a credit card with her name on and said, "If you are going to drive a car and hang out with friends, like Stella, you're going to need some cash. This is a credit and debit card to be used only by you."

Carla started to protest but was cut off by Mary before she could say a word. "I knew you were going to give me a hard time about this but please don't. Robert explained our financial status to you and if we want you to have a normal teenager's life we must give you the tools for it. A little bit of cash is just a tool, end of story."

One night after dinner Robert said to Carla, "I have dozens of pictures of me and your father from our time in the army, starting with the fun time in training camp and the not so fun time in Nam. I would like to show them to you and maybe talk about your father as the man I knew and worshipped. He was probably a lot different than the father you remember."

"I would love that. I only remember him as the man who came back from a war he couldn't forget."

That same evening, they sat down in Robert's office and he took a photo album from a bookcase. The first picture she saw of her father at Fort Hood training camp.

She could hardly believe that it was the same person she remembered as her father. This man was smiling, good looking, athletic, and surrounded by other soldiers. Robert looked at her and saw her surprise.

"This was your father at the age of twenty, a couple of months before we were shipped out to Hawaii for a few weeks before finally going to Vietnam. The guy to his left was me. Most of the pictures I have are of your father accompanied by me. We were more or less inseparable from then on."

Carla was silent most of the time Robert showed her the pictures. She occasionally asked when or where this or that picture was taken, but the look on her face was one of confusion. She kept asking herself what happened to this man to be transformed from an energetic and vibrant person to the man she knew. The emotions she felt were first anger that she was denied this man as her father, sad that she never knew this man as a father. Then anger again because of what the war had done to him.

Robert was aware of what was going on inside Carla's mind and said, "This is enough for now. Tomorrow or whenever you feel ready for it I will tell you more about your dad and what kind of man he was. You only saw the pictures but you have to know more about the person he was."

The next day Carla asked Robert to tell her more about her dad. She now had to hear what her father was like before he went to war and even during the war. She only knew what he was after the war and she needed to know more.

Robert started out by saying that he and her father became friends the first day in training camp. Robert immediately got in trouble with their sergeant when he was trying to make his bunk. Apparently the top blanket was not tight enough and no matter what Robert tried, it never satisfied the sergeant. So when he was told for the umpteenth time to do it again and when the sergeant turned his back, her father quickly fixed it. From then on they stuck together, helping each other to survive training camp.

They managed to stay together in Vietnam and ended up in the same platoon until the end of the war.

Tom, her father, was the type of guy you could always count on. Not just Robert, but everyone in their platoon knew that when there was a problem, Tom would take care of it. And when Tom was promoted to corporal after the first month everyone was happy. No jealousy. It was the right thing to do and nobody deserved it more than Tom.

With his promotion, Tom became the spokesman of the platoon and never hesitated to talk to the brass if something was wrong or a soldier was treated unfairly. He was always there for his men. Another thing he was admired for was that he would never ask a soldier to do something that he wouldn't or couldn't do himself. When morale in the platoon was low, he would find the right words or deeds to bring it up again.

Robert said, "He saved my life twice, but I'm sure there are probably another dozen or more soldiers and officers who can claim he did the same for them.

"When he got wounded in the leg, that one night we were on patrol and couldn't walk, he told to us leave him there and let the medics take care of me. That was the first time nobody followed his orders. I and Richard another guy decided to carry him back to the compound, because nobody was going to leave Tom behind."

"As the war raged on, Tom continued to be a model soldier and was given the Silver Star Medal, and later received the Bronze Star Medal, for bravery in the line of fire."

Carla was not aware that her father was a war hero and had received medals for bravery. He never mentioned any of that when he came back from the war.

Robert said. "You looked like you were not aware of all this." Carla just shook her head, Robert continued.

"That does not surprise me at all. He never bragged about anything he did."

"The first time he saved my life was during the night we were on patrol and found ourselves under fire and surrounded by enemy soldiers. I got hit in the shoulder and upper thigh and was unable to move. He took me on his back and brought me and our platoon back to base, maybe a two mile hike through the jungle. He never took a rest or let anybody else carry me, when we arrived at the camp he collapsed after the medics took me off his back."

"The second time he saved my life was when we were on patrol again and got hit by mortar fire. I woke up in the hospital, two broken legs, head wound and a concussion. The nurse told me that a corporal brought me in although he was admitted to the hospital himself with shrapnel wounds all over his body and bleeding profusely from his neck. She told me that he saved my life once more."

"I thought you had to know who your father really was, not the man who was mentally scarred for life because of the atrocities he had to endure during this senseless war. I hope you now understand that helping you is the least I can do and that it also makes me feel good, knowing that I'm doing what he would do if my child needed a helping hand. As long as I knew him, helping people was his goal in life."

This was all too much for Carla and she started to cry softly and at the same time saying, "Thank you Robert, I know I'm crying but this make me feel so good to know that my father was such a good person and admired by his friends."

Chapter 11

Spring arrived and John still did not have a cast in concrete plan of action for his famous "sex slave" project. He had everything planned except the most important part of the puzzle, where to find the right girl and how to secretly bring her to the beach house. He, of course, blamed Glenn that they didn't make any progress on this vital element of the plan. He accused Glenn of being too passive and not participating enough.

Damn right, thought. Glenn I'm not participating because I want nothing to do with this raving lunatic and his insane project. Glenn was totally convinced that this would turn in to a major disaster and anybody even remotely involved with it would have his ass on the line. So instead of actively participating, Glenn would do everything to sabotage the plan. He just had to do it without John finding out.

One Saturday Glenn was meeting his girlfriend Marissa at the Municipal pool. Marissa refused to go to the pool at Glenn's house because there was always the chance that John would show up there.

The Municipal pool was never crowded and that Saturday was no exception. When Glenn and Marissa arrived there were maybe twenty people or so at the pool. Once they were installed on their poolside chaise lounges, Glenn looked around to see if there were some other high school kids there. He spotted Stella, who he vaguely knew, with another girl he thought was an extremely sexy, attractive hot chick, one he had never seen before.

He would have remembered if he had. He casually asked Marissa who the girl with Stella was.

Marissa said, "She had no idea. Why you are interested."

"I'm just curious because I've never seen her before."

He quickly changed the subject and asked her what her vacation plans were for this summer. She said she was more than likely going to Europe for a month. Her parents would again drag her from one museum to another, see all the old castles and churches that they could find and then tell her every night how lucky she was to be able to enrich her education.

When Stella and Carla left the pool, Marissa pretended not to see them because she did not want Glenn to be introduced to that girl who seemed to have made quite an impression on him. Glenn, however heard Stella say that she liked coming there on Saturdays because it was never crowded. He thought they must come here every week, this was good to know. He wouldn't mind bumping into them on a day that Marissa was not with him.

John had already informed his parents that he would not participate in the yearly summer vacation trip with the family.

He wanted to stay in the beach house, do some sailing and fishing, hang out on the beach and relax before going to college in the fall.

He told Glenn to do the same but Glenn was in no hurry to commit himself to that. He was still hoping that this silly plan would never happen and go away.

Another few weeks went by before Glenn had the opportunity to check out the girl at the Municipal pool. That Saturday he was ready to leave his house and go to the pool when his phone rang. It was John wanting to know what he was up to and if he wanted to do something together.

Glenn said, "I am going to the Municipal pool."

John said "What in the hell are you going there for? There's never any action there."

Glenn not knowing how to defend his intent to go there answered, "Well, somebody told me that lately there is," hoping that John would pass on this so he could explore the possibilities with this beauty by himself, but no such luck.

John said, "Well, I have nothing else to do. I will meet you there."

When Glenn arrived at the pool John was already there, sitting on a beach chair waiting for him. "What did I tell you?" he asked. "Nothing going on here, as usual."

Glenn looked around and saw that the girls were not there. Either they were not coming today or they were coming later. They stayed at the pool for about an hour and were ready to leave when the two girls appeared.

Glenn said. "Hold it. Just watch the tall one in her bikini."

When the girls came out of the bathroom ready to lie out in the sun, John whispered to Glenn, "Holy shit. Where did she come from?"

Glenn said," She and Stella are here every Saturday afternoon. She must be new in town or just visiting."

John said, "Let's check her out. We hang around here till they leave then follow them and find out where she is going."

John thought she would be ideal for his project, sexy, gorgeous body, and new here or from out of town. If they stayed away from her she wouldn't know them or be able to recognize them later.

Glenn wanted to know why they couldn't just walk up to Stella and she would introduce the new girl and that was it. Why follow them in secret.

John was ready for this question and said, "No, we can't do that because that bitch Stella won't talk to me anymore. She thinks that I spread the rumor around that she is nothing but a cheap slut."

"What rumor? I never heard that rumor. What the fuck are you talking about?"

Glenn was suspicious that John wanted to talk to this girl without him as competition. But if they followed them Glenn would know as much about her as John did, so that did not make sense.

John insisted that they would not approach them at the pool when Stella was around. John of course did not want to be introduced to this new girl, and she should never talk to him or Glenn. They should stay away from her. She should not see them or hear their voices.

Glenn, as usual, did what John wanted and stayed away from her. That was probably what he should do anyway to stay out of trouble with Melissa

When the girls left, John said, "Let's follow her in your car, mine is too conspicuous and they would easily spot us following them."

The girls that day came in separate cars so they followed Carla to her house.

Glenn asked, "What now? We now know that she is not poor and lives in an expensive house in a high class neighborhood. How is that going to help us to get into her pants?"

John chose not to respond to that because he didn't know what to say without making Glenn aware of what he had in mind for this girl.

Despite the fact that he didn't get a close look at Carla he saw enough of her to feel that she was the one and he became determined that she was going to be his "Sex Slave". This was no longer a game for him. This was an obsession and he would not be sidetracked by anything that would prevent him from reaching his goal.

All the characters were in place. Now was the time to finalize an execution plan and set firm dates for the event.

When Carla got home from the pool that Saturday she found Mary in tears. She rushed to her and asked what happened.

"I'm OK. It's my sister. She was taken to the hospital this morning and they called us and told us that she had a stroke and would be in the hospital for a while. Robert called later this afternoon but they couldn't give us more details and were doing more tests but would have no further news till Monday. I have to go there and will leave tomorrow morning. But don't worry, Robert will stay here with you."

Carla said to herself. Oh no he won't. He's not going to stay to babysit me when he should be at his wife's side. No way Jose. She found Robert in his study and came right to the point.

"Robert, I strongly believe that you should go to Florida with Mary. This is not the time to think about me. I'm a big girl and can take care of myself. Ginger and I will be just fine. Please, go with her. I will feel terrible if you stayed here because of me."

Robert hesitated. "I know I should be with Mary in times like this, but she will feeling bad if we left you alone in this big house. If you had a friend who could stay here with you it would be different."

Carla got on the phone and called Stella. She explained the situation to her and asked if her Ma would allow Stella to stay with her.

Stella did not hesitate and said, "I'll stay with you."

"Shouldn't you ask your Ma first?"

"I know my mother don't worry about that."

Carla rushed downstairs and told Robert.

"Problem solved. Stella will stay here with me for the time that you are gone."

Mary's face lightened up a little and she said, "Thank you, my sweetheart, I was really scared to go by myself. This will make it a lot easier for me with Robert by my side. Thank you again that was very sweet of you."

Nonsense Carla said. "After all you did for me this is the least I could do for you. Remember you're the only people that I love and have in my life right now."

Stella moved in the next morning and Carla asked whether she preferred her own bedroom or would share the king size bed in Carla's bedroom. No hesitation there. Same bedroom.

Carla smiled and said, "I was hoping you would choose that."

That night Stella revealed some of her family's semi secrets. Her ma was not a widow but a divorcee. Stella never knew her dad, but based on what she could guess she wasn't missing a whole lot. Not that her ma told her much about him. It was just a gut feeling that he was not father or husband material. She had some aunts and uncles from her mother's side but they lived on the east coast and there was not much visiting or even phone conversation going on between them.

"So my ma and I are very close and she treats me like a younger sister, which is fine with me. She loves me as a daughter but feels that I'm mature enough to behave as an adult."

Carla and Stella had become close enough for Carla to tell her about her family and why she ran away and now felt guilty that she did. She still did not tell Stella, about her dark side when she worked the street corners or the escort business. That was still something Carla could not talk about yet.

Robert called her on Monday and the news was not good. Mary's sister had a massive stroke and the doctors were not sure at all if she would completely recover from it. He asked if it was okay for him to stay a couple of days with Mary and come back Wednesday or Thursday that week.

Carla assured him and said, "You stay as long as Mary needs you there. We are doing fine. Stella, Ginger and I are bonding and having a good time together. Please, don't worry about me. Everything is honky dory here. Getting Mary through this is more important."

He said "I'll call every day to let you know how things are progressing here.'

"Yes, please do." Carla said and they hung up the phone.

Stella wanted to know what was happening and when Carla told her that Robert would be gone for a week, she said, "Not a problem, I'm staying. The only thing we have to do is that I promised my mother that we have to go over and have dinner with her every other day, and she insisted that we bring Ginger with us."

One evening after dinner, Stella's mother asked Carla whether Stella had told her that she might not go to high school for her senior year. Carla felt like lightning had struck her.

Stella yelled at her mother. "I told you I would tell Carla, look what you did.

"Carla recovered and said to Stella, "Why didn't you?"

Stella started to cry. "I didn't know how. I didn't want to hurt you and besides it's not decided yet whether I will or not, is it?" asking her mother.

Carla, listen said her mother, "Let me explain. It could turn out good for you too. The reason I want to home school Stella is that I think I can do a better job of preparing her for college than the Jamesville High School can. I have the qualifications to do so and the idea was that I would talk to your parents. I know their not your real parents but they do for you what good parents would do for their children. I would propose that I would home school you together with Stella and I promise you that in one year you will be ready for college. That's the plan I envisioned would be good for the both of you."

All of a sudden the sky lightened up for Carla and she thought how great that would be, being with Stella all day and being tutored by her mom.

"This sounds great to me and I would love to do it, but they have already spent so much money on tutoring for me that I feel bad asking to go to this expense."

Stop right there, Stella's mother said. "Who said anything about money? The only thing I will ask for is a room in their house we can use for us. It can be the same room we used before."

Carla said, "I would still have to ask them and I don't want to do this over the phone. They have enough on their plate as it is."

"Of course, you can think about it yourself before you talk to them. Maybe after you sleep on it you may not think it's a good idea after all and prefer to attend high school anyway."

When they drove back home Stella said, "I'm sorry I didn't talk to you about it before, but with what was going on and not sure it would happen anyway, I thought I would wait before I hit you with this. But to be honest with you, I hope it happens. This will be so cool. Just the two of us together rather than sharing a class room with the Party Bimbo's."

This broke the ice and they both started giggling and Ginger jumping on the girls wanting to be part of the fun.

Robert called the next morning and confirmed the status of Mary's sister and that he would be back on Thursday but would more than likely return to Florida on Saturday. He said that maybe Carla should go back with him because this could be a long rehab program for Mary's sister and they didn't want Carla and Stella to say alone in the house for that long. He said they would talk about it when he got home.

She finally had her renewed driver's license with her picture and her birthday on it, so she was no longer bound to the house. The car they gave her to use was in perfect condition and pretty cool looking, so she could move around whenever she wanted to.

When Robert got home he and Carla discussed the situation. Robert asked what she preferred, staying in Jamesville or going to Florida with him.

Carla then explained the home schooling proposition and if he agreed to let her do it then she had to stay in Jamesville because they would start in a couple of weeks.

They wanted a head start so Carla would finish the High School curriculum in one year.

Robert noticed that Carla seemed to be attracted to the home schooling and he had to admit that he also thought it would be a good idea. He and Mary had talked about the difficulty for a student, and especially a girl, to join a new high school as a junior. In a lot of cases these girls were not accepted in the existing club and remained new and friendless for a long time. This solution would avoid that situation. He knew that Mary would be pleased with this arrangement, so he told Carla. "If that's what you want to do, by all means, it's okay with us."

Carla said, "There will be no costs involved if we can use the room we used before."

Robert felt that this would have to be resolved between the tutor and himself. He didn't want her to do this for free, but that would be taken care of when he had a chance to talk to her.

Stella and Carla were ecstatic and immediately called Stella's mom to tell her the good news. She was pleased that Robert was supportive of it and that they could start way ahead of the high school starting date. She wanted to commence with her classes two weeks after the summer vacation began. This would give Stella a two week break, and maybe they could take a short vacation.

Robert told Carla that he and Mary would probably be in Florida for several months, but he would fly back home at least twice a month. He suggested that since they would be in the house for their tutoring, Stella's mother could use one of the empty bedrooms whenever she wanted. This would eliminate a lot of driving back and forth and save time. She could stay there during the week and maybe go to her house for the weekends. This was only a suggestion and was entirely up to her.

He also told Carla that while he was gone, some bills had to be paid as they came in. The maid and gardener had to be paid cash every week. Other bills needed to be paid by check and she must be able to pay for unexpected expenses. He wanted to show her the ropes and would leave signed checks for her to use whenever she needed them. This was another new experience for Carla. Nobody had ever trusted her this way. She felt the responsibility of the trust they had in her and it made her proud to realize that they really considered her a member of the family.

The last day of school would be May 18, and they would start home schooling on June 2. This schedule would give Stella and her mother time to go to Galveston for a week. They asked Carla to come with them. She thanked them for the offer but declined, saying that she needed to go to Houston and maybe to New Orleans to take care of some issues still related to the hurricane. She also felt that Stella and her mother should have a week by themselves.

Carla wanted some time alone to think about the changes that had occurred to her during the last six months, changes that made her believe in herself and that she was capable of living a normal life. The revelations about her father being such an outstanding person helped her in this belief. She had always thought of her father as being mean to the core and that it was in her genes to be like him and she would end up like him. During her formative years she never tried to become a good person. She strongly believed in genetics and that the way she was brought up, was the way her life would be. If she had known then that her father and her mother at one time were decent people, and that they became so dysfunctional because of what happened to her father in Vietnam maybe things could have been different. She felt that now her life was heading in the right direction, and she would be forever grateful to Robert and Mary. She realized that if she had not made that phone call to them from the Houston Astrodome she would either be in jail or still working the streets.

The life she had lived seemed to be slowly fading in to her past. She thought about it less and less, and when she did she hoped that it would disappear for ever as time went by. Those were not happy times.

No matter what happened she would never go there again. But she still had one thing that bothered her and would one day need to be resolved. She had to tell Robert and Mary the truth and nothing but the truth, and some day she would.

Two weeks later and the summer vacation arrived. John had decided that the kidnapping of the girl would be done the first week of the vacation.

The plan was to keep her for two weeks at the beach house and then release her.

John had spent numerous hours watching her house and knew that her parents were going. He saw them leaving with their suitcases so he figured they would be gone for a while, which was good. Another problem came up when he saw Stella there. Every time he observed the house he saw Stella. It looked almost as if she had moved in. Well, he thought, she won't be there forever and the day she wasn't there they would strike, like late at night. This neighborhood was like dead around nine in the evening. He and Glenn would wear masks, the type that was supposed to make you look like some celebrity. They were also tight. The only masks that fit them were one of President Bush and one of President Clinton. When they put a baseball cap on they were unrecognizable. The idea was for them to wear the masks at all times when they were in the same room with the girl.

The scenario John had outlined was that they would ring the doorbell and turn their back, to the front door so the girl could not see the masks from inside the house. As soon as she opened the door they would rush in and put the bag over her head. Then they would drag her to the car. They would leave the bag over her head and force her to lie down on the back seat. One of them would have to be in the back seat with her to keep her down. They would take their masks off as soon as we got in the car. It wouldn't look too good if people saw them in a car with masks on. Once they reached the beach house they'd put the masks back on and take the bag off, so she could see where she was and hopefully not freak out when she realized that she was not in some jail cell or cellar but in a beautiful house.

"The first thing we have to do is assure her that she is in no danger and that everything will be fine. Nobody is going to hurt her and this is only a temporary situation she is in." John told Glenn.

"While you were screwing around with your little girl Marissa, I stocked the house with all the delicatessen a girl could want. Belgian chocolates, French wines, cheeses, imported cookies and I don't remember what else I bought. I spent a fortune on it. I hope she's worth it."

"All we have to do now is survey the house and wait for that bitch Stella to leave. We know she is there alone. Her parents are apparently out of town and based on the luggage they were dragging out, they will be gone for a while."

John and Glenn were taking turns watching the house, but Stella was always there, and when she left Carla was with her. John was getting nervous and wanted to find out why Stella was there day in and day out. He wanted Glenn to find out by asking Marissa about it. Glenn pointed out that it would be incredibly stupid for them to show an interest in the fact that Stella spent so much time with this girl. Glenn got more and more concerned about John's behavior and thought his obsession wiped out what little common sense he had. This venture was dangerous enough. Having a lunatic in charge could be disastrous.

Days went by and it got worse because her father showed up, God knows for how long. This waiting was driving both of them nutty, Glenn less than John because he figured if her dad stayed home there was no way they could kidnap her from her house, something he was not keen on doing anyway.

John's mind went in the other direction and he was looking for a way to get the girl when she was away from home, but that option didn't look good either because she was never alone. That meddling bitch Stella was always with here. Now these two being lesbians he could understand, much better than Brenda being one.

A couple of days later they saw the father leaving the house. They followed him and when he drove to the airport John's spirits lifted and said.

"From now on we should be at the house every minute of the day and when Stella leaves the house we must act immediately."

Stella had left the house and she and her mom had gone to Galveston, earlier that day. That same evening Carla asked Ginger if she was ready for a walk. She started to waggle her tail, a sure sign she was ready.

It was getting dark and Carla preferred to walk in the streets rather than around the lake, the walkway around had no street lighting and at this time of the day was deserted and a little scary.

John and Glenn saw her coming out of the house with the dog on a leash. They quickly put their masks on and started following her.

Glenn whispered. "What are we doing with the dog?"

John replied, "We do nothing. We grab the girl and leave the dog there. He will return home."

They slowed down and passed Carla before stopping and waiting for the girl and the dog to approach the car. When she did the two jumped out, grabbed her and before she realized what was happening they put the bag over her head and dragged her into the backseat of the car. She was pinned down by the weight of one of them. She heard the car accelerating and speeding away. The guy who held her down said, "Relax nothing bad will happen. We won't hurt you."

The car stopped and she heard other cars stopping and accelerating. There was also a scratching noise on the car door and a dog barking. Ginger, she thought. She heard one of them yelling," Oh shit! This dog is following us and he's scratching at the door. We have to let him in. People are staring at us."

The door was opened and Ginger jumped in and started growling at the one who held Carla. The other guy screamed.

"Why the fuck did you open the door and let the dog in?"

The one in back responded. "What else could I have done? Think about it. A car stopped for a red light and a dog on a leash barking and trying to get in the car and we drive off. Somebody would have taken our license plate number and called the police and we would be charged with animal abuse."

The other guy remained quite for a while and then said, "For once in your life you may be right this time."

The driver of the car seemed to be an arrogant s.o.b. He talked to the other guy like he was an idiot. A strange relationship to say the least for a team that kidnapped a girl.

Carla started talking to Ginger hoping she would relax and be quiet. She didn't want her to be hurt by one of these assholes. She told herself not to panic, just wait and see what these jerks want from me, more than likely money. The car seemed to have left town because they were driving, as far as she could tell, at a good speed and didn't stop at all. Carla started to calm down but at the same time became a bit claustrophobic with that bag over her head. She tried to tell this to the guy who was still holding her down, but he told her that they were almost there.

She tried in her mind to picture these two. One of them sounded like a young kid, and he seemed to be as scared as she was. The driver sounded more assertive and acted like he was in charge. She decided then that she would not act like a scared timid young girl but will go back to being the bitch she was when she was as a hooker in New Orleans. She was scared to death but could not show it. She remembered how she intimidated her clients as an escort girl and felt for her to survive this ordeal she must act like that. They cannot be in charge. She guessed that they must have been driving for at least 30 minutes, probably longer. It's hard to estimate time when you're in the dark and scared.

Suddenly the car slowed down and came to a complete stop. The driver got out and said," I'll open the gate and you remain in the car with her. He came back and they drove for a few seconds before he stopped again and got out of the car, probably to close that gate again. They drove less than a minute before stopping again. The car doors opened, the guy on top of her stepped out grabbed her hand and offered to help her out. This guy sounded a lot friendlier than the other guy driving the car. They took her up some steps before opening a door and entering a house.

One of them said, "I'm going to take the bag off your head, don't freak out. We both are wearing masks, not to scare you, but we need to remain unrecognizable during your stay with us."

He then lifted the bag from her head and if she hadn't been so scared she would have had a laughing fit. One looked like President Clinton and the other like President Bush.

Ginger was sitting next to her growling at both of them.

President Clinton said, "If you can't keep this dog quiet we'll take care of him."

Carla said, "Don't worry about her. Your masks are scaring her." She added sarcastically. "Being kidnapped is a new experience for both of us. We will behave better next time."

John looked surprised and thought. She has spunk I must give her that. I like girls like that, especially when they are as good looking as she is.

Glenn reacted differently and thought she wasn't scared of them. This was confusing for him. A girl being kidnapped in the night and driven to a foreign place by two masked men should be scared shitless. This is no ordinary girl, he thought. She will be trouble.

President Clinton then said, "Look its past midnight. We'll show you your quarters. They are private and have everything you need to make you comfortable. We both hope you will enjoy staying with us and this will be a pleasurable experience."

Carla calmly responded with, "May I ask you what kind of loony bin you both escaped from? You are obviously insane to even consider the possibility that when you kidnap a girl, put a bag over her head, drive her to a strange house and then dress up like presidents to expect her to call this a pleasurable experience. Now if you will show me my room I will try to sleep and hope when I wake up that this was just a bad nightmare. Oh, and by the way do I call you Mister President or do you have a name?"

John and Glenn were speechless. They looked at each other not believing what they were hearing. The driver of the car recuperated the fastest and said in a menacing tone of voice, "Listen you little bitch. We are in charge here and you will do whatever we want you to do or there will be consequences you won't like. Tomorrow we will tell you what we expect from you and I will not tolerate you talking to us like you just did, do you understand?"

"I understand, Mr. President you're going to tell me tomorrow what you want me to do. That's okay, and then

I will tell you what I don't want to do, so we can come to a compromise on what eventually I will do, I hope you understand that."

John's face got all red and he could hardly control himself. He shook with rage and finally managed to say, "Glenn take her to her room. We will deal with this bitch tomorrow.

He did not realize that he screwed up when he said Glenn instead of President Bush.

When she looked around her room and bathroom she thought. This is not the house of somebody who needs to kidnap a girl for money, so what do they want from me. She had picked up on President Clinton's mistake of addressing Bush by his real name, Glenn. She did not react and maybe they didn't even know what he did. In any case it was good information. It also showed her that she was not dealing with professional kidnapers. This could be good or bad.

Showing them that she wasn't afraid of them had rattled Clinton's cage. He obviously had expected a frightened little girl instead of a frightened bitch.

It was still too soon to judge their characters but she bet that she could influence Bush more than Clinton. Bush sometimes acted like a scared little boy, afraid of Clinton and not always agreeing with what he wanted. Interesting!

One of the first things I have to find out she thought, who are these guys, where is this place, what do they want. I better take care of Ginger and keep her away from these two freaks. I'm sure when he said he would take care of Ginger it did not mean taking good care of her.

If it's not money they want what is it? Suddenly it came to her. You stupid moron, she said to herself. You, of all people, should know what men want. They want my body.

Clinton's voice sounded angry and full of lust. They wanted me here for sex, nothing else. This was serious. If it was money she could stall them for a while, saying that she needed time to get it. Sex was different. Everything they wanted was right here.

She thought I can say that I have a disease or that I am HIV positive, but they will more than likely not believe that anyway. Saying that I have my monthly curse could give me a couple days, but I'm going to have to prove this as well. I remember one of the girls I worked with told me how she faked with her pimp when she didn't feel like working that day. Carla went to the medicine cabinet in the bathroom and found what she was looking for, Rubitussin cough medicine. She used a hand cloth and poured a generous portion of the red syrup on it, ready to show these assholes, if necessary and to let them know that sex with her was still a couple of days away.

She checked the windows in her room and bathroom but they all had burglar bars on them, so that was not her way to freedom. Her room was locked so she couldn't explore any further that night. She didn't carry her purse when she walked Ginger, so no cell phone either.

Stella would be worried when she tried to call her on the cell and house phone and nobody answered. But she had told them that she was going to Houston and New Orleans so there could be a dozen reasons why she didn't answer her phone.

She tried to go to sleep but her mind was still busy trying to find a way out of there, and also worrying about what was in store for her. In spite of the attitude she had shown earlier, the reality was that she was scared, she didn't know how crazy these two bastards were and how far they would go. She finally cried herself to sleep determined to wake up in the morning, showing no fear and not backing down.

Ginger was scratching on the door showing her that it was time for her morning ritual. She started to bang on the door until finally Bush opened it and asked why she was making this racket.

She said, "My dog has to go out to do his morning business and I could use a cup of coffee. Well, president Bush, are you opening the front or the back door so my dog can go? If not I can't be responsible for her behavior."

He opened the back door and followed her outside.

She said. "Good for you guys. You don't seem to have neighbors close by. People seeing you running around with these masks on would call the closest asylum, and you would be back there in no time."

A few weeks earlier one of the neighbors had seen her walking the dog and when she got close to him asked her a strange question. He wanted to know if she had a secret admirer or if someone was stalking her. She wanted to know why he asked that question.

He said, "For the last week or so at night there is always a car parked with a young man inside and I think he is watching your house."

Carla shrugged and answered, "If I have I'm not aware of it, but thank you for telling me.

The man said, "If you have a problem I have his license number written down."

She now knew why somebody was watching the house. She should have paid more attention to what the neighbor was saying. Since she knew that the real name of one of them was Glenn, she kept racking her brain where she had heard that name recently. She knew for sure that only a few days ago someone had mentioned that name. She just couldn't remember where it was. Eventually it would come to her she thought, and maybe there is a connection.

Bush said," I prepared breakfast. Let's go. Clinton is already there."

"Are you guys able to eat with these stupid masks on she asked?"

She didn't need an answer because she could see from the mess on his shirt and pants that it wasn't easy.

She first made Ginger her breakfast, sausages and bacon with hash browns. She was in heaven. This would beat dog food any time and she happily licked Carla's face.

Clinton made a remark about people who let their dogs lick and kiss them. He said, "That's disgusting."

Carla gave him an icy stare and said, "I rather have my dog licking me all over than getting one kiss from you.

"Well," Clinton smiled. "That will soon change, I assure you."

Carla finished her breakfast in silence. When she was finished and got up to leave Clinton said." Sit down. We have to fill you in on what we expect from you. She looked at him and said," I hope your expectations are not very high because I have no intention accommodating you or President Bush. I thought I made that clear last night. You kidnapped me, you're not after any money so what you want from me is sex, and you are not getting that from me. The only way you can have sex with me is to rape me and once you've done that and let me go I will not rest until I find you. So after you guys raped me you going to have to kill me."

She then got up and said, "You better figure it out, and for your information the charges for these three crimes are:

Kidnapping, life in prison
Rape, life with no parole
Murder, death penalty.

"And believe me they will get you. You're too stupid to get away with this. You may not believe it, but you already made so many errors and left evidence behind that will lead to you guys that the cops will ring on your door bell in no time at all.

"My parents will hire the best private detectives money can buy to help the police find you. Have a nice day," and she went upstairs.

Glenn could tell that John was furious but he also knew that he didn't know how to handle this situation. Of course, he didn't either. They looked at each other but remained silent, lost for words and not understanding what was going on. It became awkward. Finally John said, "We have to do something. She is ruining our plan; we can't let her run this show. She can't tell us that she won't cooperate. She is in our power and she must do what we tell her to do."

Glenn shrugged and said, "I hear you, but we still don't know how to handle her. We tell her something and she totally ignores it and you telling me that she is in our power is not going to change that. Just between the two of us, I believe we bit off more than we can chew and the old cliché you sometimes get what you wish for is appropriate in this case. Yes, we got her where we wanted her to be, and now we don't know what to do with her.

It's that simple. I know you're frustrated and angry but sometimes you have to admit the fact that you are losing a battle or even a war and surrender."

John jumped up and started to walk up and down the room as if looking for an answer to Glenn's analysis of the situation. He stopped his pacing and said, "I'm not surrendering. I'll teach that bitch a lesson she will never forget. Just let me think about it for a while. She stays in that room till we figure this out. She is just bluffing. She has shit for evidence."

Chapter 12

Carla was held prisoner in her room. Bush brought her meals, and walked the dog. When she tried to start a conversation with him, he apologized but said, "Clinton and I agreed that we would not talk to you until you acted reasonably."

With that he made a hasty retreat and went back downstairs.

She began to doubt the strategy she had chosen because that guy Clinton seemed to be a real bad dude and might do something radical and stupid to make a point. Should she at least pretend to do what they wanted and in order to save time play the menstruation card for at least a couple of days? In spite of the bravado she had showed last time she talked to them, she was really scared. She became more and more convinced that Clinton was not just a bad apple but that he was insane and insane people can be irrational and very dangerous.

She decided next time Bush brought her a meal, she would show him her soft side which she was sure he would tell Clinton about it. That arrogant prick would then think she had given up and would become their sex partner. She needed to be prepared to show them that she really had her period and not just try to stall them. I will show them the bloody rag and my soiled panty. She thought that will probably freak them out. To keep them interested and show my sincerity I will let them touch me. It's going to be hard to let these freaks lay their hands on me, but I believe that my life is in danger and that I need time to get out of here. I know I can do this. Other freaks have touched me in the past and I survived.

She dreaded the meeting with these two mentally challenged idiots, but her will to survive was stronger than her fear. She felt that this was her only option, hoping other more palatable options would become available after she went through with this charade.

When Bush showed up with her dinner she smiled at him and said, "I know you can't talk to me but I want to tell you that I'm willing to hear what you have in mind for me."

Bush said, "I will tell Clinton." and went downstairs.

Clinton immediately got all excited and said. "I told you, I knew she was going to cave in, go get her I can't wait to see that bitch crawl and humiliate herself."

Carla was ready for them. She had taken off her bra and the light sweater she was wearing showed her breasts with protruding nipples as if she was naked.

She made her entrance, not exactly crawling, but demure and passive compared to what they were used to seeing from her.

She said, "I.m willing to meet you half way if you would tell me more about your wishes.

Clinton said, "You already know what we want but I will tell you how all this started." He then gave her the bullshit story about the erotic dream he had and how he felt that this was something he wanted to experience in real life, so Glenn and he had put together a plan to make this happen, and when they saw her they knew immediately that she was the girl in his dream."

Carla thought. You asshole. You think I'm going to fall for this crap. But she said. "Why didn't you tell me this before? This might have been something I would have liked to experience as well. But the kidnapping part was a bit much for me, and scared the daylights out of me. You have to give me a day or two to get over this fear, and besides that I couldn't have sex with you now anyway. I have my period and I'm bleeding pretty bad."

She saw the suspicious look on Clinton's face and said, "You think I'm lying. Let me show you."

She lifted her skirt and saw the look of disgust on his face when he saw her bloody panties. He glared at her and said in disgust, "How gross. Why did you have to do this?"

Carla responded, "You wouldn't have believed me if I hadn't showed you, would you? Listen," she said, "I can't have sex with you now but that doesn't mean we can't play a little."

With that she took off her blouse and exposed her breasts to them.

Clinton was mesmerized and couldn't believe what was happening.

He said. "They are beautiful."

"Are you only going to stare at them or are you going to feel or at least kiss them."

Clinton was the first to take advantage of the offer and started fondling her breasts and kissing her nipples. Carla felt her stomach churning and bile rising into her mouth, but kept a smiling face pretending this was turning her on. She looked at Bush who hadn't moved and was still staring at her but with a look she didn't understand. It was either disappointment or disgust.

Both boys however, were highly aroused and showed a bulge in their pants. Carla playfully grabbed Clinton's crotch and started stroking him until she was sure that he had an orgasm and came in his pants.

Carla then said, "OK boys, this is enough for the first night. I'm getting horny and there is nothing you guys can do now to help me out. We will play for real in a couple of days."

Clinton said, "See, we're not as evil as people say we are. We will take good care of you."

She left them and ran upstairs to her bathroom where she retched and dumped her dinner in the toilet. She thought this cannot happen again. I need to find a way out of here. She couldn't or maybe wouldn't recall what had just happened. What was he saying about being evil? Somehow that word kept coming back to her together with the name Glenn. There must be a link between those two words. She kept repeating the words, evil and Glenn, Glenn and evil. She didn't know why these two words kept popping into her head, but felt that they were significant and was determined to find the link between them.

She thought about Stella and Robert and Mary. They were probably concerned by now that she did not answer her cell phone. Maybe I will ask Bush or Clinton if I can call them, just to tell them not to worry and that everything is fine. She went back downstairs and while walking down she heard Clinton say to Bush, "Did you see these tits? Man is she built or what? We're going to have real fun with her, I can feel it. I don't understand why you all of a sudden got shy and didn't touch her. She was asking for it."

He got excited just by talking about her and picturing her in his mind naked and more than ready to pleasure them.

Carla asked them if she could call her parents and Stella just to make sure they didn't panic and call the police or something. She said, "You can listen while I call, I won't tell them anything about this, just let them know that everything is fine and not to worry about me. I want to play with you guys until they come back which is at least a week or more from now."

She sounded convincing and Clinton said, "All right but I will be in the same room when you call and you better not try anything to make them suspicious."

She called Robert and told him that there was something wrong with her cell phone but that everything was all right. She asked how Mary's sister was doing, which apparently was not good and they expected the worse.

Robert said, "We may not be able to come home anytime soon. Mary would be unable to leave her sister at a time like this and I myself can't leave Mary under these circumstances."

"Of course you both have to stay there and don't worry about me. I'm a big girl and Stella will be back in a couple of days so I won't be alone in the house. Besides, I have Ginger to protect me."

She then called Stella and said the same thing about her cell phone not working and asked how her vacation was going with her mom. Everything was fine and they were looking forward to seeing her as soon as they got back.

See, Carla said. "That went okay. Now they're no longer worried about me and we can play our game pretty soon. I can't wait."

Then she asked, "What is the matter with Bush he didn't even touch me. He doesn't think I'm sexy enough, is he still a virgin?"

John laughed and said, "No he's not a virgin. We're juniors in college. You won't find many virgins there.

Don't worry, he'll come around. Just rub your hot sexy body against him and he'll respond."

She went back to her room and was thinking about Stella and the wonderful times they had together, and how nice it was when they were at the pool, lying in the sun, or when she was at her house just the two of them. She missed all that. Every time she thought about Stella, the words evil and Glenn popped up into her mind. There must be a link. She just couldn't put it together.

When she came down the next morning she detected tension between Bush and Clinton, like they had argued or had a disagreement. She didn't know what had caused it but was bound to find out soon enough.

Clinton spoke first and told her that they realized she had her period and sex was not on her mind. But he said lots of people have sex when their girl friend or wife has the curse and he couldn't see why they couldn't have sex with her.

Carla took a deep breath and tried to control her anger, she calmly said, "The reason I can't have sex with you or anybody is simple. I'm what they call a 'bleeder', which is a woman who has extensive blood loss when she has her period. The fact that you kidnapped me when my menstruation just started has a lot to do with it. I have no tampons with me to efficiently reduce the bleeding.

"Stuffing a rag in my panties is not doing the job. I try not to be vulgar but I'm using words you morons can understand. I need tampons to plug up the hole, do you get it." She paused and thought, I don't know how I came up with this bullshit but it seems to work.

"Now if one of you could go to a drugstore and get me some tampons and clean panties I could have this under control in a couple of days. If not then I don't know whether I will ever stop bleeding.

One thing I do know, because my doctor told me, if the bleeding continues for more than three days I have to check into a hospital and be treated as an anemic patient.

"I'm afraid I may bleed to death, and you moronic perverts want me to have sex with you. You're sicker than I thought you were. When I got up just a few minutes ago blood was running down my leg."

She ran upstairs and slammed her bed room door, waiting to see what would happen next. She thought that she had performed well, but you never know how your audience will respond.

Her audience was stunned, Glenn finally said,

"Holy shit where do we go from here? I suggest we put the bag over her head and get her back to her house as soon as possible and forget the whole thing."

John, of course, had a different suggestion and said, "Let's get her what she wants. She told us if she has these tampons she will be okay in a couple of days, didn't she say that?"

Glenn responded, "And what if she already lost so much blood that she is not okay?"

John replied, "What do you suggest we do then, take her to a hospital and explain the situation? I don't think so. You're such a joy to be with, always so optimistic and full of good ideas." Sarcasm dripped from his voice.

"We wait a couple of days and see how she feels there is time enough to take her home if she really gets sick. In the meantime, let's get her the stuff she wants. Go upstairs and ask her if there is some medicine or something else she needs from the pharmacy, and then go get it for her. You can play being the good guy."

Glenn knocked on her door and asked if she needed something else.

She said, "No just tampons, the insert type. And panties but you probably won't find those in a drug store, you will have to go to a Target or Wal-Mart store. Wait I'll give you my pair of panties so the sales lady knows what you want. Don't worry I washed them last night, they're clean. Oh one more thing. Ask the pharmacist for some medicine for menstruation cramps."

Bush cringed and already felt embarrassed that he would have to ask for all this women shit in the store.

After he left, Carla again tried to put the two magic words together but to no avail. It just wouldn't come. She felt if she could talk to Stella again on the phone she might be able to get something out of her without actually asking and without making Clinton suspicious. She thought she knew how to do this; she just had to be able to call her again.

She went down stairs and smiled at Clinton and with a sweet voice said, "I'm sorry about this morning but when a woman has PMS she can be a real bitch. I blamed you for what's happening, but you couldn't have known that I was having my period and needed my stuff."

Clinton said, "Its okay. Bush is getting everything you need and you will feel better soon."

Bush came back and gave her all the stuff she had asked for. She thanked him and gave him a kiss on the cheek. She smiled and said, "Let me quickly use these tampons and medicine. That will make me feel better in a couple of hours." She hinted that maybe tonight they could at least play a little. She might get to know them a little better and find out what they liked best for when they were ready for the sex party.

Clinton poked Bush in the ribs and said, "See she is really looking forward to it. And you could show a little more interest because she pouted and asked me whether you liked her or not. You didn't even touch her last night, she said."

Glenn said, "Let me tell you one thing. If she needs, some more of this women stuff you're going to get it. I had enough embarrassment in the shop to last me a life time, asking for this stuff with all the women listening and snickering."

John found this very amusing and said, "No you have to do it you're familiar with this shit."

Carla told Clinton that she got fed up with the TV meals they were having for dinner every night, and wanted to know if there wasn't a decent restaurant where they could get a take-out meal.

Clinton gave her a dirty look and mumbled, "You're not in a four star hotel, you know."

She responded, "OK, if that's how you feel, I don't run a high priced whore house either."

"Fine," Clinton agreed, "I get you some decent food for dinner."

"Bring a couple of bottles of decent wine, so we can celebrate a little, she said."

Back in her room she fell on the bed, and again she became depressed and scared. She put up a good front but inside she was still panicking and asked herself how this was going to end. The faked menstruation period could only be stretched out for a couple more days and then these horny maniacs are going to rape me. And in most rape cases, after they had what they wanted, the rape victim got killed and dumped somewhere in the woods.

Why is this happening to me? She whispered, with tears flowing from her eyes. Is this the price I have to pay for what I did in the past? What I did earlier in my life was not by choice. What I had until a few days ago is the life I always wanted. I wasn't born a hooker, I became one because I did not see any other options if I wanted to stay alive."

Slowly the panic subsided and she started to think more rationally. My first priority is to get out of this situation alive. I sold my body before for money.

Why shouldn't I be able to do it if my life is at stake? The big question is even if I do what they want, will they then let me go? It's not a given that I will be free then. They may think that I can possibly identify them and go to the police.

Let's take it one day at the time. What do I need to do to temporarily satisfy their lust for my body? Yesterday Clinton was more or less content with a hand job. He may want more tonight, probably more than I can mentally handle. I could hardly disguise my horror last night; I don't think I can go any further than what happened last night.

But then I may have to. I must remember that these two guys are obsessed with sex, and it's an addiction just as bad as any other drug, meaning that no matter what at some time they will stop at nothing to get it, and time is running out. She must find a way to get through this night, and tomorrow would be another day.
Clinton came back and called, "Come on down I brought you a gourmet dinner. Don't let it get cold."

"Be right there," she said. She had decided to have dinner with them, looking as sexy as possible with the clothing she had.

She entered the dining room and both Clinton and Bush stared at here with such a look in their eyes that she was afraid they were going to rape her right there. She said. "Hold it, boys, I'm hungry let's eat first." Her outfit was a pair of clean panties, a see through blouse, no bra and bare midriff, nothing else.

Her rationale was, the hornier they were the sooner it will be over. A good meal and enough wine may speed things up. She hoped it would work and that she didn't look too hot. She could have overdone it and started the orgy she wanted to avoid.

Clinton had done a good job. He had found a better than reasonable Italian restaurant and had Calamari, a salad, Scampi Fettuccini and a couple of bottles of Chianti.

Carla complimented him on his choice and added, "These are some of my favorite foods."

Clinton was in a nasty mood and said, "Well you better be worth it."

Carla answered coldly, "If you think you can buy me with an Italian meal. You better think again, I'm not for sale."

She removed her blouse and said, "Since this is the only top I have I better not spill any food or wine on it. You better eat your food or there won't be any desert." she said mischievously.

She had decided that both these guys must have an orgasm tonight. She had found out where they both put their dirty clothes, and if she could swipe their underpants with semen on them, she would have their DNA. That was proof that she was with them. This, of course, only had value if she ever got out of there, but again that was tomorrow's problem. One day at the time.

Neither of the guys could keep their eyes off her breasts and almost fought to kiss her bare ass. They gulped their food down without knowing what they were eating. Carla, of course, was savoring her food, at least pretending she was, and making comments on how delicious everything was, again complimenting Clinton on the food and wine.

She innocently asked them if her bare tits were bothering them, because she could put her blouse back on now that the meal was over, if that was what they wanted. She got from the table and said. Let me take the dishes to the dishwasher, you guys just relax."

She wasn't sure, but they both looked like they had already had an orgasm, but she could see that her job wasn't finished yet by the way they watched her every move. She exaggerated the bouncing of her boobs and the provocative way she swung her ass.

Clinton finally managed to say, "What kind of desert did you have in mind?"

She looked at him and said, "Well something similar to last night or was that not satisfying enough."

He responded, "It was okay and I know we can't have the regular sex but there are other ways to please us."

"If you had oral sex in mind," she said, "you better forget it. Sex to me is when both parties enjoy it together. Me sitting on my knees in front of you giving you a blow job does nothing for me.

"The physical condition I'm in is probably not enticing to you to perform oral sex on me, so until you are ready for that, forget it."

She sat down on the couch and said. "I think I better get dressed. You guys have that look in your eyes that tells me that I'm going to be in trouble. We agreed that

145

the big night would be the moment I stop bleeding, and we can all play without any restrictions. I told you sex with me now is impossible, unless you want to take me to the hospital or let me bleed to death."

They looked unhappy but decided they really did not have too many options, and playing with a body like hers was not exactly an unpleasant experience. They moved to the couch and sat next to her their hands all over her body, nibbling on her breasts stroking her ass while she was moaning and saying if you guys keep this up I'm going to come soon. This only resulted in more playing with her breasts, and licking every bare spot of her body, almost fighting for the privilege of kissing her ass. She moaned and groaned, faked a couple of orgasms which made them proud and they promised her that it was just a sample and they would show her in a couple of days what they were capable of in bed.

This semi orgy finally came to an end when Carla said, "You guys exhausted me I think I need some sleep."

The guys stayed down stairs to watch a basketball game on TV. She wanted to stay awake until the guys went to bed, so she could get to the laundry room and steal their shorts that were soiled with their semen. She absolutely wanted these for future evidence that she was with them in the beach house. She was able to push this night's performance to the back of her mind. She realized that she really had accomplished nothing that would lead to her escape.

Carla still had that gut feeling that told her that Stella was the key to solving the Glenn and evil link; she must talk to Stella again.

She heard the guys go to bed and hurried down to the utility room to get their shorts. She also had seen a picture of a couple with two children in the dining room, she took it to her room to see if it had any clues to who they were.

It was a picture of obviously a man and his wife with their two children Carla had no idea who they were but they could be one of the guy's parents. She decided to take the risk of keeping it and hiding it under her mattress, hoping that they wouldn't notice that it was gone.

She had a hard time sleeping. She kept thinking of a way to escape from this nightmare. She went down stairs again to check if any of the doors were unlocked. Unfortunately, that was not the case.

She went back to bed, thinking about Robert and Mary, Stella and her mother and a future, that for a short time had looked so bright and full of promises, a future she never thought was possible for her, and when it was within reach was so cruelly taken away from her. She thought, I can't let that happen, I have to fight to beat these two monsters.

The next morning she went down stairs and asked Bush, "Do you think I can call Stella one more time? Last time I talked to her she kept asking, are you okay? Maybe I should talk to her again for a few minutes, of course with you guys around."

He hesitated and looked at Clinton who nodded. He then reluctantly said that she could call but only for a few minutes. She got Stella on the phone and they talked for a minute or so. She suddenly said out of the blue, "I don't know any of these people. I remember you saying while we were sun bathing, look at these two guys staring at us, but I was lying on my belly half asleep and didn't even look up."

Stella said, "What the hell are you talking about all of a sudden? Are you drunk do you mean that one day when I mentioned these are the evil twins, John and Glenn?"

Bingo thought Carla. This is the link, she immediately pushed the off button and said, "Shit we're disconnected. Well, I really had nothing else to say anyway."

Clinton asked her. What two guys were you talking about?"

Carla answered. "I don't know. I know nobody in high school because I'm home schooled. When she wanted to explain that one of the high school juniors was pregnant and that rumor had it that one of the evil twins was the father, that's when she was cut off but I wasn't interested anyway I have enough to deal with myself."

She told them that she was still afraid she may have lost too much blood. The doctor told her to lie down on her back, which will reduce the blood pressure, so that's what she intended to do for at least today.

She went back upstairs, jubilant that she finally had something to build on. One of her questions was answered. She now knew who Bush and Clinton were, John and Glenn, juniors in Jamesville High School and by no means juniors in college.

It was time for her to develop a strategy for her escape from these two immature jerks, a strategy that would assure her safety. She was still worried that in spite of what she had just found out, they would still want to continue their insane game and use her as their sex slave. Should she let them know that she had discovered who they really were? Or should she be diplomatic and carefully tell them that the game was over and that she expected them to realize this and to take her home now? Or should she be aggressive and knock them on their asses and bluntly tell them that from now on she was in charge and if they refused to do what she demanded they would end up in jail for a very long time.

She thought about it and pondered the options and came to the conclusion that the "two by four" approach would work better than the pussy footing way. She still had to come up with a scenario that made it clear to them that they had no options.

She was aware that under no circumstances could she go to the police. In cases like that everybody involved would have to go through a severe back ground check and that was something she could not afford to happen. No matter how much proof there was, their fancy lawyers would pound on her past and they would more than likely get away with a light sentence or maybe just a parole verdict. There would be enough people saying that it was probably this New Orleans whore who was to blame by seducing two young, innocent boys with a good family back ground.

No she had other plans for these two motherfuckers. They would suffer in a very unorthodox way, something Carla would design for them as soon as she was back home. Her decision was made and she went down stairs, ready for battle. She told them that she had something very important to say, and it would be in their best interest, if they listened carefully and paid full attention to her.

Chapter 13

Clinton and Bush looked at each other and thought. What the hell do we have now?

Carla opened her speech by saying. "Listen boys, the sexual experiences I had these two nights were way below my standards and I have no desire to repeat this. I decided not to participate in the sex games that you had planned, poorly planned, I should say.

John jumped up and wanted to say something but Carla cut him off and said, "Let me finish Mr. President.

"That president bullshit also has to stop so you can take your masks off and I will call President Clinton, John and President Bush, Glenn. This should make you more comfortable, and I won't have to look at these stupid masks any longer. They were really freaking me out.

"With a smile on her face she said, another reason I can't have intercourse with you is that I could end up in jail for having sex with under age school kids."

At this point John and Glenn were looking at her like she was a creature from hell, but remained quiet. They wanted to say something but did not know where to start or what to say.

Carla continued and said, "You are really lucky that you didn't have the chance to rape me. Your high priced lawyers can now claim that technically there was no rape, because there was no penetration.

The kidnapping is an entirely different case, there is enough evidence that this actually happened, and you won't be able to dodge that bullet. That will not go away.

"If you to take me home now I will consider not getting the police involved or anybody else. Nobody but you guys and I will know what happened here.

"But soon as I'm home I will let you know what I want you to do in return for my silence. I will then show you all the other evidence that I have that would put you away, so that there is no longer any doubt in your mind that you will face serious charges if you force me to get the legal system involved."

John jumped up and said. "You bitch! You have no proof at all that we kidnapped you, and you are just grandstanding and trying to scare us."

He grabbed her arm and shook her violently, calling her a filthy slut and threatening to kill her."

Carla pulled her arm from out of his grip and said.

"Well, now I can add assault and battery to the charges, and by the way don't have to try to scare you. You are already scared shitless, and with good reason.

"I'm not going to tell you all the evidence that has piled up against you. I will however, let you in on a few stupid things you did.

"First, you don't survey a house from the same place almost every night for two weeks. Second you don't survey a house sitting in a red convertible Corvette which can be traced to you in a heartbeat. You used a different car on some nights, but that doesn't matter. I have the registration plate numbers for both cars and these cars are owned by the Witherspoon family.

"You rented a car to use for the kidnapping, a car you returned a couple of days ago. You should never use your own credit card, especially not if that car has my DNA all over the back seat.

"I could go on but we are wasting valuable time. My father can come home any day now and it would be difficult for me to explain where I was with the dog.

"Stella is also on her way back home. Same story there. She is already suspicious that I'm not telling her everything and during my last phone call I made her understand that something was wrong and John and Glenn were involved, remember when you asked me about two guys, that was you guys.

"So do we have a deal or are you waiting for the cops to show up? It's your choice.

"If I have to walk out of here, the first cop I see will have the exclusive story and the honor to arrest you."

Glenn asked. "What guarantee do we have that you won't go the police after you are home?"

She smiled and said. "You have no guarantee at all, but I will tell you why I don't want to make this public. A case like this would create a lot of publicity, my face and your faces will be in every newspaper and TV in the country. I won't have a private moment for several years to come. The media will be all over me day and night. During the trial your lawyers will ask me embarrassing and humiliating questions. Some people will even think that I'm the guilty slut that seduced you. This is the kind of shit that I want to avoid. It's not because I don't want you to be punished, but I know I can't stay out of the limelight if there is a trial. If you don't do what I ask you to do, I will not hesitate to bring this into the open. It will be your choice.

"Come on, boys, decide and make this easy on yourselves. You know I have your ass nailed to the wall and that may be a little hard to swallow for an arrogant piece of shit like John, who thinks he has the sun shining out of his ass. But you can't win them all and I think I let you guys off easy.

"Well, I'm ready. Do I walk or are you driving me home? I know this is not exactly what you had in mind, but believe me, it's the best deal you're going to get."

John realized that she had them cornered and said, "We will drive you home, but you haven't seen the last of us."

No she said. "That's right and I'm actually counting on it."

When they dropped her off a few blocks away from her house, John threatened her by saying, "Don't sleep with your windows open."

She responded. "Be careful of what you say, or you may soon sleep in a room without windows,"

"Bitch." he mumbled when they drove off.

As soon as she was in her house she called Robert to find out whether he tried to call her while she was at the beach house and also how Mary was doing and if there was any change in her sister's condition.

Mary was not doing very well, she had begun to realize that her sister was slowly slipping away and she had a hard time dealing with this.

Robert had tried to call her but was not too concerned because she had told him that she was probably going to New Orleans.

She then called Stella, and got an earful from her friend who said, "You called me and started talking to me then changed the subject and says things that made no sense. Then you hung up on me. I tried to call you back but you never answered the phone."

Carla said. "We were cut off and I couldn't get a connection when I tried to call you again."

"Well," Stella said, "We will be home tomorrow. I'll call you soon as we get in, and if it's not too late I'll come over."

Carla was happy, of course, that she was home again, but unhappy that she had to let those creeps go. She was determined to make them suffer severely for many years to come, maybe more suffering than being in jail. They will not have a happy life, she swore. I escaped their cruel plan because I was assertive and lived on the streets before, but what if they had picked an innocent timid, young girl? They would have gone ahead with making this kid a sex slave and raped her. This girl would never fully recover from such an ordeal and be a mental case for the rest of her life. No, they will pay dearly for what they tried to do. They are going to wonder why their lives all of a sudden turned to hell, but they deserve it, and I'm going to make sure they get it.

Carla was going to set up a meeting with them and explain what was expected of them and what the consequences would be if they didn't comply with her demands.

She would demand $50,000 within a week in cash. This she would tell them was for sexually abused women in the neighborhood. Noncompliance would result in a visit to both their parents to inform them of how their sons were getting their kicks. And if they didn't come up with the cash she would also inform the authorities.

If for any reason they thought that the best way for them was to get rid of her, the consequences of that stupid idea would be severe. A detailed write up of what had happened was in the hands of three different lawyers, in the event that something would happened to her, disappearance, accidental death, or anything that looked suspicious, these sealed documents would be handed over to the local police, the FBI, and the County sheriff.

Other evidence that was in her possession was that this whole plan was known to some of their high school friends. Rumor had it that the evil twins were up to something nasty, this was circulating in school.

She also would claim that her DNA was found in the back seat of the car they had rented, and was certified to be hers.

She also would say that John's semen was on her panties, which she kept frozen for future DNA tests if needed as evidence.

There were also the phone calls on John's cell phone, calls that could be traced to the beach house location.

She also had that picture she swiped from the bedroom in the beach house showing the Witherspoon family.

What she was not going to disclose were the surprises she had planned for them in the future, surprises they would definitely not cherish.

She met with them on neutral ground, a cafeteria in the Mall where everybody could see them.

Carla opened the talks by saying, "When you let me go and I promised not to go to the police, you do remember that I said there would be other consequences? I need you to give me $50,000 by next Friday, cash."

Both guys protested and said that was not fair plus she never said that was one of the conditions.

"That's true I never said that, but I'm saying it now. If you don't show up here by next Friday, both your parents will be informed."

"There is no way we can come up with that kind of money in one week." they both claimed.

"Maybe I forgot to tell you," Carla said, "we are not negotiating here. These are the conditions.

This is not blackmailing. This money will help the abused women in this area to get out of situations that people like you put them in. So stop whining and get me the money, Friday next week."

John said, "You are a real bitch."

She replied, "You haven't seen anything yet. This is what happens when little boys want to play with a smart girl like me.

"Now let me tell you what kind of evidence I have that if used will put you guys away for the better part of your lives. Once that penetrates your thick skulls, maybe you will agree that I'm offering you a bargain."

She then told them about the letters in the lawyer's possession, about the DNA in the car, the semen in her panties, the phone calls that could be traced to John's cell phone, the family picture, and the rumors in school, rumors that they created for themselves yourselves.

"That, with my neighbor's testimony that he saw you spying on me just before you kidnapped me, will do the job.

"If there are no further questions, I'll see you next week, and don't forget my present. I'm counting on it."

John and Glenn walked away from her looking like two kids who had just been reprimanded by the school principal and told that he wanted to talk to their parents. Their bravado was gone and they didn't know what hit them. Their lives as they knew it seemed to have disappeared and they were lost. Nothing like this had ever happened to them and nobody had ever prepared them for something like this. They felt miserable and saw no way out of it.

They had the impression that every one looked at them as if they knew what they had done. Getting $50,000 in one week would not be easy but they both had an account and assets in the stock market they could sell, so coming up with the money was not a big deal. Their parents did not keep a close look on their accounts. This was not a major problem. They were more concerned about the veiled threat that bitch had hanging over their heads. What if she talked to the police anyway?

Should they talk to the family lawyer or to their fathers? Neither of these options sounded very good at this time. This would be the last options and only if the police were involved.

What would they do if she had an accident, even an accident that they had nothing to do with? Her lawyers would automatically inform the authorities. She had told them that this security measure would be in place for the next ten years. They would live in fear for the next ten years. Even when she got sick, these assholes might find it suspicious and could follow her instructions. How were they going to live with this sword hanging over their heads for the next ten years?

Glenn solemnly said, "She has us by the balls, and I'm afraid she is going to squeeze hard."

John with his usual macho attitude said, "We'll get the bitch somehow, she's not going to get away with this shit, I won't tolerate it."

Glenn looked at him angry and suddenly erupted.

"You fucking arrogant asshole! You're the one who got us here. I tried for over a year, telling you that this was a stupid boneheaded idea that was doomed from the start. But no, mister fucking know it all had it all planned and said it was foolproof. Only a couple of days ago I again said, "Let her go now" but again you knew better.

"Come Friday I'm going to pay her the money, my part of it, and I will tell her that from now on it's no longer us, it will be you and me, separate units. I've had enough of you. I blame myself for letting you dominate me, always doing what you wanted, no matter how stupid it was. It's over. I'm no longer your puppet. We're done, John."

John immediately thought. He's flipped, he's over the edge. I always knew he would be a liability. This could be dangerous. I need to calm him down, getting mad at him is not going to help. I must pretend that I agree with him and that this is entirely my fault, apologize to him, everything to put him at ease.

He said, "Listen to me Glenn. I'm sorry I lost it a minute ago. You are right. I should have listened to you from the beginning. It was a stupid idea and you saw it right away.

"On Friday I will tell her that I take full responsibility and that I more or less forced you into this plan. I will also apologize to her and let her know that I'm very sorry for what I did and did not mean to harm anybody.

"We will show her that whatever punishment she has in mind will be okay with us. We, at least I, deserve to pay the price and face the consequences of it.

"She may cut us some slack if she feels that we are sincere and are sorry for what we did."

His speech had some effect on Glenn and he seemed to calm down and agreed with what John proposed to do. John felt that he had Glenn back under control, but that this was only a temporary situation. He could flip again any time and do something stupid by telling either the police or his family what we did. He had to take measures that this would never happen. Glenn must be back completely under his control or be silenced one way or the other. He was too much of a risk. He must gently remind Glenn of the fire they had set on Melissa's house which might make him think twice about his relationship with John.

On Friday the two boys showed up, each with an envelope with $25,000 cash inside. Carla immediately sensed the friction between them, and when Glenn said that John had something to say to her, she saw a look of hatred in John's eyes. John spoke up and told her that he regretted what they did to her, and if there was anything he could do to ease the pain they had caused her, she should just ask and they would do it.

Carla thought it sounded like Glenn had forced John into these apologies and promises. Knowing John they were all false and he still hated her for what she was doing to him.

She coldly said. "No, I have what I wanted and I will let you know if there are any other demands."

John then said. "So it is all about the money isn't it?"

"No," she responded. "If it was about money I would have gone to your family and asked for at least several million dollars."

She then turned her back on them and left them without another word.

"What do we now? Glenn whimpered.

Nothing, I suppose, John said. "What do you want to do, go and kiss her ass every morning? I personally hope I will never see her again."

Glenn thought. Yes, that would be ideal but I'm afraid that will not be the case.

The relationship between John and Glenn had changed since the day Glenn blew his cool. They still saw each other on occasion, but it was no longer a close friendship. Before, when you saw one you saw the other. This bothered John more than it did Glenn. John was uncomfortable if Glenn was not close to him. He was worried that Glenn could do something stupid that would jeopardize his safety.

Carla, in the meantime, had devised a scheme that would create a change in status for the evil twins. It needed some more time on her part to make it work.

She also had to go to Houston to recruit a team willing to execute it. She needed the cash from the two sex maniacs to put it in motion.

Chapter 14

Stella arrived the next day and spent the night at Carla's house, telling her about the good time she had with her mom and how relaxing the beach and the sun was. They had a real good time, and it was nice to be with her mother talking about everything that was happening, the past, the present and mostly their future.

"And what did you do, other than making phone calls that made no sense and were freaking me out?"

"Sorry," Carla said. "I was in an office when I called you and was trying to multitask, talking to you and answering questions, so the guy got all pissed off and started to be sarcastic and asking whether he should come back when it would be more convenient for me, so I put you on hold and lost you.

"I told you, I had to go to New Orleans to settle all sorts of things having to do with Katrina and my parent's deaths. On the way back I stopped in Houston because the FEMA people owed me some money, which I didn't get."

"When are we starting our classes? She asked.

Stella said, "Ma needs to reapply for some certificate, but they assured her she would get it next week, so we will start the Monday after. That will give us another ten days off."

Carla said, "Good because I have to go back to Houston for a day or two that will work out great."

Stella asked. "Is everything all right with you? You sounded so uptight on the phone, I was worried about you."

Carla asked, "Have you ever had to deal with Government Agencies? If you had, you would understand why I was tense, they are driving you nuts." Stella seemed happy with this explanation and didn't push any further."

"Maybe ma will let me come with you to Houston for a day or so."

Carla said. "That will be great. I don't have that much to do there anyway, so we can visit some of the tourist attractions. Ask your mother, and we can leave Sunday morning. I can do my stuff on Monday morning and we can come back Monday evening." Carla's business was in the Montrose area, known for a certain kind of business, but they would stay in the hotel Derek just across from the famous Galleria shopping center."

The hotel was expensive but Robert had insisted that they should stay there.

"My treat," he said. "Just charge it to your credit card."

Sunday they went to the Space Center, which they found very impressive, and after that had lunch in Kemah, right on the bay watching the sail boats go in and out of the marina. That night they had dinner at Papasito's, Carla's treat because it was Stella's first decent Mexican meal, and because Carla felt like doing something nice for her friend. She was hoping that one day they would be close enough for Carla to tell her everything; Someday maybe, but not yet.

They decided that after dinner they would have a drink in the hotel bar and go to bed early, because it has been a fairly long day. In the morning Carla went to take care of her business downtown and Stella went exploring the Galleria. They would meet for lunch in the Galleria. Carla established everything she needed to take care of and was reasonably sure that her plan would be carried out by the people she had met this morning.

After lunch they drove around the Medical Center and couldn't believe the number of hospitals and other medical facilities they saw.

Stella said. "No wonder that so many overseas patients are coming to Houston for treatment."

They arrived back in Jamesville around six and found to their surprise that Robert had come home. Carla immediately wanted to know if something had happened, Robert assured here that it was still a status quo, but since there was really nothing he could do there he decided to come home and see if everything was OK with you guys. I got a little concerned after our last phone call. You just sounded tense and maybe there was something that you couldn't tell me on the phone.

She gave Robert the same spiel she gave Stella about dealing with a Government Agency. She then asked. "Why didn't you call me? We were in Houston. We could have picked you up at the airport and driven home together."

"No," he said, "I arrived early in the morning and didn't want to cut your visit to Houston short. I'm sure you both had a good time together. I did all right. I had a limo drive me home so I didn't even have to drive myself. I was a little concerned when I couldn't find Ginger but I called Stella's ma and found out that she was babysitting her. I went over there and thought this was a good time to talk about the home schooling arrangement, so don't worry about that, we sorted every thing out and you guys are ready to go.

"Stella and her mom can stay in our house for as long as they want. Mary and I don't know when we will be back so we are very grateful that Stella and her mom are willing to stay here with you. We were not thrilled to have you here all by yourself."

Carla was moved by how much they seemed to care about her. With all the worries they must have with Mary's sister, they still found time to make sure she would be all right. Again she had a hard time not crying. That guilty feeling took over and she thought, would they still love me this much if they knew everything about me? She was afraid that this would not be the case. She would understand if their affection for her changed.

The next day she called John and Glenn and arranged to meet with them at the food court in the Mall on Friday at 2PM. They wanted to know why but she said just told them to be there and hung up.

John called Glenn and asked him if she wanted him also to meet on Friday. Glenn affirmed that yes she expected them at 2PM. Neither of them knew what she wanted, so they had to live in fear until Friday, wondering what was going to happen. Glenn passively accepted it, knowing that she had the power and nothing would change that.

John, of course, reacted angrily and cursed. "That bitch is ruining my life and I'm not going to let that continue. This has to stop." If only he knew how to stop her from controlling his life. He didn't, but he convinced himself that he would find a way and that she would pay dearly for the humiliation he felt.

When Glenn and John got to the food court, Carla was already there. When they sat down she didn't give them the time to ask any questions but said, "Listen and listen real good. Rumors are flying around in the high school circle that an orgy took place at John's parent's beach house, just a couple days ago. I know that I haven't said a word to any one about it, so one of you morons must have been bragging about something that didn't even happen. But this is water under the bridge and it can't be undone. Now comes the part that I want you to listen to. If my name is mentioned with regard to this rumor, you are both as good as dead. I will not hesitate, I will not ask you questions, I will go to the local police, the FBI and the County Sheriff and explain in detail what went on at the beach house. Kidnapping, rape, assault, all of this will be documented with the evidence I have. The result will be that both of you will be arrested and put in jail with no chance of bail.

"Have you paid attention or are you already undressing these two hussies in back of me, trying to get your attention? I'll leave now and you won't hear from me again but I hope you understood me. Now you can get to these two teenage hookers. They both drooling, they must be desperate."

She left the two in a state of shock, each accusing the other of spilling the beans and both denying that they did. In spite of the seriousness of this situation they couldn't help but look at the girls next to them. They were both excessively made up; both dressed scantily to draw the attention of every horny guy who was within a mile. One of the girls asked them which one of them was the lucky guy with this good looking chick.

John angrily said. "She is no chick and believe me, nobody wants to be the lucky one with that bitch."

The girl said, "Sorry I asked. I must have touched a nerve." and turned around.

"Wait John said." "I'm sorry I didn't mean to be so rude. I'm John and this is my buddy Glenn. You mind if we come over and sit with you girls?

They nodded and made room for them at the table. John asked. "Where are you girls from? You are definitely not from this Podunk town. We would have noticed for sure."

The girls looked flattered and one of them said. "I'm Tracy and this is my friend Cindy. We're both from Biloxi Mississippi. We just graduated from Biloxi High School and we needed a little vacation break before going to college. What about you guys?"

Glenn felt he had to say something and blurted out, "We're more or less in the same boat. Just graduated and also waiting to go to college, but we live here and are not on a vacation trip."

John piped in and said. "Where are you going from here and what the hell are you doing in Jamesville?"

Cindy fielded this question by saying. "It wasn't our intention to be here but my driver, she looked at Tracy, said let's go this way that looks on the map like it's a short cut. We are actually on our way to Corpus Christi. My brother lives there and I promised that if we were in the neighborhood we would visit with him."

"Well," John said. "You're at least another three hours driving away from Corpus Christi."

Cindy said. "Well we're in no hurry. If there is some action here we could spend the night."

John asked. "What kind of action are you looking for?"

Tracy said, "We're party girls. We're ready for anything that's exciting and fun, the wilder the better."

John and Glenn looked at each other and John said. "Well we can definitely create a party for you girls."

Cindy asked. "Where would the party be, and who would be there?"

John explained that they had a beach house, not far from Jamesville and was on the way to Corpus. The party he proposed would be just the four of them. It's a very nice house right on the beach. It has a swimming pool, a spa and unlimited booze, grass and coke if you want some."

"We could go to a nice Italian restaurant first or start partying and take out some food. What do you think are you girls up to it?"

Tracy and Cindy looked at each other, smiled and Cindy said. "Let's go. Sound good to us."

John said, "One of you can come with me in my car and Glenn can come with you in your car so you won't get lost."

Cindy said. "I'll come with you and Glenn can drive our car."

The girls seemed properly impressed with the red Corvette and figured this might be fun. These guys obviously have cash to spend. This assignment could turn out to be lucrative, their boss had told them. Just make contact with the guys, tell them you're college students, have sex with them and come back. There will be a $500 bonus for each of them.

This has worked out as planned so far and there could be other additional benefits. They decided to play it by ear and who knows what will happen.

They got to the house. Ready to party, by this time the boys were so excited that sex was the only thing on their mind. Drinking and drugs would come later.

The girls had a chance to talk to each other privately and agreed that this should be milked for whatever they could get out of it. The boss didn't need to know about the fringe benefits that came with the job. There must be some valuable stuff in a house like this. First give them what they wanted and that was getting laid.

They had one glass of champagne and were carried off to one of the bedrooms, the sex was a "slam bam thank you mam" deal, and that seem to make John and Glenn more relaxed and put them into a party mood. They offered to take the girls out to dinner and then come back to the house, change partners and get into some serious partying.

The girls agreed with anything they wanted and had already made plans that after dinner and more sex, drinking and drugs the guys would fall asleep. They had brought some heavy duty pills, mixed with a drink, would put them to sleep almost immediately.

This would give the girls all the time they needed to look around and see what there was that could easily be sold. They would not spend the night there but haul ass and drive back to Houston and their job was done.

The party turned into an orgy, but that didn't upset Cindy or Tracy. That was part of the job and nothing they had not done before. Everything went as planned, but they were disappointed with the stuff they found. They took a gas credit card that would supply them with free gas for a couple of days, and about $200 in cash.

They slipped out of the house in the middle of the night without a problem and were back in Houston early in the morning. They called their boss and reported that everything went as planned.

The boss then called the phone number the lady had given him and reported that everything was executed as requested by her. He said he would call Jamesville High School in a few days and give them the message as per her instructions. She told him that his money would be mailed to him the same day and hung up.

A few days later the phone rang in the Jamesville High School nurse's office and the nurse picked up. Before she had the chance to say hello, a man's voice asked if she was the nurse of the high school.

She cheerfully responded. "I sure am. I'm Nancy Williams and..."

The caller interrupted her. "I don't give a rat's ass what your name is. Are you the nurse?"

"Yes," the cheerfulness gone from her voice. "What can I do for you?"

He said. "I'm Anthony Fonse and I'm the owner of an Escort Service in Houston."

She cut him off and said. "I'm sure I'm not interested in anything you want to sell me."

He then raised his voice and said. "I'm not selling anything; I have information about two of your students that I think you should know. Two of my girls took a couple of days off, about a week ago and ended up in Jamesville in the mall. They were sitting at a table in the food court when two teenagers boys, approached them and started to talk to them.

"To make a long story short the girls ended up partying with these guys in a beach house somewhere, drinking, screwing and probably using drugs."

The nurse again interrupted him and said. "Why are you telling me this? I have absolutely no interest in what a couple of your whores are doing." He now yelled at here will you shut your trap and let me finish what I have to say."

Frightened she said. "Please, go on."

"That's better. I have my girls checked every month for possible infections or diseases, because I run a clean business and I don't want any problems. A report came back with the results of these tests, and one of the two girls was diagnosed positive with the HIV virus. As a nurse you should know that this disease is highly contagious. I thought it was my civil duty to inform somebody that these boys were exposed to this virus and could be infected with it. I don't know these kids and the only information she could give me was their first names, Glenn and John. She also had a glimpse of a credit card and his last name started with something like Whiter or Withesoon. She also said that one of them was driving a red convertible Corvette. Does that ring a bell to you?"

He didn't wait for an answer but said. "That's all I know and I think I did my duty and somebody like you should take it from here, goodbye."

The nurse thought. Oh my God, John Witherspoon and Glenn Evans. I'm not going to touch this with a ten foot pole. I'm not paid enough for this problem. This is the Principal's job. She went straight to his office and told him in detail what that rude pimp person had told her. The principal asked her for the guy's phone number. He said. "He needed to talk to this person and find out more details about this."

The nurse said. "I don't have his phone number. He hung up on me before I had the chance to ask him."

The principal said. "I can't believe you let him hang up on you before he gave you his phone number."

The nurse thought, you arrogant prick, but said, "Sir, I did not have the opportunity to ask him, he was a very rude man and never gave me the chance to ask any questions."

The principal said, "I'll handle it." sounding as though she was a stupid woman. Does he have to do everything himself?" He added, "Keep in mind Nancy, this is strictly confidential and you can't tell this to anybody, is that understood?"

"Of course Sir, I won't tell this to anybody."

The Principal thought, I have to inform Mr. Witherspoon and Mr. Evans about this, it's not something I cherish doing because knowing this arrogant lot, they going to try to make this all my fault, like we're not strict enough or disciplined enough, we don't teach them moral values, etc. etc. I can already hear Witherspoon saying. I knew it. I should have sent John to a private school. They would have known what to do.

These things would not have happened in a private school and I will forever regret that I let John go to Jamesville High School.

He would never even consider that it is the parent's responsibility, to instill these values in their children, not the teachers.

Anyway, he called both parents and asked them to come and see him as soon as possible. He wanted them to come at the same time, and let them decide when. He stressed the fact that it should be within a couple of days and preferably either that same day or the next. It was that serious.

They both showed the next day, and Witherspoon used to being the center point of any meeting he attended, he asked the principal in a commanding voice,

"Now, what is this mysterious event that took us away from our busy work schedule?"

The principal said. "Please, sit down." He then told them in detail what this was all about and that both John and Glenn should have a blood test done. He said. "This has been kept in strict confidence but a test is mandatory. I legally have to report this incident to the authorities but if the test turns out to be negative, I see no reason to do that."

Both Witherspoon and Evans showed disbelief and both wanted proof. They said that it was hard to believe that their sons could have been involved with a couple of hookers.

The principal became somewhat annoyed with their response. Everybody in Jamesville was aware that these two were capable of doing anything, and their parents don't have a clue. It is also possible that they are just pretending. After the fire incident they should know better. He said, "It does not matter what you believe at this point. They have to take this test immediately and I need to see the results. If you feel this is just a malicious rumor and don't want them to be tested, you leave me no choice but to report this.

"I advise that the testing should be done, but you are the parents, and the choice is yours."

Witherspoon said, "I still don't believe that John and Glenn would have intercourse with a couple of prostitutes. But you leave us no choice. We will have the test done in Houston."

When they were outside his office, Evans said. "We should talk to our boys and hear their side of the story. I think we should get together, the four of us, without telling them why we want to talk to them. This way they can't prepare a story just in case there is any truth to all of this."

Witherspoon reluctantly agreed and asked Evans to come to his house that same evening. | Evans agreed.

John and Glenn were told that they couldn't go out that night because their fathers wanted to talk to them. Both John and Glenn thought that they wanted to talk about visiting several colleges before deciding where they wanted to go.

After dinner Glenn asked his Dad if they should talk now. His Dad then told Glenn. "We're going to John's house because John's father and I wanted the four of us together for this talk."

Glenn got scared and his first thoughts were that the bitch had talked to their parents, about the kidnapping and the rest of it. He wanted to talk then.

But his Dad said, "No we will talk when we are all together."

When the four of them were together, John's dad said, "We're not going to ask you questions for now. We just want to tell you the position you're both in. There is a good possibility that you are infected with the HIV virus. This was caused because you two had sex with two hookers from Houston a few days ago, and one of these two ladies has the HIV virus. Since you apparently had sex with both of them, there is no way of telling which one of you could have the virus. You both could be infected. We, Mr. Evans and I, have decided to take you to Houston tomorrow to have you tested so we know where to go from there."

Both guys were stunned, confused and scared. Not only were they in big trouble with their family, they could very well have a disease that could kill them. John tried to say something but his father waived his hand and said, "Shut up, John, I'm not done talking. You will not only be tested for HIV, you will also be tested for drugs and alcohol and you will have a psychiatric evaluation done. When Mr. Evans and I were informed about this we decided to hire a couple of private investigators and instructed them to interview your friends, girls you dated, teachers, coaches, in short everybody you have had contact with.

"We wanted to know how these people would rate you as human beings.

"We also asked them to check out the beach house for evidence that would substantiate there was a party held recently. Both detectives reported back to us, with a preliminary report. Mr. Evans and I were shocked with what these people found out.

"Among the people you had frequent contact with, nobody liked you. You were tolerated because you came from a wealthy family and always had money to entertain them.

"Most of them hated you, and were afraid of you. The girls were impressed by the social status your family had, but none of the girls you slept with said that there was any affection or love involved.

We have taken into account that some of these people are jealous and will say nasty things about you for no other reason. But when all the people interviewed are unanimous in the evaluation of your character and behavior, there obviously is a problem.

"The beach house was a mess, dirty glasses all over the place, bedrooms and bathrooms with dirty linen on the floor. On the table in the living room, there were marijuana joints, small quantities of cocaine and ecstasy.

All signs of an orgy were present and since you are the only one who has access to the house, you and Glenn obviously are involved.

"If you both are lucky and test negative for the HIV virus, Mr. Evans and I have agreed that you will be committed to a rehab center for the duration of the summer until you go back to school.

"Since you are both 18 years old and considered to be adults, we can only commit you with your consent. You can refuse to go there. The consequences of that would be that, since you are legally adults, we as your parents would have no obligation to provide you with housing or any of the other necessities to keep you in good health. In other words we can kick you out of our houses.

"Now, this is the situation you created. We suggest that you go to a rehab center where hopefully they can teach you how to live a normal and productive life.

"Now, will you please tell us your story of how you guys got involved with two hookers from Houston?"

John asked Glenn, "Is it OK for me to start and you interrupt me whenever you feel like it."

Glenn nodded and said, "Go ahead. After all it took place in your father's house."

John started by saying, "We were not aware that the two girls we met in the mall were hookers. They told us they were on their summer break after finishing high school in Biloxi, and wanted to party before going to college in the fall.

"They were good looking sexy girls, ready to party and on their way to Corpus to visit one of the girl's brothers. It was perfect we all would have a good time and the next morning they're on their way out of here. It couldn't be better. How were we to know that they were professionals? They never asked or even mentioned money. We took them to dinner and that's all the money we spent on them.

"You said that the principal received a call from a guy informing him that one of the girls was tested and was positive for the HIV virus. Why would he guy who runs a whore house do a thing like that? Guys who are running a prostitution ring don't do this. He said he was doing his civil duties. This does not make any sense at all."

His father agreed, but he said, "That does not explain the drugs we found in the house. Even if you were not aware that these two girls were escorts, it does not justify you trashing our house and you and Glenn using drugs. That worries us a lot more than you guys sleeping with hookers. The fact that you two are known as 'the evil twins' does not exactly enhances your reputation in the community, and makes us wonder what other dreadful things you did, unknown to your parents."

John rebutted with, "Dad we're not addicts. We never used drugs; the girls brought them to the house. I'm not an addict and these drugs are not mine."

"His father said, "The drug test tomorrow will tell us the truth. Neither one of you is going out tonight. We're leaving at seven o' clock tomorrow morning."

The boys realized that protesting under the circumstances would be futile.

Glenn, though, asked his father what exactly is a psychiatrist evaluation?

"I'm not a psychiatrist," his father said, "but I do know a little about it. It's basically a mental analysis of somebody who has shown signs of unusual behavior, problems with relationships, acted disruptive, substance abuse, and coping with the real world in general. A comprehensive psychiatric evaluation may take two days, so they may keep you overnight in the hospital.

"We'll find out tomorrow. After the blood and urine tests they will ask you a lot of questions, and based on this preliminary assessment will decide on the duration of the actual evaluation."

At the same time rumors were flying around the high school campus that John and Glenn could have been infected with the HIV virus because they had sex with a couple of prostitutes. The contents of the rumor progressed from "could have" changed to "they do have".

The high school nurse only told her friend, and insisted that she must keep it a secret, so her friend told it to just one of her friends also stating that it was a secret and not be told to anybody else. It only took a couple of hours for everyone in school to know about it.

Carla found out from Stella and thought. News travels fast in Jamesville. She said to Stella, "From what you told me about these two jerks, it's not surprising, is it?"

"Not really," she agreed. "I just hope it didn't infect some other girls."

Carla knew that would not be the case, because the boys were not infected with HIV. The test would show that, but the boys would be in serious trouble regardless, and that was Carla's ultimate goal, getting them in trouble and making their lives miserable.

She would leave them alone for the next few months, and then decide what she would do with them. Their punishment was far from over. There was more to come because their debt to society was far from being paid.

Sometimes she asked her self the question. Why am I so obsessed with the punishment of these two guys? There must be thousands and thousands just like them.

Was it because she was their target as a kidnapping and rape victim, or was that the excuse she needed to get even with the men who had used her in the past, and who felt that it was all right to mentally and physically rape her, because they paid for it? If that was the case she should feel guilty for focusing her anger on the two boys. They should not be punished for what all the other perverts did to her.

It was complicated. John and Glenn deserved to suffer for what they had done to her, or what they had planned to do. What if some other innocent girl had been their victim? No, she shouldn't go soft on these two sex maniacs, at least not yet.

They tested negative for the HIV virus but positive for several illegal substances. In addition a Comprehensive Psychiatric Evaluation would have to be done, requiring them to stay overnight in the hospital.

Their fathers decided to go back to Jamesville and return the following day. They had not told their wives anything of what was going on and were not looking forward to breaking this to them, but they had to be informed now and become part of the decision making process.

When they got home they found out right away that they were too late. The news had already reached them through the Jamesville grapevine. When told that their boys were still at the hospital they demanded to go back to the hospital that same night.

It took all their husband's persuasive powers to convince them that it made no difference going that night or the next morning. The boys were in the psychiatric ward and there was no visiting while they were having the evaluation. The first time they could see them would be late the next afternoon.

The wives finally succumbed to the logic after some choice words for their husbands for not telling them the day before that their sons could have a disease which, if not treated properly, could be fatal. Both husbands pleaded that they didn't want to upset them for something that may not be there in the first place, and they said the tests showed that they did the right thing. That made the two mothers angry, and they demanded to know who gave them the right to decide what they should or shouldn't know. Both guys apologized and said. "Yes, you are right we should have told you earlier."

The next day they got to the hospital and saw the psychiatrist. He said, "I'm not finished with the evaluation yet. I suggest you go out and have a nice long leisurely lunch and come back around three o' clock. I will then be able to give you some preliminary results, but keep in mind they are preliminary. A full written report usually takes ten to fifteen days. I'm aware that you want the boys to start college in the fall, but due to the substance abuse I must insist that they participate in a three month rehab program. I therefore will speed up the report and issue it in one week. This report will guide the rehab counselors in selecting the proper programs. Normally they do their own psychiatric evaluation, but they will accept ours, and this will give them the opportunity to start the rehab program immediately."

Both parents were not happy that they had to wait anther six hours, but they had no other options than to go and have lunch. During lunch both families talked about the why's and when's of their kids' latest behaviors, not knowing that this had been going on for years. They just weren't aware of it or unconsciously would not acknowledge it.

None of the four was actually ready to admit that their son's behavior was different than any other teenager boy. Inside they did, but parents have a hard time admitting that to themselves. They probably felt that the other boy was the instigator and that their son was the innocent one in these situations.

As it is common for parents to question themselves when it becomes necessary for a son or daughter to be psychiatrically evaluated this process was slowly entering their minds and questions arose.

- What is wrong with my child?
- Is he not normal?
- Did I do something wrong?
- Did I not pay enough attention to him?
- Is this just a phase he is going through?
- What can we do?
- Could the doctors be wrong?

These were questions that were difficult to answer and for most of them there was no answer.

When they finally went back to the hospital the nurse told them that the doctor would see them in half an hour. This annoyed Mr. Witherspoon Sr. to no end and he started complaining. "Who the hell does he think he is? They're all the same. Only their time is valuable." He went on and on until his wife asked him politely to shut up because he was embarrassing her and making a scene. Strangely enough, he did shut up, which was very possibly the only time in his life that he paid attention to what his wife had to say.

When the doctor arrived, he said, "I have to talk to you parents separately because of the patient/doctor confidentiality. So who wants to come with me first?"

Witherspoon answered that the Evans family could go first because he had to make some important phone calls.

When Glenn's family followed the doctor Witherspoon's wife said, "Are your phone calls more important than your son's well-being?"

"Of course not," he said, "but you are acting silly. What the doctor is going to tell us now will be the same thing as it will be an hour from now."

The psychiatrist, now with Glenn's family in his office, said, "As I previously mentioned what I'm going to tell you is preliminary and further test results could drastically change this evaluation. Please, keep this in mind. I'll start with the bad news that way you have something to look forward to that will improve the situation. Your son is a drug addict. He is addicted to Marijuana, Cocaine and to a lesser degree Ecstasy. All these drugs showed up in the test at a level that indicates a frequent and longtime use. This is not a one time or occasional user. We're talking about a strong addiction. I can't say for sure but there is a good chance that a three month's rehab program will not be long enough. Unless your son is one hundred percent with the program and willing to do what is requested of him, it will not work. The statistics are against him. Very few with an addiction like your son has, succeed in three months.

"Now somewhat better news, the drugs he is addicted to have the highest rate of recovery, meaning it will be hard but not impossible. Other drugs like Heroin would be much worse and could take years of rehab.

"The psychological test shows that your son is not of the aggressive type who will not take instructions well. He is smart enough to realize what his life will be if he stays on drugs. Unfortunately the nonaggressive type people are also eager to please other people, like friends, girl friends and I'm sorry to say, drug users. The best environment for Glenn would be a rehab center far from home, separated from John but still within distance for you to visit. Support from his parents during rehab is very important. You have to remember he feels lonely, separated from his family, friends, in unfamiliar territory, not allowed to leave the facilities, deprived of his freedom. The whole thing will make him feel like he is a prisoner, but he also knows that they can't keep him there if he doesn't want to stay. The temptation for him to bolt will always be there and some can't resist and do flee. The consequences of an act like that are that when you do go back, you have to start from scratch. Rehab, no matter how luxurious some of these facilities are, is still difficult.

"This is about all I can tell you right now. You will receive a complete written evaluation report within the next five days. I suggest you look for a rehab center during that time. Believe me; he will not make it without a complete recovery. Don't make light of the condition he is in.

"One more thing that I suspect is that he has an Attention Deficit Disorder. This will make rehab more difficult. Rehab is very repetitious and people with ADD have a difficult time absorbing instructions that are given over and over again. They lose interest and their minds wander off.

"You are allowed to check Glenn out and go home. If there is anything else you want to discuss with me, please feel free to call me."

The doctor then talked to the Weatherspoon's and gave them almost an identical report with regard to the drug problem. The preliminary psychiatric evaluation was different with respect to the behavior.

"John," he explained, "was aggressive and unwilling to accept orders or instructions from his peers. Rehab will be very difficult for him and you will have to instill in him that his options are limited. Recovery is a must for him. I'm afraid that the first time something is not to his liking he will just leave and come home. You have to make it clear to him that this is not an option. Every time he quits the program he has to start from scratch. This will, of course, prevent him from going to college this fall. Both he and Glenn have an IQ that would indicate that their grades in school should be substantially higher than what they are. This is more than likely caused by the drugs, a brain on drugs does not function well.

"It's up to you parents to let him understand that drugs will ruin his life. With your support and background, a successful future for him was almost guaranteed. Continuing to do drugs will ruin his and your lives."

The psychiatrist was not sure that in spite of this warning Mr. Witherspoon was convinced of the seriousness of the situation. In the past, everything was always resolved either with money or his family connections. A drug addiction, however, was not that easy to fix. He also knew that this was all he, as a doctor, could do. From here on it was up to the patient and the support he would get from his family.

The two boys talked to each other a day after they were released from the hospital and as predicted Glenn was very worried and scared, and willing to do what the psychiatrist recommended. John was opposed to it called it all bullshit and felt that the psychiatrist was just trying to scare them. He said to Glenn, "You know we're not addicts. We can quit anytime we want. I'm going to convince my dad that I don't need a rehab center to stop using drugs. I don't want to go to a facility with nothing but losers in therapy. No way."

What actually happened was that when their parents checked out the different rehab facilities, the upscale facilities all offered a 30 day program. Contrary to what the doctors recommended they decided that was where both John and Glenn would be going, together to the same center. A major mistake! Their reasoning was that the most expensive rehab facility must be the best one. A mistake!

This, of course, became common knowledge in Jamesville, Monica, John's sister, told her friends that he was in a rehab center in Arizona and her father said that it was a damn country club for people with lots of money. Each patient has his own room and bathroom, wide screen TV and CD and DVD player. She also heard her dad say to her mother that it cost $54,000 a month and that the place was teeming with celebrities.

When Carla found out, she thought that was definitely insufficient punishment for these amateur rapists. I need to do better than that.

A month later when John and Glenn returned to Jamesville from their so called rehab program, they were received by their "Party Bimbos" like heroes and a party was already organized for the following night. It was as nothing had ever happened and their way of life continued without missing a beat.

Stella told Carla about the reception for the two drug addicts and the party they had organized. Carla innocently asked, "Do you think we could be invited or crash this party?"

Stella said. "Everybody is always invited, but why the hell would you want to go to a wild party like this? They're all going to be drunk, on drugs and most of them half naked."

Carla said, "While you were in Galveston, something happened."

She then told her about the neighbor who informed here that somebody was surveying her house almost every night. He had given her the car's description and license plate. She then started digging and found out that it was John Witherspoon's red Corvette. She then became more alert and watched the traffic on her street, and saw a red Corvette very often driving through her street. She didn't know what to do about it, he wasn't breaking any laws that she know of.

And then it stopped, so she forgot all about it. Yesterday the car was there again, and now she wanted to know why he was doing this. She was going to ask him face to face. She thought a party with lots of people around would be a good place. She didn't want to be alone with this creep. She didn't trust him, but she also wanted to show him that she was not intimidated by him or his cronies, so if they went there she wouldn't have to confront him by herself.

Stella said, "OK let's do it, these creeps never scared me. They just disgust me. I can pretend for a little while and mingle with my favorite crowd while you talk to Johnny wonder boy."

When they arrived at the house, the party was already in full swing, and as Stella predicted, most were drunk or high and sex seemed to be the favorite sport. Carla spotted John who was surrounded by a couple of the Bimbos, when she got closer to him and he saw her, he stared at her in disbelieves and said" What the fuck are you doing here, who let you in."

She said calmly, "I need to talk to you in private so can you come out front alone or do you want me talk to you with an audience."

He followed her outside, and once there he sneered. "So what do you want?"

She answered, "I want to remind you that I'm keeping close tabs on you and your buddy Glenn and if your behavior gets out of control. You're both toast. Your latest caper with the two prostitutes falls definitely in that category. One more like that and you will find yourself again in some very unpleasant circumstances."

John wanted to shake her but she held up her hand and warned him." Watch out, assault and battery charges will only confirm what's in your psychiatric evaluation report. This time you may end up in a court appointed rehab center, not to be compared with the country club you just came from. Be careful John, and remember I'm still in charge."

"What do you want from me?" he asked. "Is it your life's ambition to make our lives miserable?"

She smiled and said, "Yes, that's about right. I want your lives to be as miserable as the life of the girl you wanted to rape would have been."

She turned around and went back inside to find Stella and got out of there. Stella was curious to know how the encounter went. Carla told her that she asked him why he was cruising down her street and observing her house, and if she saw him again would report it to the police. She said, "He laughed and sort of hinted that the Jamesville police were smart enough not to harass a member of the Witherspoon clan and wouldn't pay any attention to her. She said that she wasn't talking about the local police. She would go to the County sheriff or the FBI. He had seemed to consider that a little more of a threat but still told her that she didn't have a case and couldn't prove any of that shit. I don't think he will keep doing it though, but I will keep an eye on it."

"Did he say why he was doing this?" Carla asked.

"He never admitted that he did it. He said that I wasn't that much to look at for him to be following me. Come on, let's go home and do some studying before you're mom gets on our asses tomorrow morning."

John was angry and needed to talk to Glenn. He wanted to know how she knew what was in the psychiatric evaluation report. He wouldn't be surprised if that dumb shit had said something about it to his girlfriend Marissa, and then of course everybody would know.

When he confronted Glenn, he said he hadn't talked about this with anybody. John knew that he would say that but he knew him well enough that he could tell if he was lying. This time he couldn't.

He then told Glenn about his conversation with Carla and what she said with regard to their future and her plans to make their lives as miserable as she could. "I don't know yet what I'm going to do with this bitch but this can't go on much longer. I know she claims she has these documents with her lawyers that whenever the authorities get a hold of them, we go to jail. I know all that, but there must be a way to get her off our backs. She is totally ruining our lives.

"I thought of seeing a lawyer ourselves and explaining part of what we did and finding out what he has to say about it. He's bound by the client/lawyer confidentiality agreement. He can't tell anybody any of what we tell him."

Glenn asked, "Do you have your family lawyer in mind or, for instance, going to Houston and pick a lawyer, because even with the confidentiality agreement, I'm not sure your family's lawyer wouldn't tell your dad. What do you think?"

John said, "It has crossed my mind that this weasel could just do that.

"We can go to Houston, pick a lawyer, pay cash and not even tell him our real name, tell him our story and listen to what he has to say, see if there are any options, and what he recommends we do. We still don't have to do anything he says, we will at least know whether there is anything we can do, or that we are fucked and she has us by the balls.

"We can't do anything for at least ten days. My father has decided that I'm going with him to New York. He is considering a business venture there and he needs to talk to people who could become business partners. He said it would be good experience for me to see how this is done. I have no choice. I can't afford to piss him off more than he already is with me. I'm sure you understand."

Chapter 15

Carla and Stella were in class when the phone rang and Stella's mother picked it up. She listened for a few seconds, and then with a sad look on her face said, "Carla, Robert wants to talk to you."

She handed the phone to Carla and nodded to Stella to leave the class room.

"Carla," Robert said, "I have some bad news. Mary's sister passed away a couple of hours ago and of course Mary is taking this very hard. I don't know if you can get away from your schooling, but if it is possible we would like you to come here for a day or two. Mary feels that besides me, you are the only person she is close to and you would be a big support for her."

Carla Said, "I'm so sorry, poor Mary. I'll be on the next plane I'll call you back to give you the details, can you pick me up at the airport or do I take a taxi?"

"I'll pick you up at the airport. Just let me know what flight you are on."

Carla told Stella and her mom, and it was, of course, no problem. They said, "Let us make the flight arrangements. You go pack your bag and we'll take you to the airport."

On the way Stella's mother said to Carla, "Please tell Mary and Robert how sorry we are for their loss and if there is anything we can do for them, just give us a call."

"Thank you Mrs. Baker. I'll tell them and I'm sure if there is something you can do, I'll call you."

"Carla, could you just call me Janice. We know each other long enough and I would prefer it."

"Of course," Carla said. "I just thought you were my tutor and I didn't want to be disrespectful."

"You're not."

Stella laughing said. "Can I call you Janice to?"

"No young lady you can call me ma."

Stella said, "I knew the same rules wouldn't apply for all students."

Robert was waiting at the gate when she arrived and said, "Thank you for coming, you will be such a support for her, she was so relieved when I said you were already on a plane."

Mary and Robert were staying at her sister's house and Mary was waiting there for them. As soon as she saw Carla she started to cry and held her with her arms around her. "I'm so happy you could come."

Carla didn't know whether these were tears for her sister's death or because it meant so much to Mary that she was there for her. Robert just stood there, not exactly knowing what to do with two sobbing ladies on his hands. He was a wise man, so he did or said nothing until the crying started to diminish.

Mary finally calmed down and was able to talk about her sister's last days in the hospital, how she had suffered for a long time, and maybe it was time for her to go. Being in pain and lying in the hospital was not much of a life. But it still is hard on the survivors to have peace with that concept, and to agree that it was best for her.

The funeral was held the day after Carla arrived, and they planned to go back home the day after. Robert would go back to Florida maybe a week or so later to take care of everything that needed to be done when a single person die, and you are the only family member left.

There was nothing that needed to be done immediately, so he could go back whenever it was convenient for him. There was a Will and Mary would inherit every thing she had, Robert would have to find out what that really was. They had no idea.

Carla talked to Janice and told her when they would be coming back. She offered to pick them up, but she drove a small car and did not feel comfortable driving Robert's big car, Carla said, "That's okay. Robert prefers the comfort of a limo anyway."

They arrived back at the house around noon, and Janice and Stella had prepared lunch, which brought tears to Mary's eyes.

She said. "We are so blessed to have friends like you; Robert and I are so used to living by ourselves that we forgot how much more rewarding it is if you have friends who care about you."

Janice responded, "You are so right. Stella and I have lived like that for a long time and now with Carla and Stella being close friends, my life has changed for the better."

"Well it's time for us to go home, but tomorrow we'll be back and are going to hit the books again, School break is over for you girls and for me as well, of course."

Carla stayed downstairs because she felt that Mary needed company other than Robert, sometimes women need to talk to other women. This was the case here. Mary needed to talk to some one about her sister, some one who didn't know her when she was a young girl growing up with her sister Mary. Talking about things they did together, little secrets they hid from their parents, boys they had a crush on. The longer they talked the easier it became for Mary. She looked like she enjoyed reminiscing about the memories she had from their youth.

They talked for hours until Mary said, "Oh my lord! It's six o' clock and I haven't even thought of what we are having for dinner."

Robert, who just walked in, said. "That's all taken care of. I've made reservations for the five of us at Michael Angelo. Yes, I know there are only three of us, but I invited Janice and Stella to meet us there at seven."

The dinner was exactly what Mary needed, a nice place with people around her. Robert knew what he was doing. Staying in the house would not have been good for her.

While this was going on, John and Glenn had found a lawyer in downtown Houston who could accommodate them on short notice. They were now on their way to talk to him. They had decided to tell him what happened, with some exceptions, they would tell him that the young lady came to the beach house of her own free will, and nobody forced her to come and they would not talk about the sex slave obsession John had.

The lawyer's office looked impressive. An elegant very good looking young lady sat at the reception desk and told them that Mr. Levy would be with them shortly and to please have a seat. She asked if she could get them something to drink but both boys declined the offer.

The office kind of intimidated them and was not what they had expected it to be when they picked the lawyer on the internet. They somehow envisioned a shabby office run by a shady character nothing like this imposing suite. This gave them an uneasy feeling that maybe, this was not the kind of lawyer they needed.

When they were ushered into the actual office and were greeted by the lawyer, their self-confidence disappeared altogether.

The lawyer asked in a booming voice. "Well what can I do for you? You were somewhat mysterious on the phone about the nature of your problems. I suggest that you start by telling me exactly what happened, and I mean exactly. If you leave things out or bend the truth somewhat my advice would be worthless and your money would be down the drain.

You tell me the story and I will ask the questions as we go along. Will that work?"

They both said, "Yes that will work just fine."

John took the lead and told him, not in detail, what had transpired at the beach house. This took about fifteen minutes and the lawyer did not ask a single question. Then Levy said. "This is an interesting story, but I specifically asked you to tell me the whole story. What you just told me is part of a story, and only the part you wanted me to know about. If you can't or won't tell me everything, I want you to leave my office and I will bill you for the time I listened to this bullshit. So what will it be?

"Since this affects both of you, I'll leave you alone for a few minutes. You can discuss it and if you decide that you can't tell me everything, just tell my assistant at the front desk to invoice you for two hours of my time. She will know what to do."

They looked at each other. Glenn said, "Now what? Do we tell him everything or get the hell out of here?"

John sighed. "We have to know what our options are. Let's just tell him everything. He is still bound by the client/attorney confidentiality agreement."

At that time the lawyer walked back into his office and asked what they had decided.

Glenn answered this time. "I'll tell you the whole story." It took him approximately forty uninterrupted minutes. He looked embarrassed and sort of relieved that their secret was in the open.

The lawyer looked non-judgmental but stern. "It seems to me that your victim is someone you should not have messed with in the first place. This girl not only outsmarted you, she has you by the proverbial balls. She also seems to want revenge for what you tried to do to her, which is not surprising. What is surprising is that she is very good at it for such a young girl. She shows a lot of maturity and intelligence.

"What I'm going to say to you now will most likely hurt the macho image you had of yourselves but you guys picked the wrong girl, because I have the feeling that you're not in the same league as she is in."

This was not exactly what the boys wanted to hear. Levy sensed that they were disappointed and asked. "What is it that you want from me? If she has all the evidence that she claims she has, and this case goes to court you are looking at a long jail term. I can't sugarcoat this, these are very serious accusations."

John asked, "Is there anything we can do. Can she continue harassing us and we can do nothing to stop her?"

"Yes," said Levy, "that's basically what it amounts to. She was very smart to choose three different legal entities to receive the documents she entrusted to her lawyers.

"You asked me if there are any options. There are always options but in this case the only option that will let you completely off the hook is to buy her out. Offer her enough money she can't refuse.

"Another option is for you guys to hire a good criminal lawyer and then go the local police and tell them exactly what your lawyer coached you to say.

"You won't go free, but your sentence will be reduced because you voluntarily admitted guilt, and a deal could be made between your lawyer and the District Attorney. But again you will have to do some time. These charges are too serious. No D.A. will allow a lesser sentence than ten years in prison to start with.

"The rape charge could be dropped but the kidnapping will always be there. The sexual harassment charge could be challenged by your lawyer, but I don't think they will drop that one.

If I were in your shoes, I would try to offer her money, probably plenty of money. I assume money will not be a problem for your family."

Glenn said, "Our families don't know anything about this."

Levy continued, "I think you guys are going to need all the help you can get, and, no offense, but I don't think you can handle this by yourselves. She has all the aces in her hand. Think this over before you get getting into more trouble. I know that the Witherspoon family can afford to pay almost whatever it takes to keep her quiet."

John felt like he had been hit by a train and stammered, "How do you know we are part of the Witherspoon family?"

The lawyer laughed, I knew before you came out of the elevator. If you want to keep your identity a secret, don't use your own car to go somewhere. Don't use your home phone, especially not when you deal with a criminal lawyer. We like to know who we are dealing with. Now if there is anything else I can do for you, just call me, but until you decide what route you're going to take, no lawyer can help you.

"My suggestion at this time is, go talk to the girl and find out if she at least would consider a monetary settlement. Maybe she is. After all she took fifty grand from you, so who knows, she may want more."

When the boys left the office, their spirits weren't very high. It finally dawned on them that they were in a lot of trouble with very little chance to get out of it unscathed.

They were also worried that somebody else could know their secret and the more people who knew the bigger the possibility of it to becoming public.

They agreed that they should have a talk with Carla. You never know she might be in need of money and willing to make a deal.

Neither one had much hope that she would sell out. She just wasn't that kind of a person, but they figured they had nothing to lose. They figured wrong.

After discussing how they should present their proposal to Carla, they agreed that Glenn should talk to her. They knew that both were persona non grata with her, but Glenn was more likely not to become abusive.

Glenn called her and said that they had a proposal to make. She immediately cut in and said, "You guys are not in a position to make me a proposal, so spare it. I'm not interested in what you have to say."

Before she could hang up on him, Glenn quickly said, "This proposition could make you very rich."

There was a long silence before Carla slowly asked, "Are you bastards offering me money?" She got agitated at that point and menacingly said, "Now I'm really pissed off. You assholes just extended your sentence and she slammed down the phone."

John who had been listening on the phone extension exploded and yelled, "That fucking bitch! She's crazy! I'm going to kill that slut. There's no other way, she won't listen to reason so we have to get rid of here."

Glenn got scared. When John was in a state like this, out of control, everything was possible. He tried to calm him down but John kept screaming and repeating that he was going to kill her. One way or the other, he couldn't let that bitch decide what they could do with their lives or how to live their lives.

Glenn said, "Let her digest this for a while and I'll call her one more time and ask her what she wants us to do. So hopefully she can offer us something we can live with and we can all forget this episode of our lives."

John still ranted, "You can go and kiss her ass if you want, but I'm done talking to her. I'm going to ignore her completely and do what I have to do."

Glenn thought. This moron still doesn't realize that she is the one who decides what we can do or not and that we are her puppies who will do what she says, or spend the rest of our lives in jail.

Killing or hurting her will just speed up the process of going to jail. I have to stop this idiot from doing another one of his insane impulsive stupid deeds, like the one that put us in this predicament in the first place. He was now convinced that he had to talk with Carla again, maybe even warn her that John was losing it and that she could be in danger.

She must have some idea of what she wants from us. She must realize that she can't spend the rest of her life finding ways to punish us, there has to be an end to this.

197

After a number of calls from Glenn, Carla agreed to talk to him again. They would meet in the mall, usual place.

Glenn asked her if there was something he and John could do to erase their debt to her. She responded that there was something she wanted to suggest, but their attempt to bribe her made her so mad that she was going to withdraw this option.

"The fact that you asked me in person made me change my mind and I will give you an opportunity to make things right. If you guys are willing to join the Peace Corps and sign up for two years of service, either in the Middle East or Africa, I will destroy the evidence, and you are off the hook. I'll give you a week to think this over. After a week the offer is off the table. Go and talk it over with the maniac."

Glenn said, "I thought you had to have a college degree to join the Peace Corps."

Carla corrected him and said, "No that is not true. You have to be eighteen old and willing to work. It is true that they prefer college graduates but it's not mandatory. Even if there were a problem, I'm sure your family could pull enough strings to make them accept you."

Glenn was quiet for a while and then said, "I can't speak for John but I'm willing to accept this. Now what will happen if I accept but John doesn't?"

She said, "I thought about this and if that is the case, I will rewrite the documents that are with my lawyers. And you will have such a minor role in it that after you finish your two years in the corps you will not even be charged with any of this. You have my word on it."

Glenn was almost sure that John would not accept this offer, and he would be furious when Glenn told him that he already accepted the opportunity to clean his slate and join the Peace Corps.

When he reported to John and explained the conditions and mentioned that this was the only offer there was, John proved Glenn right in assuming that he would refuse to do this. He said, "She's out of her fucking mind if she thinks for a second that I'm going to spend two years of my life in Africa. Screw her."

Glenn said, "Well I accepted the offer and am willing to join the Peace Corps for two years. You can do whatever you want but I made my decision and will put an end to this situation. I feel like you. I can't live with the idea that at any time I could go to jail, maybe for the rest of my life. I think it's a small price to pay for what we did."

John's reaction was fierce and hateful. "Get the fuck out of here you miserable piece of shit! You were always a coward and could never be trusted. When the going gets tough, people like you start running, so get out of my face. I will never talk to you again. As far as I'm concerned, you're dead."

Glenn felt really bad but still was sure that he made the right decision. If John could control his temper he should make the same decision. Unfortunately he would never be able to do so.

Glenn that night went to see his parents, and after dinner explained to them what his plans for the immediate future were. He assumed that his parents would try to talk him out of it but unexpectedly they supported him and said this was an excellent idea that would put him back on track. They, more so than the Witherspoon's, knew that their son was struggling with problems they were not aware of, and felt that two years in an environment focused on helping people would be exactly what he needed.

Glenn was relieved, and happy to get the full support from his parents, this would make this so much easier.

Glenn called Carla to let her know that he would definitely join, and that his parents were fully supporting him. He informed her that John was not willing to join the Peace Corps. He also warned her that John was out of control and that she should be careful. Carla said," I didn't expect John to do so. He will have to deal with the consequences.

She told Glenn that she expected him to file an application with the Peace Corps immediately and to keep her informed of the status."

Carla had something in mind for John but she was going to consult with a lawyer first. She needed to know that what she wanted to do was legal, and is she could do it without somebody doing a background check on her. She didn't want a lawyer in Jamesville, and went to Houston for legal advice.

She told the lawyer what had happened to her and why she went on a private crusade rather than report this to the local police. The lawyer's first reaction was that she shouldn't do this on her own and to let the legal system handle it. He said," You're too young and without experience to tackle a dangerous situation like this."

She finally made him understand that with her past and outstanding warrants for her arrest, she could not expect to get a fair trial in Jamesville. Their lawyers would destroy her in court and a local jury would be biased in favor of the hometown boys, especially rich local boys. "No," she said, "I thought this through and that is not an option." He understood, but was still doubtful of the wisdom of her handling it the way she was.

He then asked what he could do for her. She explained what she had in mind for John. She wanted to take him to court for harassment. She told him about his surveillance of her house, driving slowly through the street she lived in, almost every day. She said that she had pictures, taken by her neighbor, from his parked car, She was afraid. He was a drug addict and was known to have a bad temper. He had been charged with assault, drunken driving, and in general a bad apple who acted like the laws of this country did not apply to him.

"I know that this is probably not enough to get him convicted, but I want him to be harassed, ordered to come to court several times, disrupt his life style, embarrass him, make him mad and most important fuel his hatred for me. Can you do this?"

He answered, "Yes, I can do this, but it will cost you money and you won't get a conviction, it will be a nuisance court case, and I will ask you again do you really want to do this?"

She said, "Yes, I don't care about the money. I just want to send him the message that his troubles are not over and that I will continue my crusade against him."

The lawyer said, "If that's what you want, I can do it but I need all the evidence that you have, pictures, statement from your neighbor, anything else you can think of. I also need a $5,000 retainer fee to start the procedures.

"I will check on these warrants for your arrests and see if they can even be used in court. Maybe they can be dropped if you are willing to pay a fine. I'll let you know in a couple of days."

Carla asked, "Is there even a possibility that they can be dropped?"

He said, "There is even a possibility that they are erased. After Katrina a lot of serious charges disappeared, lost with no trace that they ever existed. We'll see."

Carla was impressed with the no-nonsense approach. He seemed to be all business, no bull, just facts. She was trying not to get her hopes too high on the disappearance of the warrants for her arrest, or paying a fine, it was too much to expect.

Back home and trying to cram two school years into one kept her more than busy, but doing this together with Stella made it fun and the days flew by. Janice was an excellent teacher and made it easy to learn new things. With only two students, she never advanced to the next subject unless she was convinced that they both had a full understanding of what they had covered until then. She kept both girls assured that they would be ready and well prepared for college. Until recently Carla wasn't sure that she wanted to go to college, but that had changed and they now wanted to go to the same college. That's how close these two had become. They felt so comfortable with each other that it was hard to believe that they had met only four months previously.

Carla kept saying to herself that someday soon she would tell Stella about her past, but not yet.

One evening when just Robert, Mary and Carla were having dinner together, Robert said, "Carla, we have to have a serious talk with you."

Carla almost blurted out, "I wanted to tell you." convinced that they had found out, but she kept silent and waited for the other shoe to drop.

Robert saw her discomfort and said, "Don't worry, it's nothing bad, we actually hope that you will accept it." Carla's face brightened and she waited for Robert to continue. "With the death of Mary's sister, Mary and I have been thinking. We are getting older as well and nobody lives forever. You are now the only person that is dear to us and we thought that we could become even closer. To make this short we are asking if you would consider being adopted by us, to become a real part of our family."

They both peered at Carla and saw a confused but happy look on her face, and didn't know what to make of this. Carla quickly said, "I'm so honored that you asked me to become a part of your family. But you only know me for such a short time. Maybe you're doing this because you are still emotional about your sister's death."

"No, Carla "said Mary, this has nothing to do with my sister. We have kicked this around before we went to Florida. We just weren't sure how you would react because we were aware that this is a major decision on your part, and that it was possibly too soon for you to make such a decision.

"Please, take all the time in the world to think about it. There is no rush, we won't change our minds. We don't want you to feel obliged to do this. If you don't want to, nothing will change. We still think of you as part of this family anyway."

Carla said, "There is nothing that I can think of that would make me feel better than to be with you for the rest of my life. You know I never had the security and the love I received from you and I can't thank you enough for that. I just don't feel I can accept this unless you know more about me. I have done things that I regret and am not proud of. I'm ashamed of the things I did.

"I believe I must first have the courage to tell you all of my past. If after you know all that, you would still adopt my as your daughter I would be the proudest girl on this planet. Right now, I still struggle with it and don't even know if I will ever have the courage to tell anybody my past."

Robert said, "Sometimes we've all done something that under normal circumstances we would not do, but at the time we didn't have any other options. People do what they have to do to survive or stay sane. Sometimes we are forced by uncontrollable conditions to do bad things."

Mary then said, "I can't see you doing anything so bad that we couldn't handle and that would change anything about our feelings for you. We already think of you as our daughter, and there is nothing a child can do that a parent couldn't forgive and forget. If you can't tell us now, you eventually will and you will see that nothing has changed. We will still love you as much as we do now."

Robert added," We would love you to say yes now, but we understand that you want to resolve these issues for yourself. When you're at peace with them and you feel you can tell us, do so, but if you never tell us we would still want you to be our daughter. I did things in the war that I can never tell anybody, not even Mary. We just have to live with it."

Later, Carla's lawyer called and said, "I have good news for you and bad news. The good news is there are no warrants for your arrest outstanding. The bad news is that your name is still in the system with a status of inactive. What that means is that when a lawyer has a serious case he could dig until he found out why your name was in the system. Due to the Katrina chaos, he may never find out. With the nuisance case we have, he will get nowhere. The county clerks would not give him the time of the day for a case like that, and without their help, he could not find your name in the system.

"If you ever want to pursue the kidnapping case, get yourself an experienced New Orleans lawyer and let him try to find you in the system. If he can't, no lawyer from Houston will ever get it, and you won't have to worry of being arrested."

She thought that was good news, because she would never take the other case to court. She had decided that she was the judge and jury to hand out their punishment.

Glenn called her and said that he was accepted into the Peace Corps and could be called upon any day. He also asked her to forgive him, I'm really sorry for what I did and I should never have been party to this insane and immoral idea. I honestly tried to convince him to forget this stupid caper, but that's no excuse. I should have refused to help him.

He also told her again. Be careful, John is very angry and when he is like that he doesn't know how to stop and does stupid things. Stay away from him.

She thanked him and said she was very happy that he chose to change his life style, and wished him good luck.

Her lawyer called her and said, "Mr. Witherspoon was summoned to appear in court two weeks from now. He expected a call from John's lawyer any day now asking for his agreement to postpone the first hearing, a request he would refuse. We will agree to a postponement when we are in court. I'm sure they will ask for one, this way your friend will be in agony for the next two weeks and then start all over again until the hearing."

Carla said. "That's okay with me. Do you think I'm being exceptionally cruel?"

"I'm not judging you, but if someone would kidnap me and then try to rape me, I would probably be a lot meaner than you are and mercy would not be on my mind in a situation like this."

Stella asked Carla, "What is it that you are running back and forth to Houston for?"

"Sometimes it's for the closing of my parent's affairs and other times it is when I go and see my lawyer."

"Stella," she said, "I have something I wanted to tell you for a long time, but never had the guts to do so. You are the best friend I ever had and I was afraid that by telling you what happened to me, you would judge me and never want to see me again. I now know you better and I feel I can tell you everything and you will keep it a secret. So here we go." She told her everything from the kidnapping and what happened while she was in captivity and up to the revenges she had in mind.

"This is why, when I called you, it sounded like I was crazy and you had no idea what was wrong with me."

Stella's face showed all possible emotions, disbelief, amazement, shock, anger and most of all pity for what her friend had to go through. She didn't say anything at first, she just drew Carla into her arms and started crying and holding her tight, as if she was never going to let go of her.

When she finally stopped sobbing she managed to say over and over again how sorry she was for what these sick, spoiled, rotten bastards did to her.

When Carla assured her that she was okay Stella started to ask questions like, "Why they weren't in jail, what did the police do, just let them go free? I don't understand this. They should be locked up for ever, perverted bastards like that should not be walking the streets like nothing happened."

Carla said, "Stella, this may sound strange to you but I never reported it to the police. You and my lawyer are the only people who know about this and you have to promise me that you will keep this a secret. I owe you an explanation for why I did not report this. I simply couldn't.

"Cases like kidnapping, rape and assault draw a lot of attention, the press and television. I can't afford this because I would end up in jail before they did. My past would be made public and their lawyers would have a field day exposing me. It would definitely weaken my accusations and they would probably walk away with a mild sentence or parole. I believe the punishments I have in store for them will be more effective and will hurt them more than the sentence they would get from the courts.

"My past is not something I'm proud of and I promise in time I will tell you everything of the life I led in New Orleans.

"Telling you what happened at the beach house took all the courage I had. I was so afraid that I could lose you as my friend. That's why it took me so long to telling you this."

Stella shook her head and said, "Nothing you ever do will stop me from being your friend, I only have one real friend and nothing will ever change that. You're like the sister I never had. I know you will tell me everything when you are ready to do so, I'm okay with that.

"One thing you have to let me in on is how to punish these bastards I want to be part of this, big time."

Carla asked, "Are you sure? I sometimes feel uncomfortable with what I'm doing. I know its peanuts compared to what they wanted to do with me."

"Exactly," Stella said, "They deserve to be doing hard time in jail."

She then asked, "What have you done so far to make them feel miserable?"

"Carla explained the plot with the two hookers and the fake HIV situation and what she was planning now with John, stalking her and dragging him into court next week in Houston. My lawyer knows the whole story but doesn't know if John's lawyer knows what happened at the beach house. He assured me that he won't tell him anything but if he knows what happened there, he will use that as bait without actually saying anything in court."

Stella said, "We have to find an excuse for my mother to skip class that day." Carla said. "I feel guilty that I have to lie to Janice but I have to be there, otherwise the charges will be dismissed."

"Stella asked, "Can I come to? I really want to be there with you."

"Of course you can come if you want to."

They met their lawyer outside the courthouse, then after the mandatory metal detector inspection went to the assigned court room. John and his lawyer were already there. John stared at both of them and whispered something to his lawyer, and when he looked back at Carla she gave him a big smile, looking very much at ease with the situation, contrary to John who looked unhappy and nervous. He was probably thinking that this was just a charade and that he was going to be charged with kidnapping and possible rape and assault. That bitch had tricked them and his lawyer was not prepared for this. He got more and more agitated, and if looks could kill Carla would be dead. He looked at her and Stella with hate and anger.

The bailiff announced. "All raise the Honorable judge Tony Calderon will preside." When they were all seated again he said, "First case on the docket is Carla Jones versus John Witherspoon."

John's lawyer asked the judge if they could approach the bench. The judge nodded and John's lawyer asked for an extension of the hearing, claiming that he was not given enough time to prepare for this case.

The judge replied, "I don't know if the opposing party is amenable to a delay."

Carla's lawyer said, "We would, with the stipulation that Mr. Witherspoon does not leave the state of Texas during that extension."

The other lawyer said, "I have to confer with my client."

The judge said, "You have five minutes to do so. You can all go back to the court room."

John's lawyer told John about the condition, and John responded loud enough for the judge and everybody nearby to hear. "That bitch knows that I want to go to college in Colorado. She's just fucking with me."

The judge stood up and called to the two layers Chambers and bring the accused with you. Once inside his he turned to John and said. "If you use that kind of language in my court again, I will put you in contempt and have you arrested on the spot and put into jail with no bail. Is that understood?

"I'm aware that your family has a lot of clout in Jamesville, but we are in Houston where nobody gives a rat's ass about the Witherspoon family." John wanted to say something but the judge cut him off.

"You are only allowed to talk if I ask you a question, and I didn't, did I?"

John again opened his mouth but his lawyer practically pulled him outside the judge's chambers and into the courtroom.

John was so agitated and out of control that he kept on ranting, calling the judge senile and the two lesbian bitches were just doing this to get his ass in trouble. All this was recorded by the court clerk. The bailiff had heard everything and promptly reported this to the judge, this no nonsense judge did not hesitate and ordered the bailiff to arrest John and lock him up.

John yelled at the bailiff to keep his fucking hands off him and two more police officers were needed to put the cuffs on him. The judge announced that the court was adjourned and a date would be set for a new hearing.

Carla asked her lawyer. "What happens now?"

He said, "He will be in jail for at least a week, but with this judge and him trying to avoid arrest, probably two weeks without bail. The case will be reset maybe three to four weeks from now. I will inform you."

Stella said, "Wow, this was exciting. What would have happened if he hadn't behaved like a lunatic?"

Carla said, "He most likely would have gotten a month or so of probation or maybe just a warning. She smiled, but you can always count on that asshole to get into more trouble."

Due to John's violent and abusive behavior the judge ordered a drug test for him and when the results came back positive for cocaine, marijuana, and crack, John was given a choice between a three month rehab program, in a rehab center to be selected by the court, or three months in jail. John decided to go to the rehab based on the experience he had with the previous rehab center. He soon found out that there was no comparison between the country club type rehab center and the center assigned by the court.

After a couple of days at the center he had already decided that he was not going to spend three months in a rat hole like this. He also vowed that his enemy number one, Carla the bitch, was going to disappear from this earth. He was determined to kill that girl.

Carla's lawyer informed her of the court decision, but to be careful. "These rehab centers are not guarded like prisons and the patients can walk out anytime they want. However, if he does, there will be a warrant for his arrest. But you know as well as I do that the Jamesville police force are not going to look very hard to arrest him. If you see him you should call the County Sheriff and inform them that he is around, you can also call me and I will take care of this."

When Stella heard this she said, "From now on we are going to be like Siamese twins. Wherever you go I go, no exceptions. We better start brainstorming and come up with a new plan to get him out of circulation or at least far away from here."

Chapter 16

John's first days in rehab were mainly focused on. How do I get out of here and where can I go from here? He knew that once he was in Jamesville he would be relatively safe. It would not be a safe haven forever but it would do for a while. Not being able to live in Jamesville for the rest of his life didn't bother him. That was never his intent anyway.

He had a respectful trust fund waiting for him when he turned 21, but that was another two years off. He was not going to wait two more years to get rid of Carla. This was a high priority and had to be taken care of, as soon as possible. He had to plan this carefully. The moment he killed her he must be able to get out of the country. Tentatively, Brazil was the place he had decided to go. The beaches and the sexy looking girls had a lot to do with his choice. He talked to his lawyer and asked him what the consequences would be if he left the rehab center.

"I can't believe you are even considering doing that." the exasperated lawyer said. "You'll spend 3 months in jail and I'm sure the judge will add 6 months of probation to it. My advice is don't do it."

"I hear you," John said, "but you're not the one rotting in this hell hole."

"No," he answered, "I'm not. I'm also not the one who behaved like an asshole in court. And one other thing if you're not satisfied with me as your lawyer, please feel free to fire me." John thought about doing just that but that wouldn't change anything.

He must consult a financial adviser on how to get his hands on his trust fund money before he turned 21, because without this money all his plans would go down the drain.

This assigned rehab center was an eye opener for him; not only because of the lack of luxury and comfort, but the majority of the patients in there were hardened criminals. Not just crack heads, but people with serious criminal records. It was difficult to understand that a felon charged with involuntary manslaughter would have a choice between jail and rehab with probation afterwards. He should be scared in an environment like this. Strangely enough that was not the case. He was actually trying to get close to these guys. He reasoned if I'm going to be a fugitive I may learn a thing or two from these thugs. Most of them must have been living underground, or out of the limelight at least.

This changed his focus on leaving rehab as soon as possible. He needed time to establish contacts with these guys and to find the right one, who when the time was right, could do the dirty work for him. None of these characters here in rehab had any intention of quitting doing drugs or becoming law abiding citizen once they got out of there. They were just biding time. A rehab center was still preferable over jail. So as soon as they were back on the street they would need cash to feed their addiction. That's where I will come in to provide the cash for certain services.

It didn't take very long for him to separate a couple of guys who seemed to have the qualifications to do what he wanted. One was a white trash individual who boasted that he was the meanest son of a bitch in the center. He was carrying a serrated 10 inch knife around and threatened every body by saying that he had no problem using it. The other guy was a black dude, big as a church, the silent type but with a rap sheet a mile long and not for misdemeanors either; Armed robbery, assault of a police officer, rape, drug dealing, and various other felonies. The fact that he was not in jail surprised all the other tough guys, who had done time for lesser convictions.

John now had to let them know that he had money and willing to use it for a job that needed to be done in the near future; he just couldn't rush this. He had to gain their trust. People like that do not trust white people with money. They feel they've been screwed by them too often in their lives.

One day he managed to sit at the table with all the bad guys. One of them said. What's a pussy ass kid like you sitting at our table for?

He responded, "This pussy ass kid wants to get out of here and I was hoping you guys could give me some pointers."

"Pointers cost money the guy said."

"Money I have but I can see that you're not interested." John grabbed his serving tray and left them. He figured some of these guys would be interested in money and would come back to me.

He was right on. The next day, the white trash guy approached him and said, "I'm Bill. What's your name?"

"I'm John, and are you here to harass me or can you help me?"

Bill looked at him. "You're not going to get very far with your attitude. You're a rookie here and we expect some respect from you kids."

"Well, I tried the friendly approach and got ignored by you guys so I tried a different tactic but that don't seem to work either." John rebutted.

"Me and Big Tom can help you if you have the cash. Don't pay attention to the other guys they're just talk, they're useless. Just let us know what you want and we we'll tell you how much it will cost you, money upfront.

"I have a feeling that you want more than just help to get out of here. You can get out anytime you want on your own. You don't need help for that. Big Tom and I are getting released three weeks from now, so if you want something done it has to be arranged and paid for before that time."

John became concerned about the fact that he was so transparent that this moron could see right through him. He would have to be more careful in dealing with these criminals in the future. They were street smart, he thought. I need to be in charge. I can't allow them to be in control. This would have to be in accordance with the golden rule he who has the gold makes the rules.

He wasn't sure yet that he could trust these people and tell them what he wanted them to do. He needed more information on their past, like a background check of some sort. Maybe my lawyer could get me that information. It's worth a try.

Before he could call his lawyer he needed at least to have their full names, maybe birthdays or Social Security numbers. Problem was how to get that kind of information. All that must be in the center's registration office, but how could I get my hands on it? This wasn't going to be easy.

He thought he had an idea on how to get their names. He went to see his counselor and said, "There are two guys out there who really are scaring me. Every time I'm near them they have something to say to me, and it's never very friendly."

The counselor asked what their names were." John said, "I believe one of them is called Bill and the other one is big Tom."

"Don't worry about these two. That's Bill Wallenski and Big Tom Clark. They are under close surveillance and they know if they get out of line they go straight to prison. They just want to show the rookies that they are the badass boys from the New Jersey ghetto and that you can't mess with them. But they're harmless, at least in here."

John had more information than he had hoped for and this was probably enough for his lawyer to get a thorough background check on them. He called the attorney and said, "I need that information today or at the latest tomorrow. These guys are dangerous and they don't seem to like me a lot. I need some information on them. Maybe there is something I can use so they will leave me alone. Call the center as soon as you get it. Leave a message with the switchboard and I'll call you back."

The next day his lawyer left a message and when John contacted him, he told John to stay away from those two guys. They both were known as dangerous and unpredictable. They had been charged with manslaughter but one was released for lack of evidence because the witness for the prosecution mysteriously had disappeared, and the other one was released on a technicality. In both cases the police and the D.A were convinced that they were guilty. They were also known as drug dealers, but again never convicted.

John thought' They seem to be ideal for what I have in mind. But the fact that they were unpredictable scared him and made him hesitant to trust them.

He would have to go slow with this but he had only two weeks to make the arrangements with one of them. He felt it was safer for him to use only one. He just had to find out which one was the better of the two for a job like this. He thought it was funny that he wanted references for the job of killing someone. It never dawned on him that he had a lugubrious sense of humor.

John's lawyer felt uncomfortable with John's request for a background check on this caliber of criminals. Something was brewing in that kid's troubled and drugged mind and he wondered if there was anything he could do without violating the client/lawyer confidentiality agreement.

He consulted with some of the other lawyers in his firm. They all said that there was really nothing he could do at this time. They said talk to John and try to convince him that it is a bad idea. But since you don't even know what it is, you probably will have a hard time being successful with that. Unless you know for sure that he is planning a murder there is nothing you can do.

John in the meantime had talked to Bill and Big Tom separately in order to get a feel for who he could trust with this assignment. It was difficult because he didn't want them to know yet that this was about killing a young girl.

He may not have a choice anymore because the last time they talked with Tom he told him if he didn't tell him what this mysterious job was all about, he could kiss his fat ass. He dealt with assholes like him before and they can't be trusted. If he can't trust the people I has to deal with he doesn't want to be involved. "Maybe you can talk skinny ass Bill into it, but I'm out. My gut tells me you are trouble."

Again, John felt that he was losing control of the situation. Now that he had no other choice but for Bill to do the job, he realized that unconsciously he preferred Big Tom to Bill. Bill gave him the impression of being a bullshit artist, not reliable. He now had to make a decision, go with Bill or forget about these two and look for some other convict. Finding someone else would, of course, delay everything and that was the last thing he wanted. So against his better judgment he decided to go with Bill. He asked to meet with him after dinner that night.

"Look, I'm going to make you a proposition. If you're interested I'll give you the details. If not, just forget I ever asked. You're okay with that?"

Bill said, "Sure, but being interested is not a firm commitment."

John bluntly said, "I want you to kill somebody, are you willing to do that?"

"The answer is yes, but I need to know more than that to make it a firm yes. Let me ask you some questions. Why, is my first question?"

John said, "I don't think this is something you need to know. I have my personal reasons and frankly they are none of your business."

Bill stood up and said, "Fair enough. I will forget that I asked." and walked away.

John ran after him and said, "Wait a minute. Let's discuss this; I'm sure we can come to an agreement."

"No," Bill answered," We won't. I need to know not only why, but all the details that led you to a drastic measure like this. Unless you're willing to tell me all of this I'm not interested."

John felt cornered but he desperately wanted a commitment from Bill, so he reluctantly said, "Okay you win. I'll tell you the whole story."

The story John told Bill was not exactly the way it happened. Carla was portrayed as a slut who had put poor John in this position and had more or less ruined his life with lies and false accusations. Bill, a master bullshitter himself, took all this with a giant grain of salt but nodded his head, saying it looked like she deserve to be whacked.

John relieved that Bill bought the modified story said. "Well where we go from here."

Bill said, "We first of all have to agree on my fee and how I will get my money, cash only of course.

From what you told me, this sounds like a fairly simple task. The thing that bothers me is the risk factor. Everybody in your little town must know that you have a grudge against that girl, and with your reputation as a violent and aggressive individual, they will assume that you would be very happy if she disappeared. You of course will make sure that you have an ironclad alibi with plenty of witnesses to vow that you were not within a hundred miles of the crime scene.

"The police will automatically suspect you because you have a motive and when these documents that are deposited with her lawyers get into their hands you will be their prime suspect. But with her no longer capable being a witness for the prosecution, your fancy lawyers will more than likely save your ass on these charges.

"The detectives on the murder case, however, are not going to give up. They will start digging into your recent past. Eventually they are going to come here and find out that you and I had a lot of private conversations.

"They're going to grill you and at the same time be looking for me. Do you see where I'm going with this? I will then become a suspect too and with my past legal problems they will put two and two together. They will fabricate enough evidence to put me in custody, and eventually put me on trial and more than likely get a conviction.

"I need enough money so that when the deed is done, I can flee the country immediately with a new name and matching passport and live somewhere happily ever after. Now you tell me how much money do you think I need for that?"

"I have no idea what to offer you for something like this, why don't you tell me how much you want."

Bill said, "Two hundred thousand dollars and consider the job done, half of it now and the balance when the job is done. Cash of course."

John was sure he was getting robbed but saw no alternative other than to accept, since he had told Bill his story, modified or not. Bill had him over a barrel and he would take advantage of it. John already had decided that he would only pay half of this money anyway. The moment Carla was history he would disappear and Bill would never see the rest of his inflated fee. That would serve him right.

The question now was that he could not get to this money while he was in rehab. He had more than enough money in his savings account but to get one hundred thousand dollars in cash he must go to the bank in person. That money was in Bonds and CD's. He had to find a way to get a couple of days off, and be allowed to leave the rehab center. He talked to his counselor but he said to forget it. They could not release him for a couple of days unless they had authorization from the court or his probation officer.

The other option was to simply vanish and return two days later and face the consequences, he was told that this usually resulted in a month extension of the program.

He asked Bill if he could wait another nine weeks to receive his first payment. Bill agreed but he wouldn't lift a finger before his first payment, basically postponing everything by nine weeks.

John was averse to this delay but could not come up with a better idea. His hands were tied while he was in this damn hellhole.

Bill, of course, was eager to get some of the money right away and asked John, "How much can you come up with now? I may be able to do some of the ground work if it's worth my while."

John thought about this and said, "I could get you twelve thousand dollars via Western Union soon as you are released." They agreed to go that way. Bill promised to investigate and prepare a plan so there would be a minimum of time lost.

Bill was released two weeks later and cashed that money order immediately, but had no intention of starting to do anything before he got the full payment. He was going to call John every week and feed him some bullshit story on how he was progressing and that would be it.

John was still busy trying to find a way to get to his trust fund. The financial adviser he had contacted told him that there were financial institutions that would loan him the money, but there was a substantial fee for this kind of transaction and nothing could be done while John was not around. The financial advisor would get all the details, so if John wanted to go this route everything would be ready to proceed.

A letter from Afghanistan was in John's mailbox, and he thought. What fucking Arab wants to send me a letter? When he saw who the sender was, his impulse was to throw the letter in the garbage can. But curiosity forced him to open the envelope and start to read the note from his ex-friend Glenn.

Dear John,

I felt the need to write this letter because at one time we were inseparable and as close as friends could possibly be. I still remember all the good times we had together and I deeply regret that so suddenly we became strangers, even enemies, to each other.

I no longer feel animosity toward you, I really never did. We were just so far apart on this one issue and I didn't know how to handle it. I know, I kept telling you that I was against this sex slave thing from the very beginning, but I must admit that I also was intrigued and in a way anxious to experience this far out adventure. I can't blame you for the fact that I was involved. I could have said no and walked away from it, but I didn't. It was my choice.

It's not for me to say, but I hope that you can see that what we did to Carla was terribly wrong and that the consequences we are now facing are justified. We should be thankful to her that she did not report us to the police. We would be in jail right now and maybe for the rest of our lives.

I sent her a letter, apologizing and asking for forgiveness. I hope you would do the same thing. It made me feel better and at peace with myself.

You can't be happy the way you feel about her. Deep inside you must know that she is not to blame for the situation you're in. You and I have brought that on ourselves. She is more of a victim than we are.

Once you realize this, you will start feeling guilty and the anger that's inside you will disappear. You will become a different and better person.

I learned a lot here in the boondocks of Afghanistan. These farmers here are content if they have the basic necessities to stay alive. Food and a roof over their heads is all they're praying for. We people in the so called civilized world, should be more aware that these people are also human beings. We just take everything we have for granted, like we deserve it and they don't.

I'm sorry; I get carried away when I think about how I behaved back then. A couple of months from now I'll be home for two weeks. I hope you will be around and we can see each other, I would like us to patch things up.

The very best,
Your friend Glenn.

This double crossing weasel would like to patch things up. After what he did to me he wants to be my friend again. Yeah, when hell freezes over. Maybe I should get rid of him as well. With his holier than thou attitude he could be a risk. He could be a damaging witness and testify that everything that's in the documents her lawyers have is the truth. This is really a risk I can't afford to take. I need to think about this some more. With the both of them out of the way, the evidence she claims she have will lose a lot of credibility without witnesses. I can't believe I never thought of this before. He would be more convincing and plausible in court than she would be. Taking care of Glenn should be easy enough. Lots of innocent people die in Afghanistan. One more is not going to raise suspicion that it was murder. This is just a dangerous place to be. The fact that he just decided to kill someone he had been friends with since kindergarten didn't seem to bother him at all.

Chapter 17

The girls had fabricated an excuse to extend their lunch break from one hour to two hours, and were having lunch in town. Janice was having lunch with Robert and Mary in the house and Mary brought up the fact that these two girls had lately become inseparable. They were always close, but now they are like twins. Janice said, "You're right it's amazing how quickly their friendship has blossomed. I'm really happy because Carla has been a very good influence on Stella. She is so mature for her age and Stella needed some maturity."

"Yes," Mary said, "They both are good for each other."

Robert agreed, "Bringing these two together has really worked out well. I think they're as close as real sisters could be. Are they still talking going to college together?"

"They are." Janice said. "But lately I have a feeling that college is not very high on their priority list. I don't want to force them but you have to think about which colleges you want to apply to! They can't just waltz in there and expect to be accepted, I'll mention that to them this afternoon."

Mary asked, "Why, did they want a longer lunch break? Did they have to do something that couldn't wait?"

"No," Janice said. "They just wanted to have lunch together. Sometimes they need an extra break, but they are doing well with their studies. I'm not worried about that. They'll be ready for college if they want to go there. I'm pretty sure that if they go to college it will be one where they are both accepted to. College is not going to separate these two. I don't see that happening."

The girls were taking advantage of being out of hearing from the house to talk about what their next move would be. John was still in rehab and after that he still faced a court hearing for the stalking charge. There would be no date set before he was released from the rehab center, which was not for another 8 weeks.

Carla was still not entirely satisfied with the kind of punishment John had to endure. She felt he deserved worse than that. But as time went by she lost some of the anger she had felt before and sometimes wondered if it was worth the effort she had to put into to make John's life miserable.

Did she really prosecute John for what he wanted to do with her or was this revenge for what happened to her in New Orleans? This was a reoccurring question and she could never come up with a satisfactory answer. If this was the case, would there be someone else after John that she judged to deserve punishment, any male that wouldn't meet her standards or did something wrong in her opinion?

Stella was looking at her and said. "Where were you, I don't like it when you isolate yourself like that."

Carla apologized and told her what was on her mind, that she wasn't sure if the path she had chosen was the right one. Wouldn't she be better off to forget this painful episode and get on with her life?

Stella said, "Look you have no choice but to go through with the stalking court hearing. Don't plan anything else at this time. Three or four months from now you may have a better picture of all of this and make your decision then. Let's go on with our lives together and forget him for the time being. We still have to qualify for college and finish high school."

Carla said, "I have good news from my lawyer. He tried every angle to find out if there are warrants for my arrest and came up with nothing. Everything that was there seems to be erased and can't be retrieved."

Carla impulsively asked Stella, "Can you spend the night with me? I want to tell you the rest of my story from when I lived in New Orleans. You have the right to know the real me. If I can't tell you I will never be able to tell anybody."

Stella was surprised and asked, "Are you absolutely sure you want to tell me this now? I can wait, you know, if necessary forever I don't have to know. Nothing will change the way I feel about you anyway."

"No, I want you to know. I feel I have the courage to tell you now, and I'm ready to face the consequences."

That night after dinner the two went upstairs, both feeling awkward. Carla was afraid of how Stella would react and Stella was curious, but also afraid of how this would affect Carla. It was obviously something important to her, something that was hard for her to talk about.

Carla finally said, "Let's get this over with before I lose the courage to do it."

Stella could sense the tension Carla was under and tried to calm her down by suggesting that they do this later but Carla insisted on doing it now.

She started by describing that the situation at home was becoming unbearable for her and at the age of sixteen she left her parents' house and worked as a waitress. She explained the so called boyfriend disaster, the escort service, the prostitution, drugs, arrests and ended with

Hurricane Katrina and how she landed in Jamesville with Robert and Mary.

During this two hour long confession Stella held Carla's hand and never once let go, but never said a word. She was not able to voice her emotions. Tears were running down her face practically the whole time Carla was talking. Carla could feel the strength of Stella's emotions vary by the grip on her hand.

When Carla stopped talking, it became eerie quiet for a moment until Stella, who looked like she was hypnotized, came out of it and simply said, "I love you so much."

That's when Carla let her emotions take over and started to cry while holding and kissing Stella. In spite of all the tears this was the happiest moment of her life, knowing that their relationship would be stronger than ever. They couldn't stop holding and kissing each other for the longest time. Even after the tears stopped flowing they were still hugging and kissing. Carla was the first to realize that there was more to this than just two friends trying to console each other. She actually was enjoying the intimacy she felt when kissing her friend that way. She slowly pulled back and looked at Stella, who acted like she was embarrassed.

Stella quickly said, "See, nothing has changed. I still love you forever and will never forget that you trusted me so much that you could divulge these horrible moments you had to live through. You know me well enough that this is something I will never tell anybody. I even hope that now that you have shared this with me you will be able to forget and we never have to talk about it again. I know this will not be easy for you, but I'm sure that you are strong enough, that giving it some time, you will be able to."

Then out of the blue, Stella said very seriously, "Do you think we had a lesbian moment while we were kissing each other?"

Carla looked horrified but said, "I don't know but I must say that it was nice and I had a hard time stopping it.

"I did too. I was upset when you stopped."

"I read somewhere a while ago that approximately 40 percent of female college students have a more or less serious lesbian relationship with a close friend, and that it usually started when one of them was in a stressful time of their life." She then jokingly added,

"If that's us that would be so cool. We could get married and we don't have to worry that some guy would separate us." This somewhat broke the tension that they experienced after confessing that they liked the kissing they had done.

Carla asked, "What I just revealed to you about my past, does it really not bother you, or change the way you feel about me as a person?"

Stella sighed, "Everything you said bothers me, but not because of what you had to do. What saddens me is all the terrible times you had to suffer through all by yourself. Not what you did, but what other people did to you is what disturbs me.

"To me you are still the same person you were before you told me your sad life story. My feelings for you are still the same. I trust you, I love you, I never had a friend like you and I'm not letting your past change our future together or my feelings for you.

"So let's try to get some sleep. Do you mind if I sleep in your bed? I need you close to me. You will have to be my comfort tonight. This was a lot to digest for me and I may have some bad dreams. Being close to you will help."

The following days, Janice noticed that the girls were paying more attention to each other than usual and when they caught the other one looking at them a smile appeared on both their faces. It was as if they had a little secret. She would probe her daughter and try to find out if it was something she should know about.

Carla had another related topic to discuss. She asked Stella if she thought she should tell Robert and Mary about the kidnapping event or even reveal her past to them. She also told her that they wanted to adopt her and that she refused because she wouldn't do something like that before she told them about her past. Stella thought that she could possibly tell them about the kidnapping now, but the New Orleans episode might be a little heavy for them to digest all at the same time. She agreed that sometime in the future she should tell them, but she would wait a little with it for now.

"Stella mentioned the college issue her mom brought up. She feels that we should start gathering information on the colleges we have an interest in.

"She's right about that but we haven't given it much thought, have we. We may be scholastically ready for college, I'm not sure if I'm mentally ready for it, and that's why I wasn't pushing it. What do you think about college?"

Carla's reply was, "I haven't given it much thought either. You understand my situation. Six months ago I didn't even go to school and now I may go to college. This is a bit overwhelming for me. I don't think I'm ready for college just now, but if you decide to go I go. Robert has been asking about it and I know he will be disappointed if I don't attend college. But if I go and can't hack it he will be disappointed too and maybe think I'm stupid. I was so focused on this revenge business with these assholes that I forgot to concentrate on what is really important."

"Okay," Stella said. "What is my excuse? I didn't concentrate either. Maybe I'm also not ready for college. You know what; let's kick this around with my mother. She took a year off between high school and college. She may give us some advice."

The next day before their class work started they talked to Janice about the college issue. Janice as usual listened, and understanding their concerns said, "I was aware that you guys were not all that anxious to look into the colleges you wanted to go to. My advice to you is if you are not sure you want to go to college right now, you shouldn't, because the courses are demanding and if you're not one hundred percent there you will flunk. One option you have is to register in a community college and take a few basic courses. That will give you some credits and prepare you for a four year college education. You can get a part-time job, which you will hate after a few months but will make you understand that you need a higher education to have a satisfying career.

"A lot of kids take this route and after one or two year's community college, they have matured and collected enough credits to register as a sophomore for their bachelor degree. You may want to consider this option. I wish I would have done it that way. I simply skipped school for one year altogether and it was very difficult for me to pick up where I left off."

Both girls looked at each other and simultaneously said, "That's a great idea that sounds wonderful!"

Janice smiled and said, "I kind of expected you to like this option."

Carla said, "I hope Robert will like this idea. I think he will."

Carla was still waiting for the right time or opportunity to tell Robert and Mary about the kidnapping. The opportunity presented itself one day when Robert asked her why she was so tense and almost incoherent that time when she called him in Florida. He hadn't been able to understand what she was trying to tell him.

Carla hesitated and thought about an explanation for her strange behavior. Then she suddenly decided to tell them what had happened.

She said, "What I'm going to tell you will upset you but please don't let it. I survived and I am the same as I was before you left." She realized that this was not exactly reassuring to them so she said, "Let me tell you what happened, but keep in mind that I'm right here with you. "One night when I was walking Ginger I was dragged into a car by two guys wearing masks."

She then tried to explain what happened next, but saw the terrified look on their faces and quickly said.

"I'm alright I wasn't hurt but the harm was done."

Both of them remained speechless and were almost in a trance unable to comprehend that such a horrible thing could have happened to this child, a child they felt responsible for. Slowly they seemed to recover of the shock and looked at her, still confused and horrified.

Carla got up and put her arms around them, "Look at me. "She said I'm fine I was never hurt or abused. Try to calm down and let me tell you what happened." She went through the whole ordeal omitting the sexual parts, and as she talked to them she saw them coming back to normal once they realized that Carla had survived this horrible experience, seemingly without physical or mental damage.

Robert was the first to ask some questions, about what happened to these guys who did this to her. He felt that they should be in jail.

Carla was prepared for this question knowing that Robert would not agree with the way she was handling their punishment and why she didn't report it to the police.

"One of the reasons I did not report this to the local sheriff was that these guys are Jamesville High School seniors who just graduated, John Witherspoon and Glenn Evans, both from influential families in Jamesville. I had no witnesses who saw them put a bag over my head and throw me in the back of a car. It was dark and nobody was around. It would be my word against theirs.

"Their lawyers would claim that this was not a kidnapping and I was just an opportunist who saw the chance to maybe bribe them or get paid for certain services. Their lawyers would do background checks and find out that I was trailer trash from the worst part of New Orleans, and from a dysfunctional family, both parents' alcoholics.

"What do you think my chances would be in court? All I would get would be humiliation, shame and your name would be dragged through the mud because you brought this piece of trash to their town.

"The reason I did not tell you all this is because it happened while you were in Florida, and I could only talk on the phone when one of them was listening to our conversation. When I finally managed to come back home you were having a hard enough time with Mary's sister in the hospital, and then the funeral. I kept it a secret because you were having enough problems at that time, and I figured my problems were over and telling you could wait a few weeks.

"I'm sorry if you feel that this was the wrong way to handle this, but I felt you had enough on your plate."

She then briefly explained that these boys were already in trouble with the law and that this would continue for a while. She did not provide any details, and luckily neither one questioned her on that issue.

Mary was crying and said to Robert, "This is entirely my fault. We shouldn't have left her by herself in the house. She should have come with us to Florida."

Carla answered, "This is nobody's fault but those two perverts. This could have happened even when you were here. I take Ginger out every night by myself. I was ambushed two blocks away from this house. You and Robert being home would not have prevented this."

Robert said, "She's right Mary. This could have happened when we were at home. I always thought this was a safe neighborhood, but you never know.

"I understand your reasons for not telling the police. I'm not entirely convinced that it's the right way to handle this,. Definitely you not being in charge of their punishment. I find that way too dangerous for a young girl. You realize that these jerks would be looking for a way to pay you back?"

Carla then explained, "Their hands were tied because of the documents with the evidence that were in the hands of her lawyers. They are convinced that I have enough evidence to put them in jail for the rest of their lives, only I know that this is not the case. The evidence I have will get them in trouble with maybe a minor conviction."

Robert shook his head and mumbled that this needed more talking between Carla and him. He obviously did not want Mary in the picture.

A few days later Janice asked Carla if she had spoken to Robert about the college issue.

Carla said, "No not yet but I will today."

Janice proposed to get Robert, and the four of them could discuss it together. Robert was home and came over to their class room.

Janice took the initiative and explained what the girls would like to do with regard to their college education. Robert thought it was a great idea. There was one caveat he had and that was that they had to promise that they would go to college after one or at most two years.

They both agreed with that and would register at the Community College as soon as they had their high school equivalency diploma.

Robert asked them what kind of a job they were looking for but they hadn't thought about that yet. Classes wouldn't be over for at least three months. Looking for a job could wait.

Robert said, "That's right unless someone offered you a job now, knowing that you can only start working when school is over."

They all looked at him suspiciously. He had something in mind. "Okay," he said, "I won't keep you in suspense any longer. You may not know this, but I still have a couple of small businesses here in town. One of them is a travel agency. During the summer months there's always a shortage of personnel. I'm sure I could persuade the manager to hire a couple of smart, good looking girls there for at least five to six months. Think about it and let me know so I can start the ball rolling."

They both looked at each other and said that would be great.

"That was quick," Robert said laughing. "I'll talk to the manager today and I think you can consider yourselves hired."

They hugged and thanked him and were in seventh heaven. Everything had fallen into place in a matter of minutes. How cool was that working in the same office?

Chapter 18

As promised, Bill called John every week to give him a status of the ground work he was doing. During the last call he said he was now planning the time and place for the execution of the project. John eagerly asked him to tell him some of the details which prompted Bill to call him an asshole and shit for brains to even ask something like that on a public phone. John was embarrassed and angry at the same time and said, "I don't pay you for calling me names."

Bill said, "That's just too bad and hung up."

A week later when he called he said before John could ask any questions. "If you ask me one of your stupid questions one more time, I will hang up on you and you can consider the agreement terminated. You got that?"

"Okay," John said, "So what's new?"

Bill answered, "The planning is as good as complete some minor details need to be worked out but I think you you'll like it.

"One more detail on the financial arrangement we had. You are not up to date on that and I expect a similar deposit via Western Union not later than this week. If I don't receive it by then all work will have to stop. I need on time deposits. I have expenses you have to cover. I'm sure you understand."

This kind of bullshit had been going on for several weeks, John not suspecting anything and Bill receiving close to $50,000 and never having set a foot outside New Jersey. He didn't even know where Jamesville was. The weekly reports were cooked up on his way to a public phone booth. Carla couldn't have done a better job herself.

John was pleased with the way he thought everything was moving forward, one more payment to Bill via Western Union and then a final payment before the actual event. There would not be any further payments after that. The deal was that after the killing he would meet Bill in Houston at Bush International Airport, Continental terminal C. Bill would bring him proof that the job was done and John would hand him the remaining $100,000. That was the arrangement. Unfortunately for Bill, John wouldn't make it since he would already be in the air on his way to Brazil.

An arrangement was already in place with the financial company that would actually loan him money with his trust fund as collateral. Soon as he was released from the rehab center he would sign the papers and receive a $1,000,000 loan at 18 percent interest, the balance of the money in the trust fund would be available to him on his 21st birthday. The interest was high but this was the best he could do under the circumstances. He didn't have to worry about money. His trust fund was close to $16,000,000.

His only worry was staying under the radar for a while. After Carla was eliminated and the lawyers had delivered the documents with the evidence to the police, he would be a wanted person. He might have to travel around in South America not staying too long in one country. He was seriously considering to checking out the possibilities of a fake passport and driver's license. That should reduce the risks substantially, especially outside the U.S. He was told that in South America if you have the cash you are relatively safe in most places.

The days went by quickly. Five more days and he would be out of there, back to the comforts of home. He had told his lawyer to postpone the hearing for the stalking case as long as he could, figuring that he would be gone by then anyway.

Bill was having the time of his life; money, drugs, booze and chicks. Man life was good. He was looking forward to cashing the last payment of $52,000. It was too bad that he wouldn't be able to collect the final $100,000 but that was just too risky. He thought about it a lot, but getting that hot needle in his arm was not in his future plans. Getting $100,000 for doing absolutely nothing was not bad. He decided that he wouldn't go near this girl.

If John wanted her dead he would have to do it himself. He didn't think John had the guts to kill her, but you never know. He would make sure that it could not be pinned on him. The moment he got that $52,000 he would go somewhere safe, far away from Jamesville, Texas, and he also should make sure he had a solid alibi for every day after John was released. He had no knowledge that John would try something similar like that. He just didn't trust the little weasel. He chuckled at this thought because it was funny when he realized he himself could be trusted even less.

Feeling guilty or being dishonest was a state of mind that Bill could ill afford. Not that it ever had bothered him before, but in this case, the satisfaction of sticking it to a spoiled rich kid was very rewarding for him. It was like a revenge for the times that he felt he was shafted by the establishment.

Bill had a strong dislike for John from the very first time he talked to him. He felt that John treated him like a second class citizen and the reason he even talked to him was because he needed something done. John acted like Bill was beneath him and people like that should be thankful for the privilege of serving him. Reflecting on all this shit, made Bill think that he should do more to even the score with John. It had to be something that couldn't be traced to him or get him in trouble with the law, maybe an anonymous call to this girl warning her that John had made a contract with a killer to take care of her. That would get his ass in hot water.

He had to give this more thought. It would feel good to get that son of a bitch in trouble. He just had to be careful and make damn sure he didn't get burned in the process, difficult decision. Maybe he will call her once he got his money. No need to jeopardize his paycheck.

John was released from the rehab center and was back home, playing it low key, staying away from the crowd he usually hung out with. Only his family was aware that he was back in town.

John, blissfully unaware of Bill's intentions was preparing everything for a quick exit out of the country. He did acquire a fake passport and driver's license which he intended to use only in emergency situations. He had wired the $52,000 to Bill and was waiting for his phone call to find out the details of the job. He wanted to check out what this moron had planned and make sure that it was fool proof. They only had one shot at it.

The $1,000,000 loan was safely deposited in a bank in Rio de Janeiro. His first class plane ticket on Continental Airlines was confirmed for the day after the killing. Everything was under control and that bitch would finally get what she deserved. His expectations for his future in South America were high. Him leaving his family and friends was a minor issue and insignificant in the grand scheme of things. His long range plans were to come back to the U.S. maybe California or Florida but definitely not to Jamesville.

At about the same time Bill disembarked at the Cancun airport and was on his way to the Marriott Beach Palace, ready for what he felt was a well-deserved vacation. He was looking forward to the Mexican beauties and tall Margaritas. He assumed that John would probably start calling him within a day or two, at the phone number of his friend in New Jersey, a friend who would convey a message to John with regard to the job he was supposed to do for him.

John waited three days before he called Bill; he dialed the number Bill had given him with an area code in New Jersey. He had hoped that by this time he would be in Houston as planned. A guy answered the phone with, "Yes, what do you want?"

"I want to talk to Bill."

"He isn't here and hung up."

John was already uptight and angry. When he called back the same guy answered and yelled, "I already told you he's not here. So what do you want from me."

John quickly said, "I need to talk to him right now. It's important. I'm John and he was expecting my call."

"Oh, you're John, I have a message for you, I took him to the airport a couple of days ago and he wrote down a note for you. Let me find it and I'll read it to you."

After a few minutes he was back. "Here it is:

"Dear John,

I gave this a lot of thought and came to the conclusion that this job is too dangerous at this time. We have to postpone this for a couple of months. I know you paid me half my fee but don't worry. I will finish the job when I feel enough time has elapsed and it can be done without consequences that could hurt you and me. So hang tight and I will call you.

Have a nice day,
Bill."

John did not have a nice day. He had a very lousy day and when he started to yell at the guy on the other side of the phone line, he made that very clear. He asked, "Where did that double-crossing motherfucker go."

"How the fuck would I know?" He got for an answer. "I dropped him off at the airport and when I asked him where he was going he said he was going to paradise and that was it. So if you know where paradise is you have a good chance of finding him. If you don't, I would say you're fucked man." With those words he slammed the phone down.

John first impulse was to call this guy back, but then he realized that would lead to nothing. The guy either didn't know or if he did he wouldn't tell him anyway.

He not only had lost his money, but all his scheduling and planning went down the drain. His money was in Brazil. He would have to cancel his flight and start planning from scratch. His biggest disappointment was that the bitch would still be alive longer than he had anticipated. This really pissed him off, but he vowed that he wouldn't give up and if all else failed he would kill her himself.

His biggest concern now was to avoid any jail time on account of this stalking charge. His lawyer had told him that the hearing was set for two weeks from now, and he strongly advised him to keep his temper under control or he would find himself in jail for a while.

All he could do now was put his feelers out on how and where to find a hit man. Jamesville was not the place to look for this type of individual. He would have to go to Houston, but he still wouldn't know where to find these people.

The next day he drove to Houston after checking on the Internet to find out were the seedy part of the city was. It looked like it was at the third Ward and the Montrose area. He knew more or less where that was so he headed out that way. He parked his car and walked to Montrose Boulevard where he saw some activity. The bars and restaurants were all fairly busy for this early evening time. He entered a shabby bar where he was promptly asked to show his ID. A sluttish looking barmaid wanted to know if his mother knew where he was.

John felt his anger getting the better of him, but was able to control it. He said smiling, "Very funny can I have a coke please?"

She brought him his coke and he gave her a twenty dollar bill and told her to keep the change. Her demeanor changed drastically and she said, "I was only pulling your leg you know."

He said, still smiling, "No harm done. I can take a joke especially from a good looking, sexy hot chick like you."

She then became extremely friendly and asked him where he was from and what he was doing or looking for in this part of town.

He couldn't outright say that he was looking for someone he could hire to kill the girl that he hated. He said, "I'm looking for some action and I was told this was a good place to start."

She looked at him and said, "You're a bit younger than the guys I normally play with, but if you come back in a couple of hours I can provide you with some action you've never had before." She made it a point to lower her see through blouse so a fair part of her tits became visible.

John thought, Oh shit, that's not the action I want right now. But maybe this is the road I have to travel to find the people I'm looking for. He made sure she saw that he was admiring her boobs, and said, "That sounds pretty good to me. Tell me what time and I'll be there."

"I'm Candy."

"I'm John. I look forward to see you tonight"

"I'm done at seven o' clock. Just wait outside; my boss doesn't like it that I date clients. I think he's jealous."

John still had a couple of hours to kill before his date. He wandered around the area walked into a few more bars. The last place he visited, some guy sitting at the bar started to talk to him. At first it was just innocent yakking, nothing of substance suddenly the guy said, "You look like you're after something. Your eyes are constantly moving around like you are waiting for someone or something to happen."

"You're very observant, and you're right. I'm looking for a guy who can do something for me out of the ordinary, of course for a substantial fee. I can't tell you exactly what I want done, because as far as I know you could be a cop."

The man replied, "I understand exactly what your saying but I can guarantee you that I can deliver whatever you want done. By the way my name is Carl, do you stay in a hotel close by so we can go there and talk about the specifics?"

John said, "Yes, I'm staying at a hotel on Westheimer but why can't we do this now? It's pretty private here."

Carl looked at him strangely and said, "I like kinky as much as the next guy but do you really want me to give you a blow job right here in this bar?"

John looked puzzled for a second or two and then said, "Shit you're a faggot!" and cursing ran out of the bar embarrassed and feeling stupid.

He had second thoughts about his date with the barmaid / hooker but since he felt more comfortable with hookers than with pretty boys, he decided to meet her at seven and hopefully she could give him some pointers, if nothing else at least he would get laid.

He arrived promptly at seven and when she walked out and saw his red convertible she said, "Wow, I like your car." She was dressed for the occasion, nothing to hide all the attributes shown, nothing left to the imagination. They agreed to have dinner at an Italian restaurant on Westheimer and just across the street from his hotel, the conversation was basically sexual oriented and that was probably the only subject she could talk about with authority and experience.

She asked him if he was interested in a threesome she had a good looking hot girlfriend she could call if he wanted to experience that. It would make it a little more fun for all of them. Usually when she had sex with a guy, he got exhausted and then it became boring for her. If she had her girlfriend with her, she could play with her and he could watch until he was ready for action again.

John, being a sex maniac, was very much interested and said, "That's fine with me". She called her friend on her cell phone and after a short conversation told John that Mandy would join them at the restaurant in about twenty minutes. They would be finished with dinner by then and could go straight to John's hotel room.

Mandy was a few years younger than Candy and looked a little more stylish. This could be fun. John thought when he saw her entering the restaurant. Maybe somewhat expensive, but after all the shit he went through lately, he deserved some fun.

It was definitely fun. The girls were good with him and when they entertained each other, the sex between these two girls aroused him to the point that the number of orgasms he had during this night exceeded everything he had in the past. The girls were going to spend the night so that they could have breakfast with him and give him some contacts for the job he needed to be done. He never told them what exactly he wanted that individual to do.

When he offered the girls payment for their performance they told them that they were amateurs and loved to have sex with a good looking guy like him. They finally fell asleep seemingly dead tired. When John woke up later the following day, both girls were gone. There was no message.

John thought, they are probably downstairs having breakfast. All of their stuff was gone too. Maybe he needed to take a shower first before he went looking for them. He had to admit that they were fun having around. He thought he should buy them something from the hotel shopping gallery.

After he showered and shaved he started getting dressed and looked for his watch. He thought that's strange. I always put my watch and wallet on the night stand. Then lightning struck. Both wallet and watch were gone. The wallet contained something like four or five hundred dollars plus his American Express card and driver's licenses, both licenses, real and fake' were gone. His golden Rolex was worth around five grand. He sat on the bed and started cursing and making threats about what he was going to do to these bitches. It then dawned on him that he didn't really know them. He would go back to the bar where he met Candy, but he was sure the whore wouldn't be there for a while.

What was the fucking matter with everybody? Was there a conspiracy that everyone who crossed his path was determined to screw him? Were they all looking for John Witherspoon so they could contribute to the global objective of ruining his life?

John didn't feel like staying any longer in Houston. He kind of gave up the idea of finding someone who would do the job of eliminating Carla and Glenn. Glenn would be the most difficult to eliminate. He thought this would be the easier of the two, but on second thought, finding someone in Afghanistan to execute this when you're in the US, this was virtually impossible. People who join the Peace Corps are usually not the kind that would kill another Peace Corps recruit. It still bothered him that Glenn could be on Carla's side, and worst scenario, could be a valuable witness for the prosecutor, knowing enough to put John behind bars. He had thought of this before, and the ideal situation would be to get rid of both of them at the same time. Problem was that Glenn was still in Afghanistan for more than a year.

All parties were present at the Court House in Houston. Since this was not a very important case and very few people were there, the judge made his entry and immediately summoned the prosecutor, John and Carla's lawyers to the bench. He said, "If there are any more disturbances like the ones we had before, I promise you that the instigator will be arrested and will stay in jail as long as I can legally hold him. Is this understood gentleman?" They all nodded, and the judge said, "Okay, then let's start the proceedings."

This was a clear cut case. There was a witness, Carla's neighbor. There were pictures taken that showed John sitting in his car watching the house. There was John's outburst during the first hearing. Nothing his lawyer said could change the facts. The verdict was six months probation and John could not come within 500 yards of her house during that time. If he violated these terms, he would be arrested and end up in jail for six months. John was wise enough not to say anything but acknowledged that he understood the terms.

When they left the court house Carla and John crossed paths on the steps of the court house. John could not resist the temptation and hissed, "You bitch I'll get you for this."

Carla managed to smile and said, "Now be nice or you may be locked up before you even leave the court house."

Her lawyer said, "Don't let him bait you. Ignore him. If he comes within the parameters the court has set for him, call the local police. That's all you have to do don't get into an argument with him."

This encounter was all John needed to make the decision that he would personally take care of her. Her days were numbered, he vowed. All he needed to do was to plan for when and where he would kill her. He was not going to rely on others any longer. He couldn't trust them. Some things you have to do yourself if you want to make sure it's done the way you want it. He struggled with the problem that if he couldn't get near her, how was he going to kill her?

His hate and anger toward her was so imbedded in his brain that he simply couldn't think straight. All logic escaped him when it concerned her. The result was that he came up with such insane ideas that were the fruits of his disturbed mind, ideas nobody would take seriously.

One of his ideas was to burn their house down in the middle of the night when everybody was asleep and he would prevent them from leaving the house by barricading the front door. Another one was to place a bomb underneath her car. A third was for him to ram her car with an 18-wheeler. None of these ideas went further then his sick brain.

Maybe I should call her and apologize for what I said at the court house he thought, and then I could carefully hint that I want to make up with her, let her know that I don't want this feud between us to go on forever. I tell her that I regret not having accepted the opportunity to join the Peace Corps like Glenn did. I tell her anything she wants to hear. I just need the opportunity to meet with her alone somewhere, and that would be the end of the bitch.

He made up his mind and did call her. The moment she picked up the phone and recognized his voice, she said, "You're violating your parole and if you don't hang up right now I will report you. I have absolutely nothing to discuss with you."

He had no choice but do what she told him to do. Anger and hate were insufficient emotions for what he felt at the time. She humiliated him and made him feel like he was not even worthy of talking to her. He felt insignificant and worthless every time he was in contact with her. Her behavior was dismantling his self esteem and he was, after all, a Witherspoon, one of the richest families in Texas. This must end soon. He could no longer tolerate the way this arrogant bitch was manipulating him. Who the fuck did she think she was?

He must go back to her house and find out how he could get to her when she was alone or when she left to go somewhere. There must be occasions that she was alone and if there was a pattern of this he should know about it and find a way to kidnap her once more. The moment that took place, the party would be over and he could enjoy his new life in Brazil.

Chapter 19

Stella was outraged when Carla told her that John had called her. "Why didn't you report him?" she asked, "That asshole deserves to be back in jail."

"Yes," Carla agreed, "I probably should have reported this to the police or at least to my lawyer.

By the way, his buddy Glenn called me also. He is home for a while his grandmother passed away and his mother is not taking it well. They gave him a leave of absence type of deal. He can stay home for up to six weeks. He wanted to see me and talk about Afghanistan but mainly to convince me, I guess, that he is a changed person. He said that he wrote a letter to John to persuade him to join the Corps but John never responded. That didn't surprise me.

"They parted as enemies when Glenn left for Afghanistan. John called him a coward and traitor and vowed never to talk to him again, so I doubt they will see a lot of each other, which will be better for Glenn than getting back under John's dominating influence."

Stella said, "To change the subject, are you aware that four weeks from now we will have completed our classes and will be high school graduates, ready to start working at the Travel Agency?"

"No," said Carla, "We won't start working right away. I have a little surprise for you. I wanted Robert to tell you himself but he insisted that I should. You and I are going on a vacation. Every year Robert gets a free cruise for two, from one of the cruise ship companies, his agency deals with. He and Mary almost never use it, and this year he wants us to have it. Everything is paid for, even the activities like wine with our meals, spa treatments, on-shore trips, everything is included.

"We have an outside suite with balcony and whatever other stuff that comes with it, things I know nothing about. I never was on a cruise so this is all new to me. The ship leaves from Galveston. We sail at night and dock in the morning on one of the islands. I believe he said we do six or seven different islands. He will give us a detailed itinerary later."

Stella was speechless. Tears came into her eyes and she finally said, "I don't know what to say this is so fantastic! Robert and Mary are such wonderful people. What can we do for them to let them know how much this means to us?"

Carla became silent and sad looking so Stella asked, "What's wrong? Aren't you happy?"

"Of course I'm happy. But I feel so bad that I can't tell them who I really am. They deserve to know, I just don't know how to tell them. Maybe I'm afraid they will no longer love me, maybe feel that I took advantage of them, which I actually did."

Stella said, "You know, Carla, you sometimes piss me off, like right now. You know they will always love you. You were the best thing that ever happened to them. They had nobody to give their love and affection to until you came along. You are their daughter now, not biologically but in every other way you are. They want to adopt you to make it like you are their real daughter. That's what they want.

"I'm not sure that telling them your past life story is the right thing to do at this time. One thing is for sure they are not going to love you less. On the contrary, they will love you more, if that's even possible. Robert, I think could handle it. Mary is a different story. It would upset her knowing what a miserable time you had to go through. It would be on her mind day and night, she won't be able to forget and it will haunt her forever.

"Think about it. Maybe in a case like this you should let sleeping dogs lie. If you tell Robert I know he would feel he has to tell Mary or if he realizes it would not be such a good idea to tell Mary you are forcing him to keep a secret from his wife. Mary is just beginning to get over her sister's death. She doesn't need this right now.

"If I was in your shoes I would learn to live with it and keep it a secret. There will always be time to tell them later if you have to."

Carla nodded and said, "I keep telling myself the same thing, but I feel it's just another excuse for me not telling them. I know at some time I will."

Nothing much happened for a couple of weeks and the departure date for their 10 day cruise was only a week away. They were busy putting their wardrobe together and looking through the ship's brochure on what they could do on board and on the excursions. They were determined not to miss anything.

A day before their departure Carla got a phone call from Glenn. He said that he met with John and although John never responded to his letter he acted very civilized and seemed to have remorse for what he had wanted to do and did to her at the beach house. He asked Glenn if he could be the mediator for a discussion between him and Carla.

Glenn said, "I'll drive my car and pick you up. We then will get John and because he can't be seen with you we will just drive around and talk about this situation we're in and how we can end this quandary. I think he sincerely means it and would like to make amends with you this time."

Carla said, "Look, I'm not sure I want to have a meeting with him. First of all it's against the law for him to come close to me. Second, I'm not sure he's remorseful for what he did and third, I'll be on a cruise ship starting tomorrow anyway. I have to think about this, I'm not at all sure I want to do this. Call me when we're back two weeks from now."

When Stella heard this she said, "You're not going to do this, are you? These jerks can't be trusted. If you get into a car with these two maniacs who wanted to rape you, you should have your head examined first. Changes are that you end up in a loony bin for even considering this.

"Why would you do this? What's in it for you? You are in control now. If you want to stop interfering in their lives you simply stop and that's it. You don't have to continue. Just forget that these two assholes are on this planet."

Carla said," Hold your horses. If I do this I will make sure that it's safe and that I will be protected all the way. Besides I haven't decided that I'm going to do it. I will call my lawyer and see how he feels about it and how I can be protected if I do. The reason I want to talk to them once more is to make them understand that when I say it's over, it's over and that means that there will be no more threats or harassments from either side. Let's forget it for the time being and finish packing. It's a good thing we're not flying with the luggage you have."

"What about your luggage?" Stella responded." It's just as much as mine."

Carla said teasingly, "Mine is all essentials. No frills. There's nothing in there that I don't need."

"Yeah right," Stella said. "Good thing Robert has a giant SUV to get us there."

This being the first cruise either one of them had ever experienced, everything was awesome, the size of the ship, the luxury of their suite, the quality and choices of the meals, all the different activities, the little duty free shops. It was a revelation, something they could not stop marveling about.

One of their favorite pastimes was sunbathing on their veranda, lying on a cushioned deck chair reading a book while sipping a cold drink, or talking with each other. The movement of the ship created a breeze. It was heaven for both of them. They also participated in a lot of the poolside activities where the younger crowd seemed to hang out, playing games, and flirting with the boys. Once they had some sort of a date going to the night club with two guys they met during the day. That didn't work out very well. The boys had a more romantic date in mind than the girls, so that was a one time thing.

Some of the excursions were really nice and interesting. In all they had a wonderful time and were determined that cruising was something they wanted to do again.

Most of the people they met around the dinner table were seasoned cruise people. When they found out that this was their first cruise, they started to describe the other ships they had been on, telling them about the quality of the service on board other ships, destinations that were a must, excursions to avoid, in short sharing their experiences with them, the good and the bad.

The last day on board they had mixed feelings about leaving the ship. They wanted it to go on for a little longer but they were also anxious to get off the ship so they could tell their families all about it and how great everything was and that this was the best vacation they ever had.

Janice, Mary and Robert were waiting on the dock when the two of them came down the gangway. After a lot of hugging and kissing, both of them started talking. Stella kept repeating to her mom that this was so awesome; she can't believe how awesome it was. Carla tried to tell Mary and Robert what a great time they had and thanked them for giving them this vacation.

After a couple of minutes of this verbal chaos Robert said, "I think we got the message that you had a good time but if we don't claim your luggage pretty soon it may well be underway back to Cancun."

They slowly got off their high and were able to tell them what a fantastic trip this has been. Both once more thanked Robert with more hugs and kisses. Robert said, "If I'm going to be hugged and kissed like that, you can go on a cruise every year."

Mary laughingly said, "Yes, you old goat, you would like that wouldn't you?"

After they got their luggage and dropped Janice and Stella off at their house, things got almost back to normal in Robert's car. Carla still had to say a few more times what a wonderful experience this had been and what a great time they had together.

Chapter 20

When Glenn told John that Carla would not be around for a couple of weeks because she would be on a cruise, John immediately saw possibilities like girl falls overboard, body couldn't be found, the ideal opportunity for him. He asked, "When is she leaving?"

Glenn said. "She already left."

John started cursing and Glenn asked, "What's the big deal. She will be back in ten days, and by the way she has not committed to talk to you. She told me to call her when she gets back. She wanted to think about it."

John had that mean angry look on his face, a look Glenn was all too familiar with. He became suspicious and said. "Are you planning something stupid again? If you are I'm out of here. You've got me in enough shit to last a lifetime I don't need any more of that."

John realized that he had fucked up and quickly said, "No I'm just disappointed, I finally got the courage to face her and apologize and I wanted this to be over and done with, that's all."

Glenn was still suspicious but said no more on the subject. "I'll call her as soon as she gets back. She gave me the date of their return."

Glenn left and John started cursing again and blaming Glenn for not telling him earlier about the cruise. He could have been on that ship and with a couple of thousand passengers she would never know that he was on board. This would have been so easy. He was imagining how he would have done it but this was all water under the bridge and it was all Glenn's fault, that dumb asshole.

He was now afraid that she would never agree to meet with him and Glenn, and he might have to come up with another scheme to get rid of that bitch.

One idea he had and liked was that he would procure a long range sniper rifle and learn how to use it by going to a practice range. When he felt ready he would hide in back of her house where she always walked the dog. He had surveyed the area and he could hide on the other side of the little lake in back of the house.

This would only be a little over two hundred yards and if he practiced for that distance it should not be a problem. He had read that some of those snipers could kill a person from two thousand yards. He actually believed that with some practice he could hit a moving target two hundred yards away.

He liked the idea of whacking her from a distance, but he also wanted to see her fear and anxiety of not knowing what was in store for her. His sick mind contemplated of raping her before he killed her. That would be the ultimate revenge and something she deserved.

Another drawback from shooting her from a distance was that Glenn would still be alive and remain a problem he had to deal with.

He could not afford to let Glenn hang around and be a danger to him. He was the only one who could get him in serious trouble. He had to be eliminated. His original plan would have taken care of it. Maybe he should put a little more pressure on Glenn to make Carla believe in John's good intentions. A reminder of the fire that destroyed Glenn's former girlfriend's house might change his attitude.

He also had a tape of conversations John and Glenn had. The tape was slightly altered so that Glenn seemed to be the instigator and in charge of this sex slave caper. He thought of anonymously mailing this tape to Glenn. Maybe this would create some goodwill from him.

Right now, let's just wait until the bitch returns from her cruise and see what she decided to do. He would react accordingly. He felt better now that everything was in his hands. No more third parties to fuck it up. It was all under his control and he liked it that way.

One evening after dinner, John's father asked him to come to his study for a little chat. John was a little anxious and asked, "What do you want to talk about Dad?"

His father said. "Just give me a minute and let me finish my brandy. I'll be with you in no time."

When his father entered the study he looked serious and said, "Let's not beat around the bushes and get to the point.

"I received a phone call from the lawyer that handles your stalking charges and he said that I should have a man to man talk with you. When I asked him what this was all about he replied that I must understand that you were his client and that the client/attorney confidentially agreement did not allow him to tell me anything. The only thing he was willing to say was that he had the gut feeling that you were on the brink of getting into some serious trouble.

"He would not tell me anything more than that. I should talk to you and try to find out what you are up to, and hopefully talk some sense into you.

"So son, what are you up to? Is it some personal issue with that girl you were allegedly stalking? Is she pregnant or what? I know that the last couple of weeks you've been distracted and not your usual self so something is bothering you."

John angrily responded, "Of course something is bothering me. I'm innocent. I wasn't stalking her, but I'm on parole and I have to be careful where I go, what I do, or I could be in jail, and you asked me that stupid question?

"How would you feel if the law prohibited you from visiting your lawyer friend, and some idiot asked you if she was pregnant, would that bother you?" Not waiting for a reaction he stormed out of the room leaving his father flabbergasted and concerned.

He was concerned for the fact that his son knew about his affair with Jane. If he knew, who else was aware of his relation with her? He thought they were discreet and secretive about their romantic escapades. This could have substantial repercussions if any of his political adversaries found out. They would have to be more careful or break up altogether. He could not take this lightly. This could hurt both of them. He needed to talk to her and work this out.

I also must have another talk with John he thought, and ask him where he heard this gossip about him and Jane. He would emphasize that Jane was the company lawyer and, of course he spent much time with her. But this was strictly business, nothing else.

When he spoke to John about his relationship with Jane, John laughed and said, "Whatever Dad. He mockingly added, I believe you. It's the rest of the Jamesville population you have to convince.

"I also don't think that Ma believes that business is the only relationship you have with Jane. Was that all you wanted to talk to me about, or have you all of a sudden realized that fathers should at least once a year have a talk with their son? If that's the case, consider your fatherly obligation done. You talked to me."

He left the room while listening to his father muttering that he was always a difficult child and lately was getting worse. He never answered his question about him getting into more trouble. He would find out eventually.

John Sr. and Jane had their discussion about how to continue their romance without it becoming public, more so than it already was. Jane thought that they should cool it for a while and only see each other far away from Jamesville. John reluctantly agreed she was the only woman he had sex with and seeing her only on out of town trips would not satisfy his needs. Jane on the other hand thought this was just what she needed. Slowly breaking up with him was something she had been thinking of for a long time. She just didn't know how to do it without jeopardizing her cushy job and generous perks. This was an ideal situation. Circumstances forced them into it. Neither of them was to blame. Perfect.

John called Glenn and asked if Carla was back yet. Glenn thought that she was, but he had not called her. He would wait a couple of days; give her some time to think about it. John was disappointed and angry that Glenn was not pushing this but realized that he couldn't show his feelings because Glenn was the only pipeline he had to the bitch.

He said, "Well let me know as soon as you have a chance to talk to her. I really want this to be over with."

Glenn said, "I will do the best I can, but as I told you before there is no guarantee that she wants to do it the way you suggested, or if she wants to see you at all. That's not guaranteed either."

After this conversation with Glenn, John was convinced that he had to come up with an alternate solution because he could not rely on Glenn to make Carla agree to drive around with him and resolve this problem. She would probably insist that this had to be done in the presence of a couple of lawyers, just to cover her ass.

He couldn't believe it was going to be so difficult and complicated to eliminate a worthless bitch like her. He was going to focus on one thing only and that was to kill her. Forget about having sex with her before. He also must forget Glenn for the time being. Just kill her and take care of Glenn later.

The easiest way he figured was to shoot her from across the lake at night, waiting until she went to bed. With the light on in her room it would be an easy shot. I'll buy a rifle tomorrow and practice for a couple of days, he thought. By the end of next week this will all be over, and I will be on my way to Rio de Janeiro.

It didn't turn out exactly as planned. It took five days before he could buy the rifle. That was the required waiting time in Texas to purchase a weapon.

Learning how to use a rifle like that was a little more complicated than he thought it would be. After a week of practice he was able to hit the target from two hundred yards but that was not the same as hitting a moving human being. It took another week before he felt confident enough to set a fixed date. He made reservations to fly out of Houston the next morning after he was finished with Carla. He estimated it would take a few days before they would start looking for him and by then he would be in Brazil under a different identity and with lots of money to enjoy the good life. If everything worked out as planned it really didn't matter whether Glenn was there to testify. If he wasn't around there would be no trial.

He went out a couple of nights to the spot he had selected to fire from to see how she moved around in her room before she went to bed. He was rewarded with a nude show. Carla undressed completely and walked around in the nude before getting into the bathroom. He could not see the inside of the bathroom because of the opaque glass windows.

He saw only a vague shadow moving around. What he did see before she disappeared into the bathroom was enough to give him an erection and an unfulfilled desire to have sex with her before he would kill her.

He tried to convince himself that he should forget the way she looked and how sexy she was. This was not the way he wanted it to go. The more he looked at here the more he wanted her.

He kept coming back night after night, admiring her body and the way she moved, postponing the execution of the woman he hated so much but wanted more than anything.

Tomorrow is the night he said to himself. This nonsense has to stop. Once she is gone I will be able to stop thinking and fantasizing about her. If I didn't know better I'd think I was in love with her, in love with a bitch who hated my guts and is determined to make the rest of my life pure hell. I don't think so.

The following night when he was in position he looked through his rifle scope into her bedroom and saw Carla and her friend Stella. He was not pleased with this development and felt disappointed, not because he

263

probably would not be able to shoot her that night but more so that he wouldn't be able to look at her walking around in the nude. He also hated it that he had to share her with her friend. He felt jealous and didn't quite understand why. He decided to stay for a while. Maybe Stella would leave soon and he would be able to see her anyway.

Shortly after he saw an unexpected scene. Both girls starting to undress and walk around in the nude. Damn it! He thought they are lesbians. No fucking wonder she didn't want to have sex with us. He kept watching, expecting and hoping to see some lesbian sex. If he was hoping to experience this, he was going to be disappointed. Both girls took a shower, put on their pajamas and went to bed, each in their own bed, both reading before they turned the lights out.

John was confused about what had just happened. They walk around in the nude, they didn't even touch each other, and they behaved like sisters. That was definitely not homosexual behavior like what he saw in the porno magazines he frequently bought. Maybe they were not lesbians after all. He packed up his gear and went home still confused and not sure what to do next.

Am I capable of killing her? He asked himself. The answer was, I don't know anymore. A week ago it would have been an easy decision. Right now I'm not sure what to do. I'm beginning to understand that love and hate are separated by a very thin line. I hate her for what she's been doing to me lately, but I realize that I started this war, and she is just retaliating.

I have to call Glenn again and find out if she wants to talk to me or not, this could change everything.

Glenn said that she was willing to talk to him, but on her terms. She is working during the summer in her father's travel agency and she just started this week and don't know yet what her schedule would be. One thing she said was that it had to be somewhere she would feel safe. She added that John was not a person she could trust.

She promised that she would call Glenn back this week on the when and where she would meet John.

A week or so ago, this response would have triggered another outburst of rage on John's part, but he now thought that it made sense that she must be assured of her safety. He still didn't understand what was happening to him. His emotions were taking over and he thought, I better be careful or I will end up on some shrink's couch with him asking me why I hate my mother. He was joking but he wasn't laughing. Why, he asked himself, do I have to be obsessed with everything I do or want in life? Why can't I be rational and act like other people? Maybe seeing that shrink may not be such a bad idea after all. He would ask his dad to give him the Psychiatric Analysis Report that he took before going into rehab. If something was wrong with him it should be in there. He never saw the report.

The next night he still went to his hiding place with his rifle hoping to see her through his rifle scope. The room stayed dark and he gave up for the night. On his way home he felt disappointed, but it slowly changed to anger and he irrationally blamed her for spoiling his evening by not being there. His emotions again took over and crossed that fine line putting him back where he hated her. That the bitch couldn't be trusted and she must be punished. The change from looking forward to seeing and admiring her, to hating and wanted to kill her, took place in less than two hours.

When he got home there was no doubt in his mind the following night she would be dead. He would shoot her the moment she showed in her room and it was dark enough for him to hide and be out of sight.

He was still hyped up and ready to pull the trigger. All the settings on his rifle were right for the distance, the scope adjusted for night vision, all set just waiting for her to show.

When she finally entered the room and was in the cross hairs of his rifle, he hesitated and thought he would wait until she was undressed. She took her time taking of her make-up first, untied her hair then got undressed and disappeared into the bathroom. He had to wait now until she got out of the shower.

When she appeared again in the bedroom totally naked water still dripping from her breasts onto her belly and her nipples erect, she was facing the window. He could see her through the scope, giving him the illusion that he could touch her if he wanted to. She was massaging her magnificent body from her breasts down to her lower belly. He was so aroused by this sexy view of her that he automatically took his rigid penis in his hand and began masturbating. When he climaxed, she was still looking outside facing him. It was almost like she was waiting until he climaxed before turning around and turning off the light.

Out of pure frustration he grabbed the rifle and fired a bullet through the window next to her room. Cursing himself for this stupid act, he scrambled to collect all his gear and got out of there.

On the way home he was well aware of what the consequences would be if they could prove that he had fired the shot. They could not trace the rifle to him because he had used his fake ID to purchase it. He still felt that he should get rid of the rifle right away. If they found the rifle in his house, ballistics would show that this was the rifle used to fire at the house and that would be enough to convict him. He needed to wipe his fingerprints from the rifle and bury the stupid thing or throw it in the Gulf of Mexico.

He decided to bury it in the woods. He knew exactly where and it was a place he could go back to and retrieve it if necessary.

He got rid of the rifle and went home. He needed to cook up an alibi for tonight. Before he left the house earlier he told his mother that he was in his room watching a movie. He sneaked back into the house and went to see his mother saying that the movie was over and that he was going to bed. She looked a bit puzzled because he never told her what he was doing or where he went, but she said goodnight without any further comment. John knew that when the police came to their house and asked where he was that night she would only remember that he was watching a movie in his room.

Fabricating an alibi was one thing. Having people like Carla and the police force believe him would be more complicated. The police would be looking for evidence and he for sure would be their prime suspect. He would have to come up with a solid alibi.

He should get rid of the clothes and shoes he was wearing that night. Put them in a dumpster on the other side of town or burn them.

His father wanted to know why he wanted to see his
Psychiatric Evaluation Report. John angry responded,
"That's a fucking stupid question. Now why would I want
to know whether I'm a lunatic, a serial killer, a sex maniac,
a retard, or all of the above?"

"No need to be vulgar." his father said and handed him
the report.

John left the room muttering, "Dumb ass." He read
the report but had a hard time translating the psycho
mumbo-jumbo into a language he understood.

Luckily there was the thesaurus on the internet
to help him out. The summary was that he had ADD
(Attention Deficit Disorder)
The symptoms are:
- Inattention
- Hyperactivity
- Impulsivity

He was also diagnosed with a type of bipolar disorder
called Hypomanic Episode Symptoms. The symptoms are:
- Inflated self-esteem
- Increase in goal-directive activities, either socially,
  work or sexuality
- Excessive involvement in pleasurable activities,
  usually with a high potential of bad consequences.

Both of these disorders can be treated with medicine
and psychiatric consultations.

The report mentioned that both these disorders,
if not treated properly, would lead to a troublesome
existence especially during the maturity phase of the
individual.

John was quiet for a time trying to digest this
information. He wandered if all of his problems could
have been avoided if he had been treated properly. And

why wasn't he treated for these disorders? Shouldn't his parents or teachers have noticed that there were problems with his behavior and attitude and that he needed help?

He had no illusions that his parents would have noticed. They hardly noticed that their children existed. But teachers should have. They were with him every day. There were enough complaints and visits to the principal's office. These were usually signs of young people in some kind of trouble. I'm surprised that they never had my parents come to school to inform them of my behavior. I will ask my basketball coach. He's the assistant principal. Maybe he will know why that never happened.

When John got in touch with his coach and asked him about it there was a long silence until the coach finally said, "Listen John, I recall this very well. The principal, the nurse and I have discussed your situation several times. The principal talked about it with your parents on different occasions but got the same negative attitude from your father.

"He knew what was best for his son, and his son was a Witherspoon and nobody in his family had ever needed psychiatric help. What you struggled with were just adolescent tribulations and you would outgrow it.

"This was as much as the principal was allowed to do. He even contacted the District High School Superintendent about this situation and was told that this was all he could and was allowed to do."

John thanked the coach for this inside information and promised to keep the source a secret. He wasn't sure what to do next. Was it too late for him to get treatment for these disorders? Was this something you had to treat when you were younger? He didn't know and decided to make an appointment with the psychiatrist who did the evaluation.

Getting rid of Carla was now no longer an important issue. Talking to her was now imperative. She had to know why he behaved like he did. This became very important to him. It may not change her behavior toward him, but she has to know.

The psychiatrist told him that it was not too late, but it would take much longer to get this under control than it would have been if treated at a younger age. He warned him of the side effects of the medicine and that it would take several months before all the symptoms were gone.

"That means that you will still have these mood swings and all the other symptoms for a while. You will not see or feel any results for six to eight weeks after you start this medication.

"Many patients, due to the disorder, don't have the patience to continue taking their medicine when they don't see immediate results. There are also side effects, and once you stop taking the medicine for a couple of weeks you have to start from ground zero. It requires a lot of willpower. And I recommend that you confide in a good friend or relative who will then become your sponsor, and can help you when the disorder takes over and you are no longer in control. Try to avoid confrontational situations. Don't get into arguments. Postpone important decisions whenever you can. Be with people who are fighting the same battle. Go to meetings where your issues are common and people are not afraid to talk about it.

"Believe me it's not easy' I don't want to discourage you, but it is better that you know so you don't expect miracles after a couple of weeks, because it's a long process."

John left the doctor's office depressed but also pleased that he had taking this first step and that he knew what was in front of him, a difficult time to say the least. He was worried that he had gotten into so much trouble that whatever he did, it would be too late. His reputation was established and nothing could change that. He felt that the only way out was to disappear and start all over in a foreign country. Strange that a couple of weeks ago that seemed so exciting and he was really looking forward to going to Brazil, now all of a sudden this looked like a prison sentence instead of a new and promising exciting life.

He was also concerned that he, at any time could relapse and become a major jerk and do the things that put him in a situation he was in now. Even if I start the medication today he thought. I wouldn't be able to control my emotions for a couple of months.

He began to compare himself with Dr Jekyll and Mr. Hyde and came to the conclusion that the only way to avoid more problems and confrontations was to check into a rehab center for patients with similar problems and stay there until these disorders were under control.

Unfortunately for him, his last example of impulsivity, shooting at a residence with a scoped rifle, put him back in jeopardy and a target for the local police. The fact that this weapon was a high powered rifle, not a BB gun, would trigger a serious investigation from the legal system. This would not be classified as a prank from some bored teenagers.

The worst scenario would be if they could prove that he fired that rifle. He would be charged with attempted murder. He must lay low for a while and not make any attempts to contact Carla or Glenn with the intent of getting together.

Soon as this blew over he would make arrangements to go to a rehab center and try to succeed this time, not just biding his time but working at it.

As expected, a day after the shooting the police appeared at John's house and asked if they could come in to talk to John and ask him a few questions. When John asked them why they wanted to ask him some questions, the corporal said. "This is in regard to an ongoing investigation and we have reason to believe that you can help us. In cases like this we ask the questions and you answer them, not the other way around. If you have a problem with that we'll ask you to come with us to the police station for questioning. It's up to you."

John thought, you arrogant prick, but said, "It's okay with me, go ahead ask your questions."

"Where were you last night between 8PM and 10PM?"

"I was home watching a movie and having a beer in my room."

"Is there anyone who can confirm this?"

"Yes my mother was home and she can confirm this, I went downstairs to get a beer from the fridge."

"Anyone else saw you?"

"Not that I know of. My mother and I were the only ones in the house last night. My father came home around 10:30 and must have seen my car in the garage."

"Do you have a rifle."

"No I don't"

"Is there anyone you could borrow a rifle from?"

"I have no idea. I don't know who has a rifle and if I knew they had one I still wouldn't know that I could borrow it."

"Would it be possible for you to leave the house last night without your mother knowing it, and get back in later?"

"I don't know but I don't think so, besides I went down twice during that period to get a beer."

"But it would be possible."

"That's it." John said. "I've had enough of your stupid innuendo questions and I refuse to answer any more questions without my lawyer being present. You can take me to the police station after I call my lawyer."

"That won't be necessary, that's all we have for the time being. We'll get in touch with you at some later date."

After they left, John called his lawyer and explained what had just happened. "They wouldn't tell me what this was all about. Maybe you can find out and let me know."

His lawyer said, "If you know what this is about you better let me know if you want me to defend you."

"I was home and I don't know why they came to me."

An hour later his lawyer called him back and said,

"You better have an ironclad alibi for your whereabouts last night. Somebody took a shot at that girl Carla, luckily nobody got hit. Can you come to my office tomorrow? We have to talk about this incident. I know you told me you were not involved but we still have to talk. The local police have you as their prime suspect. Innocent or not we still have to be ready. They're going to claim that you have a motive. You made threats that you were going to kill her. They are focusing on you."

John was sure that he had left no evidence and they didn't know where he was hiding the gun. Could they have found out through ballistics from where the bullet was fired? He became a little more nervous. Could he have left something that might have his DNA on it?

When he walked into the lawyer's office he immediately saw the concern on the Attorney's face. The lawyer said, "Tell me the truth. You can't afford to play games with me on this one. They found the spot from where the rifle was fired. They have a bunch of technicians out there looking for prints, DNA samples, imprints on the grass, shoe prints and God knows what else. They will find something. They always do especially if they have a suspect they want to nail on the cross. "So buddy, tell me what happened and what kind of alibi you have."

John knew that he had to come clean with his so he told him the truth, everything from his intention to kill her to his change of hearth and pulling the trigger out of frustration but not aiming at her room.

The lawyer did not comment or make any judgmental remarks. He asked where the rifle was, what happened with the clothes and shoes you wore, did he get rid of spare bullets, can we beef up the alibi, did anybody see him at the scene, were you drinking, smoking, eating, chewing gum anything you could have left there that could lead to you and where he parked park his car..

They spent hours going over the details, minute by minute that he was there, every move he made until the lawyer was satisfied that no stone was left unturned

When John got back home he was exhausted but still called Glenn to find out what Carla had to say about the shooting. Glenn said she refused to talk to him but Stella called him and said that Carla would not even consider talking to you any longer. She was convinced that he was trying to kill her or scare her to death. She had no doubt in her mind that it was John who had shot at her house.

Glenn said, "She's not the only one who thinks it was you. The word is even out that you were arrested, but obviously that's not the case yet. The police came to my house and asked me where I was that night, insinuating that I might have been involved. Luckily, I had a good alibi I was at a meeting and several people can confirm that."

After this phone call John's state of mind made a 180 degree turn and anger started to build up, anger mostly because things were not the way he wanted them to be. This made him feel that the whole world was conspiring against him, spearheaded by Carla and Glenn. The more his sick mind thought about the situation he was in, the more he was convinced that when Carla and Glenn were eliminated and he was safely in Brazil, all would be well and his problems would be solved.

He blamed himself for only one thing and that was that he turned soft and thought that this bitch would listen to reason. He now knew that was his mistake and he vowed it would not happen again. This time, both their fates were sealed and it would happen soon. No more delays. His original plan would be executed sometime this week.

This psychiatric bullshit fooled me and made me lose my focus on what I needed to do. My Dad was right for once. I don't need a psychiatrist to tell me what I should do and then put me on drugs that make me feel like a zombie. He can stick his medicine up his ass, to think that I almost committed myself to a rehab facility for several months. It's scary to know that a shrink can convince a normal person that he has to go through that shit when there really is nothing wrong with them.

The original plan was that once Carla had decided to talk to him, Glenn would pick him up first and then go to Carla's house and pick her up. John would sit in the back seat and as soon as Carla was in the car he would suggest that they drive to the marina. He would say that this was a bit out of town but when we get on board my father's yacht they would be safe. He would say that he felt nervous because if he got caught that close to Carla he would end up in prison.

Once they were on board he would flex cuff them and drive the boat out into the gulf. That is where he would kill both and dump them overboard. He had weights and cable ready to attach to their bodies so they wouldn't float to the surface. He had not decided yet if he would rape Carla or not, this would be a last minute decision.

The only change from this original plan was that Glenn would not willingly drive to Carla's house and that Carla would refuse to voluntarily get into a car with Glenn and John. Getting Glenn into his car would not be a problem, and once in the car he would force him at gunpoint to drive them to her house. They would wait until she walked the dog and then he would get out of the car and force her into the front seat next to Glenn. With a gun pointing at his head he would have no choice but to drive them to the marina.

He already had the route mapped out so that they would avoid going through town. This was the modified plan and this was how it would be done. He would try to find out what night she would be alone in the house. Usually her parents were in church on Sunday night, he must check that out because he preferred to have her being home alone.

He felt that he was back in control and everything seemed to be in place for the finale.

Chapter 21

Carla had just turned the lights off when the sound of breaking glass made her jump up in bed and turns the light back on. At the same time Robert ran into her room asking if she was all right.

She said, "I'm fine. What happened? I heard the sound of glass breaking and something like a car backfiring."

That wasn't a car Robert said. "That was a high powered rifle shot and it must have hit one of our windows. Let's find out which one." It didn't take long to find the room that was hit. Shattered glass was all over the room and the bullet had gone through the facing wall. They found it lodged in the wall in the hallway. Robert said, "Don't touch it. It may have fingerprints on it."

Five minutes after they called the police, they showed up and warned everybody not to touch anything and they would seal off the room until their technicians came up to do their magic.

Carla and Mary were both shaken up. Robert was calm now that he knew that nobody was hurt. His war experience came in handy in situations like this. The enemy was gone so there was no immediate danger.

He asked Carla, "Do you think this Witherspoon kid could be stupid enough to do something like this or can you think of somebody else?"

Carla said, "Of course I have no proof, but he is definitely capable of something like this. I don't think he was trying to hit me. I believe it to be a scare tactic. I can't think of anybody else who is mad enough at me to shoot me."

Robert said, "The police will ask all of us if we have any idea who could have done this but I'm sure that kid must already be high on their list of suspects."

It was way beyond midnight and Carla was debating if she should call Stella or wait to call her in the morning. She asked Robert for advice and he said.

"The chances of this happening again tonight are slim, but I think you should let her know. It doesn't matter if there is any danger to her or not. She will be pissed off if you don't call her now."

Carla smiled "You're right I'll never hear the end of this if I don't." She called, and of course Stella got all excited and wanted to come over right away. Her mother didn't think that was a good idea but also knew she would have to physically constrain her to keep her home, so she reluctantly agreed if it was all right with Mary and Robert. Stella didn't hear most of it because she was already in her car.

When Stella arrived at the Pott's house everybody was in the kitchen drinking fresh made coffee and preparing sandwiches. Nobody was going to sleep that night anyway. The police and their techs were all over the place. They already were convinced that the shooter must have been on the other side of the lake and were out there in force trying to find evidence of some kind.

So far the police had no evidence to justify charges against John, but everybody on the force was convinced that he was the perpetrator and they kept harassing him. They brought him back to the station for further questioning, with his lawyer present. They kept repeating all the questions they had asked him before, hoping that he would make a mistake and give them a different answer, this has not happened so far.

This time John lost his cool and in his belligerent tone of voice asked them how many more fucking times they were going to ask him the same fucking stupid questions. The sergeant looked at him and in a very calm voice said, "First of all I don't like this kind of language in my station and secondly I am going to ask you these fucking stupid questions as many fucking times as I want to. Are we fucking clear on that, you can go now but we will meet again."

"John's lawyer shook his head and sarcastically asked John if that outburst was necessary. Were you just trying to be funny? Let me answer my own question. No it was not necessary and no, it was not funny either, you know what it was, it was stupid with a capital S. Stupid and bordering on insanity."

Listen to me carefully John. "One more shenanigan like this in my presence and you will have to look for another lawyer. I know you feel that with the outrageous fees I charge your dad for your defense you are allowed to do whatever you want and say whatever you want. Well, you are wrong I don't need this shit. I'm not that desperate for money. I have a reputation to protect, which is far more important than you are." He left the police station without giving John the chance to respond to his lecture.

Who the fuck does he think he is? John thought. These goddamn lawyers are all the same. They just grab your money for doing virtually nothing in return. I would fire his ass in a New York minute, but since I won't be here much longer, why bother?

I need to focus on my plan; Carla's parents routine had not changed on Sundays. They have an early dinner in the city and then a meeting in church. They're out of the house from 5:00PM until approximately 8:30PM. He still needed to make sure that Glenn was around this Sunday and would join him for a ride during that time span. He would have to come up with a reason for Glenn to drive his car. He would use his mother's car, a black Suburban less conspicuous than his red Corvette.

For a while he was thinking of shipping his car to Brazil but for once common sense prevailed, and he realized that this would be too easy to trace. The date was set, this coming Sunday four days from now. He would be free at last, the bitch and his double crossing friend would be gone forever and he could finally start his new life in a different environment, far away from a family that didn't give a shit about him anyway.

He never considered that his new life could be a lot more complicated than he thought it would be. For instance, he did not speak a word of Portuguese and only the well-educated people in Brazil spoke some English. He would be all by himself, and unless he went back to school or got a job it would be hard to make friends. He had no intention of doing either one.

There will be a lot of people wanting to hang out with him, but it would only be because he could afford to throw his money around and they would take advantage of this situation.

He only saw Rio de Janeiro as sun kissed beaches with gorgeous girls half naked sunbathing and parties in famous night clubs with these same girls. He had no idea that Rio was a city with one of the highest crime rates in the world. A young kid with lots of money and no roots would be an easy target for the underground low lives of Rio.

He was a strong believer in the philosophy of live for today and to hell with tomorrow." This being another symptom of his bipolar disorder.

He had procured his father's gun from his desk in the study. That gun had been there for ages, had never been used and his father wouldn't miss it, if he even remembered that he had it.

That Sunday morning John called Glenn and asked him if he would have dinner with him that evening just for old time sakes and talk a little bit about the Carla situation. Glenn was not comfortable with this and said, "I would like to have dinner with you, but I rather not talk too much about Carla. This always seems to create tension between us."

John immediately agreed not to mention Carla at all, and he would pick Glenn up at five o clock.

John had chosen a restaurant that he knew Glenn liked a lot, maybe hoping that this would soften Glenn up a bit and get a conversation going. Lately when they talked on the phone there was a certain tension in the air. He wanted Glenn to be at ease and make sure that he didn't suspect that this was more than just dinner. He must be unaware that this was not going to end on a friendly note.

After dinner, John asked Glenn if he could drive to his house, the reason being that after dark the police always seem to stop young drivers, and lately he was not on good terms with the local cops. They probably would find something or invent something so they could handcuff me for a while and then let him go.

Glenn said, "Okay I'll drive to your house that's not a problem."

When they got to the car John said "I'll sit in the back so it looks like there is only one person in the car, they usually don't stop singles."

Glenn said, "That's fine," and thought, he really is getting paranoid. He must be in more trouble than I know of.

Soon as they were moving, John said, "I want you to drive to Carla's house." Glenn reacted by putting his foot on the brake and stopping the car. He turned around and stared into the barrel of a gun, John said "You don't have much of a choice you know so keep going before I get nervous and you don't want that when my finger is on the trigger."

"Why the hell do you want to go to Carla's house? Glenn demanded. All she has to do is call 911 and your ass is in jail. And what's with the gun are you completely out of your mind?"

"Just keep your stupid fucking mouth shut and drive. Remember, this gun is loaded and if you don't drive me there than I don't have any reason to keep you around. Get it?"

Glenn got scared and kept on driving toward Carla's house, thinking, what can I do to calm him down. He knew from experience that when John was like this, out of control, there was little or nothing anybody could do. Is he going to repeat this kidnapping thing again or what does he have in mind? Obviously nothing good.

They entered the street where Carla lived and John said. "Stop here, they were maybe a few hundred yards away from her house where they were parked. Turn the motor off; we are waiting here for a while."

"I will tell you what I want you to do. The moment she comes out of the house you start the car and drive toward here, you stop next to her. I'll take it from there. Now I want you to put both hands on the steering wheel in the position like you were driving. Don't ask me why just do it."

Glenn did like he was told and John leaned over and quickly flex cuffed Glenn's hands to the steering wheel? Glenn said, "How do you expect me to drive with my hands tied to the steering wheel?

There is enough slack so that you can drive, John replied. "Now shut up I need to concentrate." At that time a car slowed down in front of Carla's house and turned into the driveway. The garage door closed behind it'

John started cursing' What are they doing here? It's only seven o clock. They're not supposed to be here before eight o clock or later. His first reaction was to abort the operation, but then he thought what will I do with Glenn? No this must be done tonight. It shouldn't make any difference whether they were home or not, as long as Carla walks the dog by herself.

John had a small bottle of chloroform and a rag in the car which he was going to use on Carla as soon as he got out of the car.

That Sunday evening, Stella was visiting with Carla and they decided to order a pizza rather than cook or go out for dinner.

Their main topic of conversation was still the shooting. It was still a mystery to all of them why the window next to her room was the target. He must have seen the light in her room seconds before he pulled the trigger.

Carla said, "That's why I know he didn't shoot to kill me. He just wanted to send the message. Don't screw with me I can hurt you. No matter what his objective was if the cops can prove that he did it he is going to jail for a long time."

Stella said, "That's where he should be anyway."

At that time they heard the garage door opening and a car drive in. They were not expecting Mary and Robert so when they entered the living room, Carla asked is everything all right.

Yes, we're fine, Mary said "Robert just didn't feel like church tonight. He ate like a pig and can't stay awake when he does that."

Stella said. "We were just going to walk Ginger. Care to join us?" Mary said, "No, you guys go ahead Ginger gets a better work out with you two."

Carla said, "Okay let's go then before it gets too dark"

Stella said, "I need to go to the bathroom first. You take her outside because she is already jumping at the bit to go. Just wait in front of the house for me, I'll be right there." Carla went outside with Ginger waiting for Stella to join her'

Ginger, she said "stay here." There was a black SUV coming down the street that stopped right in front of the house. She looked inside and saw Glenn sitting at the driver's seat. Before she could ask what he was doing there, the back door flew open and John jumped on her and at the same time put a sweet smelling rag over her mouth.

John opened the passenger's door and shoved Carla inside the car. At that time Stella just opened the front door and saw John closing the car door. She didn't see Carla, but immediately understood what was going on.

She wasted no time and jumped on John's back, clawing at his face with both hands. She barely missed his eyes but deeply gouged his face with her fingernails while shouting, "You bastard! You're not getting away with this!" She then saw the gun in his raised hand. He hit her on the head with it and she went down, unconscious.

Robert heard the dog barking outside and thought that's strange. She almost never barks. He went outside to find out what was going on and found Stella lying on the pavement with blood all over her face and no sign of Carla. Robert called "Mary go dial 911. Tell them there is a girl badly wounded and one more than likely being kidnapped."

Mary wanted to say something, but Robert said "Call first and come outside," Mary did what she was told and then came outside. Mary was once an assistant nurse in an emergency clinic so she looked at Stella's head and said, "I think it's just bleeding badly. But I don't think there's a skull fracture. Let me get something to clean the wound." She only then realized that the kidnapped girl was Carla.

She started to cry but Robert firmly said, "Mary this is no time for tears. Go get something to clean Stella's head wound." At that time Stella groaned and slowly opened her eyes, she was barely able to tell them what had happened to Carla,

Robert said, "Don't move you were hit on the head and we don't know where Carla is."

Stella's head started to clear and her memory of what had happened returned. She said "John and Glenn kidnapped her again."

The police and the Medical Emergency crew arrived. Robert told the police what little he knew and after the medics had examined Stella she joined them and told

the police what she saw. She confirmed that it was John
Witherspoon and Glenn Evans who kidnapped Carla and
drove away in a black Suburban with Glenn at the wheel.

"Who hit you?" The sergeant wanted to know.

"John hit me with a gun, Stella answered, his face
is bleeding. I remember that I clawed his face with my
fingernails and he was bleeding pretty good."

The sergeant then began barking orders at the
officers who were with him and called the station to put
an alert out to look for a black Suburban last seen at the
scene of the kidnapping, license plate unknown but the
vehicle could belong to The Witherspoon's or the Evans.
The persons in the car were John Witherspoon and Glenn
Evans, the suspected kidnappers and the kidnapped girl
Carla Potts, Glenn is driving the car. The girl is in the
front passenger's seat while John is in the back seat. John
is armed with a hand gun.

They left a police officer at the house for the remote
possibility that they would call and make demands for
the release of the victim. It was highly unlikely that this
would happen.

Half an hour later the officer got a call on his cell
phone and informed them that the Suburban was John's
mother's car and that it was missing. The police now had
a black Suburban and a license number to look for. They
felt that if the kidnappers kept on driving they would be
apprehended shortly, traffic in and around Jamesville on a
Sunday night was not that heavy.

Two hours later the phone rang and it was the police
reporting that they had found the Suburban on the pier of
the Jamesville marina and that the yacht belonging to the
Weatherspoon's family was gone from his mooring. They
also said that there was a lot of blood on the back seat of

the car, which would indicate that Stella did an excellent job on John's face. This would make the search for them a lot easier.

The Coast guard was on alert and is searching for the vessel. They didn't expect to locate the yacht during the night because they have no idea where it was heading. More than likely it was sailing without any of its lights on.

The mood at Carla's house was grim and although Stella's head was still hurting, she was the one who tried to keep thei spirit up by saying, "Carla is a smart girl she'll find a way to escape these morons. She has done it before. I'm sure she can do it again."

This of course did not brighten the atmosphere a hell of a lot. At about three O' clock in the morning they decided to get some sleep realizing that the Coast guard wouldn't be able to find her in the dark. They probably have stopped looking for her and would resume their search at daybreak.

Chapter 22

When Carla came out of the chloroform induced sleep, she was disoriented and had no recollection of what had happened to her or where she was. The room she was in looked very small and had no windows. It was also very dark. The only light came from a tiny light bulb on the ceiling. The room looked more like a storage place than a room people would live in.

She slowly came out of the fog that was clouding her brain. She also found out that she had a hell of a headache and a faint sweet taste in her mouth. The stuff in the room was all nautical, an old anchor, something that could have been a compass, little flags and an old wooden steering wheel. Also yards of thick rope.

When her head became more or less normal and she felt the room slightly swaying, she knew that she was on a boat.

That's when she remembered Glenn driving a car and John attacking her. Oh my God, she thought. These idiots have kidnapped me again. They must be on drugs. No sane person would do this twice. She also vaguely remembered seeing Stella coming out of the house but she wasn't sure of that.

Is this nightmare happening to me for a second time, she thought. This can't be true. What do they have in their sick mind? Am I going to be their sex slave again, this time on a ship of some sort?

Where are they anyway? Should I make noise to let them know I'm awake or just stay here and see what happens?

The choice was made for her as John opened the door and said, "Surprise, I assume you didn't expect to see me again in control of your destiny, but come with me. You're friend is here with you."

Oh no she thought they took Stella as well.

When he shoved her into another room, a fairly large room with comfortable furniture and big square windows showing nothing but wavy water, she knew they were far from shore. The friend was not Stella but a handcuffed Glenn who looked at her sadly and said. "I'm sorry Carla, he held a gun to my head and had me flex cuffed to the car's steering wheel. We are both his prisoners and I have no idea what his intentions are. All I know is that he is insane."

John piped in with, "Now Glenn that's not a nice way to talk about your friend and cousin. But right now I have to go on deck and make sure we stay on course. I'm sorry, Carla, but I know how ingenious you are so just for everybody's safety I will have to flex cuff you too."

When this was done he went up to the deck. They heard him rev up the engine and felt a surge in speed. He was obviously in a hurry to get somewhere.

The real reason he was increasing speed was that he wanted to be out of range of the US Coast Guard before daybreak. He felt that the Mexican waters would be a lot safer for him.

Another serious problem he had was that he could only go from A to B if he used the GPS. He didn't know whether the GPS system was a one way device or could it track the source of the user and that way find the ·

location of the boat. He could stay close to the shore but a yacht that size sailing close to the shore might attract the Coast Guard thinking that they had a problem or were delivering drugs.

Getting lost in the middle of the gulf was also not a desirable situation, so he would use the GPS sporadically and keep it turned off most of the time.

He was aware that they were looking for him. The fact that Stella saw him and the car had erased the time he had counted on, time he thought he had if they would not have known so early that he would use the boat. He figured he would be in Mexican waters before they discovered that. He became aware that he screwed up by using his mother's car.

So far his plan had not worked out the way he figured it would. Killing two people with the Coast Guard breathing down his neck could very easily be the death penalty for him if he got caught. He decided to change strategy until he was safe in International waters.

He would apologize to Glenn and Carla for the way he brought them on the yacht. He would also cut the flex cuffs and tell them that they were his guests. He knew that this would sound like a lot of bullshit and both would be very suspicious, but that was all right. If by any chance the Coast Guard would catch up with him, they could not say that they were injured or threatened by him. He would explain his actions, and that he needed to talk to both of them and that she had refused to meet with him. He now knew that this was a stupid thing to do, but you don't get the death penalty for being stupid.

He was not overly concerned. The Gulf of Mexico was a big body of water and finding a yacht that could have gone in any direction was not an easy task.

He checked their position with the GPS and found that they were way off course, heading for Vera Cruz instead of Port Isabel. His original plan was to moor at Port Isabel after he had taken care of Carla and Glenn. He now has to change his plan and sail into Mexico. He couldn't risk entering a port or marina in Texas. This was a major setback for him because his papers and a sizable amount of money were waiting in a P.O. Box in Port Isabel. No matter where he docked he would have to go back and collect these documents and his cash.

He changed course and put the vessel on auto pilot, then went down to try to sell his story to Carla and Glenn.

He cut the flex cuffs and said that he was sorry for what he had to do, but he saw no other way to get them together and talk. He knew it was not the way he should have done it, but he was desperate to tell them his story.

Glenn was suspicious but didn't say anything, Carla blurted out, "Cut the bullshit John, We know you better than to fall for this crap. You want us to believe that you drugged me with a dangerous chemical, you forced Glenn at gunpoint in your car and almost killed Stella, just to talk to us?

"You must think that we are complete morons. Now what is it that you really want us for? You're as nervous as a kitten on a hot tin roof. You run back and forth, you look scared and are totally out of control. What the hell is going on? Oh, and by the way these bloody streaks on your face, are they part of a disguise? If they are, it's not very successful."

John was unprepared and said. "Your butch friend did that to me."

"Oh, Carla said, "Were back to our old self again. This is the John we know, judgmental, abusive, insulting, the real you. Stella did this to you. Wow you're lucky; because I'm sure she's disappointed she didn't scratch your eyes out.

"Now, you didn't answer my question what are your plans for us? Rape me and then throw me overboard? Of course you will have to kill Glenn as well. You can't afford to let him live."

John's face showed that she hit the jackpot, but he strongly denied her accusations and said that she had it all wrong. He really just wanted to talk to them.

"We'll talk later. I have to go on deck and make sure we are still on course he said. "And quickly ran up to the deck.

The Coast Guard in Galveston had been picking up signals from an unknown vessel in the Gulf but they were so sporadic that they were unable so far to locate the source. Since they were on alert to find a yacht that had left the marina in Jamesville, destination unknown, with two kidnapped victims on board, they scanned their monitors and listened to their audio systems with a specially assigned crew, focused on finding this vessel.

John's concerns had increased, bordering on panic. His goal had been to get Carla and John on board. Now that he had them he didn't know what to do with them.

His biggest problem, though, was the fact that he had no idea where he was and where he was heading. He was afraid to use the GPS for fear that the Coast Guard would track him down. With daylight only a couple of hours away, it would make it so much easier for them to locate the yacht. The sea was calm, but he couldn't see any stars in the sky. There must be a thick cloud cover, which was good because that would narrow down the visibility of the helicopters looking for them. But these clouds could disappear at a moment's notice. He had to take the risk of using the GPS more often to get to Mexico as fast as this boat would go.

He switched the GPS on and saw that for the last hour or so they have been drifting away from the Mexican coast. He needed to use the GPS. He simply was not a good enough sailor to do without it. Glenn was an excellent sailor. He could probably do it without the GPS, but he doubted that under the circumstances he could trust Glenn.

Downstairs in the salon, Carla and Glenn were discussing what options they had to get out of this precarious situation they were in. Attacking John unexpectedly and taking control was probably the only viable option they had. The problem was that he was carrying a gun. They would have to find some sort of a weapon they could use before he had the chance to use his gun. They knew that if threatened he would use the gun on them. They had to come up with something heavy to hit him on the head so they could take the gun away from him. This could work if they found something that would do the job. They started to look for it but heard footsteps coming down the stairs, so they sat down waiting for him to enter the room.

They saw right off the bat that he was in a foul mood. Nobody said anything until John broke the silence and said, "What have you two been talking about while I was out there? I don't expect you to tell me what you are planning to do, but let me tell you what my plan is. Since I obviously can't return to the Jamesville marina, or any marina in the US, I'm heading to a port in Mexico where I will put you ashore.

"My destination after that is none of your business, but I will not return to the US. You will probably never see me again after you get on shore. I know you won't miss me and, frankly, I will not miss you either. Don't be afraid that I will come after you again for whatever reason. I will be far away from Jamesville and have no intention of ever coming back."

He went back to the bridge. Carla spoke first and said to Glenn, "I don't believe a word of what he is saying. He just wants us to be assured that nothing will happen to us so we won't cause any trouble for him while he is trying to get to a safe haven."

Glenn nodded, "He has something up his sleeve. He can't be trusted I know that a couple of months ago all he could talk about was to getting rid of you for good. You're right, we must take him out. I know him well enough that when he is behaving like he is now, bad things are bound to happen."

Carla was pleasantly surprised that Glenn was so assertive and willing to take action against his former buddy. They kept looking for something heavy that could be used as a weapon. They found a large butcher's knife but realized that neither one of them would be able to stab him. The other thing that could do the job of taking him out of commission was a table lamp with a solid brass base. This was the only heavy object that was not bolted down so they would use it to hit him on the head.

Daylight broke and there was still a low cloud cover that made John feel more secure about his chances to reach Mexico before the Coast Guard spotted him. He risked another spell with the GPS and saw that he was now on course for Port Isabel. Still a long way off but at least they were going in the right direction. With a little bit of luck he would make it.

The wind had picked up and the Gulf had become a little more agitated than before, but John considered that to be in his favor. It was harder to detect a boat in wavy waters than it was when the sea was smooth like a mirror. What he needed now was some shut eye. He had been awake for more than twenty four hours. He desperately needed some sleep, at least a couple of hours. He would lock the door of the salon so the two of them could conspire to their heart's content but not do anything. He would lock himself in as soon as he put the vessel on course and go to automatic pilot with the coordinates set for Port Isabel.

Once he was out of the US Coast Guard reach and far into Mexican territory he would take care of them. Glenn would go first. He would take him on deck close to the railing, shoot him, put the heavy chains on the body and heave his body overboard. Then he must decide whether he was going to have sex with the bitch or just dump her overboard the same way as Glenn.

He would do this when the yacht was in deep water, and chances were good that their bodies would never be found.

He locked their room door and then locked himself in before he took a nap. Tired as he was he only slept for two hours and then went back to the bridge to check on their position. He quickly scanned the GPS and made a slight change of course. They were making progress and he figured to be in Mexican waters within six to eight hours. He was not familiar with any of the Mexican ports where he could dock. He needed to look at a chart because he wanted to dock in a fairly big port or marina. He also toyed with the idea of anchoring offshore and using the raft to sail to the beach, close enough to a town from where he could rent a car and drive to Port Isabel. He would collect all his valuables and immediately return to Mexico. He would get on a local airline flight to Mexico City and fly from there to Brazil.

The Galveston Coast Guard continued to monitor all GPS signals in the area and had intercepted a few hits that they assumed came from the yacht they were looking for. Based on that assumption, they were fairly sure that this vessel was moving west in the direction of the Mexican Gulf coast. They transmitted this information to the search planes who were now concentrating their efforts in that area. There still was a low cloud formation that made the search much more difficult. They had to be almost right on top of a vessel before they could see it.

It was now early morning when John entered the salon; Carla and Glen were both awake and anxious to hear what John had to say. Their plan on how to overpower John was simple. Next time when they heard him coming down, Glenn would stand behind the door with the lamp raised above his head and soon as John closed the door he would hit him on the head with it. They would then both jump on him and get the gun out of his hands. Hopefully the blow to his head would knock him unconscious.

John just told them that they were still on course and probably would be in Mexico late that same afternoon,

He heard a noise outside that sounded frightfully like whirling helicopter blades. He ran upstairs and he could now tell that there were actually aircrafts in the area, John looked all around but couldn't see them. The noise seemed to fade away as if the helicopter was getting farther away from the yacht. He couldn't tell where they were going or if they knew that he was in this area and would come back circling around until they found them. There was, of course, the possibility that the chopper was not the Coast Guard at all but one of the commuting helicopters that picked up workers on the drilling rigs in the gulf. There were hundreds of these rigs. Nevertheless he was not taking any risks. He must stop using the GPS and just keep going west. He would eventually land somewhere in Mexico. He had plenty of gas. That would not be a problem. Ending up in the boondocks in Mexico was better than being chased by the Coast Guard; he knew that he could not outrun their speed boats. He wanted to move as fast as possible, but he was already running at a high speed, very close to the red mark on the speedometer. He slightly increased the speed till the speedometer was right on the red arrow. That was as fast as these twin motors would go before blowing up.

He put the yacht back on autopilot due west and went downstairs. When he opened the door Carla stood right in front of him. He didn't see Glenn and when he closed the door he glimpsed an object descending on him that hit him on the head. He then saw Glenn raising the same object ready to deliver a second blow. Glenn hesitated for a split second, making sure that a second hit was necessary. This gave John enough time to pull the gun out of his pocket and pull the trigger. Glenn looked surprised, he dropped the lamp and fell on the floor blood painting his shirt bright red. The bullet had hit his shoulder and he was obviously in much pain.

Carla stood speechless staring at Glenn in disbelief, John pointed the gun at her and said, "If you don't get your ass in that chair and stay there, you're next. I have plenty of ammunition so don't tempt me."

He then went to check on Glenn, who was groaning from the pain in his shoulder. When John saw that he hadn't killed Glenn. He said. "You stupid bastard. You're lucky I didn't kill you." The top of his head was hurting and bleeding. He grabbed a wet towel to clean himself off a little. He said to Carla. "Get the first aid kit and see what you can do for him. Not that he deserves it, but I don't want blood all over the place." He thought. Why didn't I kill the bastard? I had the opportunity and didn't take advantage of it. Well he probably will bleed to death anyway.

So it's clear now. They didn't believe my story that I will drop them off unharmed in Mexico. They understand that this will be the end of them very soon. I have to keep them locked up for a little while longer and not give them a chance to attack me again. Next time they may succeed, although I don't think Glenn has much fight left in him. He seems to be hurting pretty bad and is losing lots of blood.

The bitch is the one I need to keep an eye on. She may be desperate after this failure to take me out. Carla was busy with Glenn, trying to stop the bleeding but her mind was focused on how she could stop this monster from killing them both, I'm sure that's what he will do as soon as he know that he is in Mexico where nobody is looking for him. She thought. I will have to act quickly and I can't fail this time.

John was thinking about an article he had read a while ago that in Iraq the US soldiers made the terrorists undress when they were jailed. Apparently when you're in the nude it lowers your spirit and you become more docile. Something to think about.

Carla said, "I don't seem to be able to stop the bleeding. He needs a doctor to remove the bullet and repair the arteries. You should set course for the nearest coast."

John laughed and said, "Well baby that's not going to happen. He'll have to wait till we're in a country where the doctors speak Spanish and that may take a couple of hours. But what if you undress and parade around in the nude. Sexy nurses always pick up a patient's spirits. John she said, "This is serious. He could die if he keeps bleeding like this." "I know it's serious," John responded. "So what are you waiting for? Get undressed. Don't be shy. We've seen you before in the nude. It's not a big deal."

She said. "You're crazy if you think I'm going to run around in the nude."

He said, "I may be crazy, but you are going to run around in the nude, starting right now. If needed I can help you with the undressing part," He grabbed her shirt and tore it off. "Do you need more help or can you do the rest by yourself."

Carla got really scared. She had seen him before like that, and he was capable of doing some crazy stuff. As long as Glenn was with her she always thought that together they could control him to a point. But with Glenn in the condition he was in now, she realized that she was on her own with this mental case.

She slowly started to undress and stopped when she had only her panties on to cover her most private area. He said, "You can keep those on you look a lot sexier with those on than with a bare ass. Since I won't be able to see you much longer like this I want to make the best of it."

Carla thought. What does that mean? It could be that he was going to put her and Glenn on shore somewhere, or it could mean that she wouldn't be alive much longer. He didn't seem to have that lust for her in his eyes like he did at the beach house, I think that he is really concerned that the Coast Guard is closing in on us and that the fear of that is over shadowing his normal sex drive. Raping her at this time is probably not a high priority.

He was thinking that if he rapes her now and the Coast Guard found them, he would face kidnapping and rape charges. She was sure that his obsession with her was still there and that he would force her to have sex with him the moment he felt he was out of the danger zone. She didn't dare think about what would happen after he raped her.

She'd rather jump overboard than let him touch her. She made up her mind that the moment she could see a shoreline and have the opportunity, she would try swimming to land. She preferred to drown rather than being raped and killed afterwards. Anyway, at least I would have given it a try, and if I make it maybe it won't be too late to save Glenn's life. She also thought of jumping overboard when they saw a ship in the distance. She had discussed this escape option with Glenn, but he told her that this wouldn't work. First these ships were all going full speed, and second they wouldn't be close enough to them to see you floating in the waves.

Glenn looked like he was unconscious or maybe asleep. She had the impression that the bleeding had stopped or at least been reduced a lot. She felt his pulse, which was fairly strong. She could see that he was breathing normally, so maybe it was just a flesh wound and no major arteries or vital parts were damaged.

She had put a blanket over him earlier and his body temperature seemed to be normal as far as she could tell without a thermometer.

When John went back to the bridge, Carla wrapped herself in a table cloth because she felt more vulnerable without clothing, even when nobody was there to see. She never felt that way in her own house when she and Stella were often nude together and neither of them found that strange or uncomfortable. But then again, nobody forced them to be nude, nor was she in constant fear that some maniac would burst into her room and sexually abuse her.

Chapter 23

Stella and Janice were, of course, at the Potts house waiting to hear from the police if there was any news. All they knew was that they were on the Witherspoon's yacht probably going full speed towards, Mexico. Nothing more. The Jamesville police assured them that any bit of news they received would be immediately called in to them. There was absolutely no reason whatsoever that the police would keep any news a secret from Carla's family.

At this time there just was no news to tell them. They repeated what the Coast Guard had told them. The few signals that they had picked up all pointed to the yacht being on its way to some place in Mexico.

Not knowing anything was torture for the four of them, each dealing with it in their own way but with a collective feeling of sadness and fear. This kind of situations plays havoc with your emotions. It's like a roller coaster. One moment you feel optimistic and everything will turn out right, and the next moment is like you will never see her again. This repeat itself over and over, leaving you confused and angry that your mind is playing games with you, games that are cruel and scary, games you don't want to play but are forced to participate in.

Mary, just getting over the grieving from her sister's death, saw nothing but doom and could not believe that this wonderful person would have to go through the same demeaning, humiliating and life threatening period twice. She could not comprehend why a human being could be so cruel toward another person. She prayed that Carla would come home safe, but also questioned the almighty why he let things like that happen to somebody like Carla, who deserved a much better life than the one she had lived so far.

Robert was very concerned and scared, also angry with himself that he had not protected her better, knowing that this lunatic had been released from the rehab center and was back in Jamesville.

He felt that he had let his dead Army buddy down by not taking care of his daughter. Carla's father would have handled this differently and would have made sure that this maniac did not have a second chance to harm his child.

Robert was depressed mainly because he felt helpless and that was an unusual experience for him. Normally when something happened to him he would take whatever action was required to fix the problem. This was different. There was nothing he could do but wait. He was also concerned about Mary. She was devastated and would not be able to recover if Carla didn't survive this.

Stella missed Carla more than life itself. She was inconsolable and wanted to talk to nobody, blaming herself for letting Carla go outside without her. She had let that bastard get away when she had the chance to stop him. The fact that he had a gun and used it did nothing to change her mind.

She locked herself up in Carla's room, constantly crying and asking Carla for forgiveness for not being with her when she needed her the most. She vowed that if something real bad happened to Carla she would not rest until she personally killed John. Jail time was not enough punishment for somebody like him.

She could not eat or sleep, nor did she want to. When the phone rang she was the first to pick it up, hope showing on her that face quickly turned to sadness when there was no news.

Janice, although not as close as the others, had come to love Carla as a second daughter and she also had bad feelings about how this would end. She didn't know John but what she did know about him did not give her a good feeling.

She was, of course, very concerned about how Stella was reacting to this, but knew that there was nothing at this stage she could say or do that would make her daughter feel better.

This small but very tight group of people was desolated and scared, waiting for news but also afraid of the news.

Chapter 24

Carla kept looking outside, hoping to see land that was near enough for her to reach by swimming. She was not a great swimmer, but if she would paddle slowly she knew that she could cover some distance, hopefully enough to reach the shore.

Glenn was awake and able to talk a little. He asked her what plans she had to escape. She told him that she would try swimming to shore soon as they came close enough. Glenn said, "I'm sorry I messed up. I should have hit him harder I don't know what came over me, but I was afraid I would kill him. It's not that he doesn't deserve it, I just couldn't do it."

Carla said, "I understand, I don't think I could have done it either. Today I believe I can. After he shot you I realized he won't hesitate to kill us if he feels that it's necessary."

Glenn said, "There's another way to get to shore without swimming. This boat has an inflatable raft on board with a small outboard motor. I know where it is stored. The problem will be to get it in the water by yourself. I'm afraid I can't be of much help. Can you get on deck or are we still locked in?' No, Carla said "He actually told me I could go on deck if I wanted to. I just didn't want to. He ripped the clothes off my body and he wants me to be in the nude when he's around. He thinks it demeans me and lowers my spirits."

Glenn said, "The crazy bastard is out of control again. You better do what he says when he's in that stage."

Carla said. "Well he has seen me nude before. If I want to escape, I better go up and see if I can find that raft."

"It's in back of the bridge so when he's at the controls he can't see you. Take a good look at it. There is a small package attached to it with the operating instructions. If you can bring that down I can help you with it."

When John saw her on deck he asked if she had decided to come up and keep him company. She replied, "I needed some fresh air. Don't worry, I won't come near you." She turned her back on him, acting like she was not interested in anything special just looking at the waves and enjoying the fresh air. She wandered to the back of the bridge where he couldn't see her and immediately spotted the cellophane-wrapped envelope on top of what looked like an oversized back pack with a little engine strapped to it. John was still on the bridge tinkering with the controls. She quickly ripped the envelope off the pack and stuffed it her panties.

She walked back to the stairs, avoiding John as much as she could, and went back to the lower cabin. Glenn was still awake and alert and enthusiastically said, "Right that's it, you found it."

While John was still safely upstairs' they opened the package and Glenn explained to her how to inflate the raft. That was the easy part. Inside the package was a steel cylinder with compressed air inside sufficient to inflate the raft. The cylinder was already connected to it. All she had to do was open the valve on top of the cylinder and the raft would be inflated in seconds with the little motor attached to it. He told her how to start the motor once the raft was in the water. The hard part was to lift the raft over the railing and drop it in the sea.

All this had to be done during the night when John was taking his nap.

Carla said, "How will I get on deck he locks us up during the night? Glenn said, "I don't know how to pick a lock but I can dismantle it from the inside. There's a toolbox I discovered when looking for a weapon in this small cabin in back of you. Locks are normally made to keep somebody out of a room not in it and that's why the screws to keep the lock in place are on the inside.

"I will try to get on deck with you to lift the raft overboard. Once it's in the water you have to jump in, climb in the raft and wait for maybe a couple of minutes to start the engine, otherwise the noise may wake him up. Once he discovers that you are gone there is no way he can find you, or spend the time even to search for you."

Carla asked, "How do I know where to go?"

Glenn said, "You have to go in the general direction of where the yacht is heading and when the sun comes up you must steer the raft in the opposite direction. Keep the sun in back of you and you will hit the shore."

"He then reminded her, that on board the raft was a flare gun with six cartridges and that she should fire the gun when it was dark and only when there was a ship, helicopter or drilling rig in sight. Even if you run out of gas before you hit land there is a very good chance that you will drift close to one of those rigs or ships. There is also an emergency ration on board. It's not much, just some water and nutrition bars. Be careful with the water. Take small sips. It may have to last longer than you expect.

"I wish I had the strength to go with you, but I can't climb over the ship's railing. I wouldn't be able to swim to the raft and crawl into it. My best bet is to wait on the

yacht. You'll make it and send the troops to my rescue.
You are a strong girl and a good person. I wish I had met
you before all this insanity took place. So let's wait till
nightfall and do it. You will have a much better chance in
the raft than swimming all the way to shore.

"I just thought about the life jackets that are on board.
I know where they're stored, right next to were the raft
is. You should put one on before jumping in the water.
They have an emergency whistle and a little red blinking
light to draw attention in the dark."

It was early evening and John's prediction that they
would be close to the Mexican shore proved to be wrong;
there was no sign of land so far. That got him concerned
and left him no other choice than to use the GPS again.
It would be dark in a few hours and he couldn't afford to
get too far off course. He switched on the GPS and found
out that he had again gone astray and was heading for
Mexico, but much farther South than where he wanted to
go. He rapidly changed course and switched off the GPS.
They had lost at least three to four hours.

Does everything have to go wrong? Every fucking
time I leave the bridge we go off course. At this rate they
would not be in Mexico before the early morning. The
fact that it was getting dark worked in his favor. The
choppers would be called back pretty soon until morning
and by then he would be out of their jurisdiction. The
search for them would be left for the Coast Guard and
would have to be turned over to the Mexican National
Security. This would not have a high priority for them.

His confidence went up again and he figured his
changes to get out of this mess were very good.

At that time he saw the half naked girl moving
around the upper deck and he was curious to know what

she was up to. He tried to follow her without her seeing him, but she spotted him and turned around to face him. "You're more of a pervert than I thought was possible for anybody to be, now you're spying on me when I'm half naked. Do you get your kicks from being a voyeur? You disgust me but you don't scare me anymore."

"She went down and told Glenn that she saw the life jackets but also that John was spying on her and looked suspicious. I think I distracted him by insulting and making him angry. We can be sure he is going to lock us in tonight, but that's a good thing he will feel secure that he can get a couple of hours of sleep."

As expected, after a few of John's preferred insults to both of them he left and locked the door.

Glenn said, "Let's wait a while until all is quiet and we are more or less sure that he is asleep. It's going to take me some time to get up these stairs and on deck."

Carla said. "Are you sure you should do this? You don't want to start bleeding again,"

I know he said. "But we really have no other options if we want to stay alive. The closer we come to Mexico the shorter our life span will be. I'm convinced he is going to get rid of us."

Carla agreed and said, "Well let's do it. I think he is in his room, hopefully asleep." Glenn had the door lock dismantled in a few minutes and they started the difficult climb up the stairs. Glenn had to rest every two steps but they made it without too much noise and everything was still quiet.

The first thing Carla did was to put on one of the life jackets just in case John unexpectedly showed up. She could jump overboard and still stay afloat if she got too tired of swimming.

Glenn was working on the belt that was tied around the raft. When the package was free he said, "let's move it to the railing before inflating it. There is a rope attached to it. Tie this around your wrist before we throw the raft in the water. That way you won't get separated from it.

Okay, Glenn said. "We can inflate now. This is the noisy part. The compressed air when released will make a fairly loud noise, so as soon you hear the hissing sound we throw it over the railing. You don't hesitate and jump at the same time. By the time you surfaced the raft will be inflated. You climb in and start the motor and steer away from the yacht. It's dark and you will be invisible from here in seconds. Starting the engine will probably wake him up but by the time he is on deck you will be gone.

"Let me get on my feet and grab one of the handles on the raft. You go on the other side and grab the handle. Soon as you here the hissing sound we lift this thing and throw it overboard and you jump. I'll count to three and open the air bottle and we're on," Before he could start counting they heard a cabin door open,

Quick Glenn said, he opened the bottle and both hoisted the raft but Carla had problems lifting her side high enough to go over the railing.

When it finally tipped over they heard John shouting, "Stop right there or I'll shoot both of you!" He ran to them and when he was close, Glenn fell on him yelling at Carla to jump. Carla hurled herself over the railing and plunged down to the raft. When she made contact she felt a sharp pain traveling from her forearm to her shoulder, a pain so intense that she had trouble holding on to the rope. She managed to crawl into the raft and saw that there was already a wide gap between the raft and the yacht. She heard gun shots accompanied by flashes but was not sure if they were aimed at her or Glenn. The yacht faded into the dark and she tried to start the engine. It was difficult because her right arm was useless. The pain was still bad and she was afraid that it was broken. When the engine finally sputtered and caught on she put it on a course that she saw the yacht was following.

She slowly relaxed somewhat and thought. Well at least I'm out of the clutches of that maniac and don't have to be afraid of being raped or killed by him. She began inspecting and opening the little compartments that were built into the raft walls. She found the emergency flare gun, the rations, and stuff to repair possible leaks, and something that looked like a watch with a wiggly needle jumping up and down. She had never seen a compass in her life and when she finally figured it out she tried to put the raft on a course straight west.

When Glenn deliberately fell on John to give Carla time to get over the railing, John fired his gun without aiming at anybody. He missed Glenn and when he started aiming at the raft it was too far out. The result was that he angrily kicked Glenn while he was lying on the deck. He said he would kill him as soon as they found that lesbian whore.

Glenn was pretty sure that there wasn't a snowball's chance in hell of that happening. Carla was gone, and John running the boat in circles was not going to change that, soon John would realize this and would head back to Mexico, his final destination with the yacht.

What would happen when they finally reached Mexico was unknown to Glenn, but he feared that it would not be a happy ending for him.

John dragged Glenn down the stairs and locked him in the storage room, in the dark without any water or food, clearly demonstrating that he couldn't care less what happened to him. Glenn was seriously wounded and urgently needed medical care. The physical effort to get the raft in the water had caused his wound to start bleeding again.

John had given up on finding Carla. It was like looking for a needle in a haystack, even worse in the dark. He had a searchlight on board but was afraid to use it. That would be an invitation to the Coast Guard.

They continued sailing to the west and when the sun came up they finally saw some mountains in the far distance, John had no idea what part of Mexico this could be or even if it was Mexico. He assumed it was but he would need the GPS to find out exactly what their position was. They could be far away from the US and Mexican border and he wanted to enter Mexico close to Brownsville.

He turned the GPS on and found that they were about fifteen miles from the coast and twenty five miles South of Brownsville. He made some corrections to get them closer to Brownsville and as they were getting closer to the coastline he needed to find a secluded stretch where he could beach the yacht, wade ashore and be on his way to Port Isabel. He had no plans for Glenn and assumed he would eventually be found dead or alive. He didn't really care.

A couple of hours later they were close to shore and John was looking for a beach not too far away from civilization but desolate enough for him to drive the yacht ashore without witnesses. His original plan was to anchor the yacht away from the shore and use the raft to get to the beach, but since the slut had stolen the raft he would have to wade from the boat to the beach. He had packed all he needed in a backpack and was ready to go. One thing that still worried him was the scars on his face. They had improved a lot but were still visible and could give him away, more so in the US than in Mexico, but he should avoid big city airports for now, even in Mexico.

He decided to stay in a small town in Mexico before going to Mexico City. He would rent a car and drive away from the border and find himself a small town where he could hide until the scars on his face were totally gone.

Luck seemed finally to turn his way. He found a little beach that looked ideal for him to land the yacht. He changed course and headed straight for the beach until the boat struck a sandbar. He didn't waste any time and jumped in the water and waded ashore. The water was only knee deep so that would dry fairly quickly and wouldn't make him conspicuous if he entered a town. He found a paved road maybe half a mile from the beach. He decided to go north, the direction of the border he assumed, and after approximately twenty minutes a bus came from behind and stopped. The driver asked him in Spanish where he wanted to go. John's Spanish was high school level so he understood the question and replied in Spanglish that he wanted to go to the Mexican/American border. The driver nodded and said "Twelve pesos."

John gave him a ten dollar bill and said. "I have no pesos," The driver nodded that it was okay and drove on.

Forty five minutes later the driver stopped and all the passengers left the bus. John hesitated but the driver said "terminal". John understood that this was the end of the line.

He was in the middle of a small town and figured that this was the last town before the border' He walked towards the center and saw a sign that said "Frontera 2

Km." He was hoping to find a taxi or rental car that would drive him across the border to Port Isabel.

He spotted a bar and went in he ordered a cerveza and asked the owner if he spoke English. The guy said" un poco"

John said," That will do" and asked if he could get a taxi or rent a car to take him to Port Isabel? The barman or owner answered that there were no taxis or rental car offices in this town, only buses. He would have to walk from there to the border or his son could drive him to Port Isabel on his motorcycle for twenty five bucks.

John wasn't too happy with this offer but understood it was the best he was going to get in this Podunk town. He said "Okay it's a deal.

The guy said," I will call him. He can be here in twenty minutes," He then pointed at his face and asked John what had happened.

John's first reaction was to tell him to mind his own business but he was aware that this was not the right thing to do, so he said. "My hot little Mexican girl friend got jealous when I kissed one of her friends too many times. The bartender thought this was very funny and asked no more questions about his face. John realized that this was a good answer for future questions of that nature.

A teenage boy entered the bar and started yapping in Spanish to the bartender who turned out to be his father. The kid turned to John and said in reasonably fair English," You want a ride to Port Isabel?

John said," Yes if you can get me there in one piece." the boy smiled and said," Not to worry. I get you there. When do you want to leave? John said," How about right now."

They took off and all of a sudden John became aware that he had a gun in his pocket. He couldn't risk smuggling that through border control. He didn't want to abandon the weapon and throw it in the bushes along the road. He must hide it somewhere where he could retrieve it when he got back from the Mexican border. Could he trust the kid and ask him where he could possibly hide a gun? He decided not to, but let him stop the bike and he would pretend to go behind some bushes to take a leak. He tapped the kid on the shoulder and told him to pull over, as soon as the bike stopped; he jumped off and ran for some bushes along the road. When he was out of sight he saw a collapsed little shack. He put the gun under a broken cement block and returned to the road. He said," I thought I was going to pee in my pants." The boy shrugged his shoulders and without saying anything resumed driving.

Getting across the border was a piece of cake. John had his valid passport with him but nobody asked to see it. Twenty minutes later they were at the post office in Port Isabel, John gave the boy forty bucks and walked inside he showed his ID and got access to his box. Everything was there. John emptied the box and left the post office looking for a car rental. He found an Avis office almost next to the post office. He wanted a plain, inconspicuous little car that he could drop off in Mexico City. Here he used his fake passport and driver's license. There was no problem and he took off within fifteen minutes, back to Mexico, again he crossed the border without any problems and now began looking for the place where he had hid his gun. The landmark he remembered was a boarded up cantina across the road from the hiding place. He saw the landmark, walked across the road and immediately found the shack. He lifted the cement block but the gun was gone. He was sure it was the right cement block because he had positioned it at a certain angle so he would recognize it. Just to make sure he lifted the two other cement blocks that were there but to no avail. The gun was gone. He was sure that nobody was around when they stopped the bike and he went into the bushes. Only one other person was there. The kid must have followed him and seen what he did and on his way back picked it up before John got there. That filthy little taco eating bastard stole my gun. He thought about going back to the bar and confronts the little prick but he was not in a position to make a big deal out of it. Being unable to do something about it made him furious. It was not that he was planning to use this gun again but it could be traced back to the bullet they would retrieve from Glenn's shoulder.

He must get out of this area as soon and as far as possible, he should drive all night and find a small hotel in Mexico City. It would be safer to hide in a big metropolitan city than in a small town in the boondocks.

Chapter 25

The news that the yacht was found with Glenn on
board but no sign of Carla was devastating for Carla's
family and friends. They feared that the worst had
happened to her, the worst being that John had killed her
or almost as bad that he still had her with him on the run.
Glenn was in the hospital in Brownsville and the doctors
estimated that he would be in critical condition for at least
a couple of weeks or possibly longer. The bullet wound
was not serious but the resulting blood loss was. Glenn
was struggling to stay alive and the odds were not in
his favor. Without him they would never know what had
happened. Again the unknown was killing them. Was she
still alive or was she buried at sea? All they could do was
waiting, maybe forever.

The police told them that the US State Department
was putting pressure on the Mexican government to
take this seriously and investigate in the area where the
yacht was found. If John went on shore there must be
somebody who had seen him, alone or with Carla. He
must have gone through the little town nearby. He had no
transportation. Somebody must have helped him to get
out of there. He was not stupid enough to stay in the area
where his boat has landed. There must be traces of him
being there. It was just a matter of asking questions from
the local police.

The US State Department told the Mexican Minister
of Justice that he should remind the local police that the
US was paying a lot of the Mexican police salaries and

that this was an opportunity for them to show that the American generosity was justified.

The Jamesville police had sent them photos of John. On some of them they had added the scratches on his face. They were hoping that the local police would go around showing these photos and that somebody would recognize him.

All this would take time because everything had to go trough the chain of command and days would go by before these photos would be in the hands of the local police.

Robert was painfully aware of this and decided to do something about it, one of his Army buddies had a small private investigation firm in Dallas and he called him and asked if he could help him out, his friend asked him all the details and after listening to what Robert said and also being aware that this girl was the daughter of his Army buddy he said. "I believe there is a small private airstrip in Jamesville I can be there in two hours."

I will call you when I approach the airstrip, meet me there and we will go together to the local police station." Robert said, "Thank you Richard," Richard said, "Carla's father was also my friend who probably saved my life several times without me even knowing about it, I'm glad I can do this for him, it will make me feel that I finally can give something back to him."

They met at the airstrip and drove to the police station where the officer in charge of the case was waiting for them. He told them everything he knew which was not much more than what Robert already knew. He gave Richard copies of the correspondence they had with the local Mexican police so that Richard at least knew who to talk to in Mexico. He also gave him copies of both photos of John. The detective said, "I'm not supposed to give you this information but I know from experience how hard it is to work with them." Richard said, "I know how to deal with them, my grand parents were from Mexico and I speak enough Spanish so I hope that will not be a problem." I have really no intention to work with them I will let them know that I'm there as a private investigator hired by Carla's father but I want to investigate this on my own and will start by talking to people in that small town of Progresso.

"I will be there early tomorrow morning and fly today to Brownsville, rent a car and drive to Matamoras where I will stay overnight and be in Progresso in the morning. I appreciate the help you gave me and in return I will keep you informed of my findings and if it's an important issue I will call you at once, same goes for you Robert he added."

He asked Robert to drive him back to the airstrip because he wanted to get out of there before dark, Robert again thanked him and was relieved with the efficiency that Richard handled this job.

He went back home to tell them that he was confident that Richard would have more news in the coming days than what they could expect from the local police in weeks.

Robert said, "he wanted to go with Richard but he was told in no uncertain terms that this was not a good idea. It would slow Richard down and he was emotionally involved which does not make a good investigator, case closed."

The latest news on Glenn was good. The doctors had upgraded his chance of survival from 40 to 60 percent, based on his vital signs improving. He still was in some sort of a coma and not awake yet. Again they assured them that as soon has Glenn could talk they would ask about what had happened to Carla.

The first positive news came from Richard the next day he already knew that John had gone through Progresso alone and was last seen in Port Isabel. He also knew that a teenager drove him there on a motorcycle he talked to the kid's father who owns a cantina in town and that was the place where John appeared first, the father of the kid told him that John wanted a taxi or rent a car to go to Port Isabel, that's how he ended up on a bike. Richard kept asking to talk to the boy but he has the feeling that the father is stonewalling him and comes up with one stupid excuse after another why he can't get in touch with his son, this makes me believe that there is more to it than they want me to know.

I'm booked in a small hotel across from the cantina and as soon as I see a motorbike in front I will jump on them and find out what it is they are hiding from me.

It took a couple of hours before Richard heard the roar of a motorcycle coming down the street and parked in front of the Cantina, Richard rushed across the street and had the kid in a grip before he could enter the bar.

It took fifteen minutes for Richard to get the complete story. The boy told him that he dropped John off in front of the post office and also that John was looking for a car rental place in Port Isabel. He knew that John was planning to return because he hid something on the side of the road when they were driving to Port Isabel.

At first the kid said that he didn't know what he was hiding but Richard could tell that he was lying and when he threatened the boy that he would report this to the local police the truth came out and the boy handed over the gun.

Richard gave the kid a fifty dollar bill and said."
You will be better off if you just forget that this ever
happened.'

He returned to Port Isabel and when he was in the
street where the Post Office was, he saw a car rental place
almost next door. he showed the agent the pictures of
John and the agent recognized the picture where John had
the scratch marks on his face. He gave him the name John
used, the type, color and license plate of the rental.

Richard also went to the post office and went through
the same routine with the pictures of John. Again
someone recognized him because of the marks on his face.
All they could tell him was that he had a safety box and
that he accessed it a couple of days ago. They, of course,
had no idea of what was in the box.

Richard called the Jamesville police and told him that
he had found the gun that John most likely had used to
shoot Glenn, he would overnight mail it to the station,
and he did not give them any more details.

He said to Robert we now know he was there, but he
was alone so Carla has to be somewhere else, I'm on his
tail and will get him I promise you that, oh and by the
way tell Stella that she made my work a lot easier, the
marks she left on his face has made all the difference every
one who saw him remembered his face because of the
scratch marks she gave him.

It was positive news in the sense that the investigator
was on John's tail, but very bad news that Carla was not
with him. This could mean that he already disposed of
her at sea. The bad news overshadowed the good news
by far. They all wanted John to be caught but given the
choice they rather have Carla sound and safe and to hell
with John.

Fantastic news came from the police who called them and reported that the Brownsville detective was able to talk briefly with Glenn and he told them that Carla had escaped from the yacht several hours before John beached the boat, Glenn assured them that she was safe on a inflatable raft equipped with a small motor and that he personally had seen her sailing away from the yacht. He also said that John had searched for her but since it was dark he was unsuccessful and had to give up. The police had given that information to the Coast Guard who was now trying to locate her using helicopters and cutters.

The atmosphere at the Potts house lightened up considerable, Robert said, "They will find her I'm sure of that." Whether he said that to assure every body else or maybe he had enough confidence in the Coast Guard abilities that he believed what he just said, either way it helped they were all more optimistic that Carla would be rescued soon.

Robert called Richard to give him the latest news but Richard was already up to date, the police had called him and he was just ready to call and ask if he had to change priorities and help find Carla instead of chasing John.

Robert said, "I thought about this too but I don't see how you could help finding her when she is floating somewhere in the Gulf."

Richard answered, "You're right if she is still on that raft I can't. But if she has landed somewhere on the Mexican coast maybe I can, let's wait today and if they haven't found her today then she may be somewhere in the boondocks. There is a large stretch on the western coast in Mexico that is for the most inhabitant and communication is almost non existent.

She may be safe and in good hands, but it could take days before the more civilized world would know that she is there.

Chapter 26

Carla was busy trying to stay on course heading northwest but found out that with currents and winds this was a full time job and not all that easy to do if you were a novice with a handheld compass and only one arm she could use.

So far she hadn't seen anything. No rigs, no boats and no choppers, but it was still dark and visibility was practically zero. She could faintly see some daylight but the sun was still invisible.

Carla's thoughts were constantly with Mary, Robert and most of all with Stella. They must be so devastated and frightened not knowing where she was and probably thinking the worst. She was afraid that the worst could still happen. She was somewhere in the Gulf of Mexico, and didn't have clue where she was heading, maybe to nowhere. It was possible that she was just floating around in circles. The little engine had stopped a couple of hours ago having run out of gas. She wondered how long she could stay alive if she ran out of water and vitamin bars or if a storm hit the raft and threw her in the water. She would probably drown and would never be found. She would never be able to tell Robert and Mary the real story of her life.

"Shit!" she shouted. Stop feeling sorry for yourself, you little wimp. If you don't believe you can get out of this mess, nobody else will. But they do, because I'm sure there are a lot of people looking to find me and they will, soon as it gets light. She was able to talk herself out of the depressed mood she was in. A few hours went by, the sun was up but she had no means of steering the raft in the right direction. The currents and the wind decided where she was going. She peered in all directions for something that looked like a rig or a boat, but so far nothing was in sight.

The wind picked up and some of the waves came over the raft's side walls. She wondered if a raft could sink because of the weight of the little engine. She bailed the water out of the raft with her hands as much as she could and was able to keep up with the waves. She was drenched and the wind made her feel cold and more miserable, if that was possible. She felt a bout of depression coming on and tried to fight it by thinking of all the wonderful things that had happened to her since she landed in Jamesville. Getting to become friends with Stella was on the top of that list, and just thinking that she might never see her again made her so sad that she couldn't stop the tears flowing down her face.

The day went by and it started to get dark again. She had very little water left and only one bar of food. She would try to fall a sleep because staring into the dark all night would be a horrible experience. She closed her eyes but couldn't fall asleep because of the cold wind. She lay down on the raft's floor to avoid the wind but that didn't help very much. The pain she felt in her arm was not making this any better. She was now convinced that it was broken.

Carla dozed off, in a state between sleep and wakefulness. She couldn't tell whether the raft was moving in a certain direction or staying more or less in the same position.

Then she heard and felt a bump against the raft and thought, it's either a big fish or driftwood that had hit the raft. But something was strange. It felt like the raft was not moving at all anymore. She sat up and discovered that the raft was stuck against a steel structure. She couldn't see what it was but it had to be an oil rig. It wasn't a ship. That much she could see. Whatever it was she felt enormous relief that she had made contact with something people had built and with a good chance were living on it. She heard noises but couldn't identify the source of them. It could be the waves crashing against the structure or hopefully some machines running above her.

She started to shout as loud as she could, "I'm down here on a raft!" She repeated this over and over again until she realized that she was too far down and the noise of the water masked her shouting. Nobody could hear her. She thought there must be a way to get up there, one of these steel rung ladders or something. The darkness prevented her from exploring. She just would have to wait until it got light enough for her to see.

This waiting would be difficult, hoping that her safety could be up there but not able to find out for six or seven hours later. She had to make sure that the raft couldn't drift away from this structure. She tied a rope that was attached to the raft to a steel beam.

After a miserable cold night it finally started to dawn and she could see more of the structure. From where she was it looked gigantic, but all she saw were steel beams, pipes and a huge platform way up there. In spite of her limited knowledge of drilling rigs this is what one must look like.

She still could not find a way to get up there. She decided to wait a little longer, and since she could not control the course of the raft she would have to swim around the structure to find the means to get up to the platform.

An hour or so later Carla knew that it was time to find out. She slipped into the water and slowly swam away from the raft in search of an access to the platform. If there was life on this structure it must be on that unreachable platform. Swimming with one arm out of service was not easy and progress was slow. Sometimes the waves carried her away from the steel structure and she was afraid that she wouldn't have the strength to swim back to it. She decided to hang on to the structure and just use her legs to swim. She soon found out how enormous this steel monster was. She had been swimming, she estimated, for fifteen minutes and when she looked back it seemed that she had barely moved. But now she had a target and felt less insecure than when she was drifting on the raft. After several breaks she thought she saw something that looked like a rung ladder, reaching from the platform into the water. When she got closer she yelled out Yes! "That's it." She grabbed the ladder and started the long climb to the platform. This also was extremely difficult with only one arm. functioning. Half way up the ladder Carla felt exhausted and realized that the lack of water and nourishment had made her weak. She was afraid that she would never be able to reach the platform, but having come this far she was not going to give up.

Several stops later she finally pulled herself up on the platform and needed to lie down for a few minutes to recuperate. When she got up and looked around she couldn't believe the size of the platform and the amount of equipment. What was eerie was that there was nobody there. It looked like a scene from a science fiction movie where the aliens took all the earthlings on their space ship and left for their planet.

It was a bit scary and she felt uncomfortable. It didn't seem to be abandoned because all the machinery looked either new or very well maintained. Carla walked around toward what resembled a building. She found a door that was unlocked and hesitantly opened it. She walked into a corridor with several doors on either side there was still no sign of life. There was light in this gangway, but only one out of four lighting fixtures was on. It was like these were emergency lights. She listened carefully and thought that she heard the humming of a motor maybe a fan or a refrigerator. She couldn't make out what it was. She continued down the hallway and opened one of the doors. The room had two beds, closets and a small bathroom, almost like a dorm in college. The beds were made and the room was clean. The more she explored the more confused she became. What happened here for everybody to leave in such an orderly fashion? She couldn't figure it out and that scared her.

The next door she opened was a kitchen with a fairly large dining room. She saw a refrigerator. She opened it and found bottles of beer, cokes, water and any type of juice you could think of. She didn't hesitate and gulped down a bottle of water without taking a breather.

Carla almost had a heart attack when without warning, a loud voice said. "What the fuck are you doing here?" She turned and faced two men dressed in orange coveralls. One was a young guy. The other was older, maybe fifty or so. He said. "Yes. Please tell us how you got here. Where did you come from? This platform was closed yesterday and everybody was supposed to be evacuated.

"We are the only two left and that was not supposed to be either. The last chopper left and we should have been on it but because of some screw-up they left us here. Now what's your story? You're not part of the crew. I never saw you before. How come they left you here?"

Carla said, "Nobody left me; I just got here ten minutes ago. I was drifting on a raft and bumped into this rig last night, but had to wait until daylight to find the ladder to get up here."

She saw the skeptical look on their faces and said,

"We can clear this up in a minute if you let me call the police and my parents. I know this sound crazy and unbelievable but it's a long story. Please let me call my parents because they don't even know whether I'm still alive."

The younger man said, "We can't call shore because the techs turned off the system assuming that there was nobody left on the rig."

Carla said "Why is everybody on shore? What happened?"

Nothing has happened yet, "Said the younger man. But there is a pretty bad storm brewing in the gulf that is predicted to turn into a category 3 hurricane by tomorrow. Every rig in its path has been closed and all personnel evacuated, except the two of us "of course."

The older man said, "You look exhausted and what's wrong with your arm?"

"She explained that she hurt her arm when she jumped from the yacht into the raft and hit her arm on the engine."

He said, "If it's broken you must support it with a sling," He went to a cabinet and produced a small table cloth and made a sling out of it. He put it around Carla's neck and arm. She thanked him and felt less pain with her arm supported like that.

He said, "You're probably very hungry. We saw you looking in the fridge. Am I right?"

She said, "Yes I'm famished I haven't eaten in almost two days."

"Well if there's one thing were not lacking, that's food said the young guy. You lucked out because I do a lot of cooking here. Just tell me what you want and I'll make it for you. You can tell us your story after you eat something. So what will it be?" "Carla said. A sandwich will be fine,"

No he said. "We can do much better than that. We have lobster, steaks, and shrimp. Whatever you want I guarantee that we have it. Okay, you won't tell us what you want, ill surprise you."

The other man said, "You don't seem to have much clothes on under that life jacket. Why don't you take a nice hot shower and I will round up some things for you, they will be men's clothes, but I'll get you the smallest sizes we have on board."

Carla was disappointed that she couldn't let Robert and the others know that she was very much alive, but was thankful that these two men were taking care of her. They didn't seem to be worried about the hurricane hitting the rig. She asked them why and they said we have been through hurricanes before on this rig with very little damage.

"Don't worry, we will be fine. We can watch the TV later and see what they predict."

Carla said," You have TV?"

"Yes we do. We can receive but we can't send out messages. Our cell phones won't reach that far. Normally we can call via satellite but not now."

After taking a shower and putting on a clean set of orange coveralls, she felt better and was looking forward to a warm meal.

When Bill, the younger one, walked in with a meal in a covered tray and put in on the table he said," Since you wanted a sandwich I made you one" he took the cover off the tray. Carla looked at it wide-eyed. "I can't believe what I'm seeing." There was cold lobster for a starter, filet mignon for the main course and ice cream for dessert. For a moment Carla stared at it and then a torrent of tears broke loose. The two men were baffled not realizing what hell this girl had gone through.

Bruce, the older man said, "listen, Honey Bill can get you something else to eat. You don't have to cry over it."

It's not the food she said. "But I'm so happy,"

Bruce whispered to Bill. "See that's why I never got married." Bill asked her "if you're happy, why are you crying?"

She said, "Only a few hours ago I was lying on the raft, cold miserable, scared and convinced that I was going to die and never see my family or friends again. Now here I am being pampered by two men I never saw before. It's overwhelming, but I still can't explain why I cried. But now I'm going to eat this fabulous looking and enticing smelling food."

She polished everything off and said, "Thank you so much and now I'll try to tell you my story before I fall asleep, I'm sorry but I haven't slept much the last three days."

Bruce said, "We understand, why don't you go to sleep first and tell us the story later"

She said, "No, I have to give you at least a short version of it," They said, "Okay, let's hear it." Meantime we'll turn the TV on with the sound down so we'll know when to expect the storm if we are still in its path.

Carla started with the first kidnapping and how she managed to bluff her way out of that. She mentioned why she did not file charges, then the stalking situation, John's behavior in court, and his mandatory rehab program.

She told about Glenn who elected to join the Peace Corp in Afghanistan, John's insistence on talking to her. His threats to kill her and then finally this kidnapping where he took her from her doorstep with a gun in his hands and how he had hit Stella unconscious and then dragged her into his car.

Carla explained how Glenn was handcuffed to the steering wheel and was forced to drive them to the marina. Now John had kept both she and Glenn prisoner on his yacht and that he wanted to go to Mexico, why he shot Glenn and how she finally escaped and landed on their doorstep. She said, "This was a short version, but at least you know the gist of it. I promise after a nap you can ask me all the questions you may have."

Bruce said, "Come with me. You can have any room you want. They are all empty but I put clean linen in this one and you can lock the door and sleep as long as you want. We have at least another ten to fifteen hours before we see the effects of the storm."

When Bruce went back to the kitchen where Bill was watching the news and the weather forecast, warning that the storm could reach category four status during the next hours. Bill said. "Do you realize that you came very close to me hitting you over the head with a frying pan?"

Bruce asked, "What did I do to deserve that?"

Bill said, "You insisted that she should wear more clothes. You may not appreciate the looks of a very pretty girl, but I do."

You pervert Bruce said, "Don't you think this poor girl has had enough of this shit already?"

Bill said, "I'm just kidding, but you must admit that she is quite a looker. Can you imagine, we never saw a girl on this rig and now out of a clear blue sky they send us Miss Universe, just to keep us company?"

Bruce said, "She is really upset that she can't contact her parents to let them know that she is safe and sound. These poor people must be thinking that she drowned or is still in the hands of this lunatic."

Bill updated Bruce on the storm status but there was nothing that they could do. Everything was secured and tied down. The emergency power generator had plenty of fuel. All they could do was wait until the storm blew over.

Chapter 27

The atmosphere at Carla's house was one of despair. The search for the raft was still on, but they were afraid that the Coast Guard might end it search in the next day or so.

Richard called and talked to Robert about the possibility that Carla could have been picked up by a small fishing boat that was still at sea. Most of these fishing boats in Mexico didn't have the communication gear that US fishermen have. Richard also said that she could be on a rig, but that they all had evacuated their people. She could be safe with no possibility to communicate.

Robert knew that all this could be true but also knew that the odds were low and that Richard was just trying to lift his spirits. Richard assured him that he was still chasing John and would not stop until he found him. He said, "This is now personal and no longer an assignment. This bastard will pay for this, no matter what the outcome is. I owe this to our friend."

Robert said, "Everybody in the house is devastated and close to realizing that they may never see Carla again. Mary is crying nonstop. I'm a wreck and I'm very worried about her friend Stella. Her mother called a doctor who came over but Stella refused to let him in her room. She said no doctor can bring Carla back and that's the only thing that can make her feel better. She is determined to suffer as much as she feels Carla has to go through. She won't eat and all she does is drink some water. She monitors the internet and watches all the news channels hoping against hope that something will happen.

"The storm brewing in the gulf is another downer and even if she is still on that raft, there is no way that anyone can survive these hurricane winds and the accompanying twenty to thirty foot waves.

Richard again said, "If she is on one of those rigs she will be okay. These things are built to withstand hurricane force conditions."

The wind had increased and the waves around the rig became larger but were still nothing to worry about. Carla woke up after a good ten hours of solid sleep and felt much better, the fact that she was not alone anymore and sheltered from the elements made her feel safe and happy, because she was convinced that she would survive this ordeal and be back with her family and friends.

The three of them had an enormous breakfast together and she asked them "Where exactly are we. I know this is still the Gulf of Mexico but where is this rig?"

Bruce answered, "We are exactly 138 miles south of Brownsville, Texas, less than two hours flight on the helicopter from Houston. Houston is where we are based and live if we're not on the rig."

Carla asked if they had any flare guns on board, if you do she said. "We can maybe draw some attention from ships or airplanes that are close to us."

Sorry Bill answered, "I don't think we have flares of that sort on board and even if we had we're not close enough to any of the shipping lanes, besides the fact that by now all vessels or airplanes are avoiding the path of the storm."

They informed Carla that the hurricane was about two hours away and that it was safer for them to go down a few levels on the rig once the storm came closer. Damage caused by a strong storm to the rig was usually on the deck. Small equipment and glass could fly around and that couldn't harm them below deck, it also won't be so scary because they wouldn't hear the winds as much below deck level.

They tried to assure Carla that there was really nothing to worry about and that she could relax because she was safe now. We can watch TV and see what damage the storm has done on the islands in the Caribbean and find out where the eye of the storm will make landfall. Once it does they could go back on deck because by then it would have passed and the worst will be over. And as soon as the winds were down the choppers would arrive to asses the damage and communications would be restored and then they could tell the world that Carla was on board, safe and sound.

The TV announcer confirmed that it was now a category 4 hurricane and it would make landfall between Brownsville and Tampico. It was on course to land approximately six to eight hours from now and about 80 miles north of Tampico. This was not a heavily populated area, so they were hoping for minimal damage.

Bruce said, "I'm glad that it's heading for an area like that but that puts it on course with our rig within the next hour. We better start moving down. We can watch TV there as well as up here and follow the hurricane situation."

There were no windows in the lounge they were in. They had to rely on the TV and the noise of the howling wind to assess the fury of the storm that was now close upon them.

Carla thought it became scary, but not scarier than going through a hurricane on land. She felt a lot more frightened with Hurricane Katrina rumbling around the New Orleans Super Dome.

Somehow the presence of Bruce and Bill made her feel that nothing bad would happen to her. She could not explain this, she just felt that way. It was probably because neither one of them looked even remotely uncomfortable or nervous and definitely not scared. They behaved like it was just another day at the office.

The TV weatherman said that winds were at 140 miles an hour and if the storm movement slowed down it could reach 155, miles which would make it a category 5 hurricane. Definitely a very dangerous storm. Carla pictured herself on the raft under these conditions, but then quickly realized that there would be no raft or Carla for that matter. They would have been gone long before.

The noise had increased so much that it was hard to talk to one another and they had to turn the volume of the TV to the highest setting. They could hear the wind roaring through the steel structure, at times with a high pitch that hurt their ears.

This battering lasted a couple of hours and sometimes they heard not just winds, but noises like heavy things being dragged around above their heads. She noticed that Bruce and Bill looked at each other but saying nothing.

Carla felt that something was wrong and they wouldn't talk about it because of her. She said,

"Come on guys. Tell me what's going on out there, I'll be more scared if I don't know."

Bill said, "We don't know for sure but we have the feeling that some of the heavy equipment is shifting around and that could do some serious damage to the rig. Not that it would put us in danger, but it could destroy the deck completely or knock some of the other equipment loose."

After another very loud bang Carla had the feeling that the room they were in was no longer level but had tilted somewhat. This was confirmed when she looked at her drink on the table. The coffee in her cup was no longer level.

Bruce watched her and said, "Yes we are tilting a little bit. Nothing serious and I expect that our stabilizers will automatically correct it." Carla asked, "What causes this to happen?" Bill said, "I can think of two highly likely possibilities. One is that one of the heavy equipments shifted and fell overboard, or second guess is that one of the stabilizer tanks is flooded and became too heavy, if it is the loss of the equipment than the stabilizer can compensate for it and we should be back to normal shortly. If one or two of the stabilizer tanks are flooded we're going to stay crooked."

Carla did not understand all he was saying but had the impression that it was more serious than what he wanted her to believe.

And just like that the wind stopped howling and it became eerily quiet. Carla jubilantly said, "Alright it's over!"

Bruce shook his head and said. "I'm afraid not and the worst is still to come. We're in the eye of the storm and depending on the size of the hurricane; this lull can last up to half an hour. But then we will have to go through the backside of the hurricane before it's over."

Bill said, "I'm going up for a minute to check the damage." Bruce went with him and when they came back about fifteen minutes later, their faces looked grim. Bruce said "This is a lot worse than I expected. The big crane toppled over and hit a lot of the rotary equipment. It's sitting on the helicopter pad so that it has to be removed before the chopper can land on the rig. I imagine that the rig will have to be towed to the dry dock for repairs." Out of nowhere the noise picked up and became as loud as before. It only took a few minutes. It sounded even louder than before and Carla had the impression that the rig tilted more but wasn't sure about that. There was another loud bang and all the lights and the TV went off. Since there were no windows, it became pitch dark until two small lights came on, enough to see each other but not more than that.

Bill said, "The emergency generator died for some reason and these puny lights run on batteries. They will only provide power for a couple of hours." Without lights or TV the room seemed more ominous and the atmosphere totally changed. It was clear that their ordeal was not over yet. Carla tried to stay optimistic and thought. It's still the Plaza hotel compared with a raft. No TV or lights is not the end of the world.

After a couple of hours they noticed that the sound of the storm seemed to lessen. After a while Bruce said, "I'll go up and see if it's safe to come on deck." He came back a few minutes later and said, "There's still a stiff breeze and heavy rain, but I wouldn't call it dangerous. Just be careful for the debris that is all over the place. None of the windows survived so there is broken glass on the floor. Let's put on some rain gear before we go out there,"

There was plenty of that and Carla was able to find a small size that almost fit her. The moment she opened the door to the deck she gasped and thought. This is a nightmare. This couldn't have happened while we were downstairs watching TV. What before had looked so efficient, all this shiny equipment, pipes going from one machine to another, cable running in trays, every piece labeled identifying what it was, now nothing but rubble. Everything was broken, stacked in heaps, pipes going from nowhere to nowhere, oil and other chemicals all over the place. Was this nature telling us that she was still in control and she could make or break us? It was a brutal show of unbridled force. Carla understood that a storm could destroy a wooden house with sheetrock walls, but here this was steel and it was bent and twisted. Huge bolts were sheared off and broken like pencils.

Bill and Bruce were just as perplexed as Carla. They had weathered storms but had never witnessed anything even close to this.

They walked around the deck, but the damage was such that there was nothing they could do. Bill said, "I'll take a look at the emergency generator. Maybe we can get it going again. It's below deck I don't know why it's not working, there's no damage there."

He came back to the deck and said, "There's nothing wrong with the generator but every time I start it the motor panel shows that there's a short and it shuts itself down. I need to find where the short is and then we will have power again."

Bruce said, "He's very good at these thing we'll have power very soon and find out on the TV when we can expect the helicopters back in the air."

It took Bill about fifteen minutes before the power came back on. All stations were on the air reporting the storm damage. Texas was spared, the hurricane had made landfall about 50 miles north of Tampico with relatively little damage. A couple of small villages were destroyed but major cities had escaped the fury of a category 4 hurricane.

"We can expect some visitors in the next two hours. Bruce said, unfortunately they can't land on this rig. We should be on deck and make ourselves visible so they can inform the Coast Guard that there are people on this rig that need to be taken off.

"Our coveralls are bright orange. If we move around on a light colored background they should be able to see us. They'll come down low because their objective is to assess the damage to the rig.

"One of us must be on deck at all times and when he hears the sound of chopper blades come get the other two and we all start dancing on the roof" Bill said, "I'll stay up here. I want to find out where that short circuit is that cut off the power."

Bruce and Carla went down to monitor the TV and hopefully find out when they could expect to see the cavalry come to their rescue.

All stations were showing the damage that the storm had caused and the general consensus was that it was minimal and could have been a lot worse.

They expected the oil rig crews to return soon after a visual inspection of the rigs. Helicopters were to set out later during the day although some of them were already in the air.

Bruce said, "I can't stay down here I need to get on deck, I'm way too nervous to watch television,"

Carla smiled and said, "I was just going to suggest we go back up there. I don't want to miss my ride."

It had stopped raining and the sun was trying to break through the clouds. The three of them were on the roof anxiously watching the sky, when finally a chopper came into sight Bruce shouted. "That's one of ours!"

The pilot brought the helicopter as close as possible. The co-pilot was shouting something with a bullhorn but it was hard to understand. The pilot repositioned the chopper and they tried again with the bullhorn to communicate. This time they understood most of what he was saying. The pilot wanted to know what the hell they were doing on the rig. That was all they understood but their response obviously didn't make it. The pilot made the universal sign putting his hands up in the air as if to say, I can't hear you. He then used the bullhorn again and they understood only the word help. The pilot turned the helicopter around and disappeared in the distance.

Bill said, "I hope he said we'll send help to get you out of there."

Carla said. "At least somebody knows that there are people on this rig who need help."

Bill said, "Well let's see if we can learn more from the TV. There is no point for us staying on the roof. The only help we can expect is from the Coast Guard. They're going to have to come by boat to get us off this rig."

Chapter 28

Back in Jamesville the Potts family and friends were still hoping for a miracle, but common sense told them that this was highly unlikely. The police in Jamesville told them that the Coast Guard had not given up and they would resume searching as soon as the storm calmed down.

They were watching TV and saw the images of the damage the storm had created and heard the commentaries of the news people about how lucky this has turned out for a lot of people. This of course did nothing for them. They were pleased that so many people were spared, but that didn't bring Carla back. The newscaster came back on and said, "We want to interrupt here and share with you a strange occurrence.

A helicopter pilot just reported a very strange sighting on one of the oil rigs. He was sent out to do visual inspection on one of his company's oil rigs before the crew could be sent back out.

This rig was supposedly evacuated yesterday and everybody was supposed to have left the rig. Imagine the surprise when the pilot spotted three people on the roof of one of the buildings on the rig. Even stranger was that one of them was a women. At the time of the evacuation there was no woman on board. The Coast Guard was alerted and will arrive there a couple of hours from now. We will keep you informed as soon as we have more news on this strange event.

Everybody in the room got quiet and was afraid to say something. Hope was written all over their faces but nobody dared to say what they were thinking except Stella who was smiling and jumping around and telling everyone. "That's her I feel it. That's Carla it must be her she's alive!"

The phone rang and it was Richard telling Robert that he was on his plane heading to the rig. He had talked to the pilot of the helicopter to get the coordinates and he figured it would take him about an hour to reach it. I'll call you when I get there, I have a Global cell phone and I'll find out if Carla is the woman on the rig.

Robert said, "To the others, Richard is on his way to the rig and we will know in about an hour. He said he'll call back soon as he gets there."

Stella kept saying. "It must be Carla! It just has to be Carla!" Her mother tried to tell her that this was possible but that she shouldn't consider it a fact. If it was not Carla the disappointment would be devastating. Stella should keep hoping but consider the possibility that it was not. Stella simply wouldn't listen and everyone in the room was afraid of what would happen to her if it turned out not to be Carla.

The phone rang exactly one hour and fifteen minutes later. Robert ran for it but then hesitated to pick up the receiver, afraid of what was coming. He finally grabbed it and heard Richard's voice shouting. "It's Carla on the rig!" Robert couldn't say a word but it wasn't necessary they all saw his face lit up like a Christmas tree and they all knew instantly that all was good.

Pandemonium set in and there were smiles and tears of joy. Stella was dancing around shouting I told you she was there!

After a while when they all calmed down a little, Robert said, "I have to call Richard back because he told me he had more news but he wanted me to tell you the big one first," He got Richard on the phone and he said, "The Coast Guard was considering lifting them of the rig by helicopter but the company pilot who found them advised against it. He said there is so much debris and equipment that is no longer tied down that he is afraid that some of it may shift during the rescue operation. It would be a lot safer if the Coast Guard used one of the fast boats to get them off the rig. It would take a few hours longer but it would make more sense."

The decision was that the Coast Guard would get there as fast as they possibly could and then take them to the closest port which was Corpus Christi. They would let the Jamesville police know when they could be expected in Corpus soon as they get them off the rig. It would take at least six to eight hours to arrive in Corpus.

There is one more thing I need to tell you Richard said. "I could see that Carla had her arm in a sling, but she was obviously not in much pain because she was waving at the plane like the two other guys."

Richard said, "How can I ever thank you enough for what you accomplished in these few days,"

Richard said, "We discussed this before and we decided that there were no thanks necessary. Besides my job is only half-done I still have to bring this maniac to justice, and I will."

Robert said, "It will take approximately six to eight hours before she arrives in Corpus and it's only a couple of hours driving for us to get there, so we don't have to hurry." Mary looked at him in disbelief and said. "What do you mean there is no hurry? Get the damn car and let's go! What if we have a flat tire or whatever and we arrive late? You're going to let her stay on the dock waiting for us?"

Janice and Stella applauded and Stella said, "I'd rather wait for a couple of hours than be five minutes late," Amen Mary said, "let's go."

Robert knew he had lost this battle and went to get the car out of the garage. The first thing they did when they arrived in Corpus was to see the Port Master and ask him the time of arrival of the Coast Guard vessel. The Port Master answered they just called me and they are still an hour away from the rig. They will call me back later to let me know when to expect them.

Robert asked, "Is it okay to come back in a couple of hours? Our daughter is on that rig."

"Yes of course said the Port Master. I know you are all very anxious to see her, the Coast Guard Captain told me a little bit about it and I'm happy for you that everything has turned out the way it did."

"When you come back and she is on board the cutter I will make a shore to ship call and you guys can talk to her." That will be great Robert said. "And thank you so much."

All they had to do now was kill a couple of hours before returning back to the docks. They decided to go to a restaurant and eat and drink the time away. They were so excited about the fact that in a couple of hours they would be able to talk to Carla. They knew that would make them feel even more that she really was back with them. They all vowed that she would be protected by them as long as this maniac was on the loose. She would get ticked off but she was going to have someone with her whenever she set foot out of the house.

Two hours later they drove back to the docks and when they entered the Port Master's office he smiled at them and said "They lifted them off the rig and she is on the boat, they figured to be here around four o clock," That was another two hours wait. The Port Master said, "Come with me there's a waiting room next door that has a speakerphone. I'll call the cutter from my office and transfer the call when I have your daughter on the line."

A few minutes later the phone rang and when Robert pushed the speakerphone button Carla's voice came through the speakers "Can you hear me, it's me Carla."

They all spoke together making such a racket that Carla couldn't understood them but that was not important at all. Just knowing that they were all there was enough. What was said didn't matter. What did matter was that they could actually talk to each other.

Since they were on a speakerphone everybody had the chance to say a few words to her. Carla said, "I was told by the Captain that we couldn't talk long because this was actually a phone to be used only for emergency situations and since I'm here I'm obviously no longer an emergency. He said I will be with you in less then two hours so I'll see you soon. One more thing, the medic here looked at my arm and said I should go to a doctor or hospital soon as I arrive. He is pretty sure it's broken and should be set as soon as possible. But don't worry it's just a broken arm. See you soon!"

Mary said, "Shouldn't we find out where the hospital is here or should we call our doctor and drive to Jamesville?"

Robert answered, "We should talk to our doctor first anyway, I'll call him right now," While he was calling the doctor, Janice said," If it's not an emergency it would probably be better if she saw your doctor and I don't think that a couple of hours is going to make a difference."

Mary agreed but said, "Let's see what the doctor tells Robert."

Robert got off the phone and said, "Their doctor would like to see her and he recommend that we bring her to his office today. If necessary, he would take her to the hospital and do the surgery tonight." That sounded a lot better than going to a hospital in Corpus Christi and having to commute between Jamesville and Corpus for checkups or whatever.

This decided, they talked about Carla and how this event could possibly affect her now that it was over. Stella said, "After she tells us all about it we shouldn't ask any more questions or even talk about it, unless she initiates it.

"If something like this happened to me that's how I would like it to be. I would probably want to talk about it once in a while, but I should be the one to take that initiative."

Mary said, "It will be hard for me not to ask questions but I think that would be how I would prefer it being in her shoes. Carla has been through so much. We must make this as easy for her as we can, I will bite my tongue every time the urge to ask questions crosses my mind."

Janice said, "It will be hard for us all not to ask her questions, but I agree that this is entirely up to Carla. If she wants to talk we listen but we don't ask questions." Mary said "I don't have to worry about Robert he never ask questions, he sometimes pisses me off that he doesn't, he comes across like he doesn't care but that's not the case, I know that."

Janice said. "Robert is a very nice person I can't imagine him not caring if somebody he knows needs a helping hand. He would be the first to offer his help."

Robert was outside walking up and down the pier, probably counting the minutes and anxious to see Carla. He couldn't believe that this ordeal had lasted only five days. To him it felt like five weeks.

At that moment the Port Master walked in. I just got a message that they are about twenty minutes away from docking at pier 4, which is something like a five minutes' walk from here. You may want to go there now.

They didn't hesitate and were out the door in a New York minute. Robert joined them and they quickly reached pier 4. A few minutes later they saw a Coast Guard ship coming around the bend heading in their directions.

As agitated as they were minutes ago, they now became very quiet. It was hard to describe what they were feeling now that they were so close to becoming reunited with the girl they had been afraid of never to see again just hours ago.

They immediately saw three persons clad in bright orange coveralls. It was easy to recognize Carla because she was about six inches shorter than her companions and also had one arm in a sling.

The cutter was now against the pier but they couldn't get closer because the gate to get to the ships moored at pier 4 was still closed, obviously for safety reasons.

The gangway was being installed and the ship's railing removed with Carla ready to sprint toward them. Bill and Bruce were right behind her and Bruce said. "Now look what's going to happen, they're all very happy to see Carla again and I bet you will see the biggest cry festival you have ever witnessed. That's how women show happiness," Shut up Bill said "You're just an old sarcastic s.o.b. Just be happy for them,"

The gate opened and Bill proved to be right. Tears were flowing before they even touched each other, tears mixed with smiling faces and hugs and kisses and each one at least once asking Carla if she was all right and if her arm hurt.

This went on for quite a while until Carla said, "I want you to meet my two friends who during the last twenty four hours transformed me from a whimpering scared wreck to a normal human being, Bruce and Bill," Without further explanation the three women turned to the two men hugging and kissing them, embarrassing the two of them to no end. They tried to tell them that all they did was feed her, something anyone else would have done.

Carla shook her head and said, "No guys you did a hell of a lot more for me than feeding me. You made me realize that my life wasn't over and that perfect strangers, like you were to me, can be good people and ready to help when help is needed. You are friends to me for ever and I hope I will be for you as well."

Both Bill and Bruce were now really embarrassed and didn't know what to say. Robert came to the rescue and said, "A friend of Carla is our friend, and I hope we will see a lot of you guys in the next few days, because I'm dying to know how all this happened. But right now we must get this girl to a doctor. I'm sure Carla knows how to get in touch with you and we will call you tomorrow and we can hopefully get together soon."

Bruce said, "Bill and I would like this very much. In the short time that we known Carla, she has become very dear to us. We definitely want to keep in touch with her."

With that they parted and hurried to the car and on their way to the doctor. Robert dropped them off at their house and he and Carla and Stella, went to see the doctor, Stella wouldn't let go Carla, Robert jokingly said, "Stella you're going to have to let her out of your arms when we get to the doctor, you know."

Stella said, "I know but we're not there yet so I can still hold her."

The doctor took X rays and after carefully examining them said, "It's a serious break and you will have to be in a hard cast for at least six weeks. But you'll be as good as new after that. We can get the surgery done to night or early tomorrow morning, it's up to you."

Carla said, "It's been a long day and I'm very tired so I would prefer tomorrow morning if that's okay with you."

"That's fine with me. How about eight o'clock tomorrow morning at the hospital?" He gave her instructions about where she had to register and said, "See you tomorrow."

They drove home forgetting the fact that they would not ask questions until Stella reminded all of them and then they just listened to what Carla said.

Mary said, "I made a cold meal for all of us. I didn't know how long you guys were going to be at the doctor's office," Carla said, "That's great I don't think I could stay awake long enough to have a big meal anyway, I promise I will tell you every thing tomorrow after we come back from the hospital. The doctor said that I will be back home by noon. They will give me a local anesthesia so I won't be dopey after the surgery."

They talked a little bit during dinner but they realized that Carla was exhausted and should be in bed, Stella told her mom that she wanted to stay with Carla and her mother said, "I expected nothing else, I knew I wouldn't be able to get you to come home tonight."

Mary said to Janice, "Why don't you stay with us? You're part of the family and we want you to be here when Carla gets back from the hospital. And besides, I wouldn't mind having some female company to night."

Janice said, "Okay I really would love to stay here."

Robert said, "The two girls will most likely stay upstairs but there is no reason why the three of us can't enjoy a good glass of champagne and have a quite celebration,"

"Now you're talking, said Mary."

Soon after, the two girls disappeared, eager to be together and talk for a while. Stella said, "Just for a little bit because you are tired and should go to sleep."

"Yes I will but I need to talk about it with you, not for very long but there are things that you need to know.

"I need to take a shower first but you will have to help me because with my lame wing everything is a chore, Stella said no problem I wanted to take a shower anyway. Stella helped Carla get undressed and then got undressed herself. Soon both girls were in the shower. Carla had taken her sling off and Stella was soaping Carla's body when Carla suddenly said, "You know, this is one of the moments that entered my mind when I felt lonely that I would never experience this again with you."

Stella dropped the soap and took Carla in her arms saying, "You will never have to miss moments like these again, I will never let you down again"

"What do you mean let me down again? You have never let me down."

Stella said, "Yes I did, I let this bastard take you away from me when I could have scratched his eyes out. She started to cry and said I'm so sorry."

Carla took Stella's face in both hands and started to kiss her tears away "Sweetheart, he almost killed you. There was nothing more you could have done." Slowly the crying stopped but neither one let go and their kissing became more intense until Carla felt a strange sensation running through her body, suggesting that this was more than comforting one another.

She hoarsely said, "We better get dried off and get into bed."

Stella had her eyes closed and murmured, "Just one more second, I could hold you like this forever."

When they finally went to bed Carla said. "We need to talk about this. When I was held captive and he made it clear to us that we would not survive, all I could think of was you. The thought that I would never see or feel you again was worse than me dying."

Stella answered, "I was convinced and determined that if you did not came back to me I didn't want to live any longer. I already was preparing myself by not eating or sleeping and figured if I continued doing that I eventually would die."

"Maybe this is not a good time to figure this out. We are both emotional and wanting to make up for the time we were separated and scared that we would never see each other again. Try to get some sleep and we'll work this out when we are back to normal. This doesn't mean that we can't sleep in each other's arms."

Carla fell asleep almost immediately while Stella couldn't get close enough to her and was still touching her until she fell asleep.

Carla woke up before Stella and discovered that they were both naked. She thought. We were not in the nude when we went to bed. When Stella opened her eyes and saw that they were both naked she looked as surprised as Carla did, not understanding what had happened during the night.

Stella made light of it and said, "We were probably sleeping too close to each other and got hot."

"Yes that's probably what happened."

Stella shook her head and said," That's what I meant, but I should have worded it a little different."

Carla said," Maybe, but we have to find out what kind of relationship we're having. Are we just really good friends or are we sexual attracted to each other or both?" When I was drifting on that raft this question came to my mind numerous times and since I was convinced that I was going to die I could be honest with myself and face reality. Under these conditions it's a lot easier than when you have to live with them.

"The trouble was that I couldn't come to a conclusion. I still don't know the answer. I know that I love you. I also know that when one day you come to me and say' I met a wonderful guy. I think I may fall in love with him, if that day arrives I don't know what I would do."

Stella interrupted and said, "I had similar dreams and I have the same fear that you will meet some guy and fall in love with him. And to me it's not a dream, it's a damn nightmare, I wake up and have to convince myself that it's just a dream and it will never happen."

They inched closer to each other and tenderly kissed each other. Their naked bodies touching each other made them realize that they might have feelings for each other more than friends usually have.

Stella said," I don't give a rat's ass what kind of feeling it is. I don't want to change it. Period."

Carla answered, "I don't even consider changing anything. I just want to know what it is. Time will tell I suppose, and just so that you know, no man in my life has ever come close to what I feel for you"

Same here, said Stella. "As you said earlier time will tell. But until we know, if a guy comes close to you his life is in danger. Now you better get ready to have that arm fixed. I like to be held with both arms."

The surgery went very well and the break was a clean one. No fractures, the doctor said. "You will be okay four to five weeks from now. Just be careful with this arm. Pretend for the first two weeks that you don't have an arm. Don't use it for anything."

They were home just in time for lunch and while they ate the subject of her working in the travel agency came up. Of course Mary and Robert said." No way. You heard what the doctor said,"

Carla replied, "Yes I heard what he said, don't use your arm. Since I answer the phone or type on the computer I don't use this arm at all, so I don't see why I can't go to work. Besides I need something to do. I can't just sit in the house doing nothing. I need something productive that will keep my mind busy."

Robert understood where she was going with this logic and he had to agree with her. She needed to keep her mind busy, not rehash what happened to her.

They all tried to act normally and wait for Carla to tell them what had happened during the four days she was gone to. After lunch Carla said." Well this is as good a time as any to tell you about my disappearing act."

They all knew what happened in front of the house so Carla started from the moment she was forced into the car. She told them that at first John wanted to come across as a good guy and claimed that he forced her to come with him only because he wanted to talk to her. When she didn't buy that and said that there were other ways to have a conversation with someone than putting her to sleep using chloroform and in the process almost killing my best friend with a blow to the head with your gun. Keeping someone locked up in storage room on board a yacht against her will was also not a good way to start a friendly chat.

When he saw that we didn't believe him he became nasty and said," Well if you never going to believe me there is no point in having that conversation. Don't think I'm going to bring you back to Jamesville. That's out of the question, I can't go back to the US but soon as we are in Mexican waters I will put you both ashore and I will continue my journey."

Glenn and Carla never believed any of that and started to make plans to get off the boat. It wasn't going to be easy because he locked us up in the cabin downstairs every time he went on deck.

Getting off the boat was optional. It was a do or die act. We both knew that this lunatic could not afford to let us live.

We realized that we didn't have much time because he became moody and mean and started to call me a bitch and Glenn was a wimp and coward. He gave up pretending to be the good guy and quickly became his usual self.

He had problems with his navigating skills, or lack of them. He needed the Global Positioning System he had on board but Glenn thought that he was scared to use it because it would give away his position. But he said that John couldn't navigate his way out of a bath tub without a GPS system, so we could end up in Timbuktu.

He ran back and forth between the salon we were in and the on deck controls. I went on deck a few times and he was always messing with the controls, desperately trying to stay the course to the Mexican waters.

Glenn suggested that we shouldn't wait any longer to make our move and should be ready next time he came downstairs. Glenn would hit him with the base of a table lamp, grab his gun and tie him up.

When we heard footsteps coming down the stairs we got in position. I would stand in front of him when he opened the door and Glenn would be to the side and hit him soon as he entered.

This turned out to be a disaster. Glenn was afraid of hitting him too hard and that he would kill him. The result was that he didn't hit him hard enough. John fell but was still able to fire his gun at Glenn and hit him in the shoulder.

Glenn fell down and was bleeding real bad, blood gushing out of his shoulder and I thought he was going to die or was dead already. John did not pay much attention to Glenn but pointed the gun at me and said. If you move an inch from were you are, I will blow your brains out. I knew he was dead serious, I started to shake out of pure angst and I hated myself for being such a coward.

He left the room and went up on deck. I didn't know what to do, but I knew the bleeding had to stop so I took a bed sheet and pressed it against the wound and just held it there for maybe an hour. The bleeding slowed down and Glenn seemed to be breathing normally.

I stayed with Glenn all night, checking his pulse and renewing the sheet, hoping to stop the bleeding, I didn't know what else to do. As the day progressed Glenn seemed to recover somewhat and was able to talk to me. He came up with the raft idea rather than me trying to swim to shore.

She told them what happened before she finally jumped overboard and how she broke her arm, the desperate times she had when the motor stopped and the waves began filling up the raft. That was the worst time, she said, because I knew that I would never see you guys again and was convinced that I would die that night.

Then when the raft hit the steel structure of the rig my hopes soared and I thought maybe, just maybe, I might survive this after all. She then told them about the swimming, climbing up the ring ladder with one hand and the encounter with Bruce and Bill and how everything changed for her. These two guys don't even realize what they did for me, but I will never forget it.

She then explained how Richard knew it was her on the rig. Yes Robert said, I wondered how he could be so sure. He had never seen you before.

Carla said. He is very resourceful. He flew that little Airplane very low over the platform and threw a metal cylinder on the deck. Bruce picked it up and it had a screw on top Bruce opened it and there was a piece of paper in it. Written on it was 'If this girl is Carla raise both hands up in the air when I fly over the platform again.' We saw him turning and, of course, six hands were reaching for the sky. When he was above us he tipped the wings of the plane up and down like he was saying, 'I got it' and flew away. That's why he was so sure it was me. He is amazing.

Robert agreed," That guy is amazing. I don't know how to thank him for what he accomplished in the few days he had to work with."

Carla said, "I know you must still have a thousand questions, but in time I'll remember more of the details and be able to tell you."

Mary said, "No, dear. Of course we have more questions but nobody here will ask you. When you feel up to telling us more we will listen but we will not ask for it. Stella proposed this and we all agreed to it and believe this will be best for you."

Carla looked at Stella with a thank you smile on her face.

It was also agreed upon that Carla would take a week off before going back to work. Robert said, "This is tentative and needs the doctors approval."

Chapter 29

While life for Carla and her family returned slowly to near normal, it would take a while for everything to get back to the way it was before. Richard was still chasing John down.

The last sighting was in Mexico City's international Airport. The trail got cold there and Richard was in Mexico City looking for a lead that would point him in the right direction, he wasn't having much luck, but Richard was not a person who would give up easily.

He didn't think that John was the type who would take up residence in Mexico. South America would be more his style. Rio, Buenos Aires those were cities that would appeal to him. Both places used to be ideal places for fugitives from the U.S. Once they were there and showed that they had enough money and wouldn't be a financial burden to Brazil or Argentina it was very hard to have them extradited and brought to justice in the U.S. Things had changed but it was still not easy to have the Brazilian government hand over a criminal to the U.S. Justice Department unless it was a murder case.

Richard was focusing on departures from Mexico City to Rio de Janeiro and Sao Paulo. There were several daily flights from Mexico City to both cities. He needed to get his hands on the manifests of the flights to these cities. For the last two days he had assumed that John wanted to get as far as possible away from Mexico and as soon as possible.

Richard knew that John was traveling under a fake name with a false passport and driver's license. He also knew the name he was using, the car rental people in Port Isabel had giving him the name and drivers license number that he used to rent the car.

Richard figured that after he got the manifests it wouldn't take long to find out where he was going.

He hit the jackpot with third airline he checked out Mark Bidwell, John's fake name, was booked as a passenger to Sao Paulo continuing to Rio the day before. Richard booked a flight on the next plane to Rio de Janeiro. He had a couple of hours to kill and decided to call Robert and asked him to let him talk to Carla. He wanted to know as much as possible about John. The more he knew the better the chance he had of finding him.

He told Robert that he was in Mexico City and on his way to Rio de Janeiro because that's where John was. He needed Robert's help. Robert should tell the local police that we knew for a fact that John was in Rio. The problem he saw was that he may not get the local Rio police to get too excited about arresting a US citizen based on what another American citizen told them You must insist that the FBI get involved.

Soon as I know where he actually is, hotel or apartment, I will go to the American Consulate and if the FBI is involved they will cooperate and get the local police off their asses to arrest him.

I want to talk to Carla. If she is in good enough shape to talk about this.

Robert said," I think she is and she wanted desperately to meet with you anyway. She wanted to thank you herself for what you have done and still do, I'll put her on the phone."

Carla came on the phone and started with," Sir I can't tell you how.

Richard cut in and said, "Stop right there my name is Richard and you were going to embarrass me with telling me how grateful you are for what I did, weren't you?"

She laughed and said, "Yes that was the plan."

Richard said, "All I did was peanuts compared to what your father did for me and Robert. This is the least I can do, and I am so sorry about your mom and dad. This must have been horrible for you.

"What I wanted to ask you is something you may not be ready for and if it is just tell me. I want to know if that asshole ever physically hurt you, slapped you around, stuff like that. Can you describe him, not physically but what makes him tick, what kind of people he likes to hang out with, does he like to show off, show that he has money, things like that will help me find him sooner?"

Carla said. "He is definitely a show off and likes to pretend that he is older than his real age. I don't think he would frequent sleazy joints. He would prefer the expensive, high class clubs, go to expensive restaurants, act like he is a celebrity of some sort." Richard said, "Great, that narrows it down quite a bit. I want you to know that I found out where he is, at least the town and country, and I assure you that in a couple of days I will know where he lives. There are two ways to punish him. One is the legal way and the other one is my way. I understood from what Robert told me that this is the second time he did this. The first time you decided that you didn't want the publicity and you took it upon yourself to make sure that justice would be done. I'm sure you had your reasons to go this route and I have absolutely no problem with that. I just need to know if you want to go that way again. Let me tell you first that if you want it the same way, you personally would have nothing to do with it. I can arrange it that he will spend a good number of years in a Brazilian prison without parole or early release. They don't believe in that nonsense in Brazil."

Carla was speechless for a minute and then said, "This is a surprise to me. I didn't think there was a choice this time around. With all the publicity in the media I thought this would go to court if they ever catch him".

Richard answered, "Yes if they catch him. But if he gets in to serious trouble in Brazil they will never extradite him. The Brazilian legal system will deal with it. We can go both ways with this. I want you to think about it and maybe talk with your lawyer or maybe your friend Stella." Carla said, "I don't want you to do something illegal and get in trouble here or in Brazil,"

Don't worry about me he said, "I'll cover my butt and nobody will ever know I had anything to do with it. It would actually be easier than bringing him back home. I'll call you back in a few days. By then I will know where he lives and what his plans are. I'll be on a plane in less than an hour on my way to Rio."

Carla was flabbergasted and knew Richard wasn't kidding. She definitely had to think about the choices he gave her and she wanted to discuss this with Stella, because Stella knew why she didn't want the publicity or the unwanted attention she would undoubtedly get from the media.

Stella was just as confused about this development as Carla was and said I wished this guy would be a little bit less efficient and put the motherfucker in jail without letting you decide what to do. Carla defended Richard and said, "He just want to know what I want. He gave me a choice."

Stella said, "I know he's a terrific guy, I was just kidding about him being less efficient I bet he has another option, kill the son of a bitch. He just doesn't want you having to make that choice. But I'm sure that's an option and if you would have said that you were raped or repeatedly physically abused, that's what he would have decided without giving you the choice.

Without really knowing Richard I believe he could do this without regret, he feels so much in debt to your father that if he knew you wanted this he would kill him without hesitation."

Carla shivered and said, "I could never make that decision, knowingly being the one who decides on the execution of another human being." Stella said,"

I know that and so does Richard. That's why he didn't give you that option."

Stella proposed that they should see her lawyer and find out what he thought about the available options Richard had offered her.

Her lawyer could not give much advice. He said, "The law is very clear on that. A fugitive from the laws of this country residing in a foreign country should be returned to the US by the foreign authorities for sentencing in the US. You can't legally make a decision on this nor should anybody else. If the fugitive breaks the law of the country he resides in then that country can try him locally and there is usually not much the US legal system can do about it. But as I said before, you are not even involved in that process. My advice to you is to stay out of this and the private investigator should turn this over to the US legal department. I'm well aware that a court trial in the US could have consequences for you. I believe they will be minor but I can't guarantee that. Some reporter may start digging and strike pay dirt that would expose your past and the newspapers would have a field day with it.

"The best scenario for you would be for him to do something real stupid and illegal and be arrested in Brazil. They won't extradite him. He would serve time in Brazil and after that he would be released. As long as he stays outside the US nothing will happen.

"I wish I could have given you better advice but unfortunately that's what it is." Carla and Stella returned home not much wiser and still not knowing what to decide.

Carla wanted this all to be over. If she could be sure that John would stay in Brazil and never bother her again she would tell Richard to forget it and come home. She knew however that she would never feel safe if he was on the loose, letting him be free was not an option. He needed to be punished.

Richard called her again and asked her if she had made a decision yet. She hesitated and finally had to tell him that she didn't know what to decide and that she had not discussed it with Robert or Mary. Richard said that was okay. He was in Rio but had not located John yet so there was no hurry at this time and he would let her know when he had found him.

Richard knew where John was. Talking to Carla he realized that a young girl like her could not and should not make this kind of decisions. He had been wrong to ask her to do this. She should not have to carry that burden the rest of her life. He would not ask her again. He would make a decision that would assure that she would be safe from John forever. He would never have the opportunity to mess with her again.

Richard thought he should have a talk with Stella. He had the feeling that Carla did not want this to end up in court and Stella might be able to confirm that. He didn't want to know why that was but if she was so adamant about it he must make sure that it did not go to court in Houston or New Orleans.

He got in touch with Stella and she said you're right. She's paranoid about her past and is afraid that the media will find out and make it a three ring circus, the fact that she lived with her parents in a trailer park in a bad section of New Orleans will be held against her. Her parent's reputation as alcoholics will be made public and she will be labeled trailer trash. She wants none of that."

Richard said, "He understood and would make sure the case would not come to the US." He also understood that he would have to be judge and jury on this case. He would have to get closer to John and learn more about him before making a decision on his punishment.

John had rented a plush beach front apartment and was living the life of a carefree, young well to do bachelor. Richard knew what night clubs he went to, restaurants he favored, the type of people he befriended and even the high class hookers he took to his apartment.

Richard would now have to enter this circle to get closer to John and learn more about him. Judging by the way he was conducting himself, Richard didn't think much of him as a human being.

He started to go to the same clubs, and occasionally to the same restaurant. He followed him during the day sometimes and noticed that he often went to a beauty parlor for both men and women. He assumed that he had some work done on the scars on his face. He chuckled and said to himself, you should have done this earlier it's too late now.

One night in one of the clubs John frequented Richard was seated at the bar when John walked in and took the chair next to Richard. John ordered a drink but the barman that night did not speak English and did not understood what he wanted, John annoyed and looked around for help but couldn't find one of his bar buddies. Richard asked can I help you.

John was surprised that this guy next to him spoke fluent English. Yes, please do. After his drink was served John asked Richard, "How he had found this place. Not too many foreigners came here. It was strictly for the locals, you don't look or sound like a local."

"Richard responded no I'm not."

John said," I'm planning to be one. I recently got here but I'm renting an apartment so that will make me a resident."

Richard said, "Well I'm planning to do the same thing but I stay in a hotel for the time being, by the way I'm Rick White"

John slightly hesitated before answering but then said, "I'm Mark Bidwell good to meet you because as you already know my Portuguese leaves a lot to be desired. Where did you learn to speak the local lingo"

I don't Richard said, "I spoke Spanish to him. That will get you by in Brazil."

Richard offered him a drink which John accepted. They started talking about foreigners, especially Americans, being accepted in Rio and what to do and more important what not to do. After a while Richard felt this was enough socializing for a first time. He said, "Well it was nice chatting with you but I got to go. My real estate agent invited me for dinner, so I better leave otherwise my rent may go up. I hope to see you here again. This looks like a nice place to have a couple drinks at night." Richard noticed that the scars on John's face were remarkably fainter than they were on the photos that he had. He definitely had work done on it and was wearing a light make-up.

Richard couldn't lose track of him now because it would be a lot harder to find him if those scars totally disappeared.

Richard kept shadowing John and detected a certain routine; John slept late, went to bed late and in between did not do little else other than going to the beach most of the time accompanied by a stunning girl, never the same one. Richard assumed they were escort girls or high-priced hookers. It was hard to see the difference, if there really was one. He still spent time at the beauty salon he also visited the horse and dog race tracks, in general, doing nothing useful.

Richard thought it was time to revisit the bar where they first met. He followed John and when he saw him entering the bar he waited a while before he walked in. John sat at the bar flanked by two sexy hot looking girls. When he noticed Richard walk in he called "Hey Rick. Come here and join us."

Richard immediately saw that he was either drunk or on something. He was acting totally different than he did the other night. John introduced Richard to the two girls, who mostly ignored him and continued talking and smooching with John. Richard said, "Look you seem to have good time and I only came in for a couple of drinks, so don't let me interrupt you."

John wanted nothing of that and said, "No have at least a couple of drinks here with us." Richard wanted to decline the invitation but felt it could be useful for him to learn more about John. Once the girls found out that Richard was not going to stay all night with them they relaxed and became more friendly.

Richard assumed correctly that John was under the influence of something, more like the John that Richard expected him to be, based on his past behavior. Now he was behaving like a High School kid, boisterous, trying to impress the girls, even telling them that the US police was after him, but that they had no idea that he was in Brazil and would never find him.

Richard cringed. He didn't want anybody to know that John was a fugitive because the local police might be interested and Richard wanted this to be his secret with no interference from the local authorities for the time being.

He needed to stop this moron from saying shit like that. John ordered a bottle of expensive Champagne and soon became more inhibited and amorous with one of the girls. The second girl must have understood that she was not going to score that night and left the bar. John had lost interest in Richard and was committed to the girl. He wanted her to come to his apartment but she was obviously a pro and played hard to get. The longer she could keep him on the hook the higher the cost of sex would be.

Richard knew he was not going to get John's attention that night and quietly left the bar as well. He needed to talk to other people who were closer to John to feel them out.

The bar was on the top floor and the other girl was still waiting for the elevator to come up. Richard saw this as an opportunity to find out more about John. He pretended that he could be interested in what she had to offer and asked her if she wanted to join him for a drink somewhere else. She agreed and asked him where he wanted to go. He let her decide and they went to a little bar close by.

She introduced herself as Claudia and Richard said his name was Rick. "He asked her if John was a friend of hers." She answered, "That asshole doesn't have any friends. He's tolerated because of the money he throws around. He's violent. A couple of days ago I went with him to his apartment and look what he did to me." She lifted her dress and showed some ugly black and blue bruises. He kicked me and called me a cheap whore and then actually raped me.

She also had small round burns on her body. Richard asked, if they were cigarette burns. She nodded and said, "I was lighting a cigarette and he said I don't smoke and I expect people in my presence to ask permission to smoke. He went berserk and yelled, let me show you why smoking his bad for you. He took the cigarette out of my hand and squashed it out on my body." Richard asked, "Then why were you with him tonight and why didn't you report him to the police?" Look she said. "I work for an escort agency and I would be fired if I went to the police. Tonight he asked the agency for two girls to join him and they sent me and Monica, I warned Monica, but she also knows if she refuses to accompany a client she will be fired. Some of my friends had similar experiences with him and they all refuse to be alone with him. He's crazy and seems to hate girls." Are you a friend of his? Richard said," no, I only met him two days ago in that bar. We just talked to each other because I translated for him when the bartender didn't understand him. Does he have any other friends he hangs out with?"

She said, "Yes but they are just as bad as he is, they're drug dealers, pimps or other low lives. One of the guys told me that John was wanted in the US for kidnapping a girl. He never told us that so I don't know whether this is true or not. But he is definitely capable of doing something like that, I believe he is sadistic and loves to hurt people especially girls."

Richard paid the bill and the girl asked, "Don't you want me to come with you?" Richard said, "Not tonight, but I understand that I took your time," And with that handed her a hundred dollar bill.

She was all smiles and said, "Thank you very much, and if you ever want my company I'm usually in that bar around this time."

Richard left and summarized what he had just heard. He concluded that this maniac had to be stopped one way or the other. His behavior would become more violent and other girls would be abused. There were two options. One was to kill him, the other one was to make sure he was put in jail in Brazil for a long time.

Richard made his decision and felt that his Army buddy would agree with what he intended to do to make sure that his girl was safe and in the protection of good people who loved her.

A week or so later Robert received a phone call from Richard who said," Well John is in jail in Rio de Janeiro. He was arrested for possession and dealing of cocaine together with the rape and molesting of a 16 year old girl. For a crime of this nature there won't be an extradition with the US. The local DA wants a life sentence but John, of course, got himself a first class lawyer, so he will probably get 20 to 25 years in prison. As you may know there is no such a thing as shortening the sentence for good behavior in Brazil. He will be in jail for a long time. You can assure Carla that her nightmare is over and that he is out of her life forever."

Robert called Carla and Stella into his study and said, "I just received a phone call from Richard telling me that John is in jail, he then proceeded to give them the details."

Stella was the first to react by saying, "This is fantastic news and will serve the bastard right. He deserved it."

Carla looked like she couldn't believe that this was finally over but when she saw everybody smiling and Robert starting to open a champagne bottle she realized it was for real. She ran to Stella, hugging and kissing her while crying and smiling at the same time.

Chapter 30

Stella and Carla were back at work and at the same time looking for a college that would accept both of them and also allow them to live off campus. Most colleges do not allow first year students to do this, but eventually they found one not far from home that accepted them. Both girls had changed their minds about skipping a year before going to college and were now ready to start in the fall.

Carla and Stella were still wrestling with the question of the love they had for each other. Was it just that or was there more to it? But they still could not believe that this was a Lesbian relationship. Both declared that it was not a big deal what other people called it. It would not change their relationship one way or the other.

What scared them the most was if indeed they were known as lesbians how would their family react?

Stella was sure that it would not affect her mother all that much but Carla knew that Mary was very religious and would not take this very well. The last thing that Carla would do was to hurt Mary.

Not knowing how to handle this, they both agreed to do nothing for the time being and handle it at a later time. They were not happy with this decision but sometimes you have to live with a less than perfect situation. Also some secrets fall into the category of "Let sleeping dogs lie"

The two also wondered how Glenn and John were doing, Glenn would be still in Africa for a few more years doing mission work and John was behind bars for a long time in Rio de Janeiro. Glenn was happy with the work he was doing and was engaged to a girl he had met at the mission and would come home at the end of the year to get married.

John on the other hand was not happy and angry that he was surrounded by criminals who could only speak Portuguese and showed no respect for the American millionaire who ranted and raved that he would find a way out of this shithouse and go back to the US to kill the two bitches who had put him there.

None of John's sinister plans were known by the girls and the chances that he would ever have the opportunity to execute these plans were probably slim or none existent.